Won't Be Long Now

Books by Elizabeth Hardinger

ALL THE FORGIVENESSES

WON'T BE LONG NOW

Published by Kensington Publishing Corp.

Won't Be Long Now

ELIZABETH HARDINGER

KENSINGTON PUBLISHING CORP.
kensingtonbooks.com

This book is a work of fiction. Names, characters, businesses, organizations, places, events, and incidents either are the product of the author's imagination or are used fictitiously. Any resemblance to actual persons, living or dead, events, or locales is entirely coincidental.

To the extent that the image or images on the cover of this book depict a person or persons, such person or persons are merely models, and are not intended to portray any character or characters featured in the book.

JOHN SCOGNAMIGLIO BOOKS are published by

Kensington Publishing Corp.
900 Third Avenue
New York, NY 10022

All Kensington titles, imprints and distributed lines are available at special quantity discounts for bulk purchases for sales promotion, premiums, fund-raising, educational or institutional use.

Special book excerpts or customized printings can also be created to fit specific needs. For details, write or phone the office of the Kensington Special Sales Manager: Kensington Publishing Corp., 900 Third Avenue, New York, NY, 10022. Attn. Special Sales Department. Phone: 1-800-221-2647.

Library of Congress Control Number: On file

ISBN-13: 978-1-4967-5876-7
First Kensington Hardcover Edition: May 2026

ISBN-13: 978-1-4967-5878-1 (ebook)

10 9 8 7 6 5 4 3 2 1

Printed in the United States of America

The authorized representative in the EU for product safety and compliance
is eucomply OU, Parnu mnt 139b-14, Apt 123
Tallinn, Berlin 11317, hello@eucompliancepartner.com

A memory is what is left when something happens and does not completely unhappen.

Edward de Bono

Your pain is the breaking of the shell that encloses your understanding.

Kahlil Gibran

Book One

Chapter 1
The State Fair

Growing up, I was what the family called an odd-wad. Meaning, I had a hard time getting out of my head. I lived there most of the time, and I only visited the outside world when I had to. Short visits, because they usually hurt.

The first time I remember thinking for sure I was not like other people happened at the Kansas State Fair. It was held every year in Hutchinson, where Mother, Daddy, and I lived among a nest of little ranch houses on Halsey Drive. I've always heard that those houses had been built during the war to lodge the men training at the navy air base outside of town. Daddy'd bought the little house on the GI Bill with no down payment.

That day at the fair, Daddy was demonstrating WonderWare stainless, greaseless, waterless pans inside the Industrial Building, and I was standing on tiptoes watching. It was 1952; I was five years old. Sawdust rose everywhere, and I smelled straw, animal dirt, and caramelized sugar. It was hot, and there was a lot of noise, almost as if the sounds were a solid mass that pressed against my face. People walked by, and above my head they were talking, hollering, whistling. They were eating things on sticks, opening their mouths and snatching the food out of the air like birds. Babies were crying. Balloons popped. Through the giant doorways came carnival sounds—tinkly music, the scratchy voices of sideshow barkers, the grinding gears of the rides, the shouting, the screams.

It was a lot.

Behind Daddy was a stack of a couple dozen cardboard boxes. "WonderWare Waterless Miracle Cookware" in huge black letters. The table had a bright cloth tacked to the front and sides. The wooden top was scarred and discolored from long use.

Daddy was a scrawny, homely guy. His face was bony like the cow skulls you see in old-timey cowboy coloring books. The skin on his face was pocked, and his hair was buzzed close on the sides and back, slicked in front into a flattop. Mother cut his hair. I can't tell you what color it was because I never saw it longer than a half an inch. Light-colored.

But the worst thing was his teeth. Crooked like he had gotten hit in the mouth with a bowling ball, and yellow from smoking—I used to scream/laugh every time he pretended to swallow a lit cigarette and make smoke come out his ears. You saw flashes of silver when he talked. He talked funny. He swallowed the beginnings of certain words with a gulp, not only when he was doing the pans but all the time.

Daddy was so homely and he struggled so hard to talk, it was a wonder how good a salesman he was. Maybe Mother was right—people bought his pans because they felt sorry for him. In my mind, he was just Daddy. His looks were normal, just like everything in my life was normal. Besides, with his job, he was home in the daytime sometimes, and he knew more songs and jokes and tricks than any other adult I knew. His whole face lit up when I laughed. He would sit and play jacks with me for as long as I wanted, ride me on his back, skip rope with me, play hopscotch with me on the street in front of our house, play tetherball with me in the school playground, pop popcorn and make purple Kool-Aid and pineapple upside-down cake. He was a great dad. He never wore out.

A knot of people had gathered around the table. Daddy talked and swallowed, talked and gulped, his hands never still. *Waterless!* he said, stretching it out. I seem to remember that he had a microphone on a stiff wire around his neck, but according to Mother he never did. Somehow he was loud enough for everybody to hear him, but they leaned in anyway. *Waterless pans! Right here today! Folks* (he gulped), *you don't have to drown your food before you cook it!* He smiled, winked, ran his fingers along the rim of a frying pan like he was checking for nicks on a fruit jar. *You don't have to boil your chicken, your beef, your pork till it loses all that flavor you paid good money for!* He pointed. *No ma'am, nossir, you don't have to lard it up neither! No fats, no oils, no shortening, no grease!* He ran a middle finger over the cooking surface, snapped his finger, gulped. *No greasy* (he said "greezy") *feeling in your mouth, no grease on the tablecloth, no grease on the wall!*

I was proud of having a famous Daddy.

Now he deftly produced a match, lit a flame on a portable gas burner, and placed the bare pan on the fire, all the while blathering about fried chicken. He told the joke about deviled eggs (*I call them,* gulp, *fancy baby chickens*). Then he placed his hand on the pan and jerked it back (*owee! hot!*), and I put my own fingers in my mouth.

Daddy reached under the table and pulled out a thick, dripping steak on a fork. He dropped the steak into the pan, and quickly he produced a damp white towel to wipe the table. The steak sizzled, and he forked it around, lifting it to show it wasn't sticking. *No grease! No water! Just look at that beautiful crispy!* The meat snapped and smoked. At the perfect moment, he forked it out with one hand and lifted the pan with the other, holding it up like a mirror, turning it so everyone could see. Quickly he lowered the pan and dropped the raw side of the steak onto the hot surface. *Stainless! Greaseless! Waterless!*

A murmur passed through the crowd as the aroma of the meat filled the air. I felt light-headed. My toes curled.

Daddy slid the steak onto a bright white platter and pierced the meat, releasing a string of blood. Then he cut it, slice after slice, each as thin as a silver dollar. People oohed and aahed as he fanned out the slices, revealing the tantalizing red interior. A couple of men snorted.

You know the rest. He picked a few big men near the front and gave them each a slice on a toothpick, teasing them for a moment before he dropped it into their mouths. *Tender?* he said, as if their faces didn't already show the answer. Then he grabbed the towel (*ladies, this is the,* gulp, *best part*) and wiped the pan to reveal the shiny silver finish. He lifted the pan over his head, turning it this way and that like a trophy. *Meat's tender, but boy, this pan is tough! Guaranteed! No questions! Any problem at all, you get a brand-new pan! For a lifetime!*

Now I was startled to see Mother weaving through the crowd. She had a head scarf tight around her head, and her eyes were hidden behind giant sunglasses. She was wearing a threadbare wash dress and no lipstick.

Where had she been? Hadn't she just been here, standing next to me? I looked down: a little semicircle of flattened lipsticked cigarettes. Where had she come from just now? What was she carrying?

"Mother!" I jumped up and down. "Daddy—"

Daddy shouted, pointing at Mother: "It's one of ours, all right! A happy customer! Madame, come forward!"

"Madame"? I opened and closed my mouth. I looked around and saw a man glancing at me. I realized he had been sneaking looks at me for a while. I felt my stomach fold. My face felt as if someone had smeared it with the smell of wormy dirt. I didn't know why.

Mother walked up to the table. I saw now that she was holding a dented pan.

Daddy grabbed it up. He made a joke about her clobbering "the old man." He asked her name.

Mother turned red and lowered her eyes. "I dropped it down the basement stairs."

I wanted to say *But we don't have a basement*, but something told me not to. My tongue felt dry. I couldn't stand it when things didn't make sense, couldn't stand it. As I'd grown, I'd noticed how my folks would say things that they knew perfectly well—and I knew perfectly well—did not add up. Little things, like telling me a TV show was over when it wasn't, that we were out of cookies, that the store was closed, that if I closed my eyes it would soon be morning—and they were flat *lying*, something Mother spanked *me* for. My out-of-town cousins, too, loved lying to me, sending me hunting for left-handed monkey wrenches or making me kiss a rabbit's foot to make the foot of the absent bunny grow back. Especially my cousin Joan, who loved to torment me.

Now I was baffled and enraged. Why was Mother saying we had a basement? Did she think I was stupid?

But the incident just went on, as if we actually had a basement, and my feelings made no difference. They never did. Why would they?

Daddy gulped. "Well, I'm afraid—I didn't catch your name?"

"Mildred," Mother said, as if her name actually was Mildred when in fact it was Dixie.

"Well, Mildred," Daddy said, "I'm afraid (gulp) I'll have to give you a *brand-new pan*!" He grabbed one of the boxes and handed it to her, and there was a murmur in the crowd as she took it and held it in front of her chest like a shield.

People turned to look at Daddy as he started winding up his

pitch (*nine ninety-five down* (gulp), *nine ninety-five a month*), and pretty soon people lined up to sign the paperwork, and out of the corner of my eye I saw Mother standing off a ways in the wide doorway, smoking.

I felt tiny, impossibly tiny. It made no sense. It was like, did I even exist.

The vendors' parking lot behind the 4-H building was a maze of thick, black electrical cords, and I stumbled over them as Mother dragged me to the round-shouldered green Nash.

She pressed the car door open, and, standing behind it, she smacked the backs of my bare legs with a hairbrush. She was gripping my wrist with her free hand as I tried to twist out of her reach. I was only prolonging things, but I couldn't seem to help it.

I was angry, humiliated, and, at the same time, suspicious—she wasn't hitting me as hard as she could. It stung all right, but it didn't burn. This punishment was kind of a lie, just as surely as if she had said it in words and not actions.

She finally stopped and leaned on the car's chrome door trim, resting her face on the back of her hand. She threw the hairbrush into the dim interior. Then she straightened and untied the scarf, freeing her luminous hair, which framed her face like a halo in the golden early evening. You could see the natural red streaks among the brown. She scrubbed her scalp with the fingertips of both hands.

Standing with her legs slightly apart, she gave me that look she had—*that* look, you know the one—the glare that somehow combined rage, revulsion, and indifference and portended unimaginable chastisements. I had learned (she had trained me) to dread that look. It seemed she knew just when to deploy it. It made me not only stop doing evil (or start doing the thing she wanted) but also shrivel into dust, into nothing. Just from the look.

"Stop crying," she said. "Your dad will be here any minute."

I'm not crying, I wanted to say—it was the truth—but that was talking back, and backtalk always got my face slapped, so I ducked my head and said it to myself. Why was she lying? When the truth was so obvious? It made no sense.

She bent and slapped the wrinkles out of the back of my skirt. "I told you to *stand there* and *not say one word.*" Her voice rose. "Didn't I? Well, didn't I?"

I tried to think back to when the two of us had first arrived, when Mother was standing next to me in the crowd, her hand on my shoulder. But with the noise and the smells and all those people, if she had said anything I didn't remember it. Or it had just sounded like the usual *behave yourself.* I hadn't noticed when she left. One moment she'd been there, and the next she was coming back, carrying the pan that supposedly had fallen down basement stairs we didn't have.

"I hate the fair," I said.

She frowned. "Don't be ridiculous. We don't *hate* anything."

Now I heard Daddy whistling through his teeth like he always did, and then he was standing there, with the low sun behind him. He looked like a giant. His good shirt hung in the crook of his elbow, and he held three Pronto Pups between his fingers. In his other hand he was carrying three bottles—two beers and a grape pop. His face was shiny with sweat.

He tossed the corn dogs to Mother and bent over and scooped me up. He pressed a cold bottle against my neck, and I yelped. They both laughed.

I felt tears coming on, and I kicked his knees until he set me down.

"See what Mother did?" I raised my skirt and turned around. Three little welts were just visible on my legs. "Gave me a whippin'. With the hairbrush."

Daddy's smile faded. He put his hand on Mother's arm. "How come?"

She frowned and pulled away. "You saw what she did in there. I told her— "

"Oh, Dixie. We've talked about this. They *know.*" He took her elbow. "They know the game. They don't care. They want the folderol."

I think Daddy knew it was easy to distract me with a new word. I couldn't get enough words. "Folderol" wasn't new, but it was one of his favorites. I loved that word. I loved the way my tongue felt when I pronounced the liquid *l's* in the middle and again at the end. I loved that it started with *f*, like the naughtiest word I knew. "Falled-er-all."

"They want to be, you know, seduced," he went on.

Now the sting of the hairbrush and my reflection on "folderol" evaporated. *Seduced,* I whispered; not only a new word but also the key, I sensed, to understanding what was happening. It felt like a moment when anything was possible—maybe a moment when they would let me into their world, a world that was glimmering just on the threshold of my consciousness, a world I longed to be a part of, make sense of.

Seduced.

Mother pulled away and glared at him. "Little pitchers," she said.

It was maddening, that phrase. I'd heard it a thousand times. I was not that little. I was not a pitcher.

The moment passed. But at least I had a new word, a new concept. *Seduced,* I repeated in my mind. *Seduced, seduced,* they *want* to be *seduced.* Even the word *want* in this context was intriguing.

Now Daddy reached under the front seat and pulled out a church key. He snapped open all three bottles and caught the caps on his forehead like a circus seal. He smiled with all his crooked teeth, tilted his bottle to his lips, and took three deep swallows as the caps cascaded off his face.

Mother laughed, and I saw the two of them exchange a radiant look. I felt a longing deeper and sadder than I could begin to comprehend.

"I *hate* the fair," I said in my mind.

"Goodness gracious," Mother said to me, laughing. "What a face! You better hope it doesn't freeze that way."

Another lie. She must think I'm stupid. She must think I like being laughed at.

I crawled inside my head, where there were soft, tender whispers and sinuous colors. Things made sense in my head, and it was where I felt I belonged.

Chapter 2
Harriet

My first friend was Harriet Easterday. We met in first grade when the alphabet had us sitting at adjacent desks. She was wearing a knife-pleated blue skirt and a white blouse with a Peter Pan collar. (No stiff net petticoat that flared out the skirt; they weren't popular yet.) She had on Buster Brown penny loafers and white anklets. I was wearing a dress Mother had made. I loved that dress—it was white cotton with poodles on the full, stiff skirt—and I had insisted on wearing it. The bodice was tight, and the waist hit me just below my ribcage, and I felt my midsection pressing against resisting cloth all the way around. But I loved those preening, long-necked poodles. As for the tennis shoes I wore, the midsole trim was ragged where I had picked off bits of rubber; in places, it was only crumbs. No socks.

When it was her turn to introduce herself, Harriet told us she had moved to town that summer from Boulder, Colorado, which I heard as "Bolder" and was immediately enthralled. She had two brothers and a sister, all older. Her parents were professors. She liked to ski, snowshoe, sled, swim, ride horseback, snowball fight, fish, build snowmen, and roast hot dogs at a bonfire next to the pond after ice skating. Her favorite food was hot dogs, and her favorite color was red. As she talked I got excited like a puppy, and I did what I always did when that happened: I rested my hands on my lap and twiddled my thumbs, something I learned by watching my grandma. If she wasn't crocheting or tatting or snapping beans, or reading her Bible or ladies' devotional, Grandma twiddled her thumbs. She also had the habit, while sitting, of crossing her legs and shaking one leg. She also always saved a little piece of meat to eat with her dessert, and when she made a pitcher of Kool-Aid she added a can of frozen lemonade concentrate. These are a few of the many things I'd memorized about her. I know now that she loved me and I loved her—the simplest of feelings—but I had no language for it then and therefore no idea of what it was.

When it was my turn, I stood next to my desk and said a few words, but my voice was too loud, I could tell. I swallowed and cleared my throat. The other kids tittered. I started over, lowering the volume of my voice as Mother had taught me. I was born in Hutchinson, I announced, my father sold pans, my mother worked at Central Foods part time, I was an only child, my favorite thing was reading. I started to list the books I had read, and after the third one (*Black Beauty*), Mrs. Schreiber gently said, "Thank you, Billie. Debbie?" I thought I heard a little buzz drift among my classmates.

At lunch I was sitting alone, going over in my mind everything that had happened that morning, when Harriet sat down next to me. I glanced around. There were other vacant places.

"I *love* hamburger patties," I said, and four or five kids looked up and stared. Too loud again. Harriet flinched the tiniest bit but covered it up by unfolding her paper napkin. She glanced at me and stuffed it into her collar.

We ate in silence for a minute. "What are your folks professors of?" I said.

"Dad teaches geology at Wichita U, and Mom teaches biological sciences at Juco."

"It's *Wich*ita, not '*Which*ita.'" I noticed she called them Dad and Mom. Daddy had taught me to call my mother Mother, out of respect, and she had taught me to call him Daddy. "Dad" and "Mom" sounded foreign to me, a little palsy-walsy, modern. Exotic.

Harriet clanged her fork on the metal tray. "Don't be mean. I can't help it if I'm new."

I got a lump in my throat. I couldn't say "I'm sorry," because what I'd said was true, not mean, but clearly—

"*Any*how," she said, "where do people go to ski around here?"

I laughed.

"What's funny?" She popped the round paper lid off her little bottle of milk.

"We don't have any mountains. Just fields."

She frowned. "That's not funny." She held the saltshaker over her milk and poured in at least a tablespoon.

"How come?"

She didn't answer. I repeated it, thinking she hadn't heard, but she busied herself with her food.

It went on like that. One moment I felt needed and useful, providing information about her new town, and the next, I was embarrassed but not sure why.

She finished first and left the table without a word. I sat for a while and fretted. What had I done wrong?

When I got to the playground, I waved to her, but she pretended not to see me. The swings were all taken, and the height of the slippery-slide scared me, so I leaned against a tree and ruminated. Other kids didn't like me, I knew that already. I suspected that even my cousins, who had to like me because I was family, didn't like me. I didn't know why. I went over everything I had said to Harriet, and I didn't understand why she seemed to distance herself, if that was what she was doing. It had to be something I said. I vowed not to say another word the rest of the day.

In the afternoon Mrs. Schreiber had each of us, one at a time, stand and read from the Dick and Jane reader, which was ridiculously simple and repetitive, and I quickly read through two pages, and she said, "Thank you, Billie" again, and had me sit down. My face burned. After everyone read, she divided us into two reading groups. Harriet and I, along with a handful of other kids, were in the Bluebirds group. Everybody else was in Redbirds. We all understood the significance of the labels, although Mrs. Schreiber acted as if our assignment was random. Another lie I didn't understand.

Soon the Redbirds gathered in a circle in the back of the room next to the bookshelves and began working on flash cards while the Bluebirds sat at their desks and filled out spelling work sheets. I finished mine and sat with my hands folded on my desk. The air was hot and still in the little room. It felt as if there were a hundred people looking at me. I was exhausted.

I took refuge by closing my eyes and visualizing myself at home in our little house on Halsey Drive. In my mind Daddy was off selling pans or playing cards, and Mother was washing clothes and running the sweeper, filling the house with the smell of bluing and old dust. I watched as she collapsed into her chair and grabbed a cigarette as if she were drowning for the smoke. She lifted a can of beer to her mouth, and her throat bobbed as she drank it down like water. Over the course of a day the empties would line up on the coffee table, and the giant rainbow glass bowl with the frilly edges would fill up with cigarette butts. Sometimes she would fall asleep in her chair. Like any other kid, I assumed what went on at our house went on everywhere.

Meanwhile I saw myself play on the floor with my plastic animals—the galloping white horse, the grazing brown horse, the sleeping lamb, and the little man standing in the plastic puddle, holding a coiled rope—and the white plastic fences. I was probably too big to play with these things—so Mother said—but I still liked rearranging the fences, jumping the horses over them, and walking the man around, checking things out. I liked making up stories about the man and the animals and acting them out. The lamb, made of chalk, taken from the nativity set and out of scale with the others, just lay there and slept.

I liked it when Mother was dozing and the house was quiet. Sometimes I sneaked into the kitchen and stole a spoonful of brown sugar from the cupboard. Then I would wipe the spoon on my shirt and put it back in the drawer.

The next thing I knew, Harriet poked me in the side. I raised my head, blinking and headachy, just as Mrs. Schreiber arrived at her desk in the front of the room. The Redbirds were breaking up and returning to their seats.

I flashed Harriet a grateful look, and she smiled.

I was so relieved I felt about to burst. I was certain I would have gotten into trouble for falling asleep in class, and Mother and Daddy would have been called into school and told; but Harriet had saved me. Maybe she liked me after all. Tears were coming, and I pinched my nose to stop them, I gritted my teeth, I swallowed and swallowed. I had emotions beating on the inside of my body all over, scraping along the rawness, screaming to get out. This was nothing new, but it left me breathless nonetheless. My toes curled and uncurled inside my tennis shoes, rubbing against the sweaty foot sand. I sensed that crying in school would mark me among my peers. I would never be able to live it down. Nobody had told me that, but I knew it nonetheless.

Mrs. Schreiber looked down at her desk, gathering papers. "Bluebirds, hand your work sheets to the person in front of you." By the time she looked up, I had wiped my nose on the back of my wrist and was ready to go read with the other Bluebirds.

A couple of weeks after school started, Harriet's mother called my mother and invited me to come to their house after school on a Friday to play with Harriet. Their house was in Hyde Park, a leafy neighborhood in the northwest part of town full of huge old houses.

Harriet and I entered by the back door. Her mother sat at the kitchen table, grading papers. Her dishwater blond hair was pulled back in a ponytail, something I had never seen on a grown woman. All the women I knew kept their hair short and permed. Even Mother had had hers cut. She cut mine, too, in a little bowlish cut she called a "windblown"; she had gotten tired of wrestling with me to untangle it every time she washed it. She'd never known any girl who was so tender-headed.

"Oh, hello, girls," Mrs. Easterday said, looking up. A stack of papers was at her elbow, along with a steaming cup of coffee. It smelled divine; there was no under-smell of burnt clay like we had at our house.

On the counter were two salad plates, each with a square piece of white cake and strawberries.

"This is Billie," Harriet said.

Harriet's mother stood up and straightened her skirt. "I'm happy to meet you, Billie."

"Me too."

She had us put our things on a polished bench in the living room and then seat ourselves at the long dining table to have our snack. It was quiet and cool in the living and dining rooms, and soft underfoot, with thick wall-to-wall carpeting. The heavy drapes cascaded to the floor in pretty curves. The house smelled like sweet wax. There were ashtrays set out, but you could tell only company smoked in the house.

Harriet's mother carried in our plates and glasses of milk, for which I thanked her for the second or third time; I sounded oily to myself. My neck kinked in shame. I glanced at her face, but her expression seemed neutral.

"Harriet tells me you're in her reading group," she said.

"That was supposed to be our secret," Harriet said, narrowing her eyes at her mother.

I gasped, expecting Harriet's mother to slap her for talking back. Quickly—to forestall the punishment, to distract everyone—I said, "I taught myself how to read when I was three."

Mrs. Easterday's brows lifted. "How did you do that?"

"I don't remember, actually. It's just patterns." Now it entered my mind that, improbable as it seemed, Harriet wasn't in trouble for giving her mother a dirty look. "Astonished" doesn't begin to describe my reaction. I felt the blood in my brain humming.

"That's amazing. Really." She stared at me.

I felt myself go all hot, in pride and shame.

"Well, I'll leave you to it," she said, and she returned to the kitchen.

The smell of the strawberries revived me. "I love strawberries," I said to Harriet. "But my mother can't stand them."

She poured a small stream of milk onto the berries, licking the overflow off the rim of the glass. She didn't mention or explain what she'd said to her mother.

I touched the cake with my fork. It was dense, unlike any cake I'd ever seen. "What kind of cake is this?"

"Just pound cake from Dillons."

"What's pound cake?"

She rolled her eyes. "I don't know, that's just what they call it. Why don't you try it?"

I put a morsel on my fork and slid it between my teeth. It

was fine, heavy but with a delicate crumb, and it had sponged up some strawberry juice. I rolled it around on my tongue before I swallowed it.

When we finished, Harriet said, "Want to see my room?"

The stairs were carpeted, too, and the banister was made of some kind of dark, grainy wood I'd never seen before. As we climbed the steps I ran my hands along the banister and made a mental note to look up the name of the wood when I got home. "We have this giant dictionary," I said to Harriet. "Mother buys it at the grocery store. You get one section at a time, and you thread it through these metal spindles. It's huge."

We had reached the top of the stairs. "Do tell," Harriet said.

My mouth was already open to describe the thumb index and tell her how fun it was to run your thumb along it, but I said no more. Mother had told me that not everyone would sit down and read a dictionary like you read a book, and maybe she was right.

As we walked down the hall we stopped by Harriet's sister's room. A willowy blonde like her mother, she was lying in bed, chewing gum and looking at a magazine. When she saw us she stood up and walked over to the door. She had on hip-hugger pants and a crop top, and you could see her belly button. She looked like a teenager.

"This is Billie," Harriet said. To me she said, "This is Evelyn. She's in sixth."

"Grade?"

Evelyn gave me a dismissive look and said to Harriet, "Suck in your stomach, fatso, your blubber is sticking out." She flicked Harriet's stomach with her finger, blew a pink bubble, and closed the door.

I wrinkled my nose, and Harriet shrugged. "'Suck in your stomach, suck in your stomach,'" she said, her voice high-pitched and nasal, approximately like her sister's. Then she lowered the pitch. "'Pleasingly plump.' 'Baby fat.'" I understood her to be imitating her parents.

"Oh! My mother uses 'pleasingly plump,' too."

"You're not fat; stop pretending." Her voice sounded angry.

"'Do you eat to live, or live to eat?'" I tried to make my voice sound funny like Harriet's, but it only sounded squeaky. "That's what my cousin Joan—"

"Boorring," Harriet said. For a second I thought she had slapped me—I felt the sting on my cheeks—but she had only spoken, and now as she walked she was swaying her hips and snapping the middle fingers of both hands.

As we passed the doorway to the boys' room I caught a glimpse of bunk beds; the floor was strewn with clothes, empty pop bottles, dirty dishes, scattered notebook paper, all kinds of balls, and all kinds of things to hit balls with. The boys had some type of practice after school every day, Harriet had told me.

Her room was the last one down the hall. In contrast to the impression I had of the other rooms, Harriet's was tiny—barely more than half as wide as it was long. A small iron bed stood in the far corner, partially blocking the one tall, narrow window. I squeezed past Harriet to check out the view from the window. It was glorious—one giant tree close to the house, swaying in the breeze, and, beyond it, the pitched roof of another big old house and more trees.

No wonder it was so cool here. At our house, the trees were only sprigs, and the view out my window was the clothesline and the chain-link fence, and the house was hot unless you were right in front of a fan.

"This was the maid's room, back when people had maids," Harriet said.

I blinked and pictured the pen-and-ink illustration of Cinderella from a book we had at home. To stop the whole story from telling itself in my mind, I pushed up the window, and a cooling breeze entered the room. I stuck my hands out as far as the screen permitted, and the moving air refreshed my underarms.

An odd thing happened then. As I felt the air on my skin, the words went through my mind, *The air refreshed her underarms.* It was as if my mind was narrating what was happening. I was startled. It wasn't unusual for me to re-create a day's events at night in bed—imagining different outcomes—but this was new. It was like an echo. I wondered if everybody else experienced this. Why had no one mentioned it? I longed to ask Harriet, but I was afraid. As things stood, she seemed to be drifting away from me a little at a time. When I turned around, she was sitting on the bed. I sat next to her. *(She sat next to Harriet.)*

"They kept a china bowl under the bed to use the bathroom in, and they had a pitcher and bowl on the dresser for washing up." She had one knee bent, grasping it with both hands. She was rocking a little.

"Chamber pot," I said.

She looked distracted. "What?" *("What?")*

"That's what they called the—"

"Want to see my Colorado stuff?" She walked two steps to the wardrobe and reached up to grab a wooden box on the very top of the piece. The box had a hinged lid and a keyhole, and it looked heavy. I stood up to help her, but she shook her head, keeping the box close to her chest before setting it on the bed.

(All this echoed in words in my mind.)

From under the mattress she retrieved a curly key and unlocked the box with a click. "Don't open it, I'll be back." She hurried out of the room.

I had no idea where she was going. I suspected she was hiding the key in a new place. But wouldn't she need it to lock the box again when we were finished? I sighed in exasperation. Her behavior was as much a mystery to me as everybody else's. I'd always hoped that when someone was your friend, you wouldn't have to figure them out all the time. I thought things would be natural, like with cats or horses, or even Grandma.

As my mind echoed it all, I ran my hand over the top of the box to clean off the dust there. I lifted my skirt and wiped my grimy hand on my thigh, and then I busied myself studying the bed quilt. The pattern was Lone Star, one of the hardest, a single star in the middle, its light rays radiating diamonds on diamonds on diamonds outward. Grandma had told me it was a *trial*, getting patchwork points just right—that's how she talked, old-fashioned and biblical. She'd made a lot of quilts—hundreds, I'd guess.

I talked to myself as if Harriet was there to hear me: *She's the kindest person I know, but she's not sickly sweet, not condescending, you know? She's real, if you know what I mean. It's hard to explain. She treats everybody the same.* Harriet already knew I always spent a month in the summers at Grandma and Grandpa's house, eighty-some miles away in Wiley, but I'd never told her those had been the best times of my life.

Grandpa, he's sweet, but he's got a lung disease and mostly sleeps in his chair in front of the fan in the front room. He has the thinnest arms I've ever seen on a man. He drinks his coffee out of a saucer, and after the first sip he smacks his lips and says, "That's good eats" and winks at me. He always has a nickel for a banana-sicle at Nelson's Market, and he taught me how to play dominoes. But mostly he sleeps in his chair or in the back bedroom. I wanted to tell Harriet all about them, and about my cousins, my aunts, my uncles. I wanted to talk for hours about them, because it made them real to me and less like people I visited who seemed to be only putting up with me. But I couldn't predict what Harriet might do or say, and I was afraid she might drift away permanently.

I ran my fingers over the stitches in Harriet's quilt. Machine. Grandma hand-quilted hers, and she was in a quilting group where they all sat around a wooden frame and worked on the same quilt to give to poor people. I went with her a few times. The ladies talked and talked, and sometimes they sang hymns. You would have thought, me being a little kid, that I would be bored listening to old women talking all afternoon. But I wasn't, not by a long sight. If you listened, it was like walking through their houses, their families, their lives. Being with Grandma and her friends, I realized sitting there on Harriet's bed, you felt natural, too. You didn't have to wonder what they were thinking. They just were.

Now I heard a noise in the hall and lifted my skirt to peek at the dust smear on my leg, worried that it might show through the fabric. I licked my fingers and tried to thin out the dirt. Just then Harriet returned. I threw my skirt down, but I couldn't tell from her expression whether she had seen me. I wanted to explain, but how could I do that without admitting I had seen the sticky dust all over the box? If her mother was like mine, she would be embarrassed that company had seen something dirty in her house. To say something, or to try to finesse it—that was a deep and frustrating mystery to me.

"What are you doing?" Harriet said.

"Just looking at your quilt. Did you know it's a Lone—"

She bounced onto the bed and threw open the box. She grabbed the top item, a wrinkled scarf, and tossed it in the air, evidently not interested, but I caught it and began examining it.

"What is this material?" I said.

"Silk, dummy." (*"Silk, dummy," Harriet said.*)

Silk. It felt like it might dematerialize in my hands at any moment. In a few places you could see where a scuff had separated the threads. I started to smooth out the wrinkles but thought better of it, fearing I might make a hole or there might still be dirt on my fingers.

"Colorful Colorado The Centennial State" was printed on a banner across the top of the scarf. In garish colors of purplish red, dark yellow, and white, against a background of lime green, were scattered cowboys, Indians, bucking broncos, saddles, boots, deer, cabins, tipis, stone buildings, and craggy mountains, as well as famous people (Kit Carson, Buffalo Bill) and places of interest (various forts, the Garden of the Gods, Pikes Peak). Nothing was to scale; it was as if a child painted it.

"Where's Bolder?" I said.

"It's not on there."

"How come?" When *"How come?"* echoed in my mind, I almost thought Harriet could hear it. I peered at her sideways, but she gave no sign.

She ignored me, seemingly focused on emptying the box. She scattered things on the bed—bead necklaces, leather coin purses, key chains, postcards, silver charms, magnets, a pair of pink sunglasses, tiny mugs—most of them bearing the names of Colorado towns and attractions. Souvenirs. I tried to look at each of them, I wanted to, but there were so many they began to congeal in my vision into a colorful blob. I tried to blink away the blurriness. I was panting. My arms felt prickly.

"Here it is!" Harriet said. "My rock collection! Just look, Billie!" She pulled out a flat cardboard box divided into small partitions with glassine windows, each containing a little rock. Clearly, this was the treasure.

"Oh. Yeah." I was more interested in her excitement than in the rocks. I was curious to know why she seemed so thrilled with the collection, which held little interest for me. After all, rocks could be found all over the outdoors, even in driveways.

"Look, obsidian," she said, pointing. "And here's amethyst, and blue calcite. *No*, don't *touch*."

I jerked back my hand.

"I don't let anybody touch my collection," she said amiably. "Here, you can hold these." She reached into the box and grabbed a small leather pouch, and the contents burbled when I caught it. I loosened the drawstring and poured out several smooth stones. *(. . . and poured out several smooth stones.)*

Still staring at the box, she said, "Those are tumbled and polished. They're okay, but they're for tourists." She wrinkled her nose.

I rolled the stones in one hand. They were smooth and cool to the touch, much nicer feeling, I guessed, than the odd-shaped, rough stones in the box. And whereas it hadn't hurt when she called me dummy—obviously, I wasn't dumb—it did hurt that she saw me as someone with no appreciation of the finer things.

"Crocodile jasper—isn't that cool?" she said.

I felt a spark in my backbone. A new word! I guessed by her tone and the context that "cool" referred to something other than temperature. Not having older siblings, I hadn't heard it used that way before. "Yeah," I said, nodding. "Cool."

The box contained forty little cubbies: five rows of eight rocks each. I noticed one was missing, and I asked her about it.

"Oh." She hesitated. Then she leaned toward me and whispered, "It's a worry stone. I keep it under my mattress to have something to rub on when I can't sleep. It's— "

"I have a worry *doll*!" I almost shouted. "My grandma made it for me. It has a crocheted dress and a hat, and it's, like, this big." I held my fingers apart about three inches. "You're supposed to tell her all your worries, and then they go away. Her face is worn off."

"What kind of worries?" *("What kind . . .")*

"Oh, you know." Now my voice went low. I was out of breath. "School, stuff like that."

"Really," she said, her eyes accusing me. "*You* worry about *school*?"

I laughed. "You think school's easy for me?"

"Yes."

I dropped my eyes. I hated liars, but bragging was impolite. And I knew there were gradations of lies, from trivial to terrible, although applying that scale in any given situation was hard for me. Plus, I needed to learn how to lie better, and that was hard, too. People's reactions were so complicated.

Neither of us said anything for a while. We needed a change of subject, so I looked around. My eyes landed on the wavy glass in the window, and I mentioned that my cousins liked to crawl through the dormer window at Grandma's house and then out on the roof. I longed to be a part of that, but the roof slanted sharply, and it seemed to me you could easily slide right off of it. And nobody had invited me.

"Did you really teach yourself how to read?" Harriet said.

I nodded, but I couldn't make eye contact. I could tell she thought I was lying about that, but I wasn't. To me, the patterns of letters, words, sentences, and paragraphs were self-evident. The number of possible letter combinations was finite; there were lots of them, sure, but there were many more letters—a number larger than I knew—that didn't go together, and you could ignore them; for example, there was no word that started with *nh*. So reading was a process of elimination. It wasn't that hard.

I cracked my neck to relieve the tension there, and something caught my eye on the wall next to the door. It was a shelf made of two intersecting squares. The shelf held a dozen or so glass horses, all kinds, but what interested me was a flat, irregular-shaped disk about the size of my hand, resting on a little stand. I walked over and picked it up. "What's this?"

Harriet brought up her feet and lay back on the bed. "That's just something my aunt Wanda gave me." *("... my aunt Wanda gave me.")*

"It looks like a rock, but it's perfectly flat."

"Yeah, it's a slice of a bigger rock. They call it a slab. That's a polka dot agate."

I picked it up and turned it over in my hands. "It's too thin to be a *slab*." The disk itself was shaped roughly like a mountain, and the image on the flat surface was mainly wavy, pale blue stripes interspersed with cream-colored bands. Immediately it put me in mind of a blizzard. There were several brown marks; you could picture the rock as a whole, with rough brown fissures extending through it, leaving a hole behind in each slice. Then I noticed a larger mark in the lower right corner, and it assumed the shape of a standing wolf, howling. Now I noticed an irregular diagonal line defining a large blue area, and I saw that the wolf was standing on the edge of an icy lake. A wolf in a blizzard, lost and alone, looking for the rest of its pack. I felt my heart beating in my ears. It goes without saying I had never seen a rock like it; more than that, I had never imagined such a thing existed.

"Is this from Colorado?" I asked her.

She didn't answer until I looked at her. She had one knee bent, and the other leg balanced on it at the ankle. "I don't know. It was a present, like I said."

"It looks like a wolf, see?" I held it up and pointed to the mark.

She squinted. "That's the wrong side. Turn it over." *("Turn it over.")*

On the other side I ran my fingers around the edge, noting that the lip was beveled and rough, somewhat like a live edge on a piece of wood. A second look showed me it was sparkling. "What's this?"

"You don't know anything about rocks, do you?" She smirked at the ceiling.

I took a breath. "Well, my daddy doesn't teach geology."

She sat up. "Fair enough." That sounded like something an adult, maybe her mother, would say. I recognized with a start that I might be more book-smart than Harriet, but she was more grown-up than I was, more experienced, more worldly. It was as if she and I had been fencing all this time, parry and thrust, and she had won—she would always win, she knew just what to say; she had a certain grace I lacked, not to mention pound cake and siblings and who knew what else. *Fair enough*—a new concept for me. I didn't know why she seemed to like me, but I accepted it, at least tentatively, as a gift.

"It's called drusy, those sparkles," she said. "Next time you're here, I'll show you a rock book I have. There's these rocks that have, like, caves in them with amazing drusy all over the inside. It's like a house for fairies, only it's real."

Next time. I felt myself relax. It was as if all my muscles let go at once, like rubber bands, like a balloon you just untied. Yes. Friends.

"Drusy." I tucked it into the place in my mind where I stored new words.

"Some people think rocks have, you know, magic properties," she went on. "Drusy is supposed to bring 'peace of mind' and 'spiritual healing.' "

"Really." This scared me a little bit, because it sounded as if it might be against our religion. By that I mean, mine and Grandma's. She always took me to Sunday school and church when I was in Wiley. At Grandma's house I felt safe. She took things as they came, including me. She wasn't always thinking of some lie to tease me with and then laughing at me for believing it. If I came crying to her after some cousin had offered me a spoonful of ice cream that turned out to be clabber milk (who am I kidding? It was Joan), Grandma would say, "I've got me a bushel basket of green apples. Want to make pies?" or "I haven't sorted out my buttons in a long time. Want to?" or "Did you learn that Bible verse I give you? Let me hear it." She knew lots of Bible verses, and she had lots of sayings, which she repeated like the refrains of the hymns she sang while washing dishes. I can't tell you how good it felt to hear "had a fit and fell in it" or "treated as mean as a rented mule" or "slicker than snot on a doorknob" or "ugly as a fried egg in a slop bucket" for the nth time. Her homespun proverbs were like pearls on a necklace that I got to reclaim every time I was in Wiley.

Also, she didn't hit. She didn't make a thing out of it, she just didn't, as if it never occurred to her.

But a magic rock that reached into your actual life? That kind of magic was scary. A worry insinuated itself in between my eyebrows.

I carefully replaced the wolf rock in the stand and returned to sit on the bed. Harriet and I talked for fifteen minutes or so about the wonders of Colorado. She'd been to all the main attractions, she told me. The family had driven up Pikes Peak only last summer, and she loved the cold, thin air at the top, and the view of the sky and mountains all around. Getting to the top was cool; not everybody did. You had to know how to drive in the mountains, like her dad. You would see other cars stopped on the side of the road, with steam coming out of their radiators, or turned around where the road got steep and curvy; or they hit the brakes on the way down instead of down-shifting, the *last* thing you should do. Did I know there were runaway truck ramps every so often for trucks to use when their brakes failed so they didn't smash into the cars?

It felt as if I was being initiated into a secret club.

Her parents had friends who lived in the mountains, she told me, and she and the family spent many weekends there skiing and snowshoeing and stuff, and these people had a swimming pool. The eastern part of Colorado was a lot like western Kansas: boring. But then you were in the foothills, and then boom, the mountains. The mountains around Bolder were called the Flatirons, and she and her father often went rock-hunting there, although he limited the two of them to ten pounds and he kept the best ones. He brought sandwiches and orange juice, and it was the most fun Harriet had ever had. (I realized then that she was talking about one time, although when she started talking about their rock-hunting she had implied they had done it many times. I understood, though. Even though Daddy was home during the week a lot more than other fathers because he worked fairs and events, the time he and I spent together loomed large in my imagination and memory.)

Just then the cicadas started up outside, and Harriet turned her head sharply. "That's the creepiest noise. Have you ever seen one of those bugs?"

"I love them. I had one in my hand one time, and it felt kind of like sticking a fork in the toaster." I used to imagine the sound they made was the trees singing to each other, but that seemed too childish to share. *(". . . that seemed too childish to share.")*

She shuddered.

"You can see their shells if you look for them," I said. "On trees. They're brown and thin and translucent, like those celluloid Kewpie dolls you used to get at the dentist."

"Shells?" *("Shells?")*

"It's their old body when they outgrow it. They just crawl out of it and leave it there on the tree bark." I knew the word was "exoskeleton," but it didn't seem necessary to say so.

She frowned and stuck out her tongue, in the universal sign of disgust.

I felt my power in that moment. "Some people *eat* them." *Eat them* echoed loudly in my mind.

From the foot of the stairs came Mrs. Easterday's voice. "Billie, your dad's here to pick you up."

"So soon?" I said.

"Bye," Harriet said.

"See you Monday," I said.

I was galloping down the hall when I realized I sounded like a herd of elephants, and I slowed down, whereupon I tumbled onto the wooden floor. I picked myself up without looking back. I thought I heard Harriet's sister snort in her room.

I picked my way down the stairs. My arms and legs tingled. My thoughts raced. In Harriet's room, why had everything happened twice? And did she like me, or not?

Downstairs Daddy was standing by the door, wearing his nice slacks and a collared white shirt, smiling with his mouth closed, his fedora in his hand. "It was nice to meet you, Clara," he said to Mrs. Easterday.

"The same here, Bill."

"Thank you for having me," I remembered to say to her. "I had a good time."

With the formalities satisfied, Daddy and I escaped into the front yard. The old Nash looked out of place by the curb. "Race you to the car," he said to me, and we took off running.

At dinner I told Mother and Daddy that I wanted us to take a trip to Colorado next summer, and they both burst out laughing. No echoes now, but their laughter scraped against my chest.

"Ah, sugar, what makes you think I can take time off in my busiest season?" Daddy said.

"We don't have the money for something like that," Mother said. "Don't be ridiculous. Eat your green beans."

I forked my green beans, one at a time, and shoved them, one at a time, into my mouth. After three or four I gagged, but I got them all down. Sitting there at our little dinette table, I felt exhaustion steal over me, starting at my feet and moving slowly upward. It was like a worm crawling through the inside of my skin until it reached my throat. It always stopped there. It swelled up until it was squeezing my throat, and I swallowed repeatedly, but it didn't budge even when I drank the rest of my milk. May I please be excused, I said, and Daddy said yes, and I managed not to throw up until I got to the bathroom.

I went to bed soon after. It was just coming on twilight, and the cicadas were winding down; you could hear the pitch of the sawing descend, eventually separating into individual clicks. A breeze rustled the little pear tree Daddy had planted by my window. I thought about the afternoon, the sights and smells, the taste of pound cake, how the tender breeze had traced the sweat on my arms as it glided through Harriet's window in what used to be the maid's room. The polka dot agate with the lonesome wolf. How the echoing started and then stopped. All that, and the feelings, was so much. Too much. I felt myself spiraling downward, skiing along the trail of a thought, and then the thought was gone, and sleep claimed me.

All that school year Harriet and I were inseparable. We went to the fair together, we went trick-or-treating, we went to the school's fall carnival, we went to each other's houses after school. At our house, Daddy gave us graham crackers and ginger ale in a martini glass with a maraschino cherry; at her house it was always milk and pound cake with Hershey's syrup or sandhill plum jelly or strawberries. We got a big snow on December 31, and the two of us built a snowman in her front yard and took turns pushing each other down the street in her sled, and then in the backyard we interrupted a snowball fight—her brothers versus her sister and her sister's friend. We hid behind trees at first and then joined in, and afterwards her mom served us hot chocolate and doughnuts in front of the fireplace.

In the spring we spent an afternoon at Clown Town out on 17th Street, riding the merry-go-round, the whirling cages, the roller coaster, the flying airplanes, and the train; but our favorite was the pony wheel. We both loved the smell of the ponies, the way their saddles creaked, their long manes, their soft, sad eyes. Still, Harriet said, this was nothing like the real trail rides in Colorado, in fact it was childish and silly, but she loved horses anyway, so it was better than nothing. She talked about the piney smell of the trees up in the mountains, the tall meadow grasses that swished against your legs as you rode, the birdsong, the neighing and sighing and snorting of the horses, their confident, melodic, mesmerizing tread. How the tree needles thinned out the higher you went until the branches were only sticks. I was transported to a place where all my senses were gratified, where everything was nothing and nothing was everything, and I felt filled. Not itchy, not hot, not cold, not scared, not ashamed, not embarrassed, not regretful, not worried—only filled.

The echoing happened from time to time. As hard as I tried, I couldn't see a pattern except that it only happened when I was with Harriet.

Then one day, two weeks before school was out, Harriet told me at lunch that they were moving to Arizona. Her father was tired of teaching; it didn't pay enough; he had a job with an oil company. So they were moving.

I was stunned. What?

As much as she disliked Kansas after living in Colorado, Harriet told me, she *hated* the prospect of the desert with its snakes and lizards and scorpions, and it was even hotter than Kansas.

"You're moving?"

"That's what I said, don't wear it out." In a tiny part of my brain I noted that this was a mistake on her part—the saying was, "That's my name, don't wear it out"—but I didn't correct her. Most of my brain was on fire with the terrible news.

"When?" I said.

"After school's out. We're getting a moving van."

She chattered on, her cheeks reddening and her eyes brightening. She had been growing out her bangs, and she had her hair in two ponytails that day, and little wisps escaped along her upper hairline, rippling as she bobbed her head in excitement. She was still a plump brunette in a family of skinny blondes, but there were light brown sun streaks around her face.

I sat without eating, without speaking, without hearing, until lunch was over, and then I went out into the playground and pressed my face into a big elm tree and began sobbing, and when someone approached me I lashed out and hit them and screamed and screamed, and Daddy had to come and get me and take me home.

"Well, that's a shame, sugar. But Harriet's not the only friend you have."

"She is, Daddy."

"You'll make another one, you'll see. Lots of friends."

As much as I adored him, as much as I loved doing tricks and playing jacks and canasta and macaroni five-card draw poker with him, as gentle as he was with me, he didn't understand. Anything at all.

On the day the movers came, I walked over to Harriet's house to give her a going-away gift (picked out by Mother): stationery decorated with a wheat stalk, along with ten three-cent Statue of Liberty stamps. I blinked back tears as I passed the huge Mayflower truck in the driveway.

I found Harriet in her room, which was empty except for a big moving box. She was sitting on the floor, leaning back against the box. She had the rock collection in her lap. At the doorway I said hi.

She held up the rock box. "We're taking this in the *car.*"

I nodded.

I sat on the floor next to her and glanced at the wall where the shelf had been, but it was gone. I lost my breath for a moment. I had planned to steal the polka dot agate with the howling wolf, but evidently it was already packed.

I handed her the stationery and stamps. "You can write to me. I put our address on one of the envelopes."

There was a long silence.

"I hope you like your new school," I said. *("I hope you like your new school," she said.)*

"Yeah."

"Well, I better go. Bye."

I had reached the doorway when she said, "Billie, wait." She got up and opened the moving box. At the top, wrapped in the Lone Star quilt, was her wooden treasure box. The key was on a rubber band around her wrist. She unbundled and unlocked the box, and she reached in and pulled out the wolf rock. "You can have it. I don't like it anyway."

"You don't?" I took it and pressed it against my chest.

"Well, bye," she said.

"Bye," I said.

Don't picture us hugging. Kids didn't hug in those days, at least the kids I knew. We said good-bye and I left. That was it.

For weeks the scene replayed itself in my mind. She said she'd given me the rock because she didn't like it anyway. That could mean any number of things. Again and again I wondered what she meant.

Harriet did write to me, and I wrote back right away, and we began a correspondence. Every letter started with, "How are you? I am fine." On paper, the Arizona Harriet seemed off, somehow, no longer the Colorado Harriet or even the Kansas Harriet. Maybe, like me, she found it harder putting things into writing than saying them or, better yet—as in my first visit to her house—harder than fingering and pondering important talismans.

Summer went by, and gradually the time increased between our ever-shrinking letters until we just stopped. Well, not we—me. I owed her a letter, but more and more I couldn't think of anything to say. Once in a while Mother asked me about my little friend, hadn't I written her yet, and it became a thing between us. I felt guilty about not writing, of course, and so I resented Mother's nagging, but of course she never abided any expression of "bad" feelings in our home, and so of course my brain boiled with them, and, in that way, my repressed rage painted over my grief, layer by dripping layer. Harriet's absence became less tender, and Mother eventually stopped mentioning it. At the same time, maybe as recompense, Colorado, which asked nothing of me, loomed larger in my imagination. Once in a while I took out the polka dot agate and traced the blizzard streaks and the frozen shoreline with my fingertips and stroked the howling brown wolf. I thought hard about everything Harriet had told me about Colorado, and I got to where the rock itself smelled of piney woods. The word "Colorado" came to feel cool, moist, and soft in my mouth and in my mind.

Second grade was much like first grade except that I had no one to eat lunch with, no one to poke me if I fell asleep or zoned out in class, no one whose house I had been to, no one who had been to my house. And without Harriet, I had no protection or distraction from the kids who liked to pick on me. All they had to do was call me a dork or a teacher's pet or a drip or a brain or a geek or a know-it-all or a dweeb or a poindexter, or titter-snort behind my back when my hand shot up or I corrected the teacher's grammar, or stand in a knot on the playground and laugh among themselves, glancing at me, and The Thing would explode inside me—the phantasm I had managed to ignore, most of the time, when Harriet was there. The Thing had begun to evolve, which was only natural.

It was in second grade that I started calling it The Thing. You know how scientists can trace something invisible—a hypothetical construct—by recording changes in the environment as the thing passes through? They can't see it, but they can infer its presence from the waves it makes as it glides by. The evolved Thing was like that. It lived on the innermost layer of my skin. When it was awakened, it sent out feelers, and they slithered to every part of my body. They made me itch inside.

No mosquitoes or chiggers could come close to that itch. And burn! It generated a red-hot furnace inside me that traveled to my neck and face and burst through, turning the skin bright red, and it felt as if I was in that dream you always have when you're suddenly naked in public. You know the one. You just want to die.

Imagine ten thousand red ants crawling inside your skin, inside your mouth and eyes, trailing sand. That's what The Thing felt like when I was seven.

To distract myself I redoubled my efforts to learn everything there was to know. I inhaled facts, I acquired skills, I analyzed, I hypothesized, I cogitated. I couldn't carry enough books home from the library to last a whole weekend; I spent hours in thought. One night after I was in bed I heard Mother ask Daddy if he didn't think I was a bit of an odd-wad. I think that was the first time I heard that term. It killed me. It sounded like old chewing gum.

"Bite your tongue," Daddy said. That made me feel worse.

One ordinary morning my teacher, Mr. Hechenberger, pulled me aside and said I would be taking part in a special assignment. He carried my desk into the hall; it was one of those metal-frame lift-top desks with a deep storage bin underneath to hold your stuff, and an attached swivel seat. It was too small for me, really. My lap barely fit under the bin.

Mr. Hechenberger handed me a booklet and two sharpened no. 2 pencils. "Open the first page on my signal, and follow the instructions. Don't worry, it won't affect your grade. Any questions?"

Before I could answer he nodded to me, clicked a stopwatch, and returned to the classroom.

"Why am I the only one doing this?" I wanted to ask him, but I was pretty sure I knew the answer.

The questions were printed on a kind of newsprint, and the

separate answer sheet was stiff and white and filled with rows of empty circles (nowadays they call them bubbles). The instructions explained how to mark the circles, with drawings of the right way and the wrong way. I'd never seen anything like it. It looked adult, like something you would find in a bank. It felt *official* in a way no other school papers, with their pictures of puppies and kittens and baby chicks, had ever felt. I was excited.

I don't remember what-all was on that first test. Verbal, math, social studies, classification, spatial reasoning, logic, antonyms, synonyms, analogies, or all of the above. I loved analogies. A tree is to a leaf as a house is to (a) A leaf (b) A fireplace (c) A porch (d) All of the above (e) None of the above.

I seem to remember the test had five random sentences about African tree frogs; the task was to create a paragraph by numbering them in order. I felt a thrill of pleasure. Even though it was easy, I sensed that not everyone could do it, although *why not* was a mystery.

I sat at the desk in the hallway, unsupervised, tapping my feet, humming a little, having the best time I'd ever had in school. Finally, here was something hard enough that I had to think, but not so hard that I couldn't figure it out. Most of the time it was apparent which answer they wanted, and you just had to give it to them. For maybe the first time in my life, it seemed that somebody wanted my brain to work the way it wanted to.

I was deep in my head, oblivious, and I didn't hear footsteps behind me.

"*Hey* there, egghead," he said, not three inches from my ear.

I jumped up, my arms whirling, my knees slamming against the desk. I wrestled to extricate myself, twisting my skirt.

The test booklet, the answer sheet, and one of the pencils went flying. Inadvertently I jammed the other one, against all odds, about a quarter inch into my thigh. I jerked it out, embarrassed that the boy might have glimpsed my bare thigh. What if he'd seen my underpants?

A drop of dark red blood seeped from the wound.

The boy—a fourth grader whose name I didn't know—laughed at me the way boys laugh when they're scared but hiding it. A hysterical whinny, with growling bass undertones. He covered his mouth to muffle the sound. Unceremoniously he gave me the finger—a shocking, exotic violation—and without another word he made his way down the hall.

The whole incident had taken only seconds.

I retrieved the test materials and returned to the desk, sitting there trying to catch my breath. A little more blood oozed out of the hole in my leg. I touched it with my fingertip, and the drop clung there, and I licked it. It felt primitive and crude, but somehow I trusted it to help.

Then The Thing, suppressed by my earlier joy, let loose with all its fury, and I felt fire in all my cells.

But I had a task, and I felt compelled to invent some way of completing it, and so I decided that I would postpone my meltdown until I was home in my room. I told myself I would close the door and scream into my pillow all I wanted. I repeated it a dozen times until The Thing subsided.

In spite of the time I lost, I finished the test before Mr. Hechenberger returned. I had time to review the trickiest questions, but it turned out I was satisfied with my answers, so I didn't change a thing.

That year I took half a dozen standardized tests out in the hallway by myself. I didn't mention it to my folks, although years later I discovered a letter from the school referring me to a school for the gifted in Topeka. Nothing had ever come of it.

Other than the tests, nothing changed at school; I sat in the same classroom in the same seat reading the same silly textbooks and filling out the same boring work sheets.

But rumors flew, as they will, and they only confirmed my classmates' opinion that I was peculiar. It wasn't until several years later that a teacher let it slip that I was a quote genius unquote. I knew, based on the empirical evidence of my existence, that genius was just another word for odd-wad.

That same year Mother seemed to make a project of teaching me how to act normal. She seemed to think it was a matter of my deciding to ("There's nothing wrong with you; you can act normal when you want to; don't be lazy/stubborn/conceited/mouthy/bigheaded/pigheaded"). She told me, you don't *have* to answer every question. There's no law that says you *have* to tell people what grade you got. You don't *have* to make smart-aleck remarks out loud; you can just think them. You don't *have* to talk at all unless you're called on. For God's sake, just watch how the other kids act, and do the same. It's not that hard.

But it was hard. It was exhausting. And I wasn't very good at it. I hated pretending to be someone I wasn't, although at the same time I wished I was someone I wasn't: a normal person. Why did it always feel like playacting?

At night I would go over and over what had happened that day, critiquing my behavior like a hanging judge, and I prayed to Grandma's god to help me understand why I was so weird. Lord, how I wanted to understand. But I didn't, and, more and more, I saw myself as an alien dropped on my folks' doorstep.

It turned out that the very tip of the pencil I had stabbed myself with, that time in the hall, had broken off in my leg. Now, decades later, the little grayish purple dot is still there. If it hasn't disappeared by now, I guess it never will.

Chapter 3
The Garden of Eden

I had eight cousins on Daddy's side—three from his sister Wilma and five from his sister Jolene. I was the next to youngest of the cousins, and the youngest girl.

The thing is, I had gotten it in my mind that your cousins had to play with you. I think Mother probably told me that, for her own reasons. So as a little kid I spent time in the summers swimming along deliriously in my cousins' wake, gulping.

Aunt Wilma and Uncle Frank, parents to Vivian, Joan, and Frankie, lived in Wiley four blocks away from Grandma and Grandpa. Frankie was three years younger than me, and so the youngest cousin.

Wiley in the 1950s had about a thousand people, the same as now. It had two kinds of streets—brick and dirt—and downtown was two and a half blocks long. Downtown ended at the post office.

You could walk almost anywhere in town in about twenty

minutes. I believe that, over the summers of my childhood, I walked down every one of those streets. I still dream about some of the houses I walked by. It was a five-minute walk from Wilma and Frank's to Grandma and Grandpa's. I thought Grandma's house was the best house in town because it was on the street closest to the railroad tracks, and you heard the whistles day and night. I used to watch the trains go by and peer at the people inside through the windows in the dining car. One time Mother found three of us cousins playing on the railroad tracks; worst whipping of my life. I don't know how old I was, five or six.

Grandma's house was my safe place in the world. I believed in it absolutely, maybe the only place I trusted like that.

If you want to know what it was like in Wiley in the summers, go to any baby boomer Web site. You'll get more nostalgia than you can shake a stick at—tales about boomers' idyllic small-town childhoods, when we made up our own games, went to the movies for a quarter (plus a nickel for a Slo Poke), and (everyone's favorite) drank out of the hose. Stayed outside all day until the streetlights came on. Blah blah blah. I could write one myself about the hilarity of your cousins sliding ice cubes down the back of your shirt, putting millers (you may know them as moths) down your underpants, tossing grasshoppers in your face, sticking a wad of bubblegum in your hair. Sending you on fools' errands and then laughing their butts off when you came back. Tickling you until you cried. Running into the bathroom and taking a picture of you in the tub. Telling you your tadpole died and making you dig the grave and then throwing in a raw gooey egg. I thought this teasing was funny—it often made me laugh until I cried—when I was a little kid. I took it for belonging. I guess a lot of kids do.

Nor was I the only kid who got hit. The same people who glorify drinking out of the hose also post memes about how great it was to regularly get beaten with Dad's belt or otherwise harshly punished, because, after all, the OP says, they went through that, and they turned out all right. Not me. In the comments, I always look for the ones that say, "You may think you turned out all right, but you didn't."

But those kinds of things didn't go on at Grandma and Grandpa's house when I was there. They just didn't. I think Grandma was probably as perplexed by her odd little granddaughter from Hutchinson as much as anyone, but it didn't faze her. Blood is thicker than water, she often told me.

The farm cousins, for their part, lived on rented ground near Rose Hill, not far from Wiley. Aunt Jolene and Uncle Marty had five kids: Donald, Trisha, Marie, Beverly, and Mick. Sometimes when I was in Wiley, Aunt Jolene drove up in their old army-green pickup with some of her kids; and sometimes I and the Wiley cousins spent a few days at the farm. In Wiley, sometimes I slept at Aunt Wilma's, and sometimes I slept at Grandma's, with or without various cousins.

At bedtime Grandma would spread quilts out on the floor in the front room, facing the screen door, and she set up a huge floor fan blowing air on us. Naturally, we would sit up for a while in front of the fan and go *ahhhh-ohhhh-eeee* to make juddering noises, like throat singing; at least the younger ones did. I love remembering how we would lie there in the dark and talk, although I don't remember most of what we talked about.

One Fourth of July, I remember, it was raining all day and a bunch of us sat on the front porch and lit firecrackers in our fingers and threw them in the front yard. Black Cats for the bigger kids, Ladyfingers for the littler ones like me. The point was to wait until the last second to throw them, watching as the notoriously inconsistent fuses sizzled down. More than once I ended up with stung fingers. What I liked best was to unroll them—they were tightly wound pieces of paper around a line of gunpowder—and study what we presumed was Chinese writing. I pictured the people, bent over long tables, winding, winding, winding. I wondered if they tried to read the papers as they worked. I knew I would.

When some of us stayed on the farm, the farm cousins liked to throw us (me) into the horse trough, slimy with green stuff. Or they'd ride with me bareback into a field out of sight of the house and then leave me there, lost, while they galloped over the ridge. I remember the time we were wading through the creek and Joan threw a rope at me, yelling, "Snake!" I swallowed my tears as best I could, thinking them the price of admission. Grateful for the opportunity.

It was Joan who, on one visit to the farm, finally disabused me of that notion, indifferently puncturing my childish belief in the cousin imperative. Smiling, she invited me to go look at a new litter of kittens, leading me by the hand to a grassy patch out behind the barn, with me saying, "Where? Where?" At last she pointed down, and slowly I came to realize I was peering at tiny entrails and skulls with thatches of fur. Daddy barn cats like to kill their kittens just like daddy lions kill their cubs, she told me—the kind of knowledge that would bore into my brain and then come bursting out in other, inappropriate contexts. Only Joan seemed to understand how The Thing thrived on a mixture of horror and fascination, and she eagerly fed me all the horrors I could contain.

Death in general had intrigued Joan ever since she'd attended a funeral of a neighbor of theirs in Wiley. During long summer afternoons when I was five, six, seven, she doled out details like a trainer throwing fish to a sea lion. How the funeral-home people washed and curled and ratted and sprayed your hair and put makeup on you, even men, and how they put a little white New Testament in your hands and folded your hands over your stomach. How they strapped your neck and stomach and legs to the box so you wouldn't spring up in the middle of everything (I didn't know how she knew that, or even if it was true, but it got my rapt attention). How they had to split your clothes down the back to get them on you. How they sewed your mouth and eyes closed and put a wad of cotton in your bottom. How people lined up and walked past and looked at you, maybe kissed you, maybe laid their hands on your hands. I asked her many questions, but the one that bothered me most was, why did they put dead people in a box in the ground, because how could they *breathe* in there? And Joan had rolled her eyes and said that dead people didn't breathe anymore, that was what being dead *meant,* you stupid *idiot.*

I became aware of my breath. For the rest of that trip, I periodically became conscious of myself breathing and forced myself not to stop, until something distracted me and I forgot about it, until I remembered it again. Sometimes I still do that.

Still, when I was a child death remained, for me, highly abstract, until one hot day during the summer after second grade.

My stay in Wiley was coming to an end, and Mother and Aunt Wilma had decided we would wind things up with a road trip to the Garden of Eden. I had no idea what it was, but from the bits and pieces of their conversations I overheard, I assumed it was some kind of fair, and I had looked forward to it for, it seemed, months.

While Mother and Aunt Wilma got things together for the trip, I knelt on the carpet in Wilma and Frank's air-conditioned front room, watching a fat bumblebee thump against the glass in the picture window. Joan, standing next to me, was swinging a flyswatter whose business end was made of metal mesh, its eight edges covered with heavy paper and stapled all around to keep the sharp metal strands from fraying. The screen had been bent and re-bent and didn't lay flat, and it had a smell.

Joan was eleven—three years older than me—and just coming into her superpowers. She had a way of looking at you. She didn't exactly "look" at you, or "glance," or "gaze"; she stared and she glared, and she bedazzled you. With her eyes alone she held people dumbstruck. I was in awe of her. I wanted to be her.

She smacked at the terrified bee again and again with the lumpy flyswatter, snorting with each stroke, and the sounds of her breathing and the metal scratching against the glass gave me chills.

Pretty soon the bee clung motionless on the window. Then it slid downward, leaving behind pearly guts and black bits on the glass.

As the bee lay curled up on the carpet, Joan bent over and nudged it with the flyswatter. When it didn't respond, she stood there, twirling the flyswatter by its handle on one finger, singing a breathy, tuneless, wordless song.

I looked down at the bee. It now struggled to right itself. I was half afraid, having been stung on an ankle earlier in the summer; my skin had quickly turned red and formed a welt surrounded by an oval necklace of white flakes. It had burned for hours.

But now the bee was still. As I watched, it seemed to lose all its juice at once and shrank into a shell of itself. With a start I realized something that hadn't quite registered with me when I'd seen the ruined kittens: it must have *died*. Just now. Moments ago, it had been alive, buzzing against the window, and I had witnessed its actual death, and now it would never move again, never do anything again, never sleep or eat or fly or breathe. There was nothing but greasy lint to show it had ever lived, and only Joan and I knew it had died. Had been killed. Such nothingness. I shivered and lowered myself on to my stomach. I wanted to reach out and touch the remains, but I dared not. I felt a hush in my body, all my cells holding their breath. An inkling of eternity.

"Are you crying?" Joan said, pretending to be sympathetic.

"No."

"Liar."

I moved my hands to cover the sides of my face.

"*Now* you are." She smacked me on the back of my thigh with the flyswatter, called me a stupid idiot, and hooted as she ran out of the room. *("Now you are," Joan cried.)*

The swat didn't hurt very much, only stung, but the thought of the bee's body parts on my leg made me gag. I swallowed it back. The room's chilled damp heat pressed against my arms, and my cheek burned from the nylon carpet fibers. I rolled on my back and stroked the itchy carpet dents in my bare knees.

My mind went *oh oh oh oh oh,* and a tear escaped.

Just then Mother called from the kitchen. "Did you go yet? Hurry up or we'll leave you behind!"

I glanced one last time at the bee. Then I wiped my nose with the back of my hand and rubbed it on the one-piece yellow gingham romper Mother had made me. You pulled it on over your hips and tied the spaghetti straps together at your shoulders. You had to take the whole thing down to use the bathroom.

"Wait for me!" I rose awkwardly to my feet as I untied the first strap. "Wait for me!" I cried again, running, my voice rising an octave. You would think that, at eight years old, I would have known they wouldn't actually leave me behind. But I didn't know that. I just didn't.

Aunt Wilma drove, and I sat in the backseat with Joan and Vivian. Little Frankie was in the front with Wilma and Mother. He had his head on Mother's lap, and his feet on Wilma's. We were in Uncle Frank's new turquoise Fairlane, the car he drove to Wichita to his job at Boeing. It was a Saturday, and Frank and his buddies were back at the house drinking beer and pitching horseshoes. Daddy was working the Burden Fair that weekend.

Mother read from a brochure. "'Located in Lucas, Kansas,

the Garden of Eden was built by S. P. Dinsmoor in the early nineteen-hundreds.' "

"You're going to make yourself carsick, reading," Wilma said.

Mother sighed through her nose and lowered the pamphlet. "Well, evidently he invented a special kind of cement and made these sculptures out of it. I've always wanted to go."

Wilma smiled. "Now, Bill—Bill never got carsick as a kid." Meaning Daddy. "He could ride upside-down in the trunk and never bat an eye." She doted on Daddy, her little brother, and always had. They all had. I wished he was with us. And I wished there had been room for Grandma and Grandpa, or at least Grandma.

"I never get carsick either," Joan said. She crossed her eyes and flicked me on the arm with her middle finger. I said *ow*, keeping my voice low so Mother didn't hear. They all despised tattletales.

For a while we kids played horses and cows—looking out opposite windows and counting each type in passing fields to see who could count the most of each—all of us except Vivian, who always assumed, to me, an air of otherworldliness, as if she alone of us were an adult-in-waiting, which I guess she was. She was a perfectionist and a high achiever, and I truly don't remember a time when she smiled in my presence. Joan always managed to exasperate Vivian by popping her gum or hawking up a loogie.

The game palled as the cool morning air turned hot. All the windows were down now, and the air blew our hair around. Wilma, always fixed up, had a chiffon scarf loose around her hair, dyed almost black and ratted and lacquered. It looked like a wad of cotton candy. Her makeup was flawless, down to the beauty mark she penciled in near her mouth. Her pedal-pushers and sleeveless white blouse were freshly pressed, and she was wearing gold metallic sandals. Her toenails were red. In my eyes,

Aunt Wilma always looked like a movie star. Mother was only herself—pretty, but not flashy like Wilma.

We got to Lucas about noon and ate lunch in a park—Wilma's signature egg salad sandwiches, potato chips, and graham crackers coated in chocolate frosting. From a fruit jar she poured red Kool-Aid into paper cups. I noticed the ice had melted into little white logs. Joan clandestinely spit a mouthful down the front of my romper, but I remained perfectly still. I dreaded the sticky feeling that I knew would come when the liquid dried, and I hated to think people would see my romper with a big red stain. But of course I didn't say anything.

At the Garden of Eden we parked in a field across the road, and we cousins burst out of the car. There was a good-sized crowd of people wandering around the grounds in the bright sunshine.

"If we get separated, meet back at the car," Wilma said to us. "We have to be on the road by two-thirty. Oh, Billie, you spilled." She reached into her belt and pulled out a hanky, fruitlessly dabbing the stain.

"Yeah," I said.

We walked through a giant gate: a network of big bare tree branches. Larger-than-life statues of people and animals perched among the branches, looking down, bug-eyed. There was a girl on a swing, a lady hanging on to a branch, a man and a lady at the top, an angel, and giant turkeys or maybe buzzards. In the middle, the branches spelled out "Garden of Eden."

I had never seen the like (as Grandma would say, preceding it with "My stars and garters"). I touched a lower branch, and sure enough, it was rough cement like a sidewalk.

"This way," Wilma said, and we passed under the outstretched arms of a tall man and lady who were holding hands. "That's Adam and Eve."

The lady held up a big apple with her spare hand. Joan pointed and laughed, and I looked where she was pointing. I averted my eyes when I saw the lady's bare bottom. I felt myself go red.

As we all walked along a path lined with trees (real trees, not statues), I delighted in the dim, cooler air. Frankie said, pointing upward, "A snake! A snake!"

There it was: curling among the branches of a tree, a snake as big as an alligator, its mouth open, its eyes staring at me.

"It's not real, stupid," Joan said to him.

And then we were once again out in the sunlight, and I saw that there were statues everywhere—in and atop and among the real trees and the fake ones. Some of the creatures were life-size, others gigantic, others oddly small. I didn't know where to look. Statues and wrong-sized real and fake trees as far as the eye could see. But no ticket sellers, no rides, no games, no corn dog or funnel cake stands, no grandstand, no barkers, no lambs or piglets or calves in pens, no hurdy-gurdy music, no men in matching shirts patrolling the crowds, no snow cones, no smell of popcorn. Only a block or two on the edge of town full of statues and trees and winding, trampled paths. Nothing like what I was expecting.

Before I knew it, the family had scattered—Vivian and Joan together, Wilma and Mother with Frankie. I was content to wander alone.

The first thing I saw was an elf in a tree. I stared up at it.

"Boo!" A teenage boy was suddenly next to me. I uttered a little cry.

"That's Satan," he whispered, big-eyed. "The devil himself."

I rolled my eyes. "That's stupid."

He threw back his head and laughed, and then he jostled my shoulder and took off.

I was captured by a thought: If this was the devil, and this was the Garden of Eden, were these the very same people from the Bible stories I'd seen on Sunday School felt boards at Grandma's church? Mother and Daddy and I went on Christmas and Easter to the Methodist church in Hutch, but I liked Grandma's church better, because they served tiny glasses of grape juice in beautiful silver trays with holes, like muffin tins only smaller. And little floury crackers.

Now I was dumbfounded. Why had no one mentioned that this statue place was connected to Sunday School stories? Or did they, and I missed it? Sometimes I missed things when people were all talking at once, the way they talked in the car, or the way the aunts and Grandma and Mother talked, or Mother talked with her friends. She had a lot of women friends. You could hardly keep up with their conversations. I wondered how they came up with so much to talk about. They called it "visiting"—"Go play, can't you see we're visiting?" Sometimes when they got together they visited all night long. Uncle Frank always said, "All of them talking, and not a one of them listening."

I loved to hear them talk. I soaked it up. Nothing was sweeter. It was like music.

But sometimes I blinked and realized I'd missed things, or someone would snap their fingers and say, "Billie? You there?" Now, I felt smart that I'd solved the puzzle of the Garden of Eden. Truth to tell, it took my breath away to think I was standing where the real Adam and Eve had once stood. It gave me a feeling of ancient times, heavy in my bones. The very air felt ancient, thrilling. The thought of the eternally dead bee from this morning flicked across my mind.

I stood and gulped air for a while. I sneaked glances at people passing by and tried to picture them in their houses (I assumed everyone did this). I saw groups walking together, talking, and I tried to guess how they were connected. I noticed some of them holding hands. I saw a father kiss his little girl on the cheek. A mother picked up a fussy baby from a stroller and patted its back. Two teenagers linked arms. A mother slapped a child in the face; a grandfather bawled out a toddler; a father smacked a boy on the back of the head; a girl pinched her sister on the thigh. Children got tickled, nuzzled, swatted, their noses wiped. They cried, whined, complained, laughed, begged.

So much going on. I felt overwhelmed by all the handling of children, roughhousing, teasing, embarrassment, shaming, squeezing. But no one seemed to pay actual attention to the screaming going on inside everybody. They were like marionettes, acting out a play, unmindful, whirling by.

I took a deep breath and cast my eyes skyward. I saw a statue of a lady holding a baby, giant angels with their wings extended, a huge Jesus on the cross (although his curly black beard didn't look like his pictures). At ground level, one display had a soldier, chasing an Indian, chasing a dog, chasing a fox, chasing a bird, chasing a worm. I looked at that one for a long time. It must have been from some story I hadn't heard. The world seemed to have gotten bigger, and it excited and frightened me.

I spotted a live lizard darting about on the ground and followed it until it disappeared under a small triangular building made of stone. A sign on the door said "Adults Only," like the shows at the state fair with the gigantic, lurid pictures of half-naked ladies. I stood utterly still, fearing to trespass into a forbidden place.

"There's two dead bodies in there," a voice said.

I whirled and saw a figure sitting on a bench a little way off the main path. At first I thought the person was another statue, but they were doing something with their hand. Was it a man or a woman? I couldn't tell.

"You ever seen a dead body?" the person said.

I shook my head.

The person was heavy, wearing a blue polo shirt and tan pants, along with a ball cap that said "Supersweet Feeds." There was a wavy salt ring all around the cap, and you could see the wetness where the clothes touched her (or his?) fat rolls.

I decided it was a woman.

The stranger was flicking open the hinged top of a Zippo lighter with her thumb, closing it with her index finger. *Tink*, open, *click*, close; *tink, click, tink, click*. A fairy-tale sound.

The woman's things—a bag made of heavy green cloth, a round thermos, a metal gadget I couldn't identify, various oddities—were piled near her on the bench and scattered at her feet, which were clad in old leather boots missing their laces.

She sniffed, cleared her throat, and spat a gob into the grass. A man's gesture, but still I thought it was a woman. I was surprised by how vexing it was, not being able to tell for sure.

The woman fixed me with a stare. "It's Samuel P. Dinsmoor himself, and his wife Emilie. Second wife." She pointed to the stone building. "In there, the mausoleum, the both of them. Well, their corpses." She pulled out a handkerchief and blew her nose. "You aren't allowed in there."

While I absorbed this information, I felt a sharp, grainy blister on my left heel. I limped over to the bench, which was made of the same rough cement as the statues. I eased off my tennis shoe.

"I was sitting here," the woman said. *("Sitting here," the woman said.)*

"Oh." I started to rise. I was surprised to hear the echo. What was it about this stranger that had triggered the echo? I shivered.

She shrugged. "Free country." *Tink, click.*

I sat back down and glanced at the woman's face, trying not to stare at her nose. It was bulbous and lumpy, the color of bruised red grapes. I lifted up my heel and looked at the blister. The size of a dime, and broken already.

"Eighty-one when he married her, and her twenty." She seemed to be looking off into space. Her eyes were bloodshot.

I had to think for a minute. Oh, she meant the two dead bodies. Maybe she was a man after all. She could be. She gave off an odor; her hair, dark with sweat, fell in strings just past her collar. No telltale bobby pin lines on her scalp from sleeping in pin curls.

My blister pulsed, and I felt sick with thirst. Now I understood I had lost track of time. My lips were chapped, my throat was dry, and my insides felt like the powdery skin of a deflated balloon. I was dizzy.

The woman pocketed the lighter and pulled the thermos onto her lap. She unscrewed the tin top, balanced the container in the crook of her elbow, and tipped it to fill the cup with water. Without a word she passed it to me.

It might have been poison, for all I knew, or it might have been swarming with germs or dirt or anything. But I took the cup and drank it down, with my eyes closed against the sun. *(She drank it down.)* The water was cool, not cold, but I felt it branching like a tree all the way down to my stomach. The woman—it must be a woman—tipped the jug again, and again I drank. I touched my fingertips to the remaining water in the cup and flicked the drops on my face. It stung.

"Sunburnt," she said.

Now I reconsidered; the voice was too low. Why had I thought it was a woman? My mind was flooded with Joan's stories about child kidnappings. The bad guys hurt you in secret ways and then they murdered you. It seemed unlikely that this man could kidnap me in broad daylight with people around. Still.

The stranger poured water into his free hand and patted my burning cheeks, and I felt like crying. I now realized I was sunburned everywhere my skin was exposed by the romper, with the most exquisite pain high on my cheekbones and shoulders, my nose, my lips, my chin, my scalp, the area just above my knees. My skin felt as if it would crack.

"Where-at's your folks?" He gestured with the thermos and poured another cup when I nodded.

Alarms rose in my mind, and the hair on my neck rose even

as I drank. "They're coming for me in a minute. They went to the car to get cookies." My voice sounded like a croak.

"Did they now." *("Did they now.")*

I drank again, gurgling; I was a terrible liar. Now I noticed that we were more isolated than I thought. There was no one in sight. I didn't hear any children's cries and squeals.

"You must come from redheads," he said. "They're like to burn." *("Like to burn.")*

I blinked. Again I wondered, What was it about this stranger that triggered the echo? I saw he was looking at me, the tin cup dangling by its handle on one index finger. He seemed to be sizing me up.

To calm myself, I extended my arms, staring at the red skin, sniffing it, turning my thoughts from secret kidnappings and torture to the familiar sunburn torture that awaited me. I was in for pain, nausea, shivering, blisters, itching, and peeling. I liked peeling the loose white slivers that the blisters eventually turned in to, except for the sight of the sickly pink skin it exposed and my tendency to peel too aggressively into the raw places. I longed to lie down on cool sheets, ached for it.

I tried to put the pain out of my mind. That was a trick adults knew how to do. I flashed on the memory of Mother, on the day after Christmas, crouching over me on the sidewalk after I'd fallen while trying to walk on the stilts Daddy'd made me. Mother's piercing eyes blinked away snowflakes, her jaw—hard, the muscle flexing—so close I smelled her breath, her voice, hoarse with resolve, *Don't cry, you can stand this for a minute, can't you? That's all it'll take, it'll be better in a minute, don't be a bawl-baby, you can stand anything if you make up your mind to.* I remembered blinking as I realized it would only take a minute for the scrape to stop hurting, a few days for the bruise to heal. It was a revelation. *You could stand anything* for a minute, an hour, a day, a week, because then it all went away. Slaps in the face, whippings, colds, measles, mumps—they had all gone away. Whatever hurt—even feelings—would go away. You just had to grit your teeth and stand it until it was over. I saw Mother's face, her jaw, so clearly; she'd looked angry, or maybe embarrassed, shushing me.

But it was hard for me to stand things. Other kids—especially my cousins, especially Joan—for them it didn't seem so hard. I had started practicing it alone in bed sometimes, thinking of something terrible and then not crying. But it was hard.

The man on the bench broke the silence. "Now me, I'm a Dinsmoor relation, you know. By marriage. My granddad was a first cousin, twice removed, to Dinsmoor's first wife."

I wondered what a Dinsmoor was and then remembered the two bodies in the "Adults Only" building. My throat felt as if there were a metal spring inside it, uncoiling.

He didn't seem to notice I was ignoring him. "Glass-top coffins, the both of them. It's a sight. You ever see a body moldering away?"

I felt acid in the back of my throat.

"Air gets in," he said. *("Air gets in," he said.)*

I sprang to my feet, leaned over, and threw up. It was only bile. All I had in my stomach was water. I was ashamed, but I told myself it would pass in a minute.

"I'll swan!" The stranger made a sound of disgust and swung his arm to shield his clothes, ducking away from the stream as if shot.

I'll swan—something Grandma said, too. For a split second my shame gave way, and then I cleared my throat and spat on the ground, spat again. I gagged several times like a cat, but the sickness had passed. *I'll swan.* I smelled baking apples.

"Christ on a crutch!" The person pulled out a handkerchief, dipped it in the thermos cup, and handed it to me. Under his (her?) breath she muttered, "*Nasty.*" For sure it was a woman.

I surmised she'd used this same cloth earlier to blow her nose. I picked a flat-looking corner of the cloth and dabbed my mouth as I sat down again next to her.

"You got anything *catching*?" she said. There'd been a lot of polio going around this summer.

I shook my head, and then, without warning, the jumble in my mind evaporated into one question. "What time is it?"

She closed one eye and looked up. "Three, three-thirty, I reckon."

"*Shit!*" I leapt up, wincing as I worked my blistered foot back into the shoe.

"Where-at—you look peaked," she said. *Peak-ed.*

"The car. They must be waiting for me. Oh, God."

She stood and glanced at her things on the bench. She turned to me. "I'll walk you. You look green around the gills."

I couldn't think of a good reason to refuse.

The cars in the parking lot had thinned out since morning, so it didn't take long to determine the Fairlane was gone. Now I was full-on sobbing.

"Stop bawling, you'll make yourself sick," the woman said.

"They *left* me." More sobs. "They must have *left* me. Did they leave me? Where are they?" I didn't know which terrified me more—being left, or being in the company of this stranger, even if she was a Dinsmoor by marriage. I couldn't remember a time when I was more afraid. I pictured Joan smacking the bee, I saw its little corpse, and I groaned.

"Wouldn't be the first time," the woman said matter-of-factly. "Happens. They'll be back soon's they realize." She placed her hand on my back, and I recoiled at her touch even as it reassured me somehow.

She steered me to the edge of the field toward a stand of cottonwood trees. A hot wind had come up, and the glossy round leaves were clacking. I had a thing for cottonwood trees. There was a big, twisted one in the backyard of the house next door to us, and it leaned far over the fence into our yard. I loved sitting under it, reading. I imagined it was a wizened old man, a friend of mine.

The two of us sank into the cheatgrass along the tree roots. She moaned a bit, out of breath, as she settled herself on the ground. "Out of the sun anyhow." She dabbed at her upper lip with the back of her hand. "Probably just went downtown, don't you s'pose? Pop or something, hamburgers. Mayhap it's not as late as all that." *("Mayhap . . .")*

Now she pulled out a pocketknife. Sunlight glinted off the blade as she opened it.

I gulped back sobs. How long did it take to die if you got your throat cut? I could stand anything for a minute, maybe two.

As she began cleaning her fingernails, a chorus of cicadas started up buzzing in the trees. I thought about how I used to imagine the trees were singing to each other. "I like that sound. I used to imagine . . ." But then I wondered, did I imagine it, or did I actually think they were singing? How old had I been? Would I—

"Where I come up, we called 'em heat flies." She looked up. *("Heat flies.")*

I wiped my face with my palm. "Where'd you come up?" "Come up" was what Grandma would say; "grow up" was more modern. I felt like I had one foot in the past, and one in the future.

"South of here." She leaned across me—I made myself not flinch—and picked through some dry twigs on the ground. She snatched one and sat back. "You ever see what's inside of a cottonwood stick?"

I shook my head.

She fingered the knobby twig until she found a growth line and then applied the knife to it, tracing a circle around the thin gray skin. Then she snapped it, making a smooth edge. She peered at the woody stem and then held it up to me. "Star in there. Look."

"It's shaking, I can't—"

She made a *pssh* sound and smacked my hand with the stick, surrendering it. "Don't poke your gol-durn eye out."

I curled my fingers around the twig and held the cut end close to my eye like a kaleidoscope. "Oh. There *is* a star."

"Told you."

I studied the star image in the heartwood. It had five points, like a quilt block Grandma would make. "How come I never knew this before?" Now I thought, the cottonwood tree in the backyard has had this? All this time?

The woman laughed, making a sound like a car battery turning over—a ringing, wet sound, changing to a cough. She cleared her throat, coughed some more. Finally she said, "You don't find a star every time."

I hung on to the stick. I had a box at home for relics like this.

There was a long silence.

"I wish we had some water," I said.

"Wishes was horses, beggars would ride."

I laughed a little. Again I pictured Grandma. "If ifs and buts were candy and nuts, we'd all have a merry Christmas."

The woman settled her back against a tree and closed her eyes. Soon she was snoring. Now would be a good time to run away and find a policeman or someone, but I was too dry and tired to move. I took off my shoes. Four blisters now, including the killer kind on the outside of the little toe.

After a while the woman snorted and opened her eyes. "What?"

"Didn't say anything." I was still miffed that she hadn't appreciated Grandma's "ifs and buts" saying.

She glanced down at my bare feet and wrinkled her nose, but she said nothing.

"One time I got stuck in a sandbur patch barefoot," I said. "When I was little."

She murmured.

"Somehow I walked into the middle of it, and then I was stuck."

She leaned her head back and gazed at the brilliant sky.

I tried again. "Well, my cousin Joan was out there, so I said, 'Go get M—' "

"That's nothing," she said. "I was in a car wreck when I was sixteen year old and got my throat cut." She lifted her chin; a silver-white scar ran along her jawline. A long scar, wide and jagged. "Busted right through the windshield." *("Busted right through the windshield," the woman said.)*

"Lord." It came out of me unbidden. I had never said "Lord" in my life. It was taking the Lord's name in vain. I wondered if it invoked some kind of magic power or curse, but then I told myself *of course not, don't be such a child, it's not like that.*

"I was on a date—you know what that is?"

I nodded.

"Here's the funny part. When I busted through the windshield, I lost my chewing gum. Now some people come along, and they took me and him into town to the doctor's. He didn't get a scratch, but I'm bleeding like a stuck pig. Clear to the bone. Fifty-seven stitches." She lifted her chin again. "Now, out at the wreck, along comes a cousin of mine and her father, my uncle by marriage, and they get out and look over the car, and my uncle says, 'Well, whoever it was, they're dead, 'cause here's a piece of their brain'—my Dentyne, see, on the hood. And about that time"—she was laughing now—"about that time, my cousin sees my purse in the seat! And she faints dead away! And they took her to the same doctor where I was at!" She was breathless with laughter. " 'A piece of their brain'!" She cawed like a crow and then began coughing again, which gave way to gurgling. *(" 'A piece of their—' ")*

She gurgled for some minutes and at last managed to get up a gob of phlegm and spit it on the grass. She rasped until another gob came; she spat it out, and she dug into her mouth with her fingers to get the last of it. She bent over and wiped her fingers on the grass. After that, she sat and panted a while, clearing her throat and spitting, until the fit petered out.

I was sitting there with my eyes as big as big was (another thing Grandma said). I didn't believe a word of this cockamamie story. A piece of their brain. Although I could easily picture a wad of gum on the hood of the car among a puddle of blood, and what a person might think. Still.

"Thing was," she continued as if no time has passed, "thing was, ever little bit, a piece works its way out. I'll be setting there, I'll feel something on my throat, I'll think it's a gnat or a fly, and I'll swat at it, you know how you do, and I'll come up with blood, and, whaddya know, there's a piece of glass sliding down my neck in a string of blood. Comes out through the scar. Ever little bit." She was fingering the scar absently. "My sister Arlene says, 'One of these days it's gonna cut your throat, Charlotte.'" She laughed and wheezed.

I sat there with my mouth open.

She rose and walked behind a tree. In a moment I heard a hissing stream, and now I needed to go, too. I walked to the furtherest tree. My romper around my knees, I tried to cover my nipples with one hand while holding the romper with the other, my heart pounding the whole time.

"You don't have to wait with me," I told her when I got back. As I sat down in the grass, I thought about chiggers on top of the sunburn. I worried that a piece of glass might ease out of her scar at any moment. It didn't seem likely, but unlikely things had been happening all day. It hit me that this was the longest conversation I'd ever had with an adult, and she wasn't like anyone I'd ever encountered. She had managed to occupy almost all of my busy little mind.

I retrieved the cottonwood twig, and I saw that the star was still there. I stroked it with the tip of my index finger.

There didn't seem to be anything to do but wait. Surely they would be back soon.

The woman sighed and looked off in the distance. "They'll kill you dead, believe me."

"What? Who?"

"Your kin. They'll skin you, whittle you down. Peel all the 'you' off." She scratched one hammy upper arm. "Take a perry knife and peel, peel, peel." *("Peel, peel, peel.")*

"Paring knife," I said.

She seemed to ignore this. She turned fully to face me. "Too much. All my life, I'm told I'm *too much*." She stretched out *toooo muuuch* in an aggressive tone, as if she expected me to argue.

I shivered in the heat.

She gave me an odd smile. "They'll skin you alive. Mark my words."

"Who?" I said again.

"They run from it like it's fire. But it's water." *(". . . like it's fire," she said. "But it's water.")*

"What is?"

She took off her ball cap and fanned herself with it. Her hair was plastered to her skull.

She whispered, "Love." She fanned herself faster. "You know what I'm talking about. Nothing scares them as much as love."

Naturally, I was startled by this unfamiliar—unprecedented, really—degree of intimacy. What made her think I knew what she was talking about? The word "love," to me, was sort of *nasty* (i.e., about sex). I didn't know what sex actually entailed beyond hugging and kissing like they did in the movies, but this crabbed notion of romantic love, sexual love, was the only context I had for love. It meant that the first time your boyfriend said "I love you," it was the first time anybody said it, period. I thought that was the normal order of things. I myself had never heard an actual person say, "I love you." And what did it mean, *They run from it like fire, but it's water*? Who was she talking about? Skin me alive? Whittle me down? Maybe, I thought, maybe this crazy talk was what people meant when they said she was too much.

But still, I was leaning toward her, straining to understand, because all at once I felt in my throat the need to understand. She'd said, "Love. You know." But I *didn't* know, and I wanted to know, I craved to know, I sensed that nothing was more important. Fire and water.

She sighed and closed her eyes. There was a long silence.

"You ever been to Colorado?" I blurted out.

"Can't say as I have."

Now I heard car tires in the nearly empty parking lot, and I saw a flash of turquoise. I jumped up and waved my arms. "Here I am! Here I am!" Without a word I grabbed my shoes and started running.

As I neared the Fairlane, it came to me in a flash: this would become a story. For the rest of our lives, the family would talk about the time Billie got left at the Garden of Eden—like how Uncle Frank got shot in the heel in the war, or the time our cousin Donald peed his pants onstage at the Christmas program, or the time Aunt Jolene forgot to put the paddle in the ice cream freezer—and they would laugh. I could just see it, all of them looking at each other, hee-hawing. I was so wrapped up in this thought, I didn't even look back at the woman. As soon as I climbed into the car, I was haunted by the certainty that I'd asked her her name and she'd told me, but already I'd forgotten it. All I remembered was her Supersweet Feeds cap. I leaned out the car window and looked for her among the cottonwood trees, but Mother pulled me back in.

Mother was talking, explaining how they realized I wasn't with them when they stopped in some little town on the way home, and Aunt Wilma had to call Frank to come pick up the rest of them in Wilma's car while Mother drove back to get me in Frank's car, and *oh, my God, what were you thinking, scaring us like that, and what have you been doing all this time, oh, my God, look at your sunburn, stop crying, everything's fine, you're going to be fine, stop crying. I've never driven an automatic, what if I get a scratch on it, it's practically brand new, Frank will kill me.*

She pressed the foot feed too hard and the car bucked, and I slid toward the dashboard, stopping myself with my hands. I felt sick to my stomach. I tried to visualize how, exactly, Mother had failed to notice I was missing. As they were gathering at the car, had four children been just too many for her to keep track of? Had she dropped a cigarette on her lap and, by the time she got it taken care of, forgotten to check? With everyone tired and hungry, had there been a big blowup, a screaming argument, a misbehaving or bleeding child that had taken the women's attention? Had Mother said, "Where's Billie?" and Joan said sweetly, "She's laying on the floor with her head on the hump, Aunt Dixie, I think she's asleep"? Had Mother been fishing through her purse for a match? I could make up a thousand scenarios, but I couldn't ask her such a thing. She would be hurt, or angry, or both, and it would be my fault.

My mouth was wide open, I was sobbing and gagging, and I felt slobber all down my front.

Mother stopped the car. She leaned over and made a motion to slap my face—to startle me back into my senses, I think—but then held back. Instead, she shook me, though not very hard. "Stop it!" she yelled. "Calm down! You'll make yourself sick!"

Her breath smelled of beer. I gulped air, I belched, I swallowed my sobs.

"You scared us half to death," she said, more calmly. She pulled out her hanky and began swabbing my face. It felt like knives.

I closed my eyes. I wondered, if we wrecked and I went through the windshield, would I cut my throat? Would glass shards work their way out of my jaw for the rest of my life, floating down my neck in a string of blood? Again it hit me that I'd already forgotten the woman's name. Now I would never remember it. At that moment, too, I realized I had lost the cottonwood twig with the star on it.

Now I wondered whether any of it—the woman, the dead bodies in the Adults Only building, the piece of their brain, the whole long hot strange afternoon—had actually happened. That scared me. That terrified me. Actual crazy people couldn't tell the difference between what went on in their minds and what went on in real life. I was scared to death of being an actual crazy person, chained to a wall in the notorious Third Hill insane asylum over by Winfield. Oh, the stories Mother had told me about that place.

Mother got a dry tissue and continued scrubbing my face even as she went on reproaching me. I should be ashamed of myself, I this, I that. When the tissue was down to crumbs, she dropped her arms and took a breath. I was surprised to see her hands were trembling. I studied her face. In a small flash of insight I sensed she was going on and on this way because she felt bad that no one had noticed I was missing when they left.

I couldn't imagine that Joan hadn't noticed. I pictured her sitting in the backseat thrilling to the secret knowledge, a joyous witness to the event playing out. Mile after mile after mile.

Pretty soon Mother and I set out again. She told me I looked terrible and it was late and she thought she would stop at a motel for the night. Air-conditioning would feel good on my sunburn.

The floor in the small room was covered in cool linoleum tiles, brown alternating with darker brown in a checkerboard pattern. The twin beds had tan chenille bedspreads, the thin kind, and there was a blond desk with a metal chair. A dresser held an eleven-inch, black-and-white TV set, much like the one we had at home.

"You've been in motels before, you were just too young to remember." Mother closed the drapes, and the room darkened. Then she turned down the spread on the bed closest to the window air conditioner. She moved a dial on the machine, and it rattled, spraying out hot, stale-smelling air, which gradually cooled to lukewarm. "Take your clothes off and lay down. Leave your underpants on."

I perched on the edge of the bed and began untying the strings that held up my romper. After a day in the heat and wind, the knots were stiff with sweat. When I pulled on the first one, it scraped against my sunburned shoulder, and I groaned.

Mother went to work on the string, but it would not give, and I was twisting in pain. "For the love of God," she muttered. "Hold still." The two of us worked at cross purposes for a minute, me quietly squealing, until Mother leaned down and put the string into her mouth and broke it with her teeth. Something she had told me many times not to do. Did I think we were made out of money? Did I have any idea how much dentists cost?

I wriggled out of the romper and lay on my stomach on the bed, stifling sobs. You know how a burn sometimes feels so hot it turns cold, as if the skin has decided to die? That heat/cold felt creepy.

I heard Mother root through her purse and get out a cigarette. It sizzled a bit as it caught fire, and I heard her deep drag. "I walked too much today. My legs are all pins and needles."

I turned on my side. She was massaging one leg with both hands, the cigarette dangling from her lips.

"I'm thirsty," I said.

"Didn't you drink anything?" From her purse she pulled out a can of beer and an opener. "Here." She placed the cigarette in the ashtray and cupped my chin with her hand, coaxing me to sit up. She tipped the can, and I took the beer, warm, into my mouth.

The carbonation burned my tongue and palate, and I returned the mouthful back into the can. I took the can from her, breathed deeply, and drew in several small sips. But it wouldn't stay down, and I first dribbled and then spewed the little I had taken. Wherever the drops touched me, they burned the skin like fire.

Mother jumped up, limped into the bathroom, and ran the water for a long time. She returned carrying two plastic juice glasses of water. "It's cold. Don't drink it too fast, you'll give yourself a bellyache." Again she looked through her purse and this time pulled out the familiar small brown-and-yellow tin of Anacin.

"Put it in your mouth and forget it's there. Then take a big drink and swallow the water." She frowned. "Go on, it will just disappear."

She sounded like a fairy-tale witch offering me a poison potion. But I did as she said, and I gulped down both glasses, and sure enough, by the time I breathed again the pill was gone. I excused myself to use the bathroom, and I bent over the sink with my mouth on the faucet and drank until my stomach hurt.

Pretty soon she left to get take-out food and lotion.

I stood under cool water in the shower. I'd never taken a shower, only baths, and the falling water was a revelation. It felt as if my skin was steaming, and tears flowed for minutes at a time, without thought, surprisingly hot on my face. I was delirious with relief.

But when I stepped out of the water, the heat on the surface of my skin seemed to double. I ran to the bed and lay on my stomach in front of the air conditioner. I told myself, soon there would be food. I could stand it until the food got there.

I thought about what Mother said, that I had been to a motel before but I was too young at the time to remember. It was true that there were times in my life—when I was a baby, when I had my two-year birthday party where Daddy took 8-mm home movies, and other times—when probably lots of things had happened that I could no longer remember. I pictured myself trying to blow out the two candles, holding up the tiny porcelain doll Mother gave away as party favors, and pushing around the metal butterfly on wheels—the serious, adult expression on my face was hilarious—but of course those images were from the movies Daddy had taken. I had no real life memory of the party. It bothered me to think I was eight years old and had already lost a bunch of my life. Most of my life. I focused my mind, trying to look back at my earliest memories. I remembered going to the state fair, watching Daddy selling pans; I remembered afterwards, when Mother hit me with a hairbrush, but at this moment I couldn't remember why. Or maybe that had happened a different time. I remembered one time when she hit me with a flyswatter until the end flew off and the two metal prongs cut into me, but I didn't remember when that happened or the circumstances. Sometimes the pictures were there in my mind, and sometimes they weren't.

My stomach burned.

Now my thoughts fixed on the woman at the Garden of Eden. I went over and over the day, detail by detail. I was determined not to lose it. I got the idea to pretend I was writing it down. In my mind, I saw the words as I wrote them. I filled pages and pages. I wrote, *They will peel the "you" offa you*, and I felt good. Calm. I felt right, almost joyous. But then I asked myself what her name was. And what had happened to the cottonwood twig? My memory was a blank. Now I had no evidence that the woman, if she was a woman, had ever existed. If she existed.

But, I told myself, her name wasn't important, and I reminded myself that back in Hutch we had the neighbors' cottonwood shading the backyard, and there were lots of cottonwoods all over Kansas, and one of them was bound to have a twig with a star.

I heard the key in the door and smelled hamburgers.

And then it hit me. All afternoon I hadn't been hijacked by The Thing in all its glory, even with everything that had happened. It was something of a miracle. Evidently I had gotten my fill of the painful and the bizarre in the person of Charlotte. Oh! Oh! That was her name! She did exist, she was a woman, and her name was Charlotte.

Chapter 4
Daddy

We went to the Garden of Eden on a Saturday, and the next Thursday, just as my sunburn was starting to peel, I was sitting in the backyard reading *My Friend Flicka* in the shade of the neighbors' cottonwood when it happened. I was wearing the brown and white saddle shoes Mother had just bought me for school, which was to start, I think, in a couple of weeks. My heels were resting on the grass, and I was clacking the big toes together.

I had carved up all the twigs in our yard, but so far I hadn't found a star.

I heard the telephone ring, interrupting the pattern of clacks. Irritated, I narrowed my focus on the pattern and picked it up again.

Pretty soon Mother came to the back door and called me in. I looked up to see her framed in the doorway. Her face was pale, even in shadow, and her body looked broken in the middle. "A terrible thing has happened," she said.

I felt the breath whoosh out of me. "What."

"Come inside."

I stood up. "What." I thought I'd heard the familiar annoyance and regret in her voice, and it boomeranged off of me. I took two or three steps and stopped. We were about ten feet apart.

She moaned and lifted her skirt and bent over, and, holding the cloth in front of her face, she said that Daddy had died. About noon. Of a heart attack. In Goodland, far out in western Kansas, almost to Colorado.

She took a breath and dropped her skirt. She didn't meet my eyes. He had keeled over right there in the booth at the county fairgrounds, and he was gone before the ambulance got there.

She straightened up. There was nothing anyone could do. She wiped her eyes with her hand.

We both stood unmoving. The afternoon air smelled sharp like vinegar, like oncoming snow.

"What time is it now?" I guessed about two-thirty; he would still be warm, right? Maybe—

" 'What *time* is it?' " She looked lost, unsettled, angry. "What is *wrong* with you?"

She glared at me for a moment, her lips working, and then, shaking her head, she turned and walked inside, leaving the door open behind her.

"You know what I wish? I wish it was you instead of Daddy." I spoke in a normal tone, not loud. I didn't know whether she heard me or not.

I didn't have time to think about it. I had to do something about Daddy. Maybe if I stood there and didn't move, didn't disturb the air around me, time would go backward. I would still be sitting in the shade reading *My Friend Flicka*, Mother would be inside at the table drinking and smoking and listening to the radio (I guessed), and then it would be noon again, and Daddy would be at the county fairgrounds in Goodland doing his pans, and he wouldn't keel over from a heart attack. It would all have been a fever dream. Standing in the sunlight I opened my book and began reading, but, just like a cartoon character, all at once it hit me what she had said, and I threw the book to the ground and dropped to my knees and pressed my face into the grass. I began whispering, thinking somehow the words would get to him through the earth itself, bumping through ant tunnels and gliding across wheat furrows and swimming along creek beds, skimming underneath blacktop—all the way to Goodland, where I pictured him lying on a table all by himself in some kind of small room, some cold place, maybe imprisoned in a box already. But eventually I realized that the sounds coming out of my mouth weren't words at all, only noises. I had no idea what I should/would/could say to him, and I wasn't able to form words in any case. I was an animal snorting in the dirt, and, really, that suited me. To be an animal and not feel as if the air around me was about to squeeze the air out of me.

But of course, after some minutes in the sun I sat up. I swallowed and swallowed. I knew Mother would not come and get me. That was the thing—no matter what I thought or how I felt, I would always have to get up and go do the necessary thing, just as Mother did. There was an inevitability to life, things you had to do anyway, no matter what. The weight of that knowledge settled on me, and I knew it would never leave me. No matter what, you have to push yourself up, bend your knees, get to your feet, and take those steps into the place you don't want to go. I couldn't stand it. But there was nothing to do *but* stand it.

My arms felt empty, bloodless, weightless, as I walked into the house.

Mother sat at the kitchen table, and I slid into the chair opposite. She said nothing. Pretty soon I reached around the cigarette in her hand and put my hand over hers as best I could without getting burned. She pulled away and raised her hand to her mouth and took three drags in a row before she exhaled. She stared at the half-empty pack of Winstons.

She had yet to meet my eyes. "We mustn't feel sorry for ourselves," she said. "He wouldn't want that."

I folded my hands on my lap. Only minutes before, I had been feeling very sorry for myself. I *wanted* to feel sorry for myself. What was wrong with that? Now I felt crushed and confused by shame.

I struggled to think of what to say. "I closed the door to keep the flies out."

She nodded. She lit another cigarette off of the one she was smoking. In a tone of warning, she said, "He wouldn't want us to cry and carry on."

"He wouldn't." I tried to make it sound as if I agreed, but it was actually a question—he wouldn't? Wasn't that what you were supposed to do—cry and carry on—when someone in your family died? Or maybe you were supposed to wait for the funeral? Joan had told me about people bawling and fainting and pounding on walls and whatnot at funerals. Maybe that was it. Mother and I would cry and carry on at the funeral. Or not.

Quietly I began swinging my shoes rhythmically against the leg of my chair. I kept my eyes wide open; it seemed to empty out my head.

Maybe the sound of my shoes against the chair got her attention, because now she looked at me and saw the dirt on my face. "Oh, Billie, what happened?" She licked her fingers and reached toward me.

I pulled back. The tobacco smell of her fingers insinuated itself into my nose.

"Go wash up." She stubbed out her cigarette and chugged the rest of her beer. Then she opened a new one.

I walked to the sink and ran water over my hand and smeared it over my face. I looked out the window. The book lay splayed open on the ground. I imagined black ants crawling on the pages, playing among the black type, changing the words, altering the story.

"The bus leaves at seven-thirty in the morning. Let's have you wear your brown skirt and your new white blouse."

"That's only for school. You said." I was picking my way with her, trying to choose topics and words that I thought she wouldn't get angry about. "What bus?"

She answered my first remark and ignored the question. "Things have changed."

For supper we had bread-and-butter sandwiches and canned applesauce. Afterwards I went outside and got my book and fanned the pages until I was sure there weren't any ants or worms in it and brought it inside.

I went to bed while it was still light. My head was filled with things Joan had told me about dead people. I tried to see Daddy, in my mind's eye, laughing and playing cards and drinking and lifting me high above his head, but there was nothing except the words. No pictures. In the half-light I pressed my fingers delicately against the sunburn on my shoulders and rolled and unrolled the ragged edges until finally I fell asleep. I dreamed Daddy was in a coffin with a glass top at the Garden of Eden, and insects were burrowing their way in. Charlotte, the lady I'd sat with, stared at me with half-closed eyes.

In the Trailways bus the next morning, Mother sat wordless, staring out the window. Silently I played finger games ("here is the church, here is the steeple, open the doors, see all the people") and glanced at her once in a while. Telephone poles flew by.

We had eaten very little for breakfast and had talked hardly at all.

Finally I said, "I feel like I can't remember him already." I meant it as a statement of fact, a noise for my mouth to make; but I heard how whiny it sounded. I shuddered. People hate it when you whine.

Mother reached into her purse for a cigarette (you could smoke almost anywhere in those days), and when she blew out the match and dropped it to the floor, I wanted to reach down and squeeze the hot tip between my fingers. But I resisted the urge.

"When my mother passed," she said, "Daddy told me to recite to myself my best memory of her, over and over. So I'd never forget her." She took a deep drag.

I was shocked. I knew I had maternal grandparents, of course, but Mother seldom mentioned them. To me they were two frowning people from olden times, strangers peering out from a sepia photograph in an ornate oval frame. From offhand remarks I had pieced together the basics: Mother had been, like me, an only child, growing up in Wichita, and her parents had died months apart—her mother of cancer, her father of kidney disease—during her senior year in high school. She had finished the school year living with the family of her best friend, Flossie Market. Mother was the only one left in that branch of the Mosses except for an odd cousin or two in California with whom she had lost touch. And now she had told me a story, a half story—a sentence—about her father. Memorize your favorite story of your mother to help you remember her—it sounded so tender, so sweet, so human. So real.

"What *was* your memory of her?" I held my breath.

She lay her head back on the seat and closed her eyes. After a silence, I asked again.

She brought the cigarette to her mouth and shook her head. She gazed at the ceiling. "Long time ago."

The tone of her voice told me that was the end of that. I felt she was lying; she remembered. As quickly as she had conjured my absent grandparents, they vanished, before I could fully imagine them in the flesh. She was the only person on earth who could tell me anything about them, I realized. For a minute or two I tried to think of why—did she not understand how much I wanted to know about the people I came from? How hard it was for me to feel like I belonged anywhere?

But this time instead of trying to solve the mysteries that had presented themselves, I pressed my backbone as hard as I could into the seat back and told myself my favorite memory of Daddy, the story of the first time I remembered seeing him working at the fair. I relived it all: his patter, the sizzle and smell of rare meat, the lies he and Mother had told—our nonexistent basement, the phony dented pan, "Mildred"—along with the hairbrush, the corn dogs, *They want to be seduced.* It all came back to me in a moment of time, the way they used to say that dreams, no matter how long, actually played out in only seconds. I was able to see it all, smell it, touch it, hear it, taste it, as if it were happening again, in all its beauty and ambiguity. Mother and Daddy at the height of their powers. Now a speck flashed in my peripheral vision—a road sign: "Colorado 56." Just that quickly I experienced a multitude of new feelings, feelings tied to Harriet, the smell of pines, the way the smoke curled like a ribbon over Mother's head when she smoked, my cousins' pranks, Pikes Peak, Daddy's crooked teeth, the way he gulped when he talked, Dillons pound cake, the polka dot agate, notions of what a heart attack felt like.

I closed my eyes, and when I opened them I was looking at the back of the woman's hair in front of us. I followed the curl pattern this way and that, noticing how there was a small white shine at the apex of every curve, giving into swirls of gray that turned into darker gray at the nape.

Meanwhile, the bus rocked with the flapping of the huge tires on the blacktop, and the cabin reeked of diapers, cigarette smoke, sweat, peppermint candies, and diesel fuel. Staring at the woman's hair made me carsick. I tried to swallow, but saliva threatened to spill out of my lower lip. I touched Mother's thigh, and when she saw my face she hustled me to the comfort station in the back. I was ashamed to throw up because people might hear, but the dirty-mint smell of the blue fluid in the tank helped me along. Once I got going I thought I might never stop. Eventually Mother wiped my mouth with a tissue from her purse and gave me a red Life Saver candy.

That kind gesture made me careless. Back in my seat I thought about Joan's vivid descriptions of the physical aspects of death, and I asked Mother what a heart attack was, and she said it was something in your chest, which I already knew, everybody knew, but what—

She said I wouldn't understand anyway, so hush, go to sleep, and as always I didn't dare press for more information or else, I intuited, she would narrow her eyes and give me that look—the glare that turned me inside-out. And then what? Then what? It hit me: she was all I had left.

So I pressed my head against the seat and closed my eyes and pretended to sleep. Not for the first time. I willed myself to dissolve into the scent of pines, and I imagined running my fingers over the needles, a kind of rough velvet.

Mother took me with her into the low-slung buff-brick funeral home. We walked into a carpeted hallway smelling of cigarette smoke. There were three closed doors; next to each door stood a sad, solemn man wearing a black suit, like palace guards in a fairy-tale castle. Mother whispered to one of them, and he pointed her to the door at the end of the hallway marked "Office."

She and I walked in, and a man stood up and shook her hand. How might he be of service?

They began talking about Daddy's body, where it was, where they should move it to, whom to notify—the deceased this, the deceased that. The gist of it was, we couldn't afford this or that.

Mother had brought her oldest—this is Billie, she said—but there were three more at home. You understand. We want the minimum. No, not that, no, not that, no, not that. We would have to put it on payments. Send the ashes to the address in Hutchinson.

Ashes. I cleared my throat three times.

I tried to slip away through time and space, but this time it didn't work. The Thing was creeping around under my skin. Then and there I decided not to call it The Thing anymore. From now on, it would be Charlotte, after the woman at the Garden of Eden. Had that been only last Saturday? It seemed longer ago than that. Hello, Charlotte, I said to myself. I felt her inside my skin; I smelled her sweat as it dripped off her greasy hair. I felt my face and neck begin to get red. But strangely, even with all the talk of death, the dead, the deceased, the body, I felt no grief at all, only the need to remember to breathe. I still had Charlotte, and, odd as it seemed, that gave me some comfort. I think Charlotte represented my own realness to me.

I began picking at my arms, making sure not to peel the lacy dead skin too far into the raw places.

Mother waited three or four days before she called Grandma, one night after I was in bed. I overheard her saying it was too late, the arrangements were made, they could have some of the ashes if they wanted, would Grandma please call the rest of them. Mother hung up without saying good-bye. She didn't answer the phone for several days after that, and she didn't allow me to. You can imagine what happened to my spine every time the phone rang and rang and rang.

At night I cried into my pillow, scourging myself every time: bawl-baby, crybaby, he wouldn't want us to cry and carry on. In the darkness Charlotte hissed at me, as if I were some kind of monster not of this world.

* * *

Within a month Mother sold the house on Halsey Drive, and then the car. We moved into an upstairs apartment in a big old house just off Main Street not far from the Dillons at 14th. Down the street was a Duckwall's, and across the street from Duckwall's was Coberly Drugs and, I think, a Kaufman's, and later a hardware store.

Nailed on the side of the house was a wooden staircase leading to a tiny landing; the flat hollow door was stained with grimy fingerprints. The apartment had been converted from two bedrooms and a hall, and each tiny room had powdery beige walls, creaky wood floors, chipped beige trim, and tall beige ceilings, and in the living room there was a cramped 1940s kitchenette along one wall. It had a tiny fridge with a shoebox-sized freezer that made smelly ice. To wash clothes, Mother explained, you had to gather them up, traipse down the steps to the McKutcheons' downstairs (a woman and six or seven kids), through their living room and kitchen, and then down into the damp basement. So much for my romantic idea of what an apartment was. I had only seen them in movies set in New York.

Mother put in for more hours at work; she said I was old enough to take care of myself after school, which was to start in a few weeks. It was a strange time, those weeks before school started, like a dream. The apartment seemed angry, or maybe annoyed, that we were (I was) there. It was godawful hot, and I wanted to spend all my time in front of the fan, but I had a need to walk in and out of the rooms, to stare out the windows, to keep checking that the door was locked.

With Mother at work and school not started, I read, of course, or I watched black-and-white afternoon TV. One show I liked was produced in Hutchinson. I forget its name, but it starred Sammy Scarecrow and his sidekick, Herkimer P. Pushbroom. Sometimes they had kids on, singing or dancing—yet another possibility that filled me with anxiety. Imagine looking into a camera and knowing people were watching you *right now*. I was frightened for those kids. I figured they must be scared to death.

There was strangeness in the air of that apartment when I was alone there, a closeness, like a tomb or a cave or a bomb shelter.

When she was at home, Mother sometimes mentioned Daddy, or rather the need for us—meaning me—to move on. Everybody dies, she reminded me. Life goes on. He's in a better place. He wouldn't want us to be sad/lazy/afraid/mad. After a while, she stopped mentioning him altogether. She said nothing about the family.

I ask you to believe me when I say I could not ask her a single question about them, or about Daddy's funeral—when it would be, where it would be, what it would involve, nothing. I could not take that risk, and I didn't even know what the risk was. I kept expecting Mother to say something about the strange air in the apartment, but she never did, and she never said anything about a funeral. I agonized over it for weeks until I concluded that there wasn't going to be one. I had never heard of such a thing; maybe when people were cremated, you didn't have one? I remembered she had told the guy to send Daddy's ashes to us, but we hadn't gotten them as far as I knew. What if they sent them to the house on Halsey Drive? I went around and around.

In the ensuing months, Mother and I lived on the margins. We weren't dirt poor—we never went hungry or lived in our car or even imagined it (at least I didn't)—but money was always tight. For dinners we ate canned creamed corn with Vienna sausages, or dried beef gravy on bread, or beans and ham hocks, or sugar sandwiches, or grilled cheese sandwiches and canned tomato soup, or anything that came in a box (Chef

Boyardee chow mein or pizza, Kraft macaroni and cheese); what we liked to call "salad" amounted to canned pears with grated cheddar cheese, or red Jell-O with fruit cocktail. But we ate.

Every night when she got home from work at the cannery Mother groaned that her legs felt like burning lead and her feet were numb, and some guy there always looked down the front of her coveralls, and the hairnet made her look like an old lady. I had no idea what work was like for her. At eight, I could afford to be ignorant. It wasn't until a few years later that I caught a glimpse of that place where she spent most of her days. You didn't take your kids to work. Work was work.

Two or three times a week, she had her ride drop her off at Dillons after work, and she got a six-pack of Metz beer and drank the first two warm. By the third, she was usually asleep in her chair with the TV on. In the mornings I would find two or three empties on the stand next to her green chair.

She expected me to run the dust mop every day, and if she saw dust under the kitchen chairs she bawled me out, but it seemed perfunctory. Oddly, it seemed she was getting smaller day by day.

One day I made the mistake of asking her if we should apply for welfare, and she actually yelled at me, *Over my dead body. Not one dime.* I had thought I was living only in the sad little world of the two of us; but it turned out that when it came to her view of the larger world, we were part of a unit. Our world included the extended family, if only in name, and the community, if only in revealed truths. She had absorbed the scornful attitude of the circles we nominally belonged to, and so I was along for the ride. Whether I liked it or not, I was in the community although not of it. *Over her dead body* would we breach the norms. I came to understand the implications of this only years later.

* * *

Sometime during the aftermath of Daddy's death, my brain stopped narrating what was happening while it was happening—what I used to call echoing. I was relieved. But then, everything felt empty. That's all I can say. I felt empty. I became emptiness.

One afternoon I was running the dust mop under her bed and bumped into a cardboard box. "Human cremains," the label said. What? Then I understood. Charlotte began screaming, and I dropped the box and ran into the bathroom and washed my hands three or four times, and then I lay in bed and cried, one eye on the alarm clock so that I could compose myself before Mother got home.

Day by day I felt farther and farther away from Daddy, from myself, even sometimes from Charlotte.

If it seems like I'm losing the thread here, sharing only bits and pieces of that year, it's because that's what it was like. It takes a lot of bandwidth to smother the kinds of feelings I was having, and you have to sacrifice a lot to gain any kind of stability, which is the main thing you need. Somehow the year passed, I got through third grade, I turned nine, and it was summer again and time for my annual trip to Wiley.

Chapter 5
That Trip to Wiley

Everybody was nice to me during my visit to Wiley that summer. I think Aunt Wilma had told them to go easy on me because I had lost my dad. I say they were "nice," but mostly they just ignored me, except for Grandma, who kept me busy with learning to embroider. I made a sampler with a crewel rose and a cross-stitch Bible verse. She tried to teach me how to crochet and she showed me how to tat, but I just couldn't get my fingers to keep track of the stitches the way you have to. It was one thing to follow lines printed on fabric, but knitting and tatting, you're making stitches in the air.

On Thursday Aunt Wilma had me over for an epic game of Monopoly. There were six of us—besides me, there were the Wiley cousins (Joan, Vivian, and little Frankie) and two of the farm cousins (Donald and Beverly). I didn't love that game, because you could do all the smart things and still lose by a bad roll of the dice. But I loved the old-fashioned Depression graphics, the names and florid colors of the properties, the tokens, the tiny houses and hotels, the crackling sound of the dice on the board. And of course I loved/liked/hated being together with my cousins at the big old round oak table. The longer a game went on, the more we laughed/joked/insulted each other, the more popcorn we ate and Kool-Aid/iced tea/Coke we drank, and the more Grandma, Wilma, and Jolene, sitting at the other end of the room well within earshot, talked about everything in their lives—adult things like groceries and clothes and cars and food and prices and sicknesses and meals and TV and friends and neighbors; and the warmer/hotter/more scalded I felt, the more I felt I belonged, or at least was able to pretend I did.

Mother had sent me to Wiley on the bus by myself, the more (I thought) to make me feel independent and competent. It wasn't unusual in those times to send a nine-year-old on the bus, and we didn't have a car anymore anyway.

On this day in Wiley it was raining on and off. The morning had started with a gully-washer Kansas rain with big raindrops and a warm, cutting wind, and later it had settled down to passing squalls under dark gray clouds. You could hear the rain splattering the windows, and an occasional growl of thunder. It was relaxingly dim in the room.

"Well, you know, Granddaddy always told us, if you can't get what you want, take what you can *get* and *be satisfied*," Aunt Wilma said. She talked the loudest of any adult I ever knew.

I immediately adopted "Take what you can get and be satisfied" as the family motto. To myself, of course, not out loud.

"World don't owe nobody a living," said Aunt Jolene. *Not one dime*.

"There's more than one way to kill a cat besides choking him on butter," Grandma said agreeably. Meaning, I guess, people have to find some way to live, even if it's disgraceful. She wasn't the type to judge people, which was one reason I loved her beyond anyone I knew, even though I didn't know it. Love, as I mentioned, was about boyfriends. As much as I had contemplated what Charlotte (the real one, of the Garden of Eden) had said about love in a broader sense, I still didn't understand what it meant.

"Did I tell you about Earlene Brockmeier?" Wilma said.

"I heard she was poorly." Jolene sucked in her teeth, a habit she had.

"They drew a tube of blood, and it was just sludge—you know, white cells."

"I pray for her every day," Grandma said.

"And here we thought she was just trying to get attention." Wilma rattled the ice in her glass and drank several swallows.

At the table, Little Frankie said to me, "You gonna eat that?" He liked to chew the unpopped kernels.

I slid my bowl over to him.

"Give you five hundred for Marvin Gardens," Don said to Joan.

She sniffed. "You wish."

It went on like that for, it seemed, hours, as rain pelted the roof and the windows, followed by sun, followed by rain. The game play absorbed me, and the women's talk absorbed me—until it didn't. I had emptied my glass, and I felt thirsty, my mouth and lips lined with salt that I couldn't lick away. It would be simple enough to walk into the kitchen and refill my glass, but as soon as I thought of it, Charlotte awakened and began painting the inside of my skin with sand. She did that sometimes—show up without rhyme or reason.

"I'll trade you Electric Company for B & O Railroad," Frankie said.

"It's not your turn," I said. "You can't trade if it's not your turn."

"Who died and made you king?"

"Queen," I said.

Joan laughed and looked at me. "You got a cob up your butt?"

I gasped. Frankie tittered. "*Cob* up your butt!"

I stood up abruptly, jostling the board, the tokens, and the houses. Everyone looked at me. There was nothing I could say, so pretty soon I sat back down and straightened up my stuff.

At some point, apropos of nothing, I said, "If there was a Colorado Avenue, I'd buy it."

"There isn't," Frankie said.

"I said if there *was*."

"How come?" he asked.

"It's the best place there is."

"You've never been to Colorado," Donald said. I don't know how he knew that. He was apt to assert things just to see if anyone would contradict him.

"No, but my friend Harriet— "

"Then how do you know it's the *best place there is*?" Frankie said.

"She doesn't. Just ignore her." This from Joan.

I swallowed. "They have lots to do there. Skiing and stuff."

"You! Skiing!" Joan rocked back and forth, laughing.

Again I stood up, again I jostled the table. But this time, I said I was tired and walked away. On the way to the hall, I smacked into the corner trim. More laughter.

Somebody said something—Aunt Wilma, I think—but I didn't respond. Instead I backed up and then walked down the hall into Wilma and Frank's bedroom and closed the door. Three or four times I heard the word "odd-wad." Trembling, I lay on the bed, which seemed huge. The mattress was modern and store bought, firm and straight across, unlike the cotton-stuffed ticking mattresses Mother and I had, which sagged in the middle and gave you a backache. I don't know where those old mattresses came from. I think they may have been army surplus, or homemade, maybe by Grandma. Just another thing I didn't know and couldn't ask anybody without them staring at me like I had two heads.

But after a while Wilma's perfume filled my mouth and I couldn't breathe, and so I walked back to the closed door and lay on the bedroom carpet. It made my arms itch, so pretty soon I pulled them inside my blouse. Then my face began to itch, so I took off my blouse and laid it out on the floor and positioned my upper body on it, folding my arms and resting my face on my hands.

It was dim and warm and still in the room, and I closed my eyes. But I couldn't fall asleep. I heard their voices drift in through the crack under the door.

"How come she sleeps all the time?" Frankie said.

"Stewing in her own juice," Jolene said.

Vivian, sounding worried: "Is there something wrong with her, Mom? You know, in her head? Does she—"

"She just likes a nap of an afternoon," Grandma said. "So do I, come to that."

"She gets her bowels in an uproar, and then she goes and 'takes a nap,'" Wilma said. "She just wants attention."

I cringed. Wanting attention meant you were spoiled—the kind of child in movies who pouts and whines and wears dress-up clothes and hair ribbons and makes up lies about the good child, played by Shirley Temple. Everybody hated the spoiled child, including me. But attention was the last thing I wanted. Why couldn't they see that?

"I have this boy in my class," Frankie said. "He swallows rocks at recess for money."

"Who pulled your chain?" Joan said. I heard a smack against flesh. Bony flesh, like an arm.

"She *hit* me," he said.

"Stop it, you two. Don't make me come over there."

"Well, she did," he said.

"Dry up and blow away."

There was a silence. After a while the game resumed. I tuned it out and listened to the women. I caught snatches. *Well, you know, he said, "Grown women wouldn't wear pants if they saw themselves from the back." . . . Well, "I'm sorry" don't fix the lamp. . . . I told her, "That don't set well with me." . . . The whole world can go to hell, but you can just go out and eat your cow. . . . How can somebody so smart be so dumb? . . . They had twin grandsons, so they painted one of them's toenail. I don't know which one. . . . That's a crock of cranberries, and she knows it. . . . So he signed my book, "Remember me when far far off / The woodchucks die with the whooping cough." . . . He fell down, kissed his own knee, and run off. . . . Some people want to remember, and some people want to forget. . . . Every night he comes home from work, takes off his shoes and says, "My dogs is barkin' today." . . . I'm telling you, her eyes looked like two burnt holes in a blanket. . . . I'd sooner step on baby chicks. . . . She used to say, "Guess what, Grandma? I can tie my shoes." "Guess what, Grandma? I can read, I can write." I can do this, I can do that. I called it the "Guess What, Grandma" game. (Laughs.) I swan, if she's not her daddy's daughter.*

How many years of my lifetime had they been talking about me this way? Even Grandma? What did she mean, my daddy's daughter? In a good way or a bad way? I couldn't tell. Charlotte wormed her way up to my face, and it felt reddened with a fever that nothing could ease.

When I came out of the room an hour later, Grandma invited me to her house for supper. "We'll make us a peach cobbler, want to? And you can sleep on the feather mattress in the sewing room."

The next day was Grandma's day to work at the church thrift shop, and Grandpa was playing dominoes at the VFW, so while I was eating breakfast in the kitchen Grandma called Joan to come sit with me for a few hours. I told her I didn't need a babysitter, and why couldn't I just go to the thrift shop with her? There was a rule against grandchildren, she said, ever since somebody's grandson knocked over a glass shelf full of salt and pepper shakers. And maybe Joan and I could put together a puzzle or go through the button box. We could have fun together.

Things got off to a great start. The first thing Joan did was invite me to go up on the roof with her. This was an old pastime among the cousins, but I hadn't ever been invited. Of course I was thrilled.

She climbed through the dormer window, and I followed, crawling my way backwards on my hands and knees to where she sat. Trembling, I took a deep breath and blew it out as I lay down next to her. In my mind's eye I saw myself sliding down and crashing into the spirea bushes below. I had on a crop top, and I settled my back against the rough shingles, supplying just enough friction against my skin, I told myself, to keep me in place. My chest heaved for a while.

Pretty soon Joan reached into her pocket and pulled out a little wooden tube of Grandma's tiny number 10 quilting needles. She withdrew one and threaded it through the thick skin just above the palm of her hand. Then she casually stuck two others through the skin below the thumb. Turning only my head (to avoid vertigo), I studied her technique.

She fluttered her hand, watching the sun glint on the needles. "Want to?"

"How come it's not bleeding?"

She pressed her thumbnail next to the needles. "You don't have any blood or feeling. Where the skin is thick."

Under normal circumstances I would have been skeptical, fearing a prank. But there the needles were; so I took one from her. Quilting needles are short and thin and sharp, and I dug too deep and drew blood on my first try. I startled a bit, and my body swayed against the shingles. I pressed my back against them as hard as I could.

I brought my hand to my face and held it against my tongue for a minute. Joan watched but said nothing.

After a while I threaded the needle into the shoulder of my blouse, as I had seen Grandma do many times, and leaned my head all the way back, my heart thumping with anxiety.

Pretty soon I noticed it was a beautiful day, not too windy, pleasantly warm. The sky itself was a pale, washed-out blue like an old pair of jeans; scattered around were puffy white clouds with glowing velvet edges, and patches of thin gray clouds like torn cotton candy. It felt as if you could reach up and touch them. I was nine. Even with everything, the beauty in the world had never yet failed to move me.

For a long time I just lay there soaking it in. The clouds formed animals, trains, cars, people's faces. I didn't mention what I saw in the clouds, because I figured Joan would ridicule me for being a baby, but I loved looking at them as they formed and then broke up, making new shapes. It was easy to imagine that the universe was telling me something. Even the breeze talked to me, wafting outdoor smells—the spirea bushes, the last of the lilacs, motor oil, laundry detergent, cooked squash—and once in a while a puff of cool air secreted itself among the warmth, making me shiver. Somebody nearby was cutting grass with a gas-powered mower; a chicken cried and squawked; sheets snapped on a clothesline.

Minute by minute my body uncoiled inside. After all, I reasoned, the other cousins had been up here many times, and nothing had ever happened. And Charlotte seemed to be absent.

"Mother and I live in an apartment now, you know?" I said. "Well, the upstairs in an old house. A family lives downstairs. The McKutcheons."

"I know," Joan said. "Well, I didn't know the downstairs people's name."

"It's just off of Main Street. At night you hear the kids dragging Main. You know what that is?"

She rolled her eyes. "Oh, please."

I waited two beats. "She had to sell the house. And Daddy's car."

"I *know*."

"She works full time now, at the cannery. Central Foods. Her boss is named Floy Armstrong—an old guy." Having a mother who worked was odd, another thing that separated me from most of my peers, including Joan. There was something unsavory about a mother working. Not that anyone said anything to your face. It seemed you acquired these values by osmosis.

"Floy? What kind of a name is that?"

"I know." I stifled a giggle, embarrassed—and ashamed of being embarrassed. I felt tears coming and pinched my nose.

"This world is full of stupid people," she said.

"You mean people with stupid names?"

She sighed. "No, I mean stupid people. They live day after day and don't think about a thing. Stuff happens, they react, more stuff happens, they react. One damn day after another." She rubbed her chin. "God save us from living our mothers' lives all over again."

I thought how different her mother's life was from my mother's—and, for that matter, hers from mine. But I didn't want to say something to set her off. I changed the subject. "Speaking of stuff happening, did you hear about the hornets?"

"What? No."

"I was in my room, reading. It was a Saturday. A while back."

Joan dabbed her chin with the tail of her shirt.

"So I'm reading, and it's hot in there, and all of a sudden I feel this tickle on my arm." My eyes were dry now. "It was a hornet, and it was— "

"How do you know it was a hornet?"

"—sniffing my arm and wiggling its butt up and down." I gestured with my hands. "It was—"

"Probably just a wasp, or a mud dauber."

Now I slapped the roof shingles. "Damn it, I'm—"

Joan laughed. When I didn't respond, she said, "Stop pouting, you big baby."

I folded my arms over my chest. I didn't know if she was being rude or I was being boring. "Never mind."

"Never mind," she repeated, mocking.

Another long silence, and then she said, "So what happened? With the wasp?"

It all rushed out. "I looked up, and they were all over the quilt, the lampshade, in the curtains, on the walls. There was this hole in the screen, and they were just pouring in. They were crawling all over, fluttering their wings. It looked weird, like a silent movie—you know, flickering. My *room*."

"Holy shit."

I thrilled to her reaction. It felt as if she was letting me inside. "Yeah. It was so *weird*. And cool, in a way."

"And?"

I had her attention, and I felt powerful. I shrugged. "I survived."

"Tell me what happened, smart-ass. How—"

I felt my spine prickle. "You should come to Hutch and visit sometime."

Now she turned icy. "How come? I don't know anybody there."

"You know *me*. You freaking know *me*."

I started to rise, but she pressed my arm. "Lay down, you big baby. You know what I meant."

I remained in a sitting position. Wobbly.

"I expect you lost all your friends when you moved," Joan said. Her tone implied sympathy.

That brought me dangerously close to tears. I lay back down.

"Mother won't let me ride my bike over to Halsey Drive. It's too far."

"Mothers." Again a note of sympathy.

I smiled. I pulled the needle out of my blouse and carefully pressed it into the thick flesh south of my thumb. My first poke was too shallow, and as I plied the needle it broke upward through the skin, leaving a white line, a flake. I moved down, closer to my wrist, and this time I managed to hit the right depth, embedding the needle in the skin without blood or pain.

"Nice," she said.

Nice. I felt euphoric. It felt as if something I had dreamed about for years was about to happen; more than that, it felt as if I could now make it happen by force of will. If you had asked me at that moment what "it" was, I would have said it was that someone (Joan) would like me the way Harriet had. That's the only language I had for it. But really, I wanted more than to be liked, or even loved. I wanted to be known. I longed for someone to know the real me and somehow still like me, or at least accept me. I didn't want to be empty anymore, always in pain. It felt close, so close. In my exhilaration I said to her, "I have this voice in my head."

"Really." She lay on her back with her knees bent. She closed her eyes.

Her tone, rich with sarcasm, cut me. But I ventured on. "Well, it doesn't exactly say words, but yet it does, sort of." I softened my voice, wincing preemptively, fearing she would crack up or say something mean. But she acted as if she didn't hear.

I felt a twinge in my neck. Now I wanted her to know me even if she made fun of me. It dawned on me that she was the smartest person I knew—except perhaps for Harriet—smarter than any adult, smarter even than Grandma. So Joan was the likeliest to understand, and maybe that was why I was drawn to her more than anyone else, why I ached for her to accept me.

"I'm not crazy, as in psychotic," I went on. "It's not that kind of a voice. Maybe more like a, you know, a noise."

"Uh-huh." Her boredom was palpable.

"Some kind of echo, maybe, that trails along my brain synapses, kind of like a whispery kind of noise."

"Your brain *whats*?" she said, and then, "That's something you read." Her tone was derisive and accusatory at the same time.

I had gone too far to stop now. "It's like a little caterpillar crawling along a stick. Picture it. The stick is my nerve endings, the bug is the voice." I sat up and gestured with my fingers, mimicking the caterpillar walking along the stick. "It lives along the edges—where everything is tentative, contingent." I had gained traction in my thoughts; I saw the caterpillar clearly.

Joan opened her eyes long enough to roll them. "I don't know what those words mean, and I'm in eighth grade, and I bet you don't either. I bet you're not even saying them right."

I sensed she was lying to cover up a glimmer of doubt. "Okay, listen. Everything is weakest at the seams, right? That's where your clothes rip first, right?" I pointed to my armpit. "But get this: where it's weak, it's also liberating, invigorating—it lets in *air*. Ever see a stick that has split off a branch but still clings by a thread of skin? Waving back and forth, hanging on? Sure you have. Think about it. A little breeze hits it, and it waves and twirls like mad." For a split second I visualized a twig with a star inside and my mind wandered, but I forced myself back to the present, to focus on the stick analogy: the weakest point, the nerves, the noise.

"You shit-ass, you're making this shit up."

I was panting now. "So every once in a while—you know how a caterpillar lifts half its body up and twists in the air, feeling all around? You know? And then it latches onto a *whole different* stick, right? Or a leaf? On the branch above it?"

Joan squeezed her eyes together and groaned. She ran a finger along the needles in her hand.

"And it makes this little sound—you've heard it, you *know* you have. Not the caterpillar, the voice—the noise. Like, it's in the back of your head. Like, just before you fall asleep? You know? Or just before you get a headache? It sounds like tinfoil, like someone wadding up tinfoil. Or like when your mom squeezes a grapefruit in the hand juicer. It makes *that* sound. You know the one I mean."

My jaw ached. Pain radiated through my teeth. I had never articulated all this, not even to myself. It was unfolding in front of me as I was speaking.

She gave a theatrical sigh. "You have a caterpillar in your head. Right."

"Crap!" I pulled the needle out of my skin and threw it away. "It's *not* a caterpillar, it's *like* a caterpillar! Quit acting so stupid." I rubbed my palm on my thigh.

Joan shifted onto her side, facing me. She leaned on one elbow. "Where did you get this horse-pucky?"

I blew out my breath. I was tiptoeing on a wire. "Okay, I'll make it simple for you. You ever stand in front of the mirror and stare into your own eyes and repeat 'me me me me me' over and over until it doesn't make sense anymore, and you feel like you aren't exactly standing there anymore? Like you, or some other you, might be in some other place? Like there's this other world you might be a part of, and it's a million miles away but yet you're real *close* to it?"

She ran her fingers through her hair. "Like, for a second, you don't know what's real or not?"

Goose bumps. "Yes! Yes! Well, see, that's what I'm talking about. You're you, *and* you're looking at some other you, at the same time. So that's like the voice living on the edges of your brain synapses. Or noise, rather. The tinfoil noise. See?"

One by one she pulled the needles out of her hand and tossed them. "I've never heard any noise like that. That's crap."

I felt my face crumple. Softly I rubbed my palm on a shingle. It felt like sandpaper, and I envisioned how the shingle was softening the edges of the hole made by the needle. I pictured the puncture as if it were under a microscope, a gaping chasm whose edges descended like a waterfall through the seven layers of skin into darkness.

I was emptying out.

Joan narrowed her eyes. "When you're hearing these voices from some other world, maybe you could ask to talk to your dear dead dad."

"What? No, it's not some telephone." Now the cruelty of her remark hit me. It took my breath away. I visualized the framed picture of Daddy in his navy uniform that Mother kept on her dresser. She had glued a black velvet ribbon around the edges.

For a year, something in me had been trying to break through to my consciousness, and now it did—that Daddy, after a while, would have known me. He would have understood. He would have nodded and smiled with all his crooked teeth. He had been a necessary person in my life, and I hadn't realized it until now, and now it was too late.

My brain went white, and I felt myself drift. Sorrow embraced me.

"Hello? Anybody home?" Joan said.

"I don't even *like* you," I heard myself say in a shaky voice. To myself I added *you bitch*.

She snorted with laughter.

I swallowed back tears. Some five minutes, ten minutes passed. More than ever, I felt alone in the world, the universe. Desolate.

Joan let out a sigh. In a bored, perfunctory tone she said, "If your mom is working, where do you go after school?"

I took a breath. There was nothing to do but stand it. "I babysit myself. Listen to the radio, do homework."

Joan smiled. "Babysit." She shook her head. "So do you drink your mother's beer and smoke her cigarettes? Look through her dresser drawers?"

"I *hate* beer."

"So you *do* smoke." She leaned over toward me. "You nasty thing, you."

I shook my head, but then I felt her hand on my thigh, gently caressing the skin. The touch was so light, at first I thought it was accidental. I opened my mouth—to ask her to stop, I thought, but I wasn't sure; I didn't know what was happening—and Joan whispered, "Just lay back, Billie." My name in her mouth dissolved me. I felt her fingertips press a bit harder, then softer, and I broke into a sweat. Now she moved her hand, slightly cupped, upward between my legs and trailed her middle finger, curling it and pressing with her knuckle. That's all it took. As she pulled back her hand, I gasped and arched my back. A noise came out of my throat. Inside my throat it felt high, like wailing, but it came out low, like growling.

For a time, I was no longer certain there was a roof beneath me. The pleasure had hit me like a rock and then rippled through me. I had never heard of this before. I didn't know it existed. As I lay there, panting, I put together the bits and pieces of things I had heard and read and dreamed, and I knew I had just experienced something that would never leave me, something nasty and yet—

I lay there. I couldn't look anywhere. I closed my eyes but opened them again when I felt I was losing my equilibrium. I blinked unseeing at the sky.

No one said anything.

Now, even as I lay flushed and panting, the rational part of my mind awakened. Why had she done this? To stir me, or to shame me? Would she tell people? Would she throw it up to me for the rest of my life? Did she like me, or something else? Where did we go from here?

One thing I knew, much as I hated it—she was not to be trusted. What had happened was bad; I didn't know why it was bad exactly, but I knew.

At length I turned on my side to face her, but she was squinting at the needle marks on her hand as if nothing had happened. Her silence and indifference seemed deliberate and pitiless.

I started to turn over onto my back. Then my spine was charged with electricity as I felt myself beginning to slide downward.

Still on my side, I tried to clutch a row of shingles with my fingertips, but there was nothing to grab except loose grit, and for a sickening moment I teetered before I regained my purchase. I was alarmed to realize I had felt myself nearly slipping the entire time we'd been up here, but I'd been putting it out of my mind. I was good at that.

I slowed my breathing and tried to stiffen my resolve. I pictured my cousins running on the roof, playing with rubber-band guns and squirt guns and firecrackers. I told myself it was going to be all right.

I felt gravel burrowing into my elbow. I wanted to turn over on my back, but I didn't dare; I feared blank air would assert itself momentarily between me and the roof.

Joan sat up and stretched. She smacked me lightly on the knee. "You know better than to tell anybody."

I felt my arms and legs reverberate.

"It's getting chilly. I'm going in." She got on all fours and nimbly made her way up to the window. I heard her climb through. I pictured myself melting into the roof shingles, becoming one with them, and for a moment it forestalled my panic. But my arms were cold, my armpits clammy. My legs were trembling, and in a moment, I feared, they would flail and thrash of their own accord, and I would lose my grip and tumble to earth.

Inch by inch I brought up my knees until I lay coiled in the fetal position. In my mind I made myself heavy, my skin sticky like flies' feet. My eyes closed, I searched with my fingertips in widening arcs until I found a seam, and I worked my fingers into the tiny aperture. I wanted to call for help, but I couldn't afford to lighten myself by expelling air, and in any case I wasn't able to open my mouth.

I felt a cool breeze on my back. More goose bumps.

It will be fine, I told myself. *I just have to wait it out until somebody comes. I can stand this if I make up my mind to. It will all be fine.*

At the end of my visit, I rode the bus home by myself. I stared at the telephone poles as they whizzed by. In rhythm they told me, *Forget it. Never happened. Forget it. Never happened.* They stretched out their arms, but they didn't embrace me, only provided punctuation. At the same time Charlotte hissed and fizzed, slathering me with bewilderment and alarm and a clear picture of the plain, congealed, cellular fact of what had happened. I wrung her out, thinning her to a thread's depth and plastering her against the inside of my skull; I wanted to leave space in there only for the drumbeat of the telephone poles. I hoped it would work, and I imagined that if I would forget it, it really would not have happened.

Not for years and years did I tell anyone about the tinfoil noise in my head, the caterpillar crawling on my synapses, or any of that stuff, or what happened with Joan, and, even then, it was only one person.

That was *the time Billie had a nervous breakdown and almost fell off the roof and Joan had to go get the neighbor to carry her down the ladder*, to hear (overhear) the family tell the story. One of those stories about Billie—you know, *Billie*. Oh, yeah, her. We know *her*.

CHAPTER 6
COLORADO

A few weeks passed, and it was time to shop for school stuff, my favorite thing. Every year we bought the coming school year's frayed and battered textbooks at the bookstore on Main near the Flag Theatre.

That year it was hot and dusty in the back room of the bookstore as Mother and I rummaged among the books. Mother ruffled the pages to check for penises and bad words scrawled in the margins. Absently she mentioned something about Wiley. I forget the context.

I shrugged and said my trip there hadn't been memorable, there really wasn't anything to do there, the cousins were getting older, and maybe it was time I spent the summers at home and helped her take care of the house, and didn't she just love the smell of these books? They smelled like feet and mold and chewing gum and that acid they used to make paper, wasn't that cool? Just the other day, I'd read that over time, acidic paper turns yellow or brown and gets brittle, and eventually you can hardly read it, and they call that deterioration "slow fire." This kind of spontaneous disgorging of esoterica in public was just the kind of thing that made Mother wince and glance around to see if anyone was looking at us, and she didn't bring up the subject again.

(At the moment she'd mentioned Wiley, my brain, of course, had begun disgorging *forget it, never happened, forget it, never happened, forget it, never happened* while I chattered merrily on about the smell of old textbooks. I was working on how to be functionally aware of that kind of mental undercurrent without it taking up space in my actual consciousness. You could do a search on "blindsight," where people can be aware of something in their field of vision that they can't actually see; it's a result of some kinds of brain damage. But with me, it was just how my brain worked.)

Third grade, fourth grade, fifth grade—they went by. My goal at school was to disappear into the background, and sometimes I succeeded. Gradually I learned how to keep my mouth shut and smile more; when a girl at school told me I was "pushy," I didn't argue with her; I didn't say a word, even though "pushy" made me think of a cartoonish woman wearing smeared lipstick, screaming at a salesclerk. That night I got a headache that lasted until the wee hours, but at least I hadn't made another enemy. One day as I sat in a pink chair at Mother's hairdresser's house, the two of them chatting, she leaned in toward Mother and said, "She sure is quiet, isn't she?" I raised my eyes from my book and looked around to see whom she was talking about, and I was surprised to realize it was me. It felt good, although Charlotte pouted and sulked.

Grandma called every once in a while, and we talked, although I had less and less to say to her, and Mother would always remind me not to run up Grandma's phone bill. All I wanted was to crawl through the receiver directly into her chair and have her teach me how to tat, but it was as if I had aged out of all that. Gradually I forgot the Bible verses I had memorized. Every time we talked it seemed she told me Grandpa was getting sicker, and pretty soon it was all he could do to sit upright in his chair. My memory of Grandpa, the memory I told myself over and over so I wouldn't forget him, was the time at the Burden Fair when he gave me a pocketful of dimes and I spent them all playing the cranes. I got a toy camera, a plastic monkey, and a rabbit's foot. That same year in school we were required to write a real letter to a real person to practice letter-writing, and the teacher made me change "Dear Grandma and Grandpa" to "Dear Grandmother and Grandfather." I argued with her, and Mother had to come to school and make me apologize. We were supposed to actually mail it, but I didn't.

In fourth or fifth grade, my class took a field trip to Central Foods, where Mother worked. It was a huge brick building lined with windows far up near the ceiling; we walked along catwalks some ten or fifteen feet above the damp concrete floor. The room—bigger than a gym—smelled like cooked sugar mixed with the rubbery odor of a swimming pool locker room.

From our vantage point halfway up, we saw giant vats festooned with pipes and tubes, and we watched as conveyor belts carrying rows of glass jars snaked along to a spigot, which squirted each one full of shimmering purple jelly. The room echoed with clanging and shouting and hissing steam and, once in a while, a sharp whistle.

I kept my head down for fear of seeing Mother and having her wave to me in front of my classmates. It was bad enough that she worked. That she worked in this cavernous place fit only for men, that was humiliating. It occurred to me only later that she didn't want her friends to identify me, either.

For Christmas one year she got me a record player, and I listened to the same five 45 rpm records—

Elvis, "Don't Be Cruel," "Love Me Tender"
Pat Boone, "Love Letters in the Sand"
Debbie Reynolds, "Tammy"
Johnny Mathis, "Chances Are"
—over and over in my room.

Mother and I ate, drank, bathed, and slept in the same three rooms but scarcely talked about anything beyond the weather, groceries, TV, and money. We talked a lot about money. Sometime during those years I took over the bank account. I loved the trick of reconciling it once a month; having it balance out gave me a small thrill.

Gradually the apartment absorbed our scent and began to feel closer to normal.

Then one summer day when I was twelve, the summer before high school, she came home and told me we were going to take a trip to Colorado.

I was mixing up something from a box for dinner. "Yeah. Right."

She sighed and set her thermos on the kitchen counter. "What? Don't tell me you don't want to go."

"Where are we getting the money?"

She put her hand on my shoulder, and I jumped. She looked surprised for a second but then removed it. "That's none of your concern."

"Mother, please."

She set the six-pack on the counter and opened a warm beer. "I've been saving up. We'll have to take our own food, and we can't stay in fancy motels, but we're going."

There's a strange feeling you have when you've given up on something and then, out of the blue, you get it. You've talked yourself out of it, out of even wanting it, you've told yourself it was a stupid idea, you've cried yourself out. And then, when it stands there in front of you, you're—I don't know—"angry" isn't the word exactly, although it hurts like anger. It's as if you've hollowed out that particular place in yourself, and it's shrunk to the point that you can't take it in, the very fact of getting the thing you wanted more than anything. Plus, I had entered adolescence, so there was that.

I stood there stirring the macaroni as it boiled.

She took several swallows of the beer. "I thought you'd be excited."

"I'm just—surprised, is all." I looked up and gave her a smile. Was it still possible? After all this time? A little pinprick of hope.

"Oh, Lord, my back." She stretched her back and neck—I heard the pops—and then she walked into her bedroom to change. I noticed she was limping.

I felt panicky. I tried to find Colorado inside me, but it seemed to be gone. I couldn't remember what Harriet looked like. I had forgotten where I'd put the rock she'd given me, the one with the wolf looking for its pack in the blizzard. Colorado seemed far away, a dream from a long-ago childhood, a desire I had once been embarrassingly enthusiastic about.

Eventually she persuaded me it wasn't a prank, and I set to work planning the trip. I walked three blocks to the Phillips 66 station and bought Kansas and Colorado maps. At the library I checked out a photo book called *Glorious Colorado* and another one called *Your Vacation in the American West*. I was awestruck by the high-contrast photos of snowy mountains, impossibly blue lakes, picturesque rocky footpaths among lush pine and aspen trees, colorful little towns, souvenir shops, stores, diners. The people in the photos were smiling as they fished and swam and strolled and pointed to waterfalls. Mothers in smart sleeveless shirtwaist dresses, fathers in slacks and sweater vests, boys and girls in shorts and tennis shoes. Even the dogs were joyous. For me, who had never been outside Kansas, it seemed like something out of a TV show, only in vivid color. Gradually I came to imagine that it would be as I had dreamed—

a kind of liberation, a life-changing experience—and not merely an event documented in other people's photos.

I planned a route that would take us west on Highway 50 to Dodge City to see Boot Hill, then to Garden City to see the zoo, then across the Colorado line and up through little towns and foothills to Pueblo. North to Colorado Springs and Pikes Peak, back south through Cripple Creek, down to San Isabel Lake, then 76 back to Pueblo and east to home, all in six days. Every stop had some kind of attraction—waterfall, lake, forest, museum. I planned it so that we wouldn't be on the road more than two or three hours at a time, with free rest stops and small towns to visit. It would be hot, I figured. We'd take our time. We'd stop for the night by three or four o'clock. I mailed checks to reserve rooms in quaint little cabins near water. Mother came home one day with a brand new Instamatic 100 for me, with three film cartridges, and I nearly cried for joy.

I had no idea where the money for the trip was coming from. I decided to believe that Mother had saved up for it since I knew she wouldn't tell me any other story.

Every day I counted down the days. Mother took me to Penney's and Anthony's and bought shorts, underpants, bras, and shoes. At House of Fabrics we bought fabric, and Mother made sleeveless crop tops and then cut out motifs from the fabric—stylized daisies, tall thin cats, paisley spirals—and zigzagged them onto the shorts. It was the kind of thing she used to do before Daddy died, and even though I thought the matchy outfits were old-fashioned and childish for a twelve-year-old, it felt good that Mother was maybe coming out of her shell. Every time I thought about the upcoming trip, the hair rose on my arms. It felt as if I—and maybe both of us—were starting a new life. We would have snacks. We would sing in the car. It would be so cool.

Then three days beforehand, everything changed.

I was standing at the sink when Mother got home from

work. Her lips were set, her face flushed, and there were big sweat rings on her coveralls. Without looking at me, she stomped into the bathroom and slammed the door—just the kind of childish behavior she would rag me for.

Pretty soon the toilet flushed, and the water in the sink ran for a long time. In the drafty old house you could hear everything.

I walked to the door, my bare feet swishing on the wood floor. "Mother?"

"What?" Her voice sounded old and angry. The water kept running.

I pulled back and clenched my fists. Why didn't she just say what was wrong? I was so eager to please, and she would never say what would please her, beyond the material, like getting her a beer or doing the dishes. It seemed everybody was that way. What was the big secret? Why couldn't they just tell you what you could do that would make them accept you?

"I said, *what*?" Now she used a tone.

"Nothing. It's okay. Never mind."

"Get me a beer, would you?"

While I was in the kitchen, Mother left the bathroom and headed for her bedroom, stepping out of her uniform as she went. She had already removed her shoes. She looked womanly in a way I envied. I was fully developed now, but I was built straight up and down, not curvy like Mother. It was nice that people took me for older than I was, but I knew I would never be magnetic like Mother—with or without makeup, hair a mess, clothes disheveled. Wherever the two of us went, I saw men turn their heads to look at her. It used to be funny—you could almost see the oing-oings springing out of their eyeballs. But when I "crossed the threshold into womanhood" (to quote the Kotex box), the sight of grown men's heads swiveling on their necks in her wake was just gross. They might as well have been slobbering in their coffee.

I stared for a moment at the beer foam and then licked it, delicately, like a cat. I'd been trying to develop a liking for it, but it tasted like pee to me. I carried it into Mother's bedroom, careful not to spill.

She sat in front of the mirror, frowning. She took the beer and chugged three swallows, wincing as if it burned her throat. Then she lowered the can to take a breath, raised it again, and took two more deep swallows. She belched and set the can on the dressing table, and she frowned at me in the mirror. "We're having company on our trip."

My stomach folded. I sat on the edge of her bed and waited.

She picked up her brush and yanked at her hair. "He works with me. Floy mentioned the trip to him, and he asked could he tag along in case we had a flat tire, and what could I say. Damn."

I resisted the urge to say, *You could say no, thanks, I'm going with my daughter, it's all planned. We can change a goddamn tire.* "Who is this guy?" I said instead.

"His name is Clarence. He's not 'some guy.' I've known him for years. He's in line to be a shift supervisor."

"But who is he?" It dawned on me that she was lying, that this was the plan all along.

She reached for a cigarette with one hand, and with the other she raised the beer to her lips. I could feel myself about to explode, so I left before I ruined any chance of salvaging the trip.

Clarence looked at his wristwatch and nodded. "Making good time." He settled his back against the seat, stretched his arms, and let go of the steering wheel momentarily to crack his knuckles.

My backbone shuddered.

The object of a vacation is not to make good time, I thought. *Idiot.* I was not yet at the peak of my powers of sarcasm; that came later, about the time I was a senior. But I was practicing, if only in my head.

I swallowed the nausea rising in my stomach. Mother could have said, *My daughter needs to sit in the front seat, she gets carsick*, but of course she hadn't said anything. It was his car. (It was always their car.) Mother was saving up to buy a car when I would turn sixteen in four years, but until then it was the bus, the bicycle, walking, or begging a ride from a friend. For this trip we were going to rent a car (so she'd said), but no.

Clarence didn't allow eating, drinking, or smoking in the car. He didn't stop every few hours to stretch and use the bathroom and relax and get a bottle of pop and look around. He didn't follow interesting signs off the highway to see cool things. He had canceled all of my reservations at rustic little cabins on pretty lakes. He wanted to make good freaking time.

He wanted to golf with Mother while I sat and watched TV in motel rooms. Some vacation. Mother didn't even like golfing.

The first night we stopped at a Best Western on the outskirts of Limon, Colorado. Clarence checked us in to adjoining rooms. He didn't try to hide the fact that he was paying.

The moment Mother entered our room she lit a cigarette, and I headed for the bathroom. It was clean enough, although everything was old, and not in a good way. The tub caulk was streaked with crud. I knew without asking that we would eat at the attached café and it would be dismal and Clarence would not tip enough. I was already embarrassed.

But when Mother and I stepped outside again, I stopped short. The air felt light—light in the sense of brilliant, and light in the sense of weightless. I looked at my bare arms to see if they were glowing. I took a deep breath. It felt as if the air itself were empty, a sensation I had never experienced. It wasn't the altitude—we were still on the plains and hadn't yet reached the mountains—but I couldn't define what it was. It seemed I could taste the air, and it tasted cool and blue. For a moment I wanted to run and jump. But that would be childish and stupid, so I settled for gulping breath after breath.

No matter how much Harriet had glorified Colorado, nothing she'd said came close to the feeling I got just breathing the air. It seemed as if my life was changing by the minute, as if Colorado was what I had been longing for forever.

That night in bed I heard Clarence fart and snore in the other room. I turned over on my stomach and wrapped the pillow around my head and inhaled the mattress smells of bleach, cigarette smoke, and pee. I told myself he was only some guy, he was all right, it would all be fine, Colorado would redeem everything. Then I tried to generate a mental image of Daddy, but I couldn't visualize him in any real way, couldn't smell him, couldn't reproduce the feeling of his chest hairs against my cheek, couldn't hear his voice in my head. He was turning into the man in the photographs.

I wondered why. He had been a giant in my life, so how could he be fading away? I thought about our little house on Halsey. I pictured the wavy shingled sidewalls, the tiny peaked roof over the front door, the little brown dinette set, my plastic farm animals (what had happened to them? And the barn?), and the backyard with the cottonwood tree where I loved to read.

I saw myself open the front door and walk in . . . but then I couldn't remember the living room floor. I remembered playing on it for hours while Mother sat in her chair and smoked and drank and read magazines. And once in a while, Daddy would lie on his back on the floor and play airplane with me: pull me up onto his bare feet and unfold his legs and raise me up, balancing me on my tummy, holding my hands wide like wings. We called it "doing tricks." I had been well acquainted with that floor; but now it was a blank. Was there carpet? Surely not, too expensive. Hardwood? Tile? Was there a rug? I squeezed my eyes and willed myself to see that floor. At the moment it was the most important thing in my life, more important than the trip or anything. I *had* to remember what the floor looked and felt like; I knew there were brain cells where that information was stored, there had to be; and my stupid goddamn brain would not yield it. I felt that if I could only picture that floor, everything else would come back to me. In my mind I was standing just inside the doorway, reaching out my arms to try to grab something—what? My memory? Daddy? The house? I had lost so much, some things all at once and others only gradually. And then the floor itself disappeared beneath my feet, throwing me into a pitch-black chasm, where I saw myself falling and falling, flailing.

The next thing I knew, Mother was on her knees on the bed, shaking me. "You're walking in your sleep, Billie. Wake up."

I blinked myself awake in the darkness. I was half sitting, half standing on the edge of the bed. My arms fell to my sides.

"You were trying to reach up for something," Mother said. "You said something, but I couldn't make it out." She struck a match, and the light flickered against her face as she lit a smoke.

"I was?" I sank to the bed.

The tip of Mother's cigarette glowed orange. "It's the strangeness. Strange food, strange car, sleeping in a strange bed. It's all so new."

I nodded and crawled under the bedcover. Strangeness and newness—what I'd always wanted, what I'd taken in so gladly earlier in the day. I waited until she put out the cigarette and went back to sleep, and then, quietly, without moving, I wept for all I had lost, like a little bawl-baby.

The next day we stopped and looked at a waterfall for ten minutes. We got close enough that the wind carried the cold foam, dancing and whirling, to where we stood. I reveled in the feeling of the spray against my skin. I had never imagined such a thing.

The water roared as it cascaded ceaselessly down into the rocks and pools below. More water than I had seen in my twelve years put together, and still it came. You knew just by looking that it was commonplace, this miracle, that it had been here for a million generations, and it would continue without ceasing in perpetuity.

While I stood there in awe, inexpressibly sad, Clarence complained because it cost five dollars, you wasted a lot of time walking to the waterfall from the parking lot, and you got a better view from a postcard. Afterwards in the car, he complained about the heat, the food, the altitude. He talked for an hour about the grain brokerage business he used to be in before he started working at Central Foods. He lived in Buhler and drove to Hutch every day and went golfing in Wichita on the weekends. Highway 96 to Wichita was a bitch, he said, but people in Hutch kept blocking projects to make it a four-lane. Small-town small-thinkers. In twenty years, after they made it into a real highway, he said, you'd be able to get to Wichita in forty-five minutes, easy. And it would only *benefit* those Hutch merchants who were so dead set against it. People went both directions, why couldn't they see that?

In the backseat, I stared at the white crisscross creases in the back of his neck. I asked myself, *Who are you? Where did you come from?*

Clarence liked to drive fast. Nobody cared how fast you went in this hick backcountry, he remarked, accelerating to eighty, eighty-three, eighty-five. He was doing it on purpose, just like boys I knew—cousins mostly—who took pleasure in using a car to scare you. One time, when I was riding with my cousin Don, he had gunned the car and then swerved ditch to ditch on the road, singing the loopty-loop song—"Here we go loopty-loop, here we go loopty-lie"—as I screamed. He laughed and laughed and called me a pussy, a terrible word that humiliated me. Like it was girlish to be afraid of being in a wreck! And here I was, stuck for six days with this cretin

Clarence. I messed with a scrap of cuticle on my thumb. Mother always said we didn't hate anybody. Well, I hated Clarence.

We stopped in the early afternoon at another featureless motel, where he told Mother there was only one room left, but it had two beds. I shot her a look, but her face was a blank.

When he went golfing Mother begged off, saying she had a headache. As soon as he was out of the room, she brought out the little cooler—just big enough to hold a six-pack—and opened a beer. She settled in on the bed closest to the door. I tuned the TV to a game show and sat in the chair in the corner. For two beers, the two of us held a desultory conversation over the rattle of the air conditioner while I leafed through a magazine.

I thought of Clarence out golfing. Casually I asked her if his driving bothered her.

She frowned, shrugged, and then smiled. "Your daddy spoiled me for other men."

"Really?"

"I never knew anybody like him. One in a million. Turn the AC fan up, will you? It's hot in here." I got up and turned the fan to MAX; I stood facing the machine and then bowed my head so that the air chilled my scalp.

"The first time I met him, we talked for hours and hours." She lit a cigarette and blew out the match.

A miracle was happening. It wasn't the beer, it wasn't my great attitude, it wasn't the AC. Maybe it was the altitude or the distance from home. Whatever it was, Mother was talking. Real talk.

"But you know all about that," she went on. "You've heard it a thousand times."

I turned and faced her. I did know the story; Daddy'd told me. They met in Wichita, at a greasy spoon where Mother and her best friend, Flossie Market, had stopped on their way home from shopping for school clothes. Mother was seventeen and a senior. Flossie was a year older.

"When he walked in, Flossie poked me in the ribs and said, 'You ever see a homelier man in your life?'" Mother laughed. "I looked over there and said, 'Well yes, but not very many.'"

She and I both laughed.

Now she sighed. "But what a man he was. One in a million." I saw tears. She kept smoking as she related the details. Daddy had charmed her into riding with him to the airport to watch the airplanes take off and land. But it turned out to be a crop duster strip in somebody's field, and there weren't any airplanes there at night.

"He got in the backseat and pulled out two folding chairs." She opened her third beer.

I blinked. Daddy didn't mention folding chairs. I had always pictured the two of them sitting in the car. Snuggling. But folding chairs? He carried folding chairs in his car?

"He set them side by side, and we sat there looking at the stars. Oh, those stars. There wasn't any light for miles around, it was pitch dark, and the stars, you can't imagine. It felt like you could reach up and touch them. And the crickets, and the frogs . . ."

"Yeah." I'd seen stars. I'd heard crickets.

"And talk! Well, you know, I'd been on dates before. But I was shy, and it always ended up we didn't have anything to say, and there would be these long, horrible silences. I would be so embarrassed I wanted to sink into the ground. And of course, boys, they always want to make out." She shook her head. "That's no fun for the girl."

I gathered my courage and reached over to her pack of Winstons. She glanced down but said nothing, so I pulled out a cigarette and lit it. I took a tentative drag and coughed, and I blinked from the smoke, and the world seemed pretty damn decent. What I realized only later is that after a while you get over the first-timer irritation and you get your lungs trained, and then comes the sweet, sweet reward: you take the first drag of a fresh cigarette, and the hot smoke smacks you in the palate and shoots right into the reptile brain, and bam! Immediately you get both the nicotine hit and the sense of well-being. And the ritual of it, that's satisfying, too. It gives you something to do—with your hands, yes, but also with your mouth, your whole face really, your upper body. The beauty of smoking is that you don't have to compose your face in any particular way; the smoking takes care of that. And that doesn't touch how adult and cool it makes you look; watch any movie made in the 1940s, and you'll see that the twentysomething actors look like forty-year-olds with twenty-year-old faces. It's the cigarettes—the way they hold them against their palms or tilt them upward in a marbleized celluloid cigarette holder, or hang them off their lip, along with the various techniques of inhaling and exhaling, not to mention the blue haze hovering overhead in opulent ballrooms or shady night spots or long, long automobiles. They make it look like an art. Only problem is, the longer you smoke, it takes more cigarettes, morning, noon, and night, to get less of a hit; eventually it becomes less about feeling good and more about not feeling bad. That's when you could kick yourself for getting so addicted to it.

But I knew none of this then. What I knew was, smoking in front of my mother, I had crossed a big bridge. A huge bridge.

She looked at the ceiling. "But your daddy, he never ran out of things to talk about." She raised her beer. "Never in his life." She laughed a little.

"But what did you talk about? He never told me what you talked about."

She looked at me as if to gauge what I was able to hear. Then she dropped her head back and rested it on the pillows. "I was amazed to hear what came out of my mouth. Things I'd never hardly thought, let alone said out loud to anybody." Still with her head tilted, she lifted the beer, and a little stream ran down her chin. She continued as if she didn't notice it. "He asked me—I don't remember exactly. He asked me—what did I want out of life, that was one thing. What did I want out of life." She straightened up and wiped her chin absently with her fingers.

"Oh," I said, surprised. I flicked the ash from my cigarette. No one had ever asked me what I wanted out of life—no one in the family or out of it. Why would you ask somebody that? What did it even mean?

"Let me tell you, I shivered," Mother went on. "I didn't know what he *meant* even."

Now I shivered.

Mother waggled the beer can. "I thought maybe it was a line, you know, but he never touched me that night." She tipped up the can and finished it.

"What did you tell him?" I moved my cigarette from one hand to the other, observing the effect.

"I don't know. What did I want? The normal things, I guess—a husband, a house, kids."

I nodded. The normal things.

Mother leaned forward, her eyes fixed on me. "'But what do you really want? *Inside?*'" The intensity in her voice was unnatural for her. I understood she was imitating Daddy.

Now she half leaned, half fell back against the pillows. She didn't have a beer or a cigarette in her hands, and she fluttered them as if she didn't know what to do with them. She began laughing and crying at the same time. "Shit," she said finally, wiping her face with the corner of a pillowcase. She sniffed deeply, frowning and blinking, and looked around her. She picked up the can and seemed surprised it was empty.

We sat in silence. The AC fan clattered.

When she resumed talking, her voice was quieter, the words a bit slurred. I knew this stage like my tongue knew the inside of my mouth. It was my favorite. I'd often wished she was in this stage all the time—not sober, and not six or eight beers in, but just at this calm, three-beer stage. If Mother couldn't be tender—and she couldn't—I wished at least she would be calm instead of worried or angry or irritable or defeated.

"Did I tell you he talked about the war?" Without waiting for the answer, she said, "He told me, the war was so horrible, and so many people suffered so much, and so many people died, that the ones that were left had a *duty* to *live* their goddamn lives." With "lives" she widened her eyes like Daddy always did. "He knew what he wanted to do with his life—he wanted to *feel* everything. Life to him was about *feeling* things, he said to me over and over. Bad or good. Feelings. You know, emotions."

I was thunderstruck. All at once I could hear Daddy's voice in my head. We were doing tricks, and I was wobbling on his stockinged feet, and he was saying, "Do you *feel* that, Billie? *Feel* that. What do you *feel* like?" And I was laughing/crying too hard to speak, swallowing spit. And not only then. He would call my attention to just stupid everyday things—the rainbow in sprinkler spray, roly-poly bugs, our shadows on the sidewalk. He loved to make popcorn in a big round pan on top of the stove. Once he grabbed a piece of popcorn and held it close to my face. "What do you see?" I probably said, "Popcorn." He'd turned it over in his fingers until I said, "Oh! Puppy faces!" His smile was radiant. "See?" he'd said. "Isn't that the greatest feeling in the world?" From then on, Daddy and I had called popcorn puppy faces.

Mother coughed, and I came out of my reverie. "How come you're panting?" she said. "Are you sick? It's too hot in here, isn't it?" She got out of bed and laid the back of her hand on my forehead.

"I'm fine." I felt a tear on my cheek before I realized I'd been crying. "Mother . . ." I stopped, swallowed, tried to come up with the words. "What changed? When did you stop, you know, wanting to *feel* things like that?"

She stiffened. "What?"

"Or did you ever? Want to?"

She stepped back. "You . . ." She seemed about to say something else. Three times she opened her mouth, but she didn't finish.

"Me what?"

Now she shook her head. She turned and began straightening the room. She picked up the empties and dropped them into the wastebasket.

"Me what?" I said again, but Mother was leaning over the cooler and reaching for her fourth beer, and it was too late, as always. I knew I'd replay the whole conversation that night, trying to understand where it went wrong. One moment she was there, right there, with me, and then she wasn't. What had I said? Why did I always say the wrong thing?

When Clarence got back from golfing, we ate in a crummy place at the edge of the highway a mile from the motel. In the room afterwards, Clarence cranked up the AC until I felt icy sweat all over. They watched Lawrence Welk on TV. It was all very awkward, it seemed to me, but I wasn't sure I could trust my perceptions. Maybe everything was fine.

At ten, Clarence undressed in the bathroom and came out in kelly-green pjs printed with row after row of leaping trout. Without a word he lay down in the bed nearest the wall and closed his eyes.

I looked at Mother, and she shrugged. She whispered, "Do you need the bathroom first?"

I shook my head. I lifted the bedcover and crawled into our bed still dressed. After a while Mother joined me and turned out the light. The room was chilly now, and I pulled the coverlet up to my neck.

In the middle of the night, I awakened when I heard what sounded like a slap. Disoriented, I rose on one elbow and shook my head. I heard breathing. I extended my hand; the other side of the bed was empty. My heart quickened, and I felt a terrible thirst at the same time that I needed to pee, urgently.

The room seemed to rock, and the silence felt explosive.

Now I heard whispers.

Come on.

Quiet, you'll wake her up.

Dixie—

Clarence, no.

Shhh now. Come on.

No, I don't—

Come on. A groan. *It'll just—*

Quiet. Quiet.

My God, Dixie—

Shhh. All right, but be quiet for God's sake.

I couldn't listen and couldn't not listen. The sounds they were making seemed to gather in my throat and choke me. I wondered what, exactly, they were doing. Was it the same as Joan and me on the roof? Or something else? I was absurdly, angrily ignorant. And, as before, I wondered what it meant. To Mother. To him. To me.

I was trapped. I urgently needed to pee, but I couldn't, and there was nothing I could do about it. I didn't want to know what was happening, but I couldn't stop it. I needed to lie still and not make a sound, because tomorrow I would need to pretend nothing had happened. So of course Charlotte came knocking, and I pressed my face into my pillow and held my breath as long as I could. Quietly I took another breath and repeated the process. In this way I managed to suppress Charlotte and fall into a troubled sleep.

While Clarence showered the next morning, Mother and I gathered our things and packed up. Casually I said, "I'm bored. I wish we could go home. Could we go home today?"

Mother rubbed her eyes. "Me too. But Clarence—"

"Why do we always have to do what *he* says?"

Mother reached in her purse and got out a cigarette. "Stop, just stop. You know better than this."

"This isn't fun, Mother. He—"

Mother struck a pose, the unlit cigarette between her fingers. "Billie! You know you can't always have your own way. You know that. *Behave*. Stop acting like a child."

In the bathroom the water squealed off. Both of us froze for a moment.

"We only have three more days," she said under her breath. "You can stand it for three more days."

Gone was yesterday's tender mood, and now I wondered if in fact I could stand anything. I wondered whether I could stand this trip for three more days. Whether the gorgeous scenery, the breathtaking waterfalls, the mystical magical air itself, free to breathe by the lungful—whether anything at all could enable me to endure this trip for three more days. Nature (by which I meant Colorado), I realized, didn't care if we lived or died or what happened.

"I *hate*—" I started to say "him" but instead said, "this."

Mother fixed me with a glare as she lit the cigarette. "Grow *up*, would you." Her jaw was set, and I saw that lines had begun to appear around her lips. "Please."

I was paralyzed by the rage of powerlessness. And floating on the edge of my consciousness, threatening to blossom, was the budding realization that Mother, too, was powerless, and not only now. She was vulnerable in the world in ways I hadn't imagined before.

From the bathroom came the buzz of Clarence's shaver.

I couldn't stand the tension. "Listen, I'm going for a walk," I said. "You guys have breakfast without me."

Mother frowned, but said only, "Don't go too far. He'll want to leave as soon as we eat."

I grabbed my patchwork tote bag and left without another

word. I walked along the highway for a while and then turned onto a road, no more than tire tracks that disappeared into the trees. To my surprise, on the other side of the trees was a little settlement in a hollow. Two blocks of buildings lined the path, with a smattering of houses behind. The first block was made up of nineteenth-century flat-front Victorian brick and wooden buildings. All of them appeared to be abandoned, and their old-timey painted wooden signs—"Antiques," "Uniques," "Millineries," "Sundries"—were from ten or more years ago; I could tell by the cutesy Olde West lettering. Posters taped on the windows advertised the motel where the three of us had stayed last night, along with other businesses in the larger town—a tanning salon, a tattoo palace, a gas station—and a raffle held last year to support the library.

I felt cold, and I rubbed my arms. This settlement looked to be drying up. Probably the downward spiral had started when the highway went through two miles away, just like many towns back home. "Grease spots in the road" was what people called them. Browntown, a 1920s oil town where Uncle Frank was born, was gone, along with Paola, Oil City, and others. Once the oil played out, those towns lost their post offices and just folded up. Some of them had left hardly a trace—crumbling stone foundations mostly weeded over in the middle of a pasture; an abandoned grain silo. Wiley probably would have been gone, too, after the oil boom, if not for the aircraft workers—Boeing, Learjet, and Cessna—who lived there and commuted to Wichita.

But the difference was that this village was set in a spectacular mountain landscape. Backing the road and the buildings were soaring rock formations that fronted even taller mountains. This was the closest I had been to these cliffs, and I craned my neck to try to take them all in. The gray-black rock was alive with lacy strings of lichen—all shades of green, orange, gray, and white—creating jagged rows and columns and tiny caves, branching in every direction, miniature landscapes as numerous as the stars. I wondered what marvels a person might see if they could somehow be suspended on the rock with a magnifying glass. Above the cliffs the sky was azure, and white clouds were scuttling by. You could smell the pine—there must have been a million million trees, sighing in the wind—and above the timberline you could see snow. The night's sweetness still clung in the shaded air, and the air was so pure, it was as if it were scrubbing me clean. And now my mind dredged up a memory of last night, and again I heard the sounds from the other bed.

The thoughts tumbled out. *He's ruining our trip. Imagine how the whole trip could have been, with Mother opening up to me a little bit day by day. All those hours in the car, she and I could have been talking, she might have gotten dreamy, maybe we could have gotten close. But she's as bad as he is—she let him come with us, she got into his bed. Evidently she has everything she wants, and what do I have? Nothing.*

Mother was wrong—there were things a person couldn't stand for even three more days. I couldn't bear to be around that man, or in the same car with him. Not that there was anything I could do about it. "Got to stand it or bust," as Grandma would have said.

Now I was startled by three loud squawks and the flapping of heavy wings. I'd reached the far corner of the block of defunct stores, ending in an empty parking lot with a pair of pine trees grown up through the cracks. A huge glossy crow was taking off from a branch only a few feet above my face. Farther in the tree's interior, a second one made its way sideways along the branch as it emerged into a shaft of sunlight and then followed the first one. The birds hung in the air overhead, dipping their wings sharply—screaming, it seemed, at me—as I stood transfixed. Then they flew higher and perched in the other tree, bouncing on the springy limb, continuing to cry out.

"All right, all *right*," I said, crossing the road out of their way. I glanced back to see the pair return to their original spot. Maybe they had a nest there? What time of year did crows nest? Too late I remembered the Instamatic in my bag. I hadn't yet taken a photo on this stop, and the birds overhead would have made a cool picture.

I looked around to get my bearings and saw a flat-roofed, shoebox-shaped building across the road and down a ways. A sign mounted on the roof read, "Food Beer Firewood," and hand-painted posters inside the windows said "Hamberger 39¢ lb" and "Potatoe's 10¢" and "We check ID." A nickel pony ride stood next to the door, and two pickups, one red and one blue, were parked outside. Behind the store, a sheer rock wall rose. From this distance a block away, it looked close, but it might have been a mile distant.

The door to the building opened, a bell dinged, and a man, about thirty-five, came out of the store, followed by a little girl. The girl said something to him and pointed to the pony. It was the same muckledun brown color as the one in the parking lot of our Dillons store back home. The pony's legs, front and rear, were extended in the familiar gallop mode. It had pale muckledun beige socks on each fetlock.

The man—I guessed he was the girl's dad—looked at his watch and shook his head, but then he shrugged and set down the two paper sacks he was carrying. He reached into his pocket, and the girl climbed on to the ride. He put his hand behind the saddle as the pony began rocking. The girl grabbed the leather reins and spurred the horse onward, bucking up and down.

After a minute I wondered if she was already worried that the ride was almost over. I would have been. They always ended too soon.

What was life like here, day to day? As exotic as it seemed to me, the people who lived here were probably accustomed to it, just as people back home were accustomed to big, bland, sparkly Dillons stores and Kwik Shops, expansive parking lots full of newer cars and pickups, combines crawling along the side of the road, giant grain elevators and feedlots, hayrack rides and the muddy taste of catfish, punishing heat or punishing cold, wind and sleet and hail; and printed on every forehead, "Take what you can get and be satisfied."

I wondered, how do people make a living here? They must have jobs or something. It couldn't be impossible. If I lived here, would everyday life feel to me like this moment felt? This man and this girl and this pony weren't something out of a fantasy; surely they had troubles just like anybody else. Didn't they? He had somewhere to be, but he'd set down the groceries, he'd put his hand behind the girl. Not unlike Daddy. It *looked* like happily ever after. Was it? I wondered.

Now I remembered my camera, and I quickly snapped a picture just as the ride stopped. I started to cross the street—to say hello? ask them something? start a conversation?—but now the child began crying and kicking, and he grabbed her roughly and swatted her behind. His face contorted, he growled some words, and he lifted her into the cab of the blue pickup and they drove away into the woods.

I felt a chill. I wanted it to have ended differently. More than wanted. Needed.

When I got back to the motel, Clarence and Mother were drinking coffee in the room. Mother's hair was wrapped in a damp towel.

Later that day, to my surprise, we stopped at a pretty little lake, where Clarence rented tackle and fished from the shore while Mother sat on a nearby rock, sunning herself, smoking and drinking. She was wearing makeup, and she looked like a movie star from the fifties, one of the women on the covers of the splashy fan magazines I used to read while she got her hair cut—*Photoplay, Movie Story, Modern Screen.* I fancied I could see her red lips even from the dock a hundred feet away, where I sat.

I had my bare feet in the water, thrilled with the icy shock of it. I lifted them out and, on a whim, took several pictures of them. Then I put the camera down and stared at the water. I found a few flattish chalky rocks at the edge of the dock and skipped them, watching them zigzag until they dipped into the green/blue/blackness. I could tell by the way they sank that the water here was deep, over my head for sure. I had played around in the three-foot sections of a few swimming pools, but I didn't know how to swim. But that was okay. It was gorgeous right where I was.

I fixed my gaze on the current beneath me, the gentle waves plashing against the dock supports, and soon, staring at that endless rhythmic repetition of motion, I felt separated from time and space. I was enthralled, mesmerized. My God. This, *this* was what I had been looking for. *If this exists, and it does, then why—*

Just at that moment I felt thudding footsteps behind me on the dock, and I awakened from my daze. A war whoop, and three figures rushed past me and cannonballed into the water, soaking me. Another one, close behind, heaved a giant black inner tube into the water and followed it in.

It was two couples, about high school age. They didn't seem to notice me sitting there as they sped by. I pulled my feet out of the water and folded my legs. I stuffed the camera into my bag.

They splashed around, screaming. The boys lunged at their dates, yanking on the straps of their swimsuits, and the girls shrieked and pushed them away. The boys fought over the inner tube, dunked their respective heads, spewed mouthfuls of water. Every other word out of their mouths was "fuck"—*fuck you, you fucker, go fuck yourself, hey motherfucker, gimme the fucking tube, let go of my fucking hair.*

I had a sour taste in my mouth. None of that stuff was new to me (Mother didn't care what I read), but it was one thing on the page, and another when screamed right on top of me. The tranquility of the day and the beauty of the water couldn't co-exist with these people. I thought about pulling out my book, but reading didn't seem possible with all this folderol, and besides, the book might get soaked.

Now one of the boys swam over to the dock and gripped the dock close, too close, to my knee.

"Hey, little girl, wanna play?" He stripped the water from his face with his hand and pinched one nostril closed, blowing snot out the other. His eyelashes were dripping.

I lifted my knee and scooted away from his fingers.

He spread his arm backward as if to pitch a baseball and threw a big splash at me, laughing.

"Stop it, you—"

"Bitch," he muttered, and he grabbed my ankle—hard, scraping it with his nails—and pulled me into the water. I opened my mouth to scream and swallowed a gulp, choking.

I heard him screaming/laughing, and I thought my heart might burst. I flapped my arms, and someone—one of the girls, I think—swam over to me and pushed me toward the dock.

It was all I could do to raise myself halfway up, and I felt a pair of hands on my butt, pushing me the rest of the way. I lay there panting for a moment, and then I stood up and grabbed my bag and ran. Behind me I heard derisive guffaws.

In the grass, I first flopped down on all fours, gasping and gagging, and then I found a chair and turned it to face away from the water. I squeezed the tail of my blouse and pressed my hands along the length of my shorts. Pretty soon I closed my eyes, slowed my breathing, and pretended to sleep. Those kids may not even be from Colorado, I told myself, so don't assume people are like that here. Then I thought of the dad swatting the girl. I felt cold.

After a while, I heard Mother laugh and opened my eyes. She and Clarence approached me, swinging six speckled trout on a chain. "Take our picture," Mother said. Through the lens she looked happier, prettier, than I could remember. Even Clarence seemed to be in a good mood. After I took the pictures, they gave the fish to a family staying in one of the cabins.

At the souvenir shop I took a picture of the life-size wooden Indian out front. Inside, I picked up a belt made of ornately engraved silver disks, each with a turquoise stone in the center. I jingled it in my hands, but I didn't buy it. My heart wasn't in it. I still had a bad taste in my mouth.

In the car I reflected on my morning walk, and I mentioned seeing the two crows. Clarence glanced at me in the rearview and smiled. "My grandmother told me that if you see one crow, or a lot of crows, it means someone is going to die soon. *But* seeing two crows means good luck." Him having a grandmother surprised me, for some reason. And it sounded as if she was a lot like Grandma.

As if reading my mind, Mother said, "Billie's grandmother knows a thousand ways to get good luck."

I smiled. Although I wondered why she called her "Billie's grandmother" instead of Daddy's mother. Maybe she didn't want to remind Clarence that she was married before. Maybe he didn't know.

"You have to ward off the Evil Eye, she always said," Mother went on. "The Evil Eye brings bad luck. One trick is to sprinkle salt on your front steps, so the Evil Eye will be busy all night, counting the grains, and he won't get you."

We all three laughed. For the first time Clarence seemed almost human to me.

They went on to swap Evil Eye stories, most of them involving wrapping things in red flannel or wearing red clothes or tying red ribbons to the bedpost or wearing your clothes backwards. A few required pulling hairs out of people's heads and grinding them or hiding them in a fireplace or adding them to a potion, and one required a long ritual to "cleanse" an egg and then "read" its yolk. I didn't recall ever seeing my mother more real. I had no idea she had spent that kind of time with Grandma.

As for me, Grandma had only shared a few Disneyfied versions of the Evil Eye stories. Probably she thought I was too young or too (as they say) high strung.

The rest of the trip was uneventful; we made good time but missed most of the sights I'd planned on, including Pikes Peak. On the last night, Mother and Clarence had a room to themselves, but trying to memorize miles after miles' worth of beauty out the car windows had left me so exhausted I didn't have time to think about what they were doing in there. I slept so hard I didn't remember any of my dreams the next morning, except for one: a short one where I was drowning in total blackness—my lungs were about to burst—but I woke up just before I drowned.

When my pictures came back from Coberly's, I discovered I'd forgotten to advance the film after the pony ride photo, so it was a double exposure with one of the images of my feet. You could see the pony's extended front legs—they were distinctive—but they looked as if they were sticking out of my ankle. The man and the girl looked ghostly, although the sack of groceries at the very edge was sharp.

Later at home, I dug out the Colorado map, but the little mountain village wasn't on it. I was sure it wasn't a figment of my imagination, but as I sat in my hot, crumpled bed, it felt as if it might as well be.

I daydreamed about going back there, but at the same time, I pushed it away; obviously, my fantasy of someday making an escape to Colorado was an illusion, and I was no longer sure it would be the paradise I had imagined. High school was looming, with secret slang, girl cliques, men teachers, unfamiliar buildings, dates, locker room showers. Jammed hallways redolent of the sharp smell of adolescent b.o., a hand on your thigh, runs in your stockings, a million chances to make a fool of yourself.

In the time remaining before school, I started working on (what we call nowadays) my affect. I told Charlotte to get lost. I was too old for childhood things. I was going to be cool.

CHAPTER 7
HIGH SCHOOL

For some people, high school is the peak of their life. You know them—the athletes, the cheerleaders, the class officers. Usually, as they age they take up drinking or odd hobbies, and they complain about the disrespect shown by today's young people. But for me, high school was a brief fairy tale in which I was a background character, like an elf or a talking tree, just as I desired.

The academic side of high school was still not hard enough for me to take much interest in it. I did like Bookkeeping 101, where we worked with a kit that contained pretend financial reports, colorful invoices, a fake checkbook, and the like. It was like Monopoly, but you could play by yourself and no luck of the dice was involved. Bookkeeping didn't take much brainpower, but it was tricky and required attention to detail—just the kind of thing I liked. I also liked math, especially when the teacher told us math is a language that people use to describe the world, just like the language we speak. That you could use equations to define curves blew my mind, even if I found it hard to believe. I had no inclination to forsake the world of words for the realm of numbers, though, so I stopped at the level of Algebra II.

My social life in high school ranged from nonexistent to enervating to harrowing. Out in the world, sixties things were happening: Vietnam, civil rights, assassinations, free love, the Beatles, hippies, the Doors, psychedelic drugs. But for me it was like watching a movie. In Hutchinson, it was still about Pat Boone, the interstate highways, John Wayne, the world's largest wheat elevators, Lawrence Welk, and *over my dead body*. One time we heard a rumor that so-and-so had been killed in Vietnam, but it turned out not to be true. No protest marches in Hutchinson. Street drugs had yet to arrive, beer was the drug of choice, and "free love" was only a way to ruin your reputation (if you were a girl). "Women's lib" was a punchline. The sixties were all over LIFE magazine and TV, but they were nowhere in my life except by imitation. Yes, I could work up tears when the radio played "Blowin' in the Wind," and I could argue with teachers and debaters about the war, but, except for the hours I spent in my room with my radio listening to the music of the times, my life in the Age of Aquarius was, as people say nowadays, performative. I was sour, sarcastic, withdrawn, friendless; I was hiding Charlotte as best I could, but it took a lot out of me and often didn't really work. Still, my reputation as a brainiac and a weirdo got transmogrified, in some people's minds, into my being a hippie, which would have been funny—me, a hippie, what a sick joke—if it weren't so sad. I was a misfit in Hutchinson and America both.

There were many times when I found myself on the edge of a group of my peers, unable to speak, unable to think of a single thing to say that wouldn't (I imagined) cause them to roll their eyes and sidle away. To put a pleasant look on my face, I often called up mind-pictures of Colorado's green-black trees, the piney smell, the bright feeling of the air against my skin. Little wonder people would wave a hand in front of my face and ask me where I thought I was.

And there was always the money thing. The school dress code for girls, all twelve years, called for skirts or dresses, and in high school the standard among the girls included hosiery, along with girdles and garters to hold up the hose. To make money for hose (and sanitary napkins and sanitary belts), I babysat, I did ironing, I washed the neighbors' cars, I worked at Duckwall's some weekends. In addition to keeping the checkbook, I took over the bills, since Mother was apt to forget them. More than once I had to race a check to the bank. I stuck cardboard in the flats I wore to school to cover the holes. After Hutch discontinued bus service, I was grateful that the library was only three blocks from the apartment. It won't surprise you to learn the library was my haven.

I topped out at a size 14 my freshman year. Mother made most of our clothes, and luckily she was really good at it. I loved the clothes she made me, even though they had a touch of the fifties, because they made me look like an adult; and I never owned a pair of jeans, only knit pants with a phony seam down the front of the legs. If you want to know what our clothes looked like, you can Google "sewing patterns 1960s." I can remember every straight skirt, every shirtwaist dress, every dress-up suit. I remember the gray and white striped wool skirt and blazer. She had to line it, because the wool irritated my skin, and lining a complicated jacket is a bear, but she did it. Where it was turned under—the cuffs and the collar and the waistband and the hem—it still itched, but I could stand that much. I wore a white knit shell underneath it, and when I took off the jacket in class, the boys stared at my boobs. I thought, well, I'm fat and have no waistline, but at least I have big boobs.

Junior year I had a steady boyfriend for a while. I was standing next to my locker between classes one day when I caught a guy looking at me with his head tilted in a certain way and one eyebrow raised. No smile. I didn't know him, but I knew of him; his name was Stan, and he played point guard on the basketball team. Cute, with long waves of hair on top. Between seventh and eighth period, a friend of his told me Stan wanted to meet me behind the tennis court after school. I felt a whoosh of possibilities, not the least of which was the chance to present to my peers as a normal girl. But I thought it was probably a prank, so I said no, and Stan felt challenged, and you know how the rest of it went.

At first it was a thrill to wear his class ring: to cut Dr. Scholl's footpads into little squares and stack them under the giant ring to make it stay on my finger—it was a ritual much discussed by the girls—and I felt utterly cool wearing his letterman's jacket in the halls. And it worked as I'd hoped: for the first time, it seemed, I was one of the girls. I had someone to eat lunch with. For half a semester, I even lurked on the fringes of the group of popular girls who ran the school.

But actually being with Stan made me anxious. He wouldn't stop pestering me to "let him." He had an answer for every objection; he wheedled; he sulked; he sent me mash notes; he ignored me; he told me he loved me; he told me I was killing him. Parked on some dark country road, I would let him do things bit by bit, but I always stopped him short of his goal. All that making out aroused me all right, and I already had the belief that boyfriend love was actual love; but Stan didn't seem to understand that any possibility of my getting pregnant was out of the question. It would be a calamity. It would kill Mother. It would ruin my life. For her part, Mother had always pretended that sex didn't exist. She told me nothing except *don't*. She told me tales of boys getting "fresh" with her and how she had put them in their place. She expected me to know what she meant. Neither of us brought up the Colorado trip, of course, and I never even hinted to her about what had happened on the roof at Grandma and Grandpa's house. So what little I knew about sex I had gleaned from books, but they were written in such a way that you had to already understand what they were explaining. And of course I heard and overheard plenty of information (most of it wrong) in the girls' bathrooms and the hallways. The only way I knew to protect myself was not to allow Stan to touch me under my underpants, because that either caused pregnancy or led to its cause. Without context, you know nothing.

When I began to feel the pressure from him all the time, even in class, even at home doing dishes, even in my dreams, I began to fear that the time would come when he wouldn't take no for answer. I made up my mind to end it, and one day after school I gave him back his things and stood there next to my locker while he berated me and called me a bitch and a whore and a cocktease and a phony as our classmates looked on. I knew then that I had been right to be apprehensive about him.

The next day I heard he was telling people I was a lousy lay and he had only dated me because his friends on the team said weird girls like me were nymphos. When it got back to me, I was engulfed by shame and emptied of oxygen. Instantly I knew the whole debacle was my own fault. I had dived into the deep end when I should have been content with dangling my feet in the baby pool.

The only way I could get myself to return to school the next day was to tell myself how glad I was that I was now free—detached from the complicated high school social structure devoted to (I made a list) hair, clothes, shoes, breath mints, gossip, mascara, magazines, lipstick, the car-to-car etiquette of dragging Main, eyeliner, dates, note-passing, dances, corsages, invitations, parties, pop music, beer busts at somebody's uncle's farm out by Cow Creek—the whole stupid high school ranking system. In other words, normalcy. That night as I lay sleepless in bed, I reminded myself that I had never been normal, and the way to avoid this kind of public humiliation was to maintain strict control of my infernal hopeless longing for that blessed state of being. I pressed my cold hands against my fiery cheeks and replayed the breakup scene over and over.

The next day when I walked into first period, a former friend started in on me, and I gave her an icy stare and told her I couldn't care less about Stan or any of the rest of it.

As new scandals pushed mine to the background, I developed a new chief worry: my future. It was a blank. I was going to be a senior next year, time of life-altering decision-making (we were often reminded), and I couldn't picture myself at graduation, let alone five or ten years down the road. My peers were making exciting plans. Even Mother, on her first date with Daddy, surprised by the question of what she wanted out of life, had been able to answer—a husband, a house, kids. But all I had ever wanted as a kid was to move to Colorado, and now that that dream had withered, I had no idea what I wanted or wanted to do; the thought of marriage and motherhood had no appeal for me. I scored a 36 on the ACT, but even with scholarships, college was out of the question. Mother suggested I might enjoy taking bookkeeping classes at Juco; maybe I could meet somebody. But there was no time or money. We both had to work. She seemed to call in sick more and more often, and the bills kept coming.

I floated through my junior year classes on a wave of suppressed anxiety, crashing once in a while. I floated down the halls, floated to class, floated out the door at three-thirty. I was there and not there. I had to hope high school wouldn't be the peak of my life, but there wasn't actually any reason to hope.

Chapter 8
Joan's Wedding Veil

On my sixteenth birthday in 1963 I got my regular driver's license, and Mother bought us the car she'd saved up for: a 1949 Plymouth DeLuxe. I think they only came in black; anyway, ours was. In a time of Corvairs and Imperials and T-birds and Mustangs, the Plymouth seemed like a relic from an earlier century: it had round shoulders, a rounded top, round bumpers, round headlights, a chrome strip in the middle of the windshield, a green/beige stick shift in the steering column. Sort of a poor man's Depression gangster car. I could barely see over the big steering wheel, and it took all my arm strength to make it turn a corner on a dirt road (you could Google "manual steering"), and it had manual brakes, too, whose pedal I could reach only by scooting down in the seat. The car shimmied when it reached forty-five or fifty miles per hour, and the itchy green/brown horsehair upholstery was shiny in spots. I think Mother paid a hundred dollars for it. She said she was relieved we finally had a car and I could drive, because she didn't feel like driving anymore. She got too tired.

Nobody loved a car more than a sixteen-year-old in the 1960s in farm country who has graduated from the restricted license you got at fourteen, which allowed you to drive with an adult present or, if alone, drive "the most direct route" to and from school, along with "agricultural errands." (One girl I knew, who lived out on Pennington Road, kept a broken water pump in the trunk of her car so if she got stopped she could say she was on the way to Wilbeck's.) The beauty wasn't in the car itself (I didn't know much about cars); it was the freedom it gave you. It was, for me, the knowledge that, if I had to, I could drive west out of Hutch and end up somewhere where troubles melted like lemon drops. Or at least where I could camouflage myself in the wallpaper. Of course, I no longer thought that it could actually happen, but it was calming to pretend it could.

Meanwhile, I drove all over town and even dragged Main once in a while.

That summer, Mother and I drove to Wichita to Joan's apartment so that Mother could make Joan's wedding veil. It was warm that day, I remember. Joan and I lay in lounge chairs on the patio, the new kind made of pliable plastic tubes. I squirmed to distribute the tubes along my body. Two of them had separated where the back of my thigh joined my hip, and it felt as if, any minute, they might part and I might fall through them onto the concrete patio. I pictured it, like something out of an old Laurel and Hardy movie. I glanced at Joan—who was sipping her margarita with her eyes closed behind her sunglasses—and reached underneath my butt to reposition the straps. One caught a tiny hair on my thigh, and I swore under my breath.

I retrieved my drink, which Joan had made for me without the alcohol, and licked the salt on the rim. I loved this drink. It tasted like a lime slush. In spite of the pinch on my thigh and the occasional need to slap a mosquito, life seemed sweet. Joan's life.

I was on to her now, of course. Any ambivalence I may once have felt about that day on the roof had evaporated as I'd navigated the bumpy road of consent with Stan. I hadn't seen Joan or communicated with her since that day, although Mother and I kept up with things via Aunt Wilma's annual Christmas letter, which recounted Vivian's outstanding academic and extracurricular achievements, Uncle Frank's new car, and Frankie's latest hobby, along with vague accounts of Joan's misadventures; when Aunt Wilma wrote that *Joan was invited to spend two Saturday mornings at school after a party got out of hand (ha!)*, I figured Joan and her friends had set fire to a weather-worn old tractor in a pasture one night after a few beers, or actions to that effect. For Mother's part, she replied with a few sentences on the back of a card.

I told myself Joan wasn't a nice person, and I didn't care a thing about her. I felt much older, more mature, than I had been that day. I was only in Wichita today to keep Mother company and drive the car.

"It's nice here," I said, as coolly as I could, in imitation of a blasé adult tone, to show her I was above it all. "I like that you get shade in the afternoon."

Joan shrugged. She looked like a younger, hipper version of her mother, Aunt Wilma the big-haired movie star; Joan was dressed in short cutoffs, a shirt of her boyfriend's tied at the waist, and bare feet with red nail polish. Her hair was wound in a fat sloppy bun held in place with a chopstick. She wore fresh white-pink lipstick and yesterday's smeared mascara. Her arms and legs were tan. As she had since she was twelve, she looked carelessly sultry.

"You still going with that one guy?" she said.

"We broke up."

"How come?"

"You know, it got boring." I didn't want to give her any information that would come back to me weaponized.

Joan could afford to be generous. Her future was all set. She'd been living with her boyfriend, Harvey, in this ultramodern apartment in Wichita, and they were having a hurry-up wedding in two weeks. I know what you're thinking. Wasn't everybody scandalized? Didn't Uncle Frank show up with a shotgun? Didn't it just *kill* Aunt Wilma? No, of course not. All my anxiety about the possibility of getting pregnant turned out to be just another joke on me. In the sixties the actual age of consent in Kansas was sixteen; if you were old enough, there wasn't much anybody could do about it if you moved in with your boyfriend, although some friendly sheriff might have a talk with the boyfriend and hint that he was about to go to jail, and I suppose some guys believed that. And if you actually came up pregnant, you just—got married. Your folks were required to be embarrassed, there had to be some mild shaming at the wedding shower (but there would be a wedding shower), and there would be gossip—until the next thing came along. And when the baby was born, it was just the cutest thing, you could just eat it with a spoon, didn't it look just like Uncle Whosit.

And your aunt Dixie would make you a veil with lace and pearls and handmade tiny white satin rosebuds. As she worked on the veil I heard her humming on the other side of the sliding door.

When I told Joan I had broken up with Stan, she burst out laughing. "Oh, Billie," she said, with airy condescension. She laughed again as she rose from her chair and walked into the apartment. I heard her say, "How're you doing, Aunt Dixie? Ready for another beer? Wanna try a margarita this time?"

I winced. Just what I needed—trapped for two hours in the car, with Mother drunk and talkative. Or weepy. Lately you could never tell.

But I forced myself to tuck that worry away in the back of my mind. For now, it was enough to empty my forebrain and let my lizard brain take over. At sixteen, I visualized my animal brain as a raw wound that absorbed everything, even if it was only air, with a kind of frightening and delicious intensity. Especially smells, especially sounds. I took a deep breath. Wichita, a city ten times the size of Hutchinson, had a smell that was hard to identify—gasoline and oil, for sure, but also something gritty, sugary, and green. And out here on the patio through the basket-weave privacy fence, the city emitted a constant hum, a warm, breathy undertone. An occasional squeal of brakes, miscellaneous pops, doors opening and closing. Voices and splashes from a nearby swimming pool. I tingled with the novelty of it. My hormones responded to these vague inklings of urban life.

The apartment was a corner unit on the ground floor of a new pink stucco building, something I had seen only in movies set in California. Thinking about it now in my lounge chair, I was stung by the memory of what had happened an hour ago when Joan ushered us in. I had taken it all in—the carpet, the drapes, the harvest gold kitchen appliances, the grainy golden oak cupboards, the Formica countertop, the gleaming chrome fixtures, the refrigerated air. I was oppressed by envy, and I had whirled in a circle, smiling, my arms extended, in the middle of the living room, crying, "I never want to leave this place!" Dramatically I had sunk down on the sofa, tearing several paper bags lying there. Quickly I reached underneath me and pulled them out, accidentally ripping one right through the big red logo of Wichita's finest home-owned luxury goods store. Mother and Joan had exchanged a glance, and there had been an awkward silence. I felt too big for the room, as if my arms and legs would soon burst through the windows. I imagined I smelled bad, and my hair was greasy.

Now I heard the thunk of the sliding door. Joan had put on

thongs (that's what we called flip-flops then), and they smacked against her feet as she carried a drink and a pitcher. Winking, she set the drink on the wavy translucent glass top of the small round table between us. She poured herself a fresh one from the pitcher and settled into her chair.

I took a sip and was surprised to taste alcohol. I drank again, delighted. How could there be this *heat* in the middle of all that icy lime? Heat in my insides? My pleasure separated me from the bad feelings I had had earlier. "How do you make this?"

"You buy it by the bucket at the liquor store."

"Oh." And then, impulsively, "Can you drink?"

She laughed. "Well, I try."

"No, I mean because of the . . ." I made a semicircle motion with my hand over my midsection.

Joan shrugged. "Our mothers smoked and drank all during all their pregnancies, and we turned out okay, am I right?" She extended her glass, and the two of us clinked. I had a moment of pain, remembering the time when I still thought Joan might be my friend. But I knew better now, I told myself.

I gulped the drink like water. Then I groaned, took off my glasses, and pressed the meat of my hand against my right eye. "Ice cream headache."

Joan chuckled. "Self-healing."

For a few minutes we reclined in blessed silence. Then a yard sprinkler started up nearby, and I imagined I felt a few droplets on my arms. I smelled the water. The headache went away, and I felt tranquil, even drowsy. "Remember when we used to stay out at the Wirths' farm by Rose Hill? Aunt Jolene and Uncle Marty? We used to carry water out to the sheep?"

Joan yawned.

"I remember filling up buckets from the faucet in the bathtub and hauling them through the hallway and the kitchen and backing out through the door and walking past the quince tree to the trough. *Hot* water." I remembered the way my spine had kinked when the gritty buckets scraped against the porcelain tub.

Joan made a gagging sound, but I ignored it. "And then we chopped the ice in the trough with an ax. Remember that?" I sipped my drink. I didn't taste the alcohol at all now, but the belly heat remained. Beer had never done this, the few times I had sipped it to be polite.

"Christ on a cracker," Joan said. "Don't tell me you're nostalgic about tromping through sheep shit at the Wirths'."

"And the horses. Remember how they'd snort, and steam'd come out their noses?" It was like a little play in my mind, a dumbshow. I felt my lungs burning in the cold wind, my sockless feet freezing in tennis shoes. The buckets' wire bails cut into my fingers. I smelled the pungent wet wool, felt the sheep nosing my thighs.

Joan sat up in her chair. "Wait a minute. We only stayed over in the summer. Besides, they left the farm when you were—you must have been five or six. Moved to Missouri."

I blinked, and the movie in my head vanished. "It must have been a late freeze or something." She still thought of me as younger than I was. As I remembered it, I had been at least ten when the Wirth cousins moved to Missouri.

Joan laughed and lay back again. "You're so full of shit. You just make stuff up."

"But I *remember* that. I remember all of that. I remember Trisha, Donald, Marie, Beverly, Mick."

"Do you remember the outhouse? The wasps? Taking a bath in a galvanized tub, one after another, youngest ones last?"

I blinked. "Yes, all of that. I thought it was great. It was—"

"Are you even a girl?" Her tone fell on a scale between exasperated and sardonic. "Sometimes I wonder."

This brought me up short. "You don't have to be a boy to like—"

She burst out laughing. "Shit?"

"The outdoors. Animals. *Real* stuff, not . . ." I flashed on a memory of the dead kittens out behind the barn.

"Not what?"

"You know"—I searched for the right word—"*folderol.*" I gestured with one hand to indicate the patio but then swept with both hands to include the apartment, the city, the world. But even as I said it, I again felt the envy I had felt upon first seeing Joan's wedding presents stacked in the spare room—blenders and electric knives, fondue sets, towels, bedsheets, kitchen tool sets, ice buckets—all the things that represented her life going forward. Domestic bliss wasn't anything I had imagined for myself, but it was *something*. It was normal. Waking up in the morning in bed next to your husband—*huzzzbund*, the word itself chimed, so sleek and buzzy and sophisticated—and then getting up, making waffles, making plans to play cards and have cocktails later with friends, laughing at a silly inside joke, kissing him when he left for work. That was a future I could picture—it was in all the women's magazines, which were an extension of the community's norms, after all—but not for me. For me, nothingness.

"'Folderol!'" Joan screamed. "What century are you *from*?" She was slurring her words.

"I just feel this need to *do* something, you know? Like I'm supposed to be *doing* something." "Folderol" had brought with it a memory of Daddy, of his enthusiasms, his ambitions, his joy.

"You want to be rich and famous?" Joan said.

"No. I don't know."

There was an electric silence.

"What year are you?"

"I'll be a senior."

"And then college?" she said.

"And study what?" Surely she knew there was no money for college. In my world, people who had money didn't talk about it; once at a debate tournament some kids were laughing in the hallway at their judge—a volunteer from the community who had come to the event in his overalls—not knowing he had a law practice in town. And people who didn't have money, well, at least they had their pride. Not one dime, after all. It was a kind of rough egalitarianism.

"You like to read, right?" she said. "Do something like, I don't know, seventeenth-century Irish folklore—something where you know everything there is to know on earth about one teeny-tiny thing. That's you in a nutshell. Little Miss Know-It-All."

I winced. "What would I do with that?"

"Talk about it—God knows you love to talk about shit you read in books. Teach seventeenth-century Irish whatever to the next generation."

I shook my head. "I couldn't teach. I—"

"Get a PhD then. Write books that thirty-two people in the world read. Write reviews of books that twelve people read. Be the world's leading expert."

She still knew me, all right. She knew just how to fascinate me and deflate me at the same time. I had to put a stop to this. "As fun as that sounds, I don't have any money to go to school."

"Poor you. Get scholarships." She placed her hand on her little round belly and spread her fingers.

"Right." I placed my glass against my face so that the rim enclosed my lips. I sucked in air to pull the glass tight. I felt my lips swell.

"I'm serious, asshole. If you want to 'do something' so bad, you need to get out there and do it. The world doesn't owe you a living."

"Oh, really. I never heard that." Talking into the glass distorted my voice. I sounded a bit like Donald Duck. I crossed my eyes at Joan.

"You get that from your dad," she said, frowning. "*Be somebody.* Good isn't good enough for you."

I twisted the glass and pulled it away from my face with a tiny *pock* sound. "I'm not *like* that, and neither was Daddy."

Joan rolled her eyes. "Oh, please." She was looking at her diamond as she rocked her hand in the sunlight. "He was a big bawl-baby, just like you," she said. "He sold *pans* at county *fairs*, for God's sake, but what he wanted was to be some kind of a big deal. Everybody knows that."

I felt heat rising in my face. I took a mouthful of margarita and let it melt a bit before I swallowed it. Ah, that was the trick. I took another.

"He was penny-ante, Billie. Small potatoes."

I felt sick to my stomach. I tried to picture Daddy alive, lively, laughing, but I couldn't.

"Everybody loved him," Joan said. "They all babied him. But he was such a fuckup."

"*My* dad? You're talking about *my* dad?" I heard just the slightest slurring of my words now.

"Your mom kicked him out, you know. They were separated when he died."

I gasped. "Like hell."

"Everybody knows it. Ask Mom, ask Aunt Jolene. He was living in a hotel in downtown Hutch."

I narrowed my eyes at her. She could easily be lying, but logic, my old friend, told me that with Daddy gone a lot and me inside my head all the time, it would have been easy enough for Mother to keep something like that from me. But Daddy? Leave me? "I don't believe you."

Joan shrugged. "Don't then. I don't give a good goddamn." She retrieved a bottle of Coppertone from under her chair and spread the creamy lotion on her arms.

I licked the remaining grains of salt off the rim of my glass and turned it until the dregs reached my mouth. I pursed my lips and sucked in the bitter lukewarm puddle. I inhaled the smell of the lime. I felt shaky.

Now I heard the water sprinkler again, wondrously subtle, summery. I let myself sink into the sound until I felt as if I were teetering on some edge. I wanted Joan to talk me off of it or, if not, to go ahead myself and step off. I couldn't look at her; I stared into my glass and said, "Sometimes I think I was left on my folks' doorstep by aliens."

When she didn't react, I tried again. "I mean, I don't feel like I belong here. In this family. In this—you know, around here."

In my side vision I saw her sniff her forearms, recap the lotion, and set the bottle on the table.

"I feel like—like I don't *think* like other people." The words hung in the air like mist. I could almost see them, each letter swirling, in the oppressive silence. I watched them until they floated out of sight. I made one last attempt: "Know what I mean?"

Joan pointedly studied a spot on her arm. "Will you please, for once, just climb down off your fucking cross."

I moaned. *I must be feeling something,* I thought, but all I felt was a furious blankness. When would I ever learn? I would never reach bottom, because there was no bottom.

"Harvey is finishing up his degree in December," Joan said in a chatty tone. "He's already got a job."

Out of long habit, I swallowed my feelings before they could worm their way deeper into me. Must. Carry. On. "Pan Am. I heard." I joggled my empty glass. "Can I get another one?"

"You know, you could do worse than get married." She filled my glass from the half-empty pitcher. Most of the ice was melted now. "Are you still going with that one guy?"

"No, I told you. We broke up." I drank several swallows. So good.

"Too bad." Now she launched into a monologue about the forthcoming wedding. The church ceremony would be in Wiley, and then there would be a caravan to Wichita, where there would be a beer-and-champagne reception at Harvey's club. Did I want to see the dress? The top was fitted, with cap sleeves and white satin bows at the shoulders, and the skirt had daisies and pearls, and she would be wearing white satin heels and, of course, the veil Mother was making. Did I have anything to wear? Of course, Dixie would make me something, maybe a shift. Had I seen this new fabric, they called it whipped cream? So soft, and it would drape over my problem areas and disguise my (lack of a) waist.

"I'm not coming." I licked the salt and drank almost half the glass.

"And a coordinating neck scarf." Now she looked at me. "Of course you're coming. We're all expecting you."

I shook my head.

"Don't be a child."

"Do you really want to do this?" I said.

She gave me a savage look. "For fuck's sake."

"Remember when you told me you couldn't stand the idea of living our mothers' lives all over again?"

"Don't be stupid."

"You did. You said, 'God save us from living our mothers' lives all over again.' That time on the roof." I experienced a sense memory of my fingers digging into the gravel, trying to find a grip. That other memory, well, it alighted softly, light as a daddy longlegs, and I barely felt it when it drifted away. I wondered if she was remembering it, too.

She pushed her sunglasses on top of her head and rubbed her eyes. "We were kids, for Christ's sake. Grow the fuck up."

"I thought you—I felt like—"

"I don't give a rat's ass *what* you felt like. Nobody does. Why. Can't. You. See. That."

I started to get up, to go hide someplace, but when I pressed my feet to the concrete, the straps on the bottom of the chair parted, and I flailed my arms. One hand smacked the table, and I managed to grip it and gain enough leverage to twist myself upright and stand.

"You're drunk," Joan said. "Speaking of living our mothers' lives."

I wanted to slap her face, and I leaned over to do that, but on the way I felt wobbly and pulled back. I suspected she was right—I was drunk, or half drunk. How much did it take your first time with real booze, I wondered. This was not what I'd expected it to feel like—wrung out, all the juice squeezed out of you.

But if my body was uncertain, my mind was teeming, the thoughts swimming and squirming, filling the empty space inside me, making a harrowing noise. The sound was dissonant, as if you were playing a note and its half note at the same time. It ground against my spine. Charlotte. Was Charlotte, or something like Charlotte, an undercurrent in everyone's life, a river that gurgled just beneath the surface? Why did no one ever mention it? For years now, for as long as I could remember, people had ignored all this hideousness inside—the itching, the alarm, the dread, the clamor—they pretended it away. They just sat around playacting. But I couldn't, not for long anyway. It seemed I didn't know how.

My throat filled with wordless rage. It hurt. It hurt like knife blades.

It was if I was watching myself when I hooked my thumbs on the edge of the table and tipped it perpendicular to the ground, and then I pressed it against the heavy city air until it toppled over and crashed onto the patio floor. The glass shattered, and the pieces slid along the concrete like ice crystals. The table's frame wobbled and came to rest at my feet with a clang.

Joan yelled an obscenity and rolled off her chair. She high-stepped like a show horse across the patio and yanked open the sliding door. "Your daughter is crazy as a hoot owl!" she shouted to Mother inside the apartment. "She belongs at Third Hill!"

I stood as still as I could. I'd heard once that if you get pieces of glass inside you, they will work their way out of the scar, one shard at a time, as if to remind you of that special day when you fell apart. I frowned, trying to recollect where I'd heard that. It seemed unlikely to be true. And then I remembered. The Garden of Eden. Charlotte. *Whoever it was, they're dead, because here's a piece of their brain.* Pieces of glass sliding down your neck in a thread of blood.

I looked around at the scattered glass. Mother would be here at any moment. I wasn't afraid of what she would say or do, but I dreaded that look on her face. It would cut deep, deeper than anything. It always had.

Just before the wedding, Mother found a table almost like Joan's in the Sears catalog for $12.98, and she mailed Joan a check for $17.98 (the extra $5 was for the inconvenience, I guess). They had the wedding; Mother went; I stayed home.

Mother nagged me for months to call or write Joan and apologize, but I kept putting it off. Somehow, "Sorry I broke your table" didn't seem to address the issues between the two of us, let alone the issues with, well, me.

The thing was, though, Joan didn't cash the check. Mother kept asking me about it when the bank statement came. I thought about lying to her and saying the check had gone through, but I had always been a bad liar. Plus, of course, Mother bugged me constantly to call or write and apologize to Joan. After putting it off until almost Christmas, I finally wrote her a letter.

Sorry about your broken table. Mother sent you a check to buy a new one (check no. 1478, $17.98). Did you get it? It would be cool if you would cash it and wipe the slate clean. I keep having to add it to the list of outstanding checks when I reconcile the account. One thing's for sure—I'll never forget my first margarita(s), the first time I got drunk! That was quite the drive home. Thanks for another "first" in my life.

Sorry I didn't make it to your wedding. Mother says it was beautiful. I hope you'll send us some pictures. Good luck with married life.

I'm glad the baby came out all right.

Your cousin,

Billie

I read and reread the letter until I was satisfied with the degree of passive aggressiveness (not that I knew that term then, but I was well acquainted with the concept) but not enough to prove anything in the court of law I imagined myself living in, having to answer constantly for my trespasses. I considered using the assassination of President Kennedy in November as an excuse for not writing earlier, but that seemed like a chickenshit thing to do, intellectually dishonest. I did cry when he was murdered, after yelling at my classmates in the hall who were discussing it, telling them it was obviously only a stupid rumor, we weren't one of those countries where bad guys killed our leaders like that. But then the principal came on the intercom. Classes were canceled for the rest of the day, and I went home and stared at the TV and cried and cried. But still, the president seemed like someone on the TV who had nothing to do with me.

Besides, I figured if Joan didn't relish the agony I went through waiting for it, she would have cashed the damn check.

* * *

Getting the mail was my job. Sometimes on weekends I would sit on the porch after lunch, my excuse being I was waiting for the mail, but in reality I only wanted to get out of the apartment. It had shrunk over time and had become unbearably crowded when both of us were home. With two smokers now, everything in the place was coated with that sticky cigarette goo that attracts dust, which then congeals, making it gross and hard to scour off.

So I was sitting on the porch on a cold, sunny day when Joan's letter arrived. It was short. She had not picked up on my (phony) jocular tone at all. Her note was deadly serious. She didn't mention the table, the check, the margaritas, the wedding, the baby. She was formal and distant, and she said *I feel it's best if we stay out of each other's lives.*

I felt the loss almost as keenly as when Daddy died. I recalled throwing my book on the ground in the backyard of the house on Halsey Drive and rooting around in the grass, pretending somehow I was communicating with him through the earth itself. Now I scarcely recognized that girl. In spite of everything, I had believed then that somehow, at some unknown time and place, my alienation would just go away, and that Joan, somehow, would be part of it, because Joan was the only one who ever hinted, however cryptically, that she knew how I felt. Even though she, unlike Daddy, was still alive, only absenting herself from me, the loss I felt was deepened by the clear fact that she had never been in my life, not really, only flitting at the edges, skittering off my wounds, her heart and mind empty of any feeling for me at all.

But I could be wrong about that, couldn't I? It was only a letter, which I tore to pieces and threw away. Family things like that got papered over eventually, didn't they? Didn't they?

* * *

The next year I graduated at the top of my class, but I didn't march. I didn't go to the religious thing the Sunday before, either, and I didn't go to the ceremony where I was inducted into the Honor Society. All that was phony capitalist imperialist folderol, empty ritual, and I was sick of it, I told Mother. I hadn't gone to Joan's wedding, and I hadn't gone to Grandpa or Grandma's funerals. (Grandpa had died when I was in seventh grade, and Grandma went when I was a sophomore.) Everybody had given me to understand that people died all the time, and life went on, and it was our duty to be, actually, unmoved. So why belabor the pity party? And besides (so I told myself—the actual truth), not seeing them in their caskets let me, on some animal level, pretend they weren't dead.

Mother said she was too tired to argue with me, but when I was older I would regret not going to funerals and other important ceremonies. So many things only happen once.

A week after graduation I got a job at the iron and metal yard on South Main. It was a place where you bought and sold scrap iron—pipe, angle iron, car parts, miscellaneous copper, some brass, the occasional bedsprings and car batteries. I was the bookkeeper; my boss, a sweet middle-aged man, called me the bean counter. I smoked at my desk and drank coffee from a thermos, and almost no one talked to me. I was content at work. I had lots and lots of details to keep track of and almost nothing to think about. I told myself Charlotte was only a memory, a childhood conceit not worth a brain cell thinking about.

Mother worked and drank. She fell once in a while at home and got mad when I expressed concern. "Tripped over my own two feet," she would say, and she would ask me to get her a beer. She would have a cigarette lit by the time I got back.

I turned twenty, and she turned forty. Joan never cashed the check, but neither did I stop payment on it. Month after month I added it to the outstanding checks.

You could do that, it turned out. You could just keep putting one foot in front of the other and going to work and smoking and eating and sleeping, while the whole time, there was nothing inside you.

Then something happened that cracked my world open—the shrinking world inside me and the small world outside me—and all sorts of things came tumbling out.

Book Two

Chapter 9
Seven Women in a Cadillac

Certain dates in your life you never forget: when you were born, when something historic happened, when someone died. For me, it's Saturday, June 17, 1967. Whenever I notice 6:17 on a clock—it can happen twice a day—I relive what happened on that date, the summer I was twenty, and my throat closes for a moment.

I had spent the day at the library. It was ungodly hot for June. When I walked in our door, breathing hard from climbing the stairs, there was Mother at the table, her face in her hands, a cigarette trembling between two fingers. From the empty beer cans it looked as if she was on her fifth or sixth. Her breathing sounded like an animal growling, interspersed with beer burps. You could have been forgiven if you had thought she was sobbing, but when she looked up there weren't any tears. All my senses were on alert. Something was wrong.

"Where have you been all this time?" she said.

"What's wrong?"

She took a drag and coughed. Now tears came, but no words. There's always that vacillation before they tell you.

My arms turned clammy, and I couldn't swallow. I set the library books on the counter and got out a Tupperware glass, filled it at the tap, and gulped it down. Warmish, brownish Kansas tap water. I sniffed the faded blue-green plastic, scaly and smelly inside from repeated washing. The smell, or rather its familiarity, helped me stand there and wait.

In a flat voice, looking at her hands, Mother told me what had happened. Uncle Frank had called from Wiley. Vivvie, Joanie, and five of their friends, all women, had been killed in a car wreck in the middle of nowhere off of Highway 77.

I squeaked out, "What?"

It was the goddamn awfullest thing, Uncle Frank had told her. Those ladies must have had two dozen kids between them. Everybody in Wiley knew those ladies. The goddamn awfullest thing.

With the heel of her hand Mother wiped her nose.

I shook my head, blinking. "This has to be a mistake." The first step of grief, of course, is denial, although I didn't know that then. I knew nothing about grief.

Mother drained the last of her beer and waggled the can, and I retrieved a new one from the carton on the counter.

"It's true, though." She reached for the Collins Grocery church key and pressed the two triangles into the top of the can. "He called maybe twenty minutes ago."

I tried to picture Frank in their dining room where the phone was, but all I could see in my mind was something like a snowy TV screen. Couldn't picture Joan or Vivian or Aunt Wilma, or any of Daddy's family. Frank Jr., Grandma and Grandpa. Aunt Jolene and Uncle Marty and their kids at the farm in Missouri. I couldn't picture a single one. My mind kept repeating *she's dead she's dead she's dead.* It was like blows, it hurt, but it wasn't real.

I asked Mother the who-what-when-where-how-why, but she only repeated the bare facts Frank had shared—Joanie, Vivvie, five friends, middle of nowhere, two dozen kids, goddamn awfullest thing. Sometime earlier today, maybe this morning. He'd only talked for a minute. He had a lot of calls to make.

I refilled the glass, but when I tried to drink, I choked. Something was in my throat.

I stared as Mother drank half the beer in one chug. Staring at her was all I could do for a minute. I know it sounds nutty, but I was looking to her to show me how I was supposed to feel, or at least how I was supposed to act. But aside from drinking and smoking, she didn't seem to be showing me anything. It was like one of those prank videos where people walk by a statue on the street and it suddenly reaches out to grab them. Only it was backwards; even though her hands and her lips were moving, you would have thought she was a statue.

I felt sweaty and weak, so I walked over to the coffee table and switched on the fan, making it oscillate so that it would hit us both. The moving air cooled the sweat running down my legs under my skirt, and I took a breath.

I sat down and got a Kool out of the pack in my purse. With the first inhalation against my palate I felt the familiar release. I sucked hard three or four times, and I let the smoke trail out of my nose; the irritation of my nostril hairs brought some tears to the edge. I sat there, smoking and blinking and sniffling, postponing the inevitable, whatever that was.

Meanwhile Mother muttered to herself; she was already making plans. How we would drive to Wiley tomorrow. What we would wear, what food we would pick up at Dillons to take with us, had she gotten her good suit back from the cleaners, did the Plymouth have gas in it.

Some tears fell out and rolled down my cheeks, but I didn't feel them. I mean I felt them trickling hot and salty on my skin, but inside I didn't feel like crying. Instead, I felt like the time as a child when I had a tooth abscess and my cheek swelled up like a balloon; the skin had stretched so far, had become so thin, it felt like my mouth would burst.

You know what I wish? I wish I would have just walked over to the table and held Mother and been held for a while. Something tiny far inside me told me that such a gesture would have been normal. But if we hadn't done it when Daddy died—if instead we had been brave and refused to make a spectacle of ourselves—well, then, we weren't about to do it now.

At least not Mother. As for me, other deaths came back to me. The death of the bee, for Christ's sake, the dead bodies of S.P. Dinsmoor and his wife behind glass in the forbidden building at the Garden of Eden, the unattended but morbidly imagined funerals of my grandparents, and, of course, Daddy keeling over of a heart attack in Goodland and ending up as cremains in a box under the bed. And now Joan. And Vivian, too, earnest Vivian, and five other women. So much woman-flesh, so reduced.

These were my thoughts. My feelings were someplace where I couldn't reach.

Pretty soon I fixed myself a sandwich, and Mother ate her usual supper of a piece of cheese and sweet pickles and beer. We talked very little. Slowly the taut balloon inside me leaked out its air and shrank into a wrinkled lump of damp rubber/latex/polymer. At ten I went to bed; she stayed up to see if it was on the news yet.

Behind my closed bedroom door I heard the KTVH opening news theme, muted and tinny, followed by ghostly TV voices. I couldn't make out what they were saying. I turned on my fan, stripped to bra and underpants, and lay down in bed. I drifted off for a while.

A car drove by on Main Street below, honking, startling me back into consciousness. My fan blew hot air on me, hesitated, and swiveled. I reached for my cigarettes.

It was Saturday night, 11:19, and teenagers were dragging

Main, of course. I heard a car peel out at 13th, laying rubber, and the kids screamed out war whoops through the open windows. Boys, from the sound of them. I pictured them driving south through downtown, taking a left on Avenue C, and turning around in the R & B drive-in, where you could get a giant pork tenderloin sandwich for forty-five cents. Then they'd head back thirty blocks to the north end of town, and then circle through the parking lot at Sandy's (later McDonald's, later Hardee's, maybe something else by tomorrow) or the Larkland shopping center—what nowadays we would call a strip mall but then seemed new and futuristic. Carfuls of boys might park on a side street and wait for a carful of girls to pull up next to them and exchange shouts through the open windows. No cell phones, no social media, no texting in those olden days. Everything earthy, sweaty, primitive, analog.

Everybody knew the drill.

It had only been three years since I'd graduated, but it seemed like a lifetime now. Lately I had been having visions of the two of us, Mother and me, in twenty or thirty years, me a fat, graying, middle-aged woman living in the same upstairs of the same house with my elderly mother. I saw the two of us sitting there (Mother saying, "Only June, and hot as hell already"), her bent over in her green chair and me on the couch, smoking in silence, the very picture of ennui, as the fan oscillated relentlessly.

I got up to pee, and I put on a shirt to cover myself. The TV was off, and Mother still sat at the table, resting her head on her folded arms. Asleep or passed out, I couldn't tell. A soft whistling sound came from her lips. She had a cigarette between her fingers, and I noticed that the ash was long and twisty like the gunpowder snakes we used to play with on the Fourth of July. On second glance I saw that the cigarette had burned all the way down to the filter and gone out, so, evidently, this time she wasn't about to burn the house down with us in it, along with Mrs. McKutcheon and her last two children and one or two cats; in one recurring dream, I stood screaming, leaning over the railing at the top of the steps, afraid to jump, and I always woke up just before the flames reached me.

After the bathroom I returned to the couch and leaned into the one window in that room. I felt the cooling outdoor air and smelled the window screen—metallic, rusty, dusted with moth powder.

Back and forth, the fan whirred. I turned to face the room and lowered myself onto the couch.

Joan was dead. Of course she was. There was no mistake. She was dead.

It was too late forever. Too late to reconcile with Joan, too late to get to know Vivian, too late to mourn Daddy, too late to get high school right, too late to solve the puzzle that was my mother. Too late to fit in, too late to get the hell out of Dodge.

Then a picture formed in my mind—how terrified Joan must have been, in the last seconds before the end, when she realized what was about to happen. I saw her lips wide open, her teeth. How she must have dreaded the pain to come—skin, bones, muscles, organs, mouth, teeth, nose, eyes, arms, chest, hips, legs, ankles. How her throat must have curdled as the air rushed in.

I broke into a cold sweat. These thoughts were as forbidden as any I had ever had, almost sexual in their impact. I was treading on illicit territory—a starless nightscape that might, if I went deep enough, swallow me whole. I might not come back this time.

I picked up a magazine from the coffee table and folded up a corner of the cover, arranging it so that the breeze from the fan lifted it, and then it returned. It took several tries before I got it just right; I made a sharp fold and then rounded it a bit. The paper lifted, and then it made an almost imperceptible *tick* as it settled back.

Now I had the three things: the drone of the fan, the lift of the paper, the tick. Four, if you counted the breeze tickling the hairs of my arms.

After a while I'm pretty sure my breath, and maybe my heartbeat, became synchronized with the tiny world I had made: the drone, the lift, the tick, the trembling hairs. I left my body and floated naturally into a recollection of Daddy—*the* recollection—of that first time I watched him selling pans at the fair. The immediate pain of his death had dulled, replaced by the pain of my realizing, in the years since he had died, that it was Daddy who had made me feel like I belonged to the human race, at least marginally, and the best I could manage now was to pretend I was one of them. I had tried to pretend Charlotte away, but of course she was still in there.

It was silent now in the house, in the block, in the town. I scooted closer to the window and stared out at the stark landscape—the tiny backyard, the worn pathway, the corner of the garage roof, the clothesline, the giant catalpa tree, all thrown into relief by the streetlight on the corner. The tree's seed pods crackled in the wind. All of it was familiar and should have been comforting, but tonight its very serenity felt empty, like a stage set, flat and featureless. It was mocking me.

I lay back and relaxed my throat and pointed my chin upward. In the dim light through the window, I could see the eyelashes on the curve of my left eyelid. A tear clung to them, and when I felt it about to let go, I moved my head ever so slightly, redistributing the surface tension and keeping the drop suspended for a moment while I focused all my thoughts on the shimmering rainbow hidden inside the bubble. *Don't blink,* I told myself, and in that moment I blinked (of course) and the tear fell and coursed down my cheek, my neck.

Joan had died, horribly. No matter where my mind went, it came back to that. I tiptoed into the kitchen and fetched one of Mother's beers. It tasted like pee. After I drank half of it I fell asleep on the couch.

I got maybe three or four hours' sleep that night. Mother was up and dressed, humming as she made coffee, when I awoke.

My first thought was *Joan died Joan died Joan died.* My second thought was *Oh, God, we're going to Wiley. Everybody will be there.* I had a crick in my neck, and my head twanged from the little beer I had consumed.

I felt the itch start inside my skin, as if insects were crawling there. Charlotte had come calling.

On the coffee table, the cover of the magazine—all the pages, in fact—was crinkled with humidity. The little four-part world I had built in the night was gone.

I heaved myself off the couch and walked into the bathroom. I swallowed two Anacin and then took a hot bath and washed my hair and put on my white blouse and my beige linen skirt. I put cellophane tape on my bangs to hold them straight while my hair dried. Other girls I'd gone to school with were growing their hair past their shoulders and wearing it flat, a lot like hippies, but women Joan's age, as well as the fortysomethings and fiftysomethings, were still getting perms and wearing bouffants, curlered and ratted and sprayed. But I had hated sleeping every night with brush rollers raking my scalp, and I hated the gouges left by those pink plastic picks we used to hold the rollers in. After graduation I had cut my hair short. My only concession to fashion was my attempt to tame my curly bangs. There was a famous skinny British supermodel named Twiggy, whose long, full, straight bangs and boy cut and boyish body I envied, but it was all I could do to straighten those damn messy curls out of the sides of my bangs. As soon as I got hot or stressed, though, they sprang right back.

Mother was wearing her mauve jersey dress and sandals. I noticed she had painted her toenails, and of course she had applied bright red lipstick.

At Dillons the overhead fluorescent lights were buzzing, and the linoleum floor was so shiny it sparkled. I felt the buzzing and the sparkle in the back of my eyeballs. It wasn't the beer I'd had the night before, I didn't think; it was the usual way I felt when I faced some occasion when I had to dog-paddle through rooms packed with people.

We picked up two dozen assorted cupcakes for the family, doughnuts to eat on the way, and a six-pack of Budweiser; they had the new pop-top cans, so you didn't need a church key to open them. After we were back in the Plymouth, Mother sent me back in to get a second carton for the trip home.

We set out for Wiley, taking Main Street south through South Hutch to 96, in those days a two-lane blacktop. I drove. We had the Plymouth's little side vents open and the windows cracked, and the wind buffeted our faces and hair. Mother tied a scarf loosely around her head.

She had the Sunday *Hutchinson News* on her lap. It crackled in her hands as she read aloud from the front-page story—as if I hadn't already read it before we left—with its odd, cryptic details. Under the headline SEVEN KANSAS WOMEN DEAD IN CRASH, the article said that the "death car" was a white 1956 Cadillac De Ville thought to be driven by Pinky Hilyard, well-known in Butler County for her weekly radio show on radio station WNDR ("A Thousand Watts of Wonderful"), which she co-owned with her husband, Duane. The other six victims had not yet been identified at press time. The women were said to be traveling to Wichita from Wiley, a town of some one thousand people some twenty-five miles southeast of Wichita, where the victims all lived. The car was demolished after colliding with a tree; apparently there were no other vehicles involved. It wasn't known why the Cadillac was on the back road where the wreck occurred, two turns off Highway 77. Butler County sheriff Roy Klaas said the investigation would continue.

While Mother read, I time-traveled right into the house on Halsey Drive, where I sat cross-legged next to Daddy, listening to "Sergeant Preston of the Royal Canadian Mounted Police" on the radio. In my mind the image was as clear as clear (as Grandma would say). It's possible I was blind to traffic for minutes at a time, although I can't say. There weren't a lot of cars on the road.

"Seven women in a town that size, it's going to kill Wiley, just kill it." Mother folded the paper on her lap and lit a cigarette. Everybody in town probably knew at least one of the women, she said—from church, from school, from ball games, from Scouts, from the park, from 4-H, from the post office, from the garden club or book club or quilting club or bridge club, from the drugstore or the grocery store or Grandma's church's thrift shop, from the Coffee & Eats café. When you thought about it, it was the women who planned out most of the goings-on in a town like that, raised the money, made the costumes, baked the cakes, held the rummage sales, brought the refreshments, attended to the details. Wilma and Frank probably knew all those women in the wreck. Mother wondered if any of the others were related to each other, or only Joanie and Vivvie.

"You want to go to Wilma and Frank's, or Grandma's?" I asked her. Actually I doubted we would go to Grandma's. A family of some Kentucky relatives of Grandpa's lived in the house now, but I still thought of it as Grandma's house.

"How come they were on a dead-end dirt road?" Mother said. As if I knew. As if anybody knew. "It doesn't make sense. They were on their way to *Wichita*, for Christ's—"

"You want to go to Wilma and Frank's?" I said again.

"It says, it was two turns off the highway. Now how come—"

"'If you're gonna act like a turd, go lay in the yard,'" I said.

She gagged on a mouthful of smoke. "What?"

"Just something Joan used to say. 'If you're gonna—'"

"I heard you." She rolled her eyes, coughing.

"She said it all the time. It's just a joke."

"What a thing to say. At a time like this." *Behave yourself.*

You know better. There's nothing wrong with you; act normal. You can act normal when you want to.

"When's the funeral?" I said. "Will they have one together, or two?"

She shrugged. "Depends on the in-laws, I expect. Well, the husbands." She added, "Jesus, Billie," no doubt referring to the turd remark.

I hadn't even thought about the husbands. And now the children began to materialize in my mind's eye. Joan had three, Vivian had two, and a collage of their photos decorated the door of our tiny fridge. One in particular I remembered: two children standing in a kiddie pool—skinny, shivering bodies hugging themselves, hair dripping, lips purple. Offhand I wasn't sure if the ones in that picture were Joan's or Vivian's or a combination. And the others. All those kids, motherless. It took your breath away to imagine it.

And there would be parents, grandparents, siblings, in-laws, aunts, uncles, cousins, friends and neighbors, old classmates. Thighs touching in the crowded pews, stifled sobs, the sound of children being pinched and shushed, the suppressed, embarrassed laughter. The heat, the sickening smell of people and crusty carpets and wilting flowers. Breathy organ music. And, at the cemetery, the swirling dust above the freshly broken dirt. Sandburs clinging to your ankles.

I thought about it. It would take a few days to schedule the funerals. Meanwhile, grief and anger would fill the town. "We going to Wilma and Frank's?" I said again, and this time Mother nodded.

"I don't know if the Wirths will be there," she said, and then, "Look out for that bird!" Just ahead a crow, perched on a patch of gooey roadkill, spread its wings and took flight. It almost seemed to frown at me. I swerved to avoid the stippled remains, fighting the Plymouth's giant steering wheel and the drag of the tires. It was too pat, but there it was. One crow means a death.

Mother panted for a minute and then went on. "The Wirths. You remember them—Wilma and Bill's sister Jolene and her husband Marty? They had five kids. Used to live on a farm near Rose Hill? They're in Springfield now. Missouri."

"Of course I remember them," I said, irritated. Had she been oblivious to me my whole childhood? "They'd come to Grandma's in a pickup with sacks of unshucked corn and green apples." Now I flashed on an image of bushel baskets lined in oilcloth. "Jolene brought her dirty clothes to wash, too."

Mother reached into the backseat and brought out a beer. With the *pssh* I relaxed a little, and then I realized how tight my shoulders had been.

She sucked the foam off the top and took three big swallows.

A wave of nostalgia washed over me. "They used to take me back with them to the farm." In my mind I was back there, bouncing on bumpy gravel roads in the bed of the pickup, twangy country music playing on the radio inside the cab. One time we stopped at the gas station in Rock and we each got a cold bottle of pop. "I remember riding horses and wading for miles in the creek, it seemed like," I said. "And the water pump in the kitchen."

"Well, they worked hard, all of them." She had this self-righteous streak that came out sometimes when she was not yet high. It almost seemed hardwired, but of course, I thought, it was learned.

Awash in memory, I didn't catch her tone. I went blundering on. "And taking a bath in a galvanized tub in the living room, oldest to youngest, all in the same water. Trisha always used to tell me she peed in it just before me, and she would *die* laughing."

"There's no *shame* in *honest* work." Mother spoke slowly, leaning toward me, spilling a few drops.

This time I caught the tone. I glanced at her, and she glared back. "But I wasn't— "

"You'd do well to have some goddamn *gratitude*." She gulped the beer and almost choked. Then she added, "I've never taken a dime of welfare. Not in all this time since your dad died. Not one dime."

I wanted to argue with her—I didn't look down on anyone, let alone the Wirths, and it depressed me to think I couldn't ever go back to the farm again, literally or figuratively. It had only been a dozen years, but somebody else lived there now, if the house was even still standing. The countryside was littered with the corpses of broken-backed old farmhouses.

Something made me bite back the sarcastic remark on the tip of my tongue. There was no talking back to Mother.

It flummoxed me—what would happen if I *did* talk back to her? I was too big to hit; she hadn't even slapped my face since high school. What, then, was I afraid of? I mean besides the obvious—that my energy would drain out of me all at once and my body would crash and burn, and finally I would float away to whatever alien planet I really belonged on, along with my companion Charlotte.

Or maybe it wasn't fear but shame. It seemed to me that I spent almost all the waking hours of my childhood ashamed of one thing or another. That's why in bed at night, I used to enact little scenes where I said all the right things for once. But before I saw her reaction I would fall asleep into dreams where I was lost in some town or countryside, vivid with detail, where I couldn't find anything familiar at all and wandered, ashamed and angry, down dirt roads and bumpy brick streets leading to nowhere.

What I needed now was a smoke, but the wind in the car was so rough I was afraid the hot box would fly off. It seemed Mother never worried about that sort of thing.

Pretty soon she turned toward me on the bench seat, bent her knees, leaned her head against the seat back, and closed her eyes. As her face relaxed into sleep, she looked almost like she did in the snapshot I had tacked to the wall in my room. In it she was leaning back on a canvas chaise longue, in a shady yard I didn't recognize. Beautiful dappled shade. She was wearing one of those 1940s crepe dresses with horizontal pleats at the waist like a cummerbund. She had a wide smile as if she was about to laugh. Her lips were dark, and even though the photo was black and white—and slightly overexposed, so there was a thin ghostly fuzz around the objects—I knew she was wearing bright red lipstick. It was wrinkled, that picture, although I had smoothed it out as well as I could with my fingers. I had pulled it out of Daddy's wallet when we got his effects from the coroner; Mother said she didn't want it, I could have it. I'd asked her when and where it was taken. Without looking at it, she had said she didn't remember.

Now I reached over and slipped the beer can out of her hand. Almost empty. I felt peace, like a blanket, settle over me.

Pretty soon we passed the Quaker State sign just before 96 took you east and south and you turned off to Kellogg, which in those days took you to Augusta, where you turned on to Highway 77 to Wiley.

When we had driven there years ago, I remembered, I would make up stories in the backseat. My own fairy tales. I called them my car stories. I would stare at the far horizon and picture men riding horses, keeping up with us as we drove. I never told anyone, and I've long ago forgotten those tales. I never knew anyone my age who made up car stories, although I had asked. And of course they had rolled their eyes.

When I parked the car in Wiley, Mother woke up and reached for her beer. She patted the seat and her lap, and then she cleared her throat and acted as if she was looking for her purse. She twisted the rearview around, untied her scarf, poufed her hair, and fixed her lipstick. She was faded, all right, like a cut rose that has begun to wilt, but underneath, a few velvety petals emitted a sweet fragrance you could just catch, and you could tell she used to be beautiful.

It was late morning, bright, with frills of heat in the breeze. At Wilma and Frank's, the men were standing in the side yard next to the street, some of them smoking, most of them holding cans of beer or pop. One was absentmindedly kicking a horseshoe stake with the toe of his boot.

The men nodded as we approached. I heard someone say "Bill's wife."

As we walked to the house I braced myself. The heat and the drive had put a fine point on the headache left over from last night, and the cords in my neck were twanging. I took as deep a breath as I could. As soon as Mother opened the door, the smell of perfume and hairspray, combined with the sudden chill of the air conditioner on my sweaty skin, brought tears to my eyes. I blinked and set my jaw. I could stand anything for ten minutes, an hour.

Everyone looked up when we opened the door, as they always do. I pulled a tissue from the pocket of my skirt and dabbed at my eyes.

Mother crisscrossed the room, with me following behind, drifting from one group to another. Most of them were women, a few older men; some standing, others sitting. I put on a small, sad smile and hoped no one would speak to me. I felt huge, like Alice after eating the EAT ME cake, and insects were crawling around on the creamy lining of my body.

I knew how my body felt inside all right, but I didn't know how I *felt* felt, if you know what I mean. All I could think of was what I looked like to other people, the expression on my face. Was it right? Was it normal? Did it show my insides?

At length Mother led me out of the living room and down the hall into Wilma and Frank's room. The lights were off, the drapes pinched closed. I blinked to orient myself, and I saw Aunt Wilma's lips first, painted pale orange, slightly outside the lines of her mouth, like the movie stars did. Her hair was ratted. She was sitting on the bed clutching a pillow on her lap. Two of her friends were with her.

Mother walked over to her and patted her shoulder. She said something in a low voice.

Wilma flinched and reached up one hand to pick at her hair. "My babies," she said tonelessly, frowning.

Not really, I thought. There's Frankie.

It felt as if I were watching a scene in a play, and everyone had their lines.

One of the other women stood up and motioned with her head and then led us toward the door. "You're Bill's wife, aren't you?" she said. "Phyllis and me've been here all night. She's taking it awful hard."

Mother nodded, and I followed suit.

We walked back down the hall and stopped again at the entrance to the living room. I wondered where they were keeping Joan's and Vivian's bodies. Vivian's, I didn't worry about; I assumed she didn't have a visible scratch on her, because—she just wouldn't. She would be pristine, almost metaphysical. But Joan was different, I realized: she was dead in the gritty, physical way, in the way of clammy dirt and spiders and utter blackness.

I ducked into the bathroom to get my breathing under control. I stayed in there for as long as it felt decent—only one bathroom, all those people—and when I walked out, Mother was gone. Probably outside smoking and talking to Uncle Frank. I was more afraid of talking to him than to anyone else. He'd always treated me nice, and I was afraid of being—seeming—weak in front of him. I didn't want him to think less of me than he probably already did.

I parked myself in the corner of the dining area behind the foldout table, which was covered with white/beige food. I lifted a pie pan full of deviled eggs and peeked at the bottom. Yes, there was the white cloth tape with the name neatly printed—Opal Winslow. No one I knew. I popped one of the eggs into my mouth, whole. Nice and bland, a little sweet. It made me feel invisible for a moment.

People came and went, bringing food, flowers, and all the other things. The phone rang repeatedly; one of the female Kentucky cousins was answering it, writing down messages. The toilet flushed every few minutes. Occasionally my name, or Mother's, or Daddy's, or "Hutch," drifted up from the haze of voices like sudden birdsong.

After a while my attention was drawn to a nearby conversation between two men.

"The guy on KAKE said there wasn't no skid marks," one of them said. I noticed he was wearing a string tie like Grandpa used to wear. Superimposed on the shiny silver buckle was a galloping horse with a small turquoise stone in its middle.

"Well, Ray, now, it *was* a dirt road. You don't—"

"Tell me this, then—what was they doing there? Off of 77? Something stinks about this whole thing, is all I'm—"

"They'll get to the bottom of it. Give it time."

At my right, a woman in a white straw hat said to her companion, "Well, you know, it's natural the husbands want them buried next to them."

"But what about their second wives? You know they're—"

"You think so? After all this?"

"They're young, they're men," the other woman said, shrugging.

Another woman, tall and thin, spoke up. "The children, oh, God, all those children, growing—"

"That's what I'm saying. They'll marry again, mark my—"

"Poor Wilma, I don't know how she—"

"At least they didn't suffer. Killed instantly, the paper—"

"They always say that."

"It was in the Wichita paper, too."

"The Lord never gives us nothing we—"

"Well, thank God, they was saved."

"Billie, is that you?" came a man's voice close to me. "You remember me?"

I jumped, and he withdrew his extended hand. "Don Wirth," he said. "Jolene's second oldest, sister of Wilma and your dad? Aunt Jolene? From Missouri?"

"Oh, hi." I pictured us cousins in the back of the pickup among the bushel baskets. Now Don was taller, a little pudgy, and he'd gotten his teeth fixed. He resembled Daddy a bit around the eyes, although he had a self-satisfied expression I had never seen on Daddy's face. I was struck by that—that I couldn't remember having seen any ugly expression on Daddy's face, homely as he was.

"Mom couldn't come, so she sent me," Don said.

We had a five-minute exchange to establish when we had last seen each other, which petered out when neither of us could remember. We talked about the heat; the lack of rain; how it looked like harvest would be early this year; and finally the accident—all while Don eyed the food. I resisted the urge to put my fingers in my ears and go *la-la-la-la-I-can't-hear-you*. Energy was seeping out of me. It took so much energy, all this.

Don gathered a paper plate and plastic utensils and helped himself to glazed ham, creamed peas, sugared sweet potatoes, cottage cheese, and a piece of angel food cake, talking all the while. He ate standing there. Between bites he told me he used to live a fast life, with women and alcohol and whatnot, but he had repented and found the Lord. Now he sold farm equipment. Married to a great gal, three terrific kids.

He swallowed and looked me in the eye. "Do you know the Lord as your personal savior, Billie?"

I pushed another deviled egg into my mouth. Around the egg I smiled and nodded.

"Praise the Lord."

Did I live in Wiley, he asked me.

I swallowed. "Hutch. Well, Hutchinson. Eighty-some mi—"

Of course he knew where Hutch was. Did I have my own place, he asked.

No, I was living with my mother. You know what Daddy used to call these (pointing to the deviled eggs)? Fancy baby chickens.

He gave me a blank look. My mother hadn't remarried? How long had it been?

Twelve years, I told him. I was eight at the time.

Oh, yeah. Hard to grow up without a father, he imagined.

Uh-huh.

How was my mother, anyway? He'd heard she was poorly.

No, she was fine.

He wondered if I was seeing anyone.

No one in partic—

He bet I got lots of dates, cute girl like me (looking at my chest).

The eggs? Baby chickens? *Fancy* because they're *deviled,* get it?

Did I work? What doing?

Um, a scrap-metal dealer. Bookkeeping.

He himself didn't get to Wiley that much since they'd moved to Springfield, though it was only a five-hour drive. Of course, he remembered Joanie and Vivvie, but he imagined I was a lot closer to them than he was.

Well, you know, Vivian was older than me. They both were.

When had I last seen Joanie?

(My chest hurt. I felt my lips swell.)

Fancy baby chicks? I said. When he sold his pans? My dad? Bill?

Oh, he said. Oh, I get it. Yeah. Fancy baby chicks. Funny.

Then there was a silence while a string of thoughts coursed through me: yes, I remembered when I had last seen Joan. I tried to keep my mind a hard flat stone, skipping along on the surface of a nothing pond.

"Long distance," I said finally, smiling. Phoning long distance—Hutch to Wiley, Hutch to Wichita—was expensive in those days, as if that explained why I hadn't seen Joan in years. Sometimes if you say something with enough conviction, while nodding, people just pretend to understand.

"Oh. Yeah." Pretending to understand.

"Listen, I need to use the little girls' room." Never in my life had I used such a silly expression, but it came out of my mouth. I loathed myself. I needed badly to be elsewhere.

"Well, we know they're in a better place now," he said.

I wanted to punch the smug look off his stupid face, but instead I smiled with my lips closed and shuffled off.

After the bathroom, I peeked around the corner and saw that Don had left the food table.

From the kitchen I heard water hissing and spattering, the scraping and stacking of bowls, women murmuring. For a moment I wished I were one of them, working out my feelings—whatever they were—while enacting this simple duty, as needful as digging the graves. Then I felt bad. Their lives were probably as complicated and difficult as mine or anybody else's. Who was I to assume otherwise? Maybe everybody was right. I was conceited as hell.

I slipped into the kitchen. One of the women saw me and stopped scraping, and then the other two stopped what they were doing. "You need something?"

I glanced around and spied a red-and-white cooler on the floor. I reached in and pulled out an icy can of store-brand pop. I formed my lips into my small sad smile, nodded to the women, and slipped through the door to the back porch and then into the yard.

Sure enough, there was Mother talking to Frank and two men I didn't know. They were standing at the edge of the concrete walk that led to the garage.

I started toward them, but some ten feet away I realized that my can of pop didn't have one of those new pull-open rings. Now I remembered the church key hanging from the handle of the cooler by a rubber-covered wire. "Coors" in that familiar pretty script.

I said, "Oh, shit" louder than I intended, and then I froze. I couldn't move; I couldn't look at Mother. I could only stare at the can in my hand.

Time seemed suspended for a few seconds. You know what I mean. No voices, no car tires, no insects, no breeze stirring the leaves, nothing. Hot, wet air pressed against me, against my neck, like hands.

Then Frank reached into a pocket and pulled out an opener, extending it toward me. I knew I needed to walk three steps and take it, open the can, return the opener, say thank you, take a sip, settle in, listen to the talk. Easy as slipping off a log backwards (as Grandma always said). Maybe hug Uncle Frank or shake his hand, and say, "I'm so sorry." I could do that. It would be easy. No pressure. What had happened so far—neglecting to open the can in the kitchen, saying *oh, shit*—these were tiny, insignificant things. Nothing, really. Chances were, no one except Mother had even noticed how mortified I was. The men might have observed that my neck and face were red and rashy, that my hands were trembling, but likely not. I relived the conversation with Don, recalled his baffled expression when I mentioned long distance. Our whole exchange had been a non sequitur. I was an idiot.

Still, only seconds had passed. I could still redeem the situation.

Now the cold can slipped from my hand and struck the big toe of my sandaled right foot. The can bounced off my toe, hit the concrete on its rim, bounced again, and burst open, spraying the contents in a circle. Mother and the men jumped back. I slipped and fell to the ground.

Frank was the first to move, and the look on his face told me the story of my life. Burdened as he was by his own terrible losses, and maybe the sweetest man I knew, he was biting his lip to keep from laughing.

Now—even now—I thought I could salvage it. All I had to

do was laugh, giving Frank and the others permission, maybe even allowing them a moment of grace. But at the same time I doubted myself. *Would* they laugh, in a convivial way? Or would they stare at me like a lunatic? In my confusion all I could do was writhe in the grass, wishing, as always, that I could melt like ice and disappear into the earth. Then, of course, I thought of Joan being buried soon, and for a moment there were black dots in front of my eyes as in some old Donald Duck cartoon.

You thought I was kidding when I said I couldn't get out of my head. Well, there you have it.

Of course, Mother and the men immediately knelt beside me, solicitous, kind, and I felt like I might explode.

"I'm all right, leave me alone!" I scrambled up, bumping my head on someone's shoulder and biting my tongue, releasing blood. Mother grabbed me by the waist and walked me around to the back of the garage, me twisting all the while to try to loosen her grip. I was awash in sweat, and her arm felt bony. Then Mother herself slipped on the grass and had to lean against the garage, but she recovered quickly.

With the two of us out of sight, I bent over to let the blood dribble out of my mouth.

"Anything broken?" She was smiling in a crooked way. I couldn't tell if she was amused or trying to calm me down. There was alcohol on her breath, naturally.

I choked, fake-laughed, choked again. Spit, fake-laughed.

Now she frowned and handed me a tissue from her purse. "Let's walk over to Grandma's. You can wash up. They won't mind." I assumed by "they" she meant Frank and the others.

But with the mention of Grandma's, I was already hurrying away, limping and pressing the tissue to my mouth. She didn't say anything more, and I didn't look back; I knew her baffled, angry expression by heart.

I had made it two blocks to the city park when the cicadas started screaming in the elm trees. From tree to tree, now low-pitched, now high, up and down the scale, they shrieked. I closed my eyes, and it felt as if I were floating a foot above the ground, carried along by this familiar, bittersweet sound. I floated another two blocks and then turned down the alley to Grandma's house, past people's trash barrels.

Now only a few steps left to Grandma's. What used to be Grandma's.

On the back porch, the trumpet vines, wildly overgrown, smelling as sweet as sugar, had pulled the wooden lattice away from the fascia board. Fat bumblebees, drunk on nectar, floated from flower to flower. I remembered whiling away warm afternoons as a preschooler sitting on tacky puddles of watermelon juice with a flyswatter, killing flies.

I hoped no one was home. I remembered seeing one of the Kentucky cousins at Wilma and Frank's.

It would be no problem getting into the house. Nobody in Wiley locked their doors.

Inside the back door I called out, "Anybody home? Hello?" No answer. I waited a minute, my toe twanging, but the house was still.

The little utility room off the back porch had an automatic washer and dryer where the wringer washer and rinse tubs once sat. On the opposite wall the old sink still hung, where Grandpa used to shave in the morning and wash up after playing dominoes downtown with his American Legion buddies. I remembered seeing the tiny black whiskers against the white enamel.

When I stepped into the kitchen I braced myself for the brain hit I expected when I smelled the main part of the house—cigarettes, boxes and bags of musty fabric, moldy books, coffee, fried squash, and the unvented gas heater in the bathroom. But of course houses take on the smell of the occupants and their things, and my grandparents had been gone a long time. Now the house smelled of dirty clothes and towels, corn chips, tennis shoes, dogs, and something sweet/sour that I couldn't identify. For a moment I was thunderstruck, as if I'd been snatched unbidden out of time and place; was it possible I was in the wrong house? As in a dream? But no, of course not. There were the black and yellow linoleum tiles halfway up the kitchen walls, although Grandma's dusty crocheted fruit had been replaced by an avocado green and harvest gold plastic plaque of three mushrooms in graduated sizes. Mama, daddy, baby mushroom. So modern. It seemed sacrilegious.

In the dining room I called out again. No answer.

I noticed the heavy black telephone on its little wooden stand in the corner, and I remembered when I was a kid you placed a call in Wiley by picking up the receiver. An operator came on the line, and you gave her the two-digit number you wanted to reach (Frank and Wilma's number was 62), or, if you forgot, just the family's name. Did it still work that way? I reached out to touch the phone, but I jerked my hand back. I didn't want to know.

In the bathroom I bent over to rinse my mouth. As I backed up I found myself flinching automatically to avoid touching the heater, but there was no need. It was gone. You could see where the pipe had been capped off. And, you idiot, it was summer. It wouldn't have been on anyway. I heard a hundred voices say, "Boy, for a so-called genius you sure are stupid." I got that a lot.

I rinsed my mouth until the water ran clear, and then I cupped my hands and drank and drank. I sat on the edge of the tub and wrestled off my hose, and I grabbed the big bar of Ivory soap to scrub the sticky film off my feet and legs. The smell of it burned my nose. My toe was purpling already.

I took off my skirt and rinsed it out.

I walked into the sewing room, which still had the day bed where I used to sleep sometimes. Some cousin had told me that this room used to be a railway car that they'd nailed to the side of the house. I suppose it's barely possible that that's true. The room was long and narrow, and the windows were hinged on top; you lifted them up and fastened them to the ceiling. Adding a train car to a house sounded like the kind of thing the Enholms would do.

On my knees in the bed, I raised and fastened the window. I leaned my hands on the sill and looked through the screen at the side yard. Years ago there had been a row of poplar trees along that side of the yard, and I used to listen to the wind passing through them and talk—pretend to talk—to the trees. You could hear occasional words in the wind. At bedtime you could watch the stars come out. Grandma hung out her sheets, and the smell of the pillowcase as you fell asleep—

Stop. Just stop.

I was in this room for one reason: it was hot as an oven, the better to dry my wet things. I hooked the skirt on the ceiling window hasp and spread out the hose on the bed. Then I went into the kitchen to see if there was anything to eat.

Chapter 10
The Sycamore Tree

When I got back to Frank and Wilma's, a Butler County sheriff's car was parked in front. A handful of people were piling in to three cars. Mother stood on the front porch. "Look at that toe," she said as I walked up.

"Where's everybody going?"

She frowned. "I don't think you should go." Another non-answer.

I saw that the car—Uncle Frank's beige Impala—was full of men, and God knows I didn't need/want their company. But I thought they might be going to a restaurant or tavern or something, and I felt the need to escape, so I slipped into the backseat. Too late I realized I was next to Don. On his other side was Frankie. Uncle Frank was in the driver's seat, and a heavyset man I couldn't quite place was in the front passenger seat. They glanced at me, looking startled, and then at each other, but no one said a word.

I reached for the door handle, but the car was already moving. To Don I whispered, "Where are we going?"

"To where it happened. Somewhere north of Bison Creek."

"How come?"

He gave me a sharp look. "To see where it happened."

"Oh." I drew my elbows in against my sides and made myself as small as possible.

Frank eased the car through the stop sign and turned onto Highway 77 heading north. It was the same stretch of road Mother and Daddy and I had always taken to Wiley, but now my heart was in my throat because we were going to Where It Happened.

The man in the front seat with Frank—a buddy of his from the horseshoe circuit—was on his second smoke. I lit a cigarette and opened the tiny ashtray in the door. You could see my hands shake. The first drag helped.

Don sat sprawled next to me, too close. He was one of those men who oozed—oozed fluids, oozed forced bonhomie, oozed a creepy energy. I had experienced this before—on the street, at school, at work—and though "ooze" may not be the best word for it, I recognized it instantly. In those days I seemed to attract oozy men. Maybe it was some scent I gave out. I hated it; I had enough on my mind, and I didn't need to worry about some creep oozing on me. I wished Don was at the other window and little Frankie was next to me.

Frankie wasn't actually little anymore; he was fifteen? Sixteen? But when I looked at him, I saw the little boy he had been when I myself was a kid and more, I guess, impressionable. For a moment I wondered if Joan had seen me then the way I saw Frankie now, but I swallowed it back. If I had any hope of keeping my shit together, I couldn't think about her at all. Or Vivian—any of them—as children.

"What kind of mileage you get on this thing?" Don said to Frank.

"Twelve, thirteen, thereabouts."

"Your gas is awful high here. Back home they're getting twenty-nine nine. I paid thirty-two nine at a Shell in Parsons."

"That right."

Don launched into a recital of the history of gas prices in Springfield, Missouri. He added that a lot of people thought Springfield was the capital, but it wasn't. After a silence he said it was Jefferson City.

"Dad, can you crank up the AC?" Frankie said.

I let my head fall back against the seat and closed my eyes.

The next thing I knew, we were pulling up behind the other two cars, which were parked along a dirt road. I blinked and gulped air.

"You coming?" Don said.

I sat still, and he made a noise of annoyance with his mouth and crawled out the opposite door after Frankie. The car rocked slightly from the men's movements, and I felt queasy until they were all gone and the three doors slammed. So eager, they were. What impulse, I wondered, drove people to visit the scene of an accident? What did they expect to see?

After a while I opened my door and swung my legs out. Immediately I was engulfed in wind, heat, and dust. No matter how many times I had felt this, I had never gotten used to the summer heat after riding in a car that had AC. I hated Kansas summers—one day the air clung to your skin, the humidity insinuating itself into every pore, and then the next day, everything would be so dry the air robbed your skin, your lips, your eyes, of what little juice you had. Like most people I knew, I'd never lived in a house with AC.

For just a moment I slipped into my Colorado memory, when I had breathed in the sweet, clear air and felt the tree-cooled breeze. I had spread my arms wide, wanting to gather it all up—the air, the trees, the rocks, everything—and take it home with me. I had turned to Mother, and she was lighting a cigarette; the creepy guy—what was his name?—wouldn't let anyone smoke in his car. No matter; the piney mountain air had revived me.

And then I was back in the present, my thighs sticking to the vinyl seat of Frank's Impala, the sun beating down on my scalp, sweat pouring.

I rose and leaned against the open door, keeping it between me and the scene of the wreck, maybe two hundred yards away, where a knot of people were standing around under a huge tree; the sheriff was talking and gesturing. That must be the tree in question. I was relieved to see that the death car evidently had been towed.

The tree was magnificent. If I hadn't known better, I would have seen it as sheltering, cooling, comforting, its leaves waving light/dark in the wind. In fact, the whole scene would have made a great jigsaw puzzle: it looked like nothing so much as a farm auction. Daddy had taken me to a few of those in the countryside around Yoder or Abbyville or Pretty Prairie.

I closed the car door. We had parked at the base of the flood dike at my back. To the left and just ahead was a trailer house, white with turquoise trim, nearly hidden behind a grove of trees. A tractor was parked in the yard. At the end of the driveway was a homemade wooden sign with a painting of a comb and the word "Hair." Just past the sign, the road curved sharply to the right and dead-ended in another farmyard.

This second house was once painted yellow perhaps, now peeling and grayish. You could see an outbuilding with a pickup next to it.

Stretching to the horizon east and west, wheat fields and pasture, miles and miles. The wheat was nearing harvest, the grain heads glittering, nearly white.

Now I noticed the sheriff gesturing in my direction, and everyone turned to look. My face flamed, but then I guessed he was describing how the accident happened. I gasped to think that yesterday morning, the big Cadillac had been here, right in the spot where I was standing perhaps, the seven women alive and vital, maybe singing gospel in four-part harmony. And now Frank and Don and the other people were standing where those women had died suddenly and hideously. I myself didn't believe in ghostly woo-woo stuff, but Christ! How could those people stand there on that ground, knowing what had happened there? What were they looking for? Tire tracks? Globs of motor oil? Car parts? Hair? Scraps of flesh?

I felt disgust well up in me, and I turned around and climbed the short distance to the top of the dike. I looked back toward the south, down the road we (and the women) had traveled. It was a dirt road like a thousand others, flanked by fields. I gazed left and right at the dike snaking away from me in both directions.

I heard a step behind me and whirled around, uttering a cry. I can imagine what my face must have looked like.

"What the fuck, lady." The boy, a teenager, tried to cup my elbow, but I jerked my arm away. He was bony, with greasy hair and two-day stubble, and wearing grimy chinos and an old plaid shirt with the sleeves cut out. He had a red-stained bandage on his forehead and a scrape on his chin. You could smell the animal dirt on his boots, the body odor from his armpits.

He leaned his head back and stared at me through narrowed eyes. Then he reached into his shirt pocket, where there was a lone loose cigarette. He pulled it out and lit it.

Now I wasn't sure how old he was. Maybe my age, although I suspected he was younger than he looked.

I caught a whiff of his cigarette smoke and returned to the car to get my purse. I leaned my hip against the car, cigarette in hand. "I didn't mean to come," I said, continuing the conversation running in my head.

He looked puzzled.

"I didn't know we were coming *here*. Until we." Suddenly I

felt exhausted. Too drained to form words, and out of breath. I closed my eyes.

"Oh," he said.

I blinked and found words again. "You—are you in the family? Of the woman—the women? In the accident?" Now it felt as if I was talking too much, as if I had been talking nonstop.

"Huh-uh." He dropped his cigarette, stepped on it, and headed away from me, toward the grayish house on the right. After two steps, he turned back to me. "Me and my uncle." He pointed to the house.

I didn't say anything, and again he turned to go.

"Did you see it?" I blurted out.

Without turning around, he said no. Then he hesitated.

"My cousin was—and her sister—they were." My throat closed.

Somehow he got it. "That's rough," he said. "Awful rough." He was stopped now, but still he didn't turn around. He scratched his ear.

"Welp." I swallowed hard. I still had the cigarette, unlit, between my fingers.

Some seconds passed. "I got some ice tea in the icebox, want some?" His tone rose as he spoke, and by the end he sounded as if his voice were squeezed by too long a string of words.

"Yeah, okay."

He continued walking, and I had a bit of a time catching up with him.

I licked the dust off my lips. "So what do you do— " I realized I didn't know his name.

His arm brushed against mine, probably accidentally. "Me and my uncle," he repeated.

"Oh. You go to high school in Bison Creek?"

He nodded. "Graduated in May."

Several more steps on the sandy road. Now I reached into my purse and lit the Kool.

He cleared his throat. "You?"

"I went to Hutch High. I live there with my mom."

We were both walking with our heads down, looking at our feet.

He cleared his throat again and spit off to the side. "Well, I work on cars in town whenever my uncle don't need me on the farm."

"Want some company?" came a voice behind us.

Oh, hell no, Don, you creep, I wanted to say. My toe was throbbing. I was in *no mood*, as Mother would say.

Don offered his hand, and the boy took it. "Don Wirth. I'm a cousin of two of the victims. And her." Indicating me.

"Oh," the boy said.

Don fell into step with us. "And you are?"

"Um, Clayton, um, Fontenot."

"And you've met Billie, I guess," Don said.

"We're getting something to drink," Clayton said.

"Awful dry myself," Don said. "Fontenot. Sounds French. You Cajun, by any chance?"

The kitchen was hot, but it was a relief to be out of the wind. My hair was plastered to my skull with sweat. I fluffed it as best I could with my fingertips and then wiped them on my skirt. A saying of Grandma's came to me: *I must look a sight.*

The big square kitchen had three wall cupboards, stained with hand grease around the door pulls, and an eight-foot-long metal sink-and-cabinet combination. Been a long time since I'd seen such a thing. If ever. One of the metal doors was permanently bent open.

The room smelled of coffee and old food. The only decoration was a wall calendar with a picture of a waterfall; a pencil hung on the nail by a string.

Don and I took seats at the table. In the center was a blue-and-white sugar bowl, and a coffee can held a spray of spoons.

Clayton walked across the linoleum to a floor fan, turned it on high, pointed it toward the table, and retrieved three tall jelly glasses from the cupboard. Then he opened the fridge and pulled out a gallon-size pickle jar half full of dark brown tea.

"Don't have no ice." He poured us each a glass and set the jar on the table.

I took a ladylike sip and then a gulp.

"Did you want sugar?" Clayton took out a spoon and dipped it three times in the sugar. Don did the same.

For a moment the silence was relieved by the clink of spoons. Beneath the table I lifted my skirt to let the breeze from the fan hit my legs. Under my hose, my legs itched from heat and sweat. I chugged the rest of the tea in my glass.

"Billie here, she's from Hutchinson. Lives with her mother," Don said.

"Big town," Clayton said. "Never been."

"Is it? How many, Billie?"

"Forty thousand?"

"That's nothing." He looked at Clayton. "Where I'm from—Springfield, Missouri—a hundred thousand, easy. It's no Wichita, but then—"

"Oh," Clayton said.

"A lot of people think Springfield's the capital, but it's not. Guess what is."

The boy shrugged.

"Jefferson *City*." Don smiled and tossed back the curl that was hanging over his forehead.

I poured myself half a glass of tea, and we all drank for a minute. I wanted to sink through the floor and disappear. Here I was in a stranger's house with a cousin who made my skin crawl. I also needed to use the bathroom, but I couldn't imagine having the words come out of my mouth. The absurdity of my situation didn't make it any less dire.

"Now, me and the wife, we've got what they call a 'three and two,' three bedrooms and two baths," Don droned on. "New subdivision, real nice." He talked about his kids, pulled out his wallet to make us look at pictures of their gap-toothed grins, and then got on to the subject of suburban lawn maintenance. My headache, which had faded, came tinkling back.

Eventually there was a silence. The two men looked fine with it, but I was itching all over. The walls of the kitchen closed in on me.

Pretty soon Don pointed at me. "Now Billie, her father died when she was a kid." He turned to me. "How old were you, Billie?"

What I wanted to say was, *Stop saying my goddamn name over and over! I know it's how you make friends and influence people and sell farm implements, but stop it!* What I said was, "Nobody wants to hear my life story."

"Well, excuse me for living." Feigning hurt feelings.

Again he turned to Clayton. "How about you, Clay? How did you come to live with your uncle?"

Clayton winced. I didn't know if it was because Don called him Clay or because of the intimacy of the question. I said, "That's none of our business."

He shrugged. "Just making conversation."

Clayton stood up abruptly. "Want a beer?"

"No thanks," I said. "And Don here, he doesn't drink."

"Mind if I have one?" Clayton said, his hands on the back of his chair.

"Yeah, no, go ahead." I was trying to head off Don's "Are you saved?" speech.

Clayton walked toward the fridge, and I looked out the kitchen window. The glass was rippled a bit, but you could see the outline of the hulking tree through the saplings and brush that lined a slough that lay west of the house. It was a sycamore, I saw now; you could tell by the way the bark was peeling. Until I noticed the tree I had almost forgotten where we were and why we were here. I placed my fingertips, cool from the tea, onto my temples and massaged them. As a child, I liked to press my eyelids hard with my thumbs until I saw throbbing shapes and colors like a kaleidoscope. I had felt myself floating out of time and space. Now I repeated it, pressing gently. Only darkness.

When I opened my eyes I saw that Clayton was standing by the refrigerator, beer in hand. He drank half the beer and pushed the door closed.

"So you farm here with your dad?" Don said.

"My uncle." Clayton turned his chair back to front and straddled it.

"Right. I, myself, I'm in farm implements—Deere, Massey, Case. You know."

"That right." Clayton stifled a burp.

"I seen you're a Massey man." He must have been referring to the tractor parked next to the barn.

Clayton nodded. "Besides that, we got a 9N we use—"

Don's face lit up. "That's a sweet little machine."

For long minutes the two of them talked about tractors and combines and plows and spring-tooths and harrows. Clayton finished his beer, crushed the can in his hands, and left it on the table before he got another one and returned.

Don asked him about high school and then followed up with, "You play baseball, by any chance? That was my game."

"Little bit. But mainly tumbling—well, gymnastics."

"Oh," Don said, nodding. "The wiry type."

"I've seen that on TV," I said. "The Olym—"

Clayton laughed. "Well, we wasn't that good." The laugh, the irony—that was the beer. I knew it instantly. It was like he was turning into a different person, relaxed, sociable, talkative.

"Baseball was my game," Don said again. He leaned forward on his elbows. "Second base. Not to brag, but I was the best athlete on the team. Batted three-twelve my senior year. I don't mind telling you—"

"First thing Coach taught us, he said, you got to know how

to *fall.*" Now Clayton leaned forward, too, banging the table with the back of his chair. The table rocked a bit on its center post. "There's falling wrong, and there's falling right."

"Like they say, second base is the 'hot corner,' and I— "

"We spent a *month* on falling. See, you got to ease into it, twist yourself, touch lightly." Clayton rotated his hips to demonstrate. "See, you got to—to—you know, spread out the force. It's physics." He frowned. You could tell he was struggling to explain.

"Two objects having mass can't occupy the same space at the same time," Don said, beaming.

Clayton shook his head. "No, see, it's— " He took several swallows of beer. "Well, it's not as easy as it sounds. Falling right. But it can keep you from getting messed up."

I pictured myself falling wrong as hell, dropping the pop can in front of Frank and the others, and the shame hit me again full force. I touched my skirt. Although I had rinsed it out, it felt stiff from the spilled pop. I imagined ants crawling up my legs, attracted to the sugar in the pop. Charlotte, come to call. I gritted my teeth.

Don cleared his throat. "Baseball, now that's a thinking man's game."

"Sure you don't want one?" Clayton was slurring his words a bit now. His lips looked slippery, his eyes a bit unfocused. Not yet two beers in; he wasn't very experienced. Well, that figured. Only a month out of high school.

"Thanks anyway," I said.

"Me, I could only do the rings and the bars, where Coach lifts you up. Couldn't do nothing where I had to run or do a fancy dismount—no pommel horse, nothing like that." He sighed. "Polio. Ankle's messed up." He touched his right thigh.

"Did you see it happen?" Don said.

I took in a deep breath. It was all I could do to keep from howling.

"Man. I loved the rings," Clayton said. His tone was mournful.

"The accident, I mean. Did you see it happen?"

"Don, don't," I said.

"Me?" A gurgle from Clayton's throat, two or three coughs. "No. I— " He wiped his nose with the heel of his hand. "I heard it, but I never seen it. I was doing chores. Took off running—you know, toward the sound—and damn if I didn't fall down in the damn slough. Slipped and fell." He laughed a little to show he wasn't some young fool. Casually, manfully, he touched his bandages. "Had a little rain this week, slough's muddy still." He coughed again and cleared his throat.

"So you didn't see what happened," Don said.

"Next thing I know, sheriff's out there." There was a short silence. "They'd already, you know, passed on. The ladies."

I gasped and then coughed. My throat felt like sawdust.

Both men looked at me and quickly dropped their eyes. Don reached out, hefted the big jug, and poured himself—and, without asking, me—more tea. He busied himself with the sugar. Clayton played with the drops of condensation on his beer can.

I drank half the glass. Gratefully.

Nobody said anything for a while. Don, of course, broke the silence. "What about the neighbors? In the trailer?"

Clayton drank. "That would be Ruth and her brother, Russell."

"We heard they were Negroes," Don said.

"'We'?" I said. "You got a frog in your pocket?" (Grandma again.)

"They're older," Clayton said. "She can't hardly see no more. Still does hair, though, ever little bit."

Don looked confused. "You ever have any trouble with them? Being they're— "

"Ruth and Russell?" Clayton looked surprised. "No. She brings us over a pie ever little bit. Russell, he's got a blade and plows the road, winters. Sometimes she calls me over, help him get up off the ground. He falls ever little bit. Never had no trouble."

Don pressed his lips together. "Well, you know, people talk. Nobody knows what they were doing on this road, since they were going to Wichita. Doesn't make sense."

"And?" I said.

"Whoever gets the mail first brings it all back," Clayton said. "Saves a trip clear to the end of the road, where you turn off of 36."

Don widened his eyes at me. "It's not me—it's just, you know, people talk."

"Them two didn't have nothing to do with the wreck, if that's what you're getting at," Clayton said. "They never caused no trouble I'm aware of."

"For God's sake," I said to Don. "Just because they're Black—"

"Black," he said. "They didn't used to like being called that, you know. They—"

"For God's *sake*," I said again. I had had this conversation too many times. *Well I work with a guy that grew up in Alabama, and he says there wasn't any trouble until the outside agitators come in and got 'em riled up. We all got along, they knew their place, they didn't want to mix with us any more than we wanted to mix with them.* No matter what I said, I'd get *would you want your sister to marry one*? And *you know what happens to property values?* and all that shit, and there was no answer for it that would negate what the guy that worked with a guy from Alabama said the guy said. It was just Billie being her odd-wad, smartass, conceited self.

"You gonna go look at the tree?" Don said to me.

I shook my head.

"There's nothing to see, really," Clayton said. "It's all been cleaned up."

* * *

The Impala's tires spit sand as Uncle Frank pulled out and made a U-turn in the road.

"You get a chance to see the site?" he asked me.

"No, I—"

"Wasn't much to see," Frankie said from the backseat.

"You guys cool enough?" I turned the AC fan to high. I was so tired, it felt as if I was about to fold in two. At least they had let me sit in the front seat when I'd told them I would get carsick. And, thank God, Clayton had let me use the little bathroom in the old house before we left.

For a while the men talked about the heat. They disagreed about the date it had last rained in Wiley, finally settling on April something. They hadn't been aware it had rained recently near Bison Creek.

"I just can't figure it out," Frank said. "How come they was on this road. There's got to be a reason. I just can't figure it out."

"Maybe they had to use the bathroom," Frank's friend said. "You know how they are." He lit a smoke and cracked his window.

"Don't make sense, Willard," Frank said. "Why not stop at a gas station in Bison Creek? Why turn down a dirt road you don't know where it goes?"

That was his name: Willard. A little kink uncoiled in my brain.

"Maybe one of them got sick all the sudden," Willard said. "I heard two of them was pregnant."

I winced. Sometime in the night I had thought of that. But people seemed to be making stuff up, so even though of course it was possible, I wasn't taking anybody I knew's word for it. And hell, what did it matter now?

Frank shook his head. "They could've just shot a U and went back to town. What—two, three miles?"

"Gotta be a reason," Willard said. "It's almost like somebody wanted them dead."

I felt a cleaver slice through my brain, releasing buckets of blood. Wanted them dead? I fumbled in my purse for a cigarette.

"Shit," Uncle Frank said. "Not a one of them had an enemy in the world."

I wanted to kiss him.

"Well, Joanie and Vivvie, sure," Don said. "But what about the rest of them? I heard one of them was about to get a divorce."

"Jesus Christ!" I yelled. "Have you lost your *minds*?" I had meant it to come out as conversation, maybe even humor, but my voice was surprisingly loud in the car, even with the AC fan on high.

Frank leaned back in his seat as if slapped. Then his shoulders slumped. "We're all upset, honey, it's hard—"

"I'm not upset, okay?" I heard how silly I sounded. For a second I wondered if this was a dream; the whole ride, the whole day, the night before—it was all surreal. I swallowed. In an apologetic tone, I said, "Look, you're—we're—we all of us are trying to find a *reason* for something that—something that—something that doesn't *have* a reason."

I was surprised to see Frank's grip tighten on the steering wheel. "No car wreck happens without somebody screwing up. That's a fact."

Willard stubbed out his cigarette. "They shouldn't have *been* there, plain and simple. If we knew how come they was there—"

"We don't even know who was driving," Frankie said. "Everybody just assumes it was Pinky Hilyard."

"It was her car, right?" Don said.

"That doesn't prove anything," Frankie said. "When they get the blood alcohol back—"

"Drunk at seven-something in the morning?" Don said doubtfully.

"She wasn't drunk," Frank said flatly, as if that settled it.

"Well, Dad—"

"Don't matter anyhow," he shot back. "It wasn't her fault, or whoever was driving. If they wasn't on that road with a goddamn tree in the goddamn *middle* of it, none of this would've happened in the first place."

"They should cut it down," Frankie said. "We should go back there right now and cut that fucker down."

We all froze. Waiting, I guess, for someone to blame the tree itself, possessed by a tree devil. I snorted through my nose, couldn't help it. I had a picture of the five of us cutting that fucker down and hauling it to Wiley and setting fire to it in the middle of the park. Big bonfire. I saw the townspeople roasting hotdogs and marshmallows. The picture, to me, was funny. And yet appropriate to the occasion. Of all the exemplary behavior people were displaying of how one should act under these circumstances, this was the first one I liked. Of course it was ridiculous, but satisfying in its way.

I couldn't let go of it. I thought maybe, just maybe, the men would see the humor in it, too. I imagined how, at every Wiley get-together, somebody would bring up the time they had the big bonfire in the park, and everybody would laugh, rocking, throwing their hands against their thighs, howling. Eventually only a few old people would remember what the bonfire was about.

Because, obviously, it wasn't the tree's fault. And it wasn't the driver's fault, whoever it was. It wasn't anybody's fault. It just happened.

"It just happened," I heard myself say.

"The hell you say," Frank said in an angry tone, and my stomach sank.

"They were my *sisters*, Billie," Frankie said. "This is *killing* Mom."

"You think I don't know that?" I felt grit in my eyes. How did we get here? How did we always get here?

"How. Come. They. Was. There," Frank said. "Tell me that. They didn't have no goddamn business on that road."

I wanted to scream/cry. I sensed their judgment, their fury, and it felt as if the car was shrinking around me, ready to crush me. "I don't know," I muttered. "How would I know? Nobody knows. That's the point."

"I won't accept that!" Frank turned to me now, twisting the steering wheel at the same time. The two outside tires slipped off the blacktop, and then he managed to guide the car back onto the road. "I won't accept that," he said again. "Somebody knows. Somebody knows something. How come they're not talking? Somebody knows something."

"Yeah," Frankie said. "I'm sure it'll all come out."

"What all?" I said. There was a silence. I felt calmer. I took a deep breath. "Look, okay? They planned it all along, okay? Say there was an ad in the paper about a farm auction north of Bison Creek. So they figured they'd stop and take a look on their way to Wichita. Only they took the wrong turn, and they ended up—"

"Where'd you hear that?" Frank said, his eyes wide.

"I just made it up, Uncle Frank. All's I'm saying—"

"Made it *up*?"

"I'm just saying, there's *an* explanation. Just because we—"

"Made it *up*?" For a moment I thought he might reach over and smack me.

I pressed my back against the seat. "It's just an example, okay? It *might* explain it. I'm sure the sheriff will talk to the husbands, and we'll find out." I felt my teeth chattering. I stammered. For the thousandth time, I was mystified why the people around me didn't understand what I was trying to say. But it always happened. I would say something that I knew damn well was logical and true, but what they heard was stupid, ignorant, condescending, nonsensical.

"I don't know," Willard said. "He don't seem to have much on the ball, that sheriff."

"Maybe we should get a lawyer," Don said. "Or a private investigator."

For Christ's sake, I thought. But in my mind I vowed not to say another word.

We drove for a while in silence. I got sleepy, or at least dreamy. I zoned out the rest of the drive.

Frank pulled the Impala into the driveway and yanked it into reverse, rocking the car and waking me from my dream or whatever you call it. For a moment I forgot where I was, and then I remembered. I pushed the door until it latched open. Outside, the neighborhood was graying. It was just past twilight, and the cries of the cicadas were dwindling to a shuddering rasp.

Mother sat by herself on the front porch, smoking. Her lipstick looked black in the porchlight. My upper arms were cold from the AC, and I hugged myself, running my hands up and down the chilled flesh.

Chapter 11
The Historical Marker

Mother said she didn't want to get home in the dark, so we slept in the Plymouth overnight and drove back home in the morning. She drank three beers on the way home, and I had to help her climb the stairs to the stifling apartment.

I scrambled some eggs, and Mother dozed for an hour in her chair. I did a couple of loads of laundry. We got through the day.

She went to bed early, and I sat on the couch, reminiscing and smoking, and still—still—wondering how I felt, going through something like this. I know that because, years later, when I mentioned the accident to my therapist and she asked me how it made me feel, I just looked at her. I told her about the trip to Wiley and all the rest of it, and she said, No, I mean how did you *feel*? Honest to God, I couldn't tell her because I didn't know. All my feelings, even the good ones, felt the same, and they hurt.

But I'm getting ahead of myself.

First, there was Joan's and Vivian's funeral to get through.

* * *

"Of all days for it to rain."

Uncle Frank stood in the doorway of the First Methodist Church of Wiley. It had a canopy over the front to shelter parishioners, brides and grooms, and, as today, mourners, which was handy for standing under to smoke in the rain.

"Yeah," I said to Frank. I stepped over to the edge, my cigarette in the hollow of my hand.

"Well, can't be helped," he said. "You need a ride somewhere?"

I shook my head.

"Suit yourself." He lifted his suit jacket over his head and trotted to the Impala.

I was grateful he didn't press me as to why I was at the church, with the funeral still two hours away. Truth was, I couldn't bear the tense near-silence at Wilma and Frank's house, the throat-clearing, the whispering, the swallowing of tears. Let Mother and Aunt Wilma and the others sit there. Not me.

My chest was weighted with an image of Joan when we were children—she was always half a head taller—breathlessly sharing the details of the funeral she had attended, the things she'd learned about bodies. She loved to creep me out.

The rain was lukewarm at the edge of the canopy as droplets made their way to my face, my neck, my hands. I banished the picture of Joan and strained to imagine, realistically, what would happen today so that I could rehearse appropriate faces to make. I was wearing the navy blue suit Mother had made for my first job interview, and I had stuffed the jacket pocket full of tissues.

Now I dropped the cigarette into a puddle and pulled out a tissue, pressing it against my eyes so that part of it hung down and covered my mouth. That would work. Just hide my stupid face.

I heard a loose muffler clanging, tire splashes, and then brakes, and I dropped my hand. An old blue Chevy pickup. Through the rain-streaked windows I saw a man lean over to grab a basket of flowers. He opened the door, pushing it with one booted foot, and hurried to the canopy. Imagine my surprise when it turned out to be Clayton, the teenage boy from the house near the wreck site.

"It's you!" he said. He was dressed for chores.

"Hey, Clayton."

He removed his Farmall ball-cap. "I—my uncle asked me to drop these by."

"Tell him thanks, would you?"

He glanced around and then turned to me and gestured with the basket.

"Just inside the door, I think."

He returned in a minute. "Welp."

"Tell your uncle we appreciate it."

"You bet." He turned to go.

"Hey," I said. "Could you give me a ride?" I was acting on impulse. I had no idea where we would go.

"Um, sure. Where to?"

I didn't answer, only ran through the rain to the sanctuary of the old pickup. The door squawked when I opened it. I climbed up into the long bench seat and slammed the door behind me. The windows were up, of course, and it was dank and close in the cab. The air felt oily and smelled of cigarette smoke, gasoline, rust, damp animals.

When I offered him a cigarette, he didn't pocket it but lit it, and mine, with a match from a box among the detritus on the truck's broad dashboard.

"Where to?" He cracked his window, letting in the smell of the rain.

"I don't care."

He looked at me. "Well, I've got just about enough gas to get home with, and a dollar bill in my pocket."

"Sorry. How about the marker, then?"

"Marker?"

"A couple miles west of town. Turn left up here." I tuned the radio to KOMA, Oklahoma City. It was the only station we could get that reliably played rock music. With all the others, it was country western, ag prices, or men preachers with high-pitched voices. When I got it tuned, we heard the last half of "Light My Fire" by the Doors. The music felt too aggressive, so I turned the radio off. I realized I was in a vehicle driven by someone I hardly knew, and for a moment I felt this was a mistake, but there we were.

"The marker" was all anybody in Wiley called the little wayside attraction, featuring a couple of picnic tables and a plaque put up by the state of Kansas to commemorate the spot where Adelia Haughman had saved the lives of two free-staters back in the days of Bleeding Kansas, just before the Civil War.

The place looked forlorn. The monument itself was streaked with spray paint, and the ground was trampled by cars and people. The parking lot, big enough to hold six or eight cars, was littered with beer cans, trash, and broken glass. There were signs of bonfires, and behind a tree I spotted the aluminum frame and ragged webbing of an abandoned lawn chair.

"Looks like a party spot," Clayton said drily as he parked.

"Yeah," I said, shrugging. "I don't know the Wiley area all that well. I just spent time here as a kid, visiting. Everybody in town knows the marker."

I offered him another cigarette, but he shook his head, and I put the pack in my purse. I took off my suit jacket and folded it, laying it on the seat between us. The rain had slowed, and I rolled down my window and stuck one arm out, moving it up and down in curlicues like ocean waves.

Clayton reached behind the seat. I heard cardboard tearing, and he pulled out a bottle of Budweiser. He offered it to me, but I declined. He fished around on the dashboard for a church key, popped open the bottle, and took a few sips.

"It's about a woman, of all things, riding to the rescue of a couple of abolitionists about to be lynched," I said. "The marker." He didn't answer. We sat and watched rain dribble down the windshield.

"Well, anyway—thanks for the iced tea the other day."

"No problem." He chugged the beer.

I remembered the beers he had drunk that day. "Are you even eighteen yet?"

He shrugged. "Pretty soon." He gestured with the bottle. "Just getting a head start." He seemed more relaxed than the other day.

"Your uncle doesn't care?"

He smiled. "My uncle. You never met nobody like him."

"How so?"

"I don't know." He took a long drink, thinking. "He likes to bake cakes. You ever hear of a farmer liked to bake cakes? Birthday, regular, all kinds."

"Oh."

"And get this—he likes to get cleaned up and go to town and see movies in the afternoon, when hardly nobody's there. One time, I said I wanted a horse, and damn if he didn't go and get me a goddamn horse, and one for himself, too, so we could ride together." He began peeling the label off the beer bottle. "Truth to tell, he never had no kids, and I think he gets a kick out of playing like I'm his. He's my mom's brother. Never met nobody like him."

"Where do you ride?"

"Mostly on the property west of us, but they don't care. We always close the gates. They run cattle over there sometimes."

"The trailer just over the dike?"

He nodded. "Ruth and her brother Russell. Me and my uncle help them out sometimes, and she brings us a pie now and then. Just neighboring like you do. I helped him fix his baler one time."

There was a silence. Then I asked him if he knew the story behind the tree in the middle of the road.

He settled his back against the seat. "Back in the old days—thirties, middle of the Depression—why, the road went around the tree and then on north. Never bothered nobody." He gestured in an arc with the bottle. "Welp, the county wanted to widen the road and blacktop it, make it part of the new highway, turned out to be 77. Cut down the tree, straighten out the road. Now the people close by didn't want a bunch of traffic next to the house, and that tree, it had always been there in the middle of the road, since the eighteen hundreds or something, and like hell they was going to let somebody cut it down."

I pictured the magnificent tree, the instrument of death. Clayton was so caught up in the story, I think he forgot about that.

"So the county said, screw that, we'll build the blacktop a half a mile west, and you can have your dirt road, it's a driveway now, you'll have to walk clear to the county road to get your goddamn mail."

"This was Ruth and Russell's family?"

"So they put up a sign, 'End county maintenance, proceed at your own risk,' but I guess that's been gone a while. My uncle or somebody put up a Dead End sign, but the county made them take it down. 'Can't have a road sign on a private road' or some such bullshit. That's the government for you."

I murmured something and looked out the window.

"Not like I'm one of those goddamn protestors. March in the streets? Burn stuff down? Screw that." He said "protestors" like it was a dirty word.

I cringed. Who was I to disagree? I myself had scarcely participated in the sixties vibe, although I tried to, because obviously it was cool.

Clayton wound up the story. "So after while my uncle just plowed over the land north of the road and put in wheat."

"This was Ruth and Russell's family?" I asked again.

"No, it was the folks of the man she married. His name was

Adams, he was a bachelor lived there by himself after his folks passed on. How him and Ruth met, that's a story."

"Tell me." I was surprised by his loquaciousness. I hadn't known boys to talk much, except about KU basketball or their own achievements. I wondered how much beer he had consumed today.

Then it hit me. "Wait. He was a white man?"

Clayton nodded. "He went to this convention—you know, farmer convention—in Chicago. This would have been in the late forties maybe. Anyhow, one evening he goes for a walk and gets lost and ends up in the colored part of town. He wanders into this beauty salon, you know, and there's Ruth. He asks her, does she cut white people's hair. So she gives him a haircut."

"Oh." My anxiety for the two of them was rising. I recalled seeing a TV news report when I was little of a crowd of white people screaming and throwing things at a little Black girl walking to school. Mother noticed and told me to turn it off. I pestered her with questions, until finally she said, "We're not 'better' than them, I don't care what anybody says. They love their children just like we do." You can imagine how I churned on that for weeks, both the argument for racial equality and the blithe reference to loving one's children. I didn't quite understand the connection, but the two things had always been associated in my mind thereafter.

"Hello?" Clayton said.

I blinked. "Then what happened?"

"Well, he gets a taxicab the next day, goes over there—candy, flowers, the whole deal—and he asks her out." He gave me a look. "I *know*. Just goes to show you, you never know about people. I can't feature any of my people marrying colored. Course, his folks was dead by then." He shrugged. "Long story short, after writing back and forth for a while, he goes back there and they get married."

"Was it even legal?"

He shrugged again. "Well, it was Chicago." He took big swallows. "So she moves down here with her kids, and after a while she moves back, I don't know how come. He dies, she inherits, she comes back to sell the farm, can't get a buyer, decides to stay and farm it. Her brother Russell comes to help her. She still does hair, too, though I don't know how, since she can't hardly see with that one milky eye. Between the two of them, I guess they make out."

"I wonder if she gets lonesome." Were there even any Black people in Bison Creek—then or now? How did the townspeople treat her? I tried to imagine it.

He finished his beer. "She takes her coffee every morning in the front yard. So she seen the car go by and heard the crash. Called the sheriff. You thirsty?"

This shocked me back into the present. "I don't like beer," I said automatically. *She seen the car go by.*

"Just as well." He put the empty bottle behind the seat and brought out a new one. After a while, he said, "Your cousin said your dad died a while back?"

"Yeah." I lit a cigarette. The squall had passed, and the sky was lighter.

"What was he like? I never knew my dad."

I was relieved to talk about a safe subject. "He sold pans at fairs and things."

"Really? One of those guys?" He rocked his shoulders, I suppose in imitation of his idea of a fast talker.

"Life was a party whenever Daddy was around." I leaned back. "He knew all kinds of stuff—cards, card tricks, magic tricks, jokes, games, riddles. Used to swallow a cigarette and make smoke come out of his ears." I blew a smoke ring, and another, and then an odd thing happened: I felt a pang of something. Sweetness, contentment, happiness—whatever it was, it shocked me. It felt as if the rain had formed into drops of light that fell on my arm from a sparkler.

I heard Clayton say something, but I didn't make out the

words. I took a deep drag of my cigarette and tried to sustain the mood. "He was in the navy in the war. He played poker on the ship, and he sent Mother money."

"He cheat?"

The question soured the air. "No—he knew how to read people, and he was good with numbers. I get that from him, I guess—the thing with numbers."

Clayton brought out a beer bottle, opened it, and held it out to me. He gave me a sheepish smile, and it seemed like a friendly gesture, a kind of apology—or I wanted it to be. I hesitated and then took it. I closed my eyes and took a sip, and then another. It was barely cool. The third swallow didn't taste so bad. Maybe it tasted better from a glass bottle than a can? I liked seeing the bubbles behind the brown glass.

"So you work," Clayton said. "You said a welding shop?"

I shook my head. "Scrap metal. Bookkeeping and stuff." I tipped up the bottle and gulped several times. It wasn't so bad once you got used to it. I felt a tad light-headed. "Yeah, we buy and sell used pipe, copper, rebar, angle iron, car batteries, stuff like that."

He looked surprised. "I wouldn't have figured."

"How come?"

He shrugged.

"You mean you don't feature me working in a cold concrete building with gritty concrete floors? In the south part of town? Surrounded by a square block full of rusty-smelling junk?" *Me being such a refined lady and all* was what I was getting at, sarcastically, suddenly self-conscious about being in my best blue suit and surreptitiously checking my hose to see if they had snagged on the stiff triangle tears in the truck's upholstery. And the south part of town was where most of the Black people lived in Hutchinson, but in my own casually racist way, I forgot that not everyone in the world would know or intuit that. Shame swept me. I was turning out to be as big a liar as anybody.

"Something like that," he said.

To counteract my shame and with half a beer in me, I turned chatty. "My favorite thing is inventory." I explained the procedure, where I kept a spiral notebook with lists of pipe and angle iron, separated according size, in nominal lengths that I added or subtracted when we bought or sold the material.

Clayton brought out another beer and started on it.

"So it's like, say we get four pieces of inch-and-a-half by inch-and-three-quarters angle iron, ten feet long. So I go in there and write it down, bang by bang by bang, right? Now we sell an eight-foot piece. You go down the list, you find a piece bang by bang by bang, say five feet, and you line through that, and then you look for another three foots' worth and line through that. Or feets' worth." I giggled. It was embarrassing how much I loved those notebooks full of lists of numbers, how it felt as if you could flutter the pages and magically bring a sense of order and calm and cleanliness to the tangled piles of metal out in the lot. Nobody else was allowed to write in my inventory notebook.

He nodded. "That's what passes for fun in Hutch?"

Now I laughed, rocking in the seat, spilling a bit of beer, which I licked off my wrist. "The adding machine—you know, one of those heavy old things with a hundred keys and a pull handle?" I was laughing hard now. I was safely in my element now. I went on and on about the complicated process for multiplying with a mechanical adding machine, something I had mastered on my first try. At one point I looked over at Clayton, at his unfocused eyes, and I knew I was boring him to death, but I couldn't help myself. It was Charlotte, back for her encore, pressing me ever onward into the very pointy point of the pencil. A couple of tears leaked out.

Clayton yawned. "No idea what you're talking about."

"It's okay, I do." I took another drink. Almost empty now. "I sit there and drink coffee and smoke and play with my numbers. I'm the only girl. Hardly anybody bothers me."

He nodded. "How long have you worked there?"

"Big trucks, we weigh, on the big scale."

He nodded again, humoring me.

"Since graduation. So three years." I pulled out a tissue and wiped my nose. I felt as if I were slowly tipping over. I hadn't had this long a conversation with a guy since high school, or anybody probably. "It's not like I'm going to grow old working there. I'm going to move to Colorado." And just like that, I waltzed trippingly right up to the edge. To the very precipice of my secret dream, my secret self. I didn't have the words to describe the beauty, the mountains, the air, all of it, not to mention all that had happened on the trip, when my relationship with Mother had changed—deepened at bit, broadened a bit—even if we had soon fallen into old habits again. I hadn't entirely given up my dream of moving there—it depended on my mood—but as time had passed, it seemed increasingly impossible. Mother would never go, for one thing. So to talk about it made me feel like a fool. Like a fool getting naked and saying, see how ugly I am?

"You have family there? I never been."

"No, I just like mountains." I took a breath and backed away from the abyss. "Your uncle keep you busy?"

"Yeah." He put his bottle between his legs and ran one finger along the inside of the big steering wheel. "But I work a couple days a week for a guy in town, when I can get the hours. He's got me mainly changing oil, stuff like that, but what I want is to rebuild engines." His finger followed along the scalloped edge of the grip. "I never knew my dad." He grasped the wheel with both hands and tested the play in it.

"Yeah." I wiped my eyes with my fist.

He looked out his window. "Me and mom lived with her folks, and then she died. Mom. Got the cancer." He pointed to his chest.

"Damn."

"My granddad—he was mad all the time. I don't know how

come. Mom had the diabetes, too—she had to give herself these shots. I think he didn't really believe she was sick. He—you know—he acted like she was a dope fiend, going off to the bathroom to give herself a shot. If she didn't want to do something, didn't want to go somewhere, didn't feel good, he'd act like he didn't believe her. Even when she got the cancer, he said it was all in her head."

"Damn."

"Yeah." He lifted the bottle and drank. "When I got to be five or six, my grandparents give me to a cousin of Mom's and her husband. They had four kids already, so yeah, they needed another one." He laughed under his breath. "Their oldest was my same age. They put me in with him. Rex. He was pissed off all the time, too. All the time."

Strangely enough, this made me think of Joan. If you didn't know her, you might think she was pissed off all the time, too, instead of—whatever she was. Come to think of it, maybe she *was* pissed off all the time. I wondered why.

Clayton laughed again. "I come down with polio, and they put my one leg in a brace, and Rex"—laughing hard now—"that bastard used to punch me in my leg and watch it twitch. Hurt like a motherfucker." Although he was laughing, his knuckles were white around the bottle. "Now me, I never knew where I'd end up next, so I got to where I would just let things roll off my back. Old Rex, when he couldn't get a rise out of me, that made him madder. He was so stupid, you could see his rat brain working, trying to figure me out."

"Jesus, Clayton." Joan had tormented me, too, but at least I didn't live with her.

"So one day, I'm there by myself, I get ahold of his baseball glove. Now Rex, he was a shortstop, really good, best hitter on the team. He loved that glove, treated it like his baby. Kept it in his bottom drawer, with a ball in the pocket. Oiled it like a motherfucker. Man, that pocket? Black. Had that glove for two years, I think."

"How old were you?"

"Fifth grade." He tilted his head. "Anyhow, I wrapped it in a rag, and I took it and hid it out in back of the garage. Now we seen a snake back there once, and Rex, he never went back there. So it rains for three or four days straight. A couple weeks go by, time for spring practice. So Rex goes to get his glove, it's not in the drawer. He goes apeshit, screams for his mom. 'Clayton, you know where Rex's glove's at?' 'No, ma'am, I ain't seen it nowhere.' He turns the house upside-down, no glove. So maybe a week later, me and Debby—she was two years younger—we're sitting at the kitchen table working a jigsaw puzzle, Rex comes running in, hollering for his mom. Runs into the kitchen, throws the glove on the table, soaked through, flat as a pancake, mold on it. Puzzle pieces fly everywhere, he's yelling his head off. Debby screams, their mom screams." Now Clayton was laughing so hard he could scarcely get the words out.

"Oh, my God. Then what happened?"

"This is the best part! He slammed it so hard he banged his hand on the table. Busted his thumb, his fucking thumb! And two bones in his hand!" As he said this, Clayton struck the steering wheel, accidentally honking the horn. He rocked with laughter. "Well, of course they got him another one, and he oiled it up and stuffed a ball in it, but his hand was too busted up to play the rest of the summer. When the cast come off, he squeezed this rubber ball all day and half the night. Like a demon. Spring come, he starts playing again, still fields okay, new glove's okay, but it's like he forgot how to *hit*. Thumb don't fit right on the bat no more. He makes the JV team, but he keeps getting into fights, cussing out umpires. Finally they kick him off the team." Clayton wiped his eyes with the back of his hand. "After that, they give me to my uncle."

"He ever figure out who ruined his glove?"

"Busted his own fucking hand, the cocksucker."

I felt a headache forming around the edges of my buzz, like

lace on a hanky, like a worm crawling through my brain, whispering. I felt like a child again, unanchored to anything solid.

"Before I left, I went through all their puzzles, and I took out one piece from each one." He looked at the bottle in his hand. "I shouldna did that. Debby was a sweet girl, and she loved them puzzles."

I shrank back. I realized I didn't really know this kid. I had talked too much, told him things. I felt smarmy, as well as vulnerable.

"Fuck her," he said. "Fuck the whole family, except my uncle." Grunting, he threw his beer bottle out the window. He smiled as the bottle smashed against a tree, and he was still smiling when he looked back at me.

I dropped my eyes. It was ugly, just ugly and brainless, breaking things for no reason and leaving the mess for other people to deal with. The violence of it disturbed me. A cold trickle crept up my spine. I brought up a knee and put my hands around it, interlacing my fingers. It was a meaningless gesture, more like a nervous habit, but it relieved the tension I felt.

I heard his door squawk open and felt the seat bounce as he hopped out of the truck. "It's nice out. Come on. I won't hurt you." Was he angry? He sounded angry.

I climbed down from the truck, relieved to be out of the confined space. But when I looked around, except for the marker there was nothing but the road and the empty countryside. I followed Clayton to the marker, where he stood silently reading the text.

A Cry for Freedom

In 1858, in the now-abandoned town of Lost Saddle, three miles northeast of this site, six so-called Border Ruffians led a raid from Missouri across Spotted Dog Creek into Kansas. The men burned down the offices

> of the newspaper *Our Cry for Freedom* and took two men, including the editor, hostage. They dragged the men into a nearby woods, stripped them of their clothing, and prepared to hang them. Little did they know that the clearing they had chosen for their crime was a scant 20 yards from the cabin of Adelia Haughman, a staunch abolitionist. The female Jayhawker came charging through the trees on her stallion, Lightning, a revolver in each hand. She shot dead two of the Ruffians and, galloping at full speed, pulled the naked victims onto her horse and rode them to town. Despite the setback, the newspaper continued to publish. Three days later it ran a four-column photograph of Haughman and her two naked passengers as they rode into town. Parts of the photo were blacked out so as not to offend the sensibilities of readers. Four of the Ruffians escaped to raid another day.

"Never heard of her," Clayton said.

"Nobody has. That's how come there's a marker, I guess."

He ran two fingers over the raised letters on the cast metal plaque. "People die," he said. "They just die, and eventually everybody that knew them dies, and then it's just words on a fucking marker." He looked around, picked up a baseball-sized rock, and heaved it at a tree. I watched as he hunted more rocks and threw them, cursing when he missed.

Now my headache blossomed. I was afraid of him, a little bit, yes I was, I admit it. I walked over to him and hooked my arm through his. To distract him I began to tell him almost everything I knew or thought or dreamed about Colorado. Even as he pulled away and resumed throwing rocks, he listened closely, nodding, asking questions. He had never been to the mountains, nor gazed into blue/green/black lakes, had never tasted trout, never smelled summer air scented with snow.

After a while he seemed to lose interest in the rock throwing; he got another beer—I declined—and we sat at a picnic table. He didn't know what lichen even was, he told me, let alone how it made intricate and delicate patterns against the face of giant boulders. And a waterfall—that must be something to see. He'd sure like to look through my pictures. He didn't know there was any such thing as a double exposure. It sounded interesting. For that matter, he'd never used a camera. He sure would like to learn how.

It felt as if time had gone hazy; we were (or I was) in a sweet dream. I told him about Harriet and her rock collection. I told him everything I could remember that she had done in Colorado—skiing, snowshoeing, ice-skating, bonfires. It seemed he couldn't get enough of my Colorado fantasy, and the more he responded, the more I revealed to him. He sat and drank, smiling and listening.

I felt a longing I couldn't identify. The closest I could come was that I wanted to take some kind of leap. I wanted to get closer to him. I took a deep breath. "I remember once when this bee died," I said. "Joan, my cousin, the one in the wreck? She killed it with a flyswatter, and I don't know why, but all of a sudden I realized, it's dead. Forever. That was—"

"Shit," he said, his eyes widening. "The funeral." He smacked his hand on the table.

"I didn't want to go anyway."

He stared at me. That stare. You know the one. I had said the wrong thing for the millionth time in my life. I had taken a leap and fallen far into the place where only Charlotte lived.

I stood up and started walking to the truck. My legs felt like rubber.

"Billie?"

"Just take me back to town, okay?" I pulled open the truck door.

He walked to the driver's side and peered at me across the

cab through the open windows. "I'm sorry. About your cousins."

"I know." I climbed in and raised my leg and kicked the inside of the door, leaving a mud smear. My suit jacket lay crumpled on the seat.

I exhaled with relief when he said, "Where to?"

I had Clayton drop me off downtown, and I walked to Frank and Wilma's house the back way, composing myself as I walked. Only a couple of cars were parked at the house. The funeral must have still been going on. The rain had let up, and now the air felt steamy.

Inside the house, the table had a clean cloth and some candles, but no food yet. I heard kitchen noises and walked into the doorway. Two aproned women were working without a word, their backs to me, preparing the food. One was quite tall; both were brunettes going gray.

"Hi," I said.

The tall woman whirled around, uttered a squawk, and placed her hand on her chest. "You scared me. Didn't see you there." The serving spoon in her hand dribbled some kind of noodle casserole on the floor. The other woman bent to wipe it up.

"I'm sorry, I—"

"You're Bill's daughter, aren't you?" the first woman said. She lifted her hand to her head to smooth her hair. "Your mother was looking for you." She looked closely at my wrinkled suit, my stockings, my muddy shoes.

I made a face that I hoped looked apologetic. "I—we—I went for a ride to clear my head, and we got lost."

The tall woman raised her eyebrows and then turned around and resumed her work, but the other one stood at the sink, absently scrubbing the metal strip at the edge of the counter, watching me.

"Where's everybody at?" I said.

She looked at her watch. "Cemetery by this time, most likely."

"Right."

Now she turned away to open the tap and rinse out the dishcloth.

I quickly slipped out of the house. I walked to the Plymouth and sat in the front passenger seat with the door open and smoked one cigarette after another. In my mind I went over my conversation with Clayton. I felt shaky, headachy. Sad and embarrassed.

Pretty soon the cicadas started up. I opened my mouth and sang with them, softly, tunelessly. I sang about someone who was wandering, lost, in a flat, featureless, unending plain. She wanted to go back to some other place, but she realized you can't go back, because there is no path. In your rambling, undoubtedly you crossed and crisscrossed that very spot but never recognized it. That's because it wasn't a place at all, it was time itself. *Where am I?* you asked, as if time were a place whose whereness you could go to. If only you could step on that exact spot, that very time, where all the pain started, you could drop to your knees, spread your arms, howl at the sky; but you were lost, and the air swallowed your cries as if you were nothing, no one, nowhere. This was the conversation I'd wanted to have with Clayton, or anybody, but of course I'd blown it. I sang with the cicadas until I heard tires on the brick street and looked up. There was the giant black hearse, there were the cars. There were the people.

I knew the first words out of Mother's mouth would be, "Where were you?" and I was right.

CHAPTER 12
THE VOICE OF THE PEOPLE

"Well, folks, you're tuned to 780 on your AM dial, K-WOW, a Thousand Watts of Wonderful. We're coming to you from Wiley, Kansas, in a special radio simulcast with AM-1240, Wichita. We're beaming the show today throughout south-central Kansas because the subject of today's broadcast is of regional interest. I'm Duane Hilyard. I'm the owner of K-WOW, and the husband of Pinky Hilyard"—here he stopped to clear his throat—"who for years—I guess fifteen, sixteen years, right, George?—hosted a call-in show on this station. As most of you know, we lost Pinky two weeks ago today. And Wiley lost six other women, too—all of them in a terrible car accident over by Bison Creek."

"Do we have to listen to this? We already know all this." I picked at a pimple on the back of my shoulder.

"Be quiet, I can't hear," Mother said.

". . . their way to Wichita. There weren't any other cars involved, as far as we know now."

"It's just morbid," I said.

"Shut *up*, or leave the room."

"It's obvious he's reading it," I said, and then, when Mother glared at me, "Okay, okay." I couldn't not listen.

". . . start off with a call from Wiley. Go ahead, you're on the air."

"Duane, we're so sorry. We all of us loved Pinky. She was so special."

"Thank you, thanks very much."

"Her and Marjean, was they sisters? Cousins? People—"

"No, no relation. Pinky was helping Marjean get started on her singing career. She had a heck of a voice, Marjean did. Just a beautiful voice. The two of them, Pinky and Marjean, they were real close."

"Well, people was wondering."

"Thanks for calling. And now we've got a special guest. Do we have him? Yes, we've got Clyde Mellecker. Clyde's the husband of Gloria Mellecker, one of the victims. Clyde, how are you doing? Can you hear me okay?"

"I can hear you. I'm doing all right."

"Thanks for talking to us this evening, Clyde. Now, you and Gloria, you have five children, is that right? And what are their ages?"

"Well, the oldest is going on nine, and the youngest is just a baby."

"Is that right." He sighed. "Tell us, how are they doing?"

"Well, I don't think it's hit them yet. Her sister's here taking care of them. She brought some toys and whatnot."

"Uh-huh, uh-huh. And, Clyde, you farm eight miles south of Wiley, is that right?"

"That, uh, that's right."

"Tell us, Clyde, how did you, you and Gloria, how did you two meet?"

"All right. Well, my best friend in high school, Virgil O'Connor, he was her big brother. I seen her around the house, you know, little redheaded kid? Well, she was in this project—school, 4-H, something—where you write to a soldier in the war—excuse me, Korean conflict? You got the names off of this list." He cleared his throat. "Anyhow, so she wrote me this letter."

"Letters from home mean so much to our servicemen. What branch were you in?"

"I made it home, but Virgil, he didn't, KIA. Navy, fire control. So when I got home I went around to the house, and I *was* Virgil for them. They just claimed me."

"And Gloria was how old at this time?"

"Fifteen, thereabouts. They just glommed on to me."

"I can hear you smiling over the phone, Clyde."

"For Christ's sake," I said. Mother shushed me.

"Me and Gloria, we'd take walks, pick up milk at the store, that kind of a thing, but we never had what you'd call a date."

"They treated you like their son."

"Yeah. But me and her, there was something there, though we never talked about it. Talked about everything else, though. She was a talker."

"How'd you—"

"On graduation night I just bam, just asked her to marry me. That was it. Damn, we was happy, me and her."

His voice faltered on the last few words. There was the sound of a receiver in a cradle, and then a dial tone went out over the air.

"I think we lost him." There was a silence. "Now I have here a statement from the Butler County Sheriff's Office. They don't think there was another car, they don't know how come Pinky and her friends were on that dirt road, they don't know what caused the crash, other than she lost control of the vehicle. Seems like they don't know very much, here two weeks later."

Mother shook her head and took several swallows of beer.

I smoked.

". . . I tell you what, it's a pure mystery," the caller, a man, was saying. "They wouldn't have turned off the highway for just no reason, I tell you what."

"That's right. Not a one of those women had any connection to the people who live at the end of that road. Seems like something was up, had to be."

"What are you thinking—some kind of a crime?" the voice went on. "Somebody flagged them down and forced them onto that road? With a gun? A robbery? Maybe a—an assault?"

"Thing is, nothing came up missing," Duane said. "What does that leave us with? Go ahead, caller. You're from Wiley?"

"Rose Hill," said the man. "I heard one of them was getting a divorce."

"No sir, that's not true at all. Not at all. And even if it was, so what? What does it have to do with the wreck?"

"Maybe some kind of a suicide attempt? Or somebody had a nervous breakdown?" His voice went high at the end.

"Good grief," I said.

"And—a new caller. We're not here to just repeat gossip, folks. What's your question?"

"Did they check the car out? Was the brakes working? The footfeed?" This voice was ambiguous, but likely a man.

"I can tell you, there wasn't one thing wrong with that car," Duane said.

"Anybody check out the husbands? Where was *they* at when this happened?"

"Husbands?"

"How about the Hilyards? They have any enemies?"

"Well, I'm Duane Hilyard myself. And I can tell you neither me nor my wife had an enemy in the world. I'll take the next caller."

"Duane?" came a woman's voice, angry. "I don't know how you can set there and take this abuse. I've knowed you and Pinky half my life, and there wasn't a nicer person in town than Pinky Hilyard. God bless her."

"Well, thank you," Duane said. "It's so hard to believe that these fine Christian ladies just all died like that. One minute here, the next, gone, seven of them, just like that. There has got to be more to this story. Go ahead, caller."

"How come you're on the radio talking about this?" the caller said. "They ain't even cold in the ground yet, and you're— "

"You'd be surprised the calls and letters we've gotten at the station," Duane said. "You'd be surprised. There's a lot of interest in town. All over, for that matter. It's a national story. They're talking about having a special."

I lit a cigarette off the old one.

"I heard there was an open container." A woman's voice, young. "That true?"

"No, ma'am. No open container, no alcohol in any of them's blood."

"Well, I heard there was."

"No, not at all. Next call, please."

"What about the children? Why aren't we talking about them? Eighteen children without their mothers. What are they telling the children?"

"I suppose that all depends on their beliefs," Duane said. A click.

Now a man came on. "I think you-all are getting into some weird stuff. It was just an accident, that's all. A terrible thing, but that don't mean it's somebody's fault."

"We're just trying to understand how it happened," Duane said. "If we just knew how come they were there. That road, the way it was, with that tree practically in the middle of it, and so close to that dike, it was like an accident waiting to happen."

"What about them people?" said the next caller. "The ones that live there? Not to be prejudiced, but I seen them on TV and they was colored."

"For God's sake," I said.

Mother glared at me.

"Well now," Duane said, "there's no reason to think any of the neighbors had anything— "

"I'm just saying— "

"I know, I know. It's a mystery, sure enough."

"Welp, I hope the sheriff's looking into them, that's all I'm saying."

"I'm sure he's— "

"Because I drove by there today to have a look. Those ladies had no business there. There's got to be a reason."

"All right. Thanks for calling. Do we have the sheriff? We don't? All right. All right. We're going to fit in a commercial here. You're listening to a special broadcast . . ."

"Turn it off, will you?" I said.

"Leave the room if you don't want to hear. Go to bed."

"I can't *not* hear it."

"Close the door. Turn on your record player."

"That's not what I mean."

"Hush, they're starting again."

". . . and we're back, live. Go ahead, caller."

"Duane, it's a tragedy, a town this size. Feels like we got the heart kicked right out of us."

"That's what I said," Mother said.

"Well, that's right," Duane said. "The heart kicked right out of us."

"What I don't get is, how come all this guessing and gossiping about this and that? Because things like this, they just happen, it's just random, there isn't necessarily some big reason for it. When your time's up— "

"I hear what you're saying, but nobody wants to think their loved one was taken in such a brutal way just—at random. Know what I mean? The children are gonna ask, 'How come my mother died like that? How come God let her die?' We need to give them a reason. Thanks for calling."

"Duane, have they done lie detector tests?" the next caller said.

"On who?" Duane sounded bewildered.

"Everybody that was there, to start with."

"What would you ask them?"

"What they *know* about this that they're not *telling*. The husbands, too. Somebody knows something."

"All right, well. Thanks for calling. I don't know what good that would do, I really don't. The neighbors, the husbands, they're in the dark just like the rest of us. But if anybody out there knows how come Pinky and her friends were on that road, please contact Butler County. I'm hoping that somebody can help us understand. I'm not looking to blame anybody. I don't think it's anybody's fault, necessarily. But I just feel like, there's got to be something we're not seeing. Everybody in Wiley wants answers. This was too big of a thing to just be random." Several seconds elapsed before he continued. "We will stay on this story." He repeated the call letters, followed by the catchy "A Thousand Watts of Wonderful" jingle.

A different male voice began the weather forecast. I leaned over and clicked off the radio.

"It does make you wonder." Mother finished her beer and set the can next to the empties on the coffee table.

I lit a cigarette and took a deep drag.

"I said, it makes you wonder," Mother said.

"I'm going to bed. I'm tired." I walked to my room and stood for a minute next to the bed. With the cigarette dangling from my mouth, I rummaged in the tangled sheets, trying to straighten out the creases. The cigarette fell into a fold, and I clawed through the bedding until I was able to retrieve it, minus the hot box. With my open hand I slapped at the glowing embers on the sheet. One spark flew off and stung my arm.

I licked my arm and then sank onto the edge of the bed.

I fell back on my pillow, turned on my side toward the wall, and drew up my knees. After a few moments I was able to force my face into immobility, and I lay with my arms tight around me. I tried to make my mind a blank, but I kept hearing the voices on the radio—so familiar and yet so alien. Did I sound like them—harsh, judgmental, prying, angry? When you boiled it down, who was I, anyway? What did I believe? Was I Charlotte, or was Charlotte me, or what? Two weeks in, and still it felt like the ground had been yanked out from under me.

The next day Mother and I both slept late and didn't have much to say to each other. While she smoked and drank, I sat on the couch and smoked and read the special commemorative edition of the Wiley paper that was published the Wednesday after the wreck. It had profiles and photos of each of the dead women.

Pinky Hilyard had raised money for every good cause there was, the piece said, and she had a great sense of humor and laughed like a rooster. Marjean O'Neal had a big voice, bigger than Patsy Cline's, some people said. At twenty-two, Marjean already had three kids. Gloria Mellecker, redheaded mother of five, was famous for her chicken casserole. She collected joke knickknacks, like the myrtlewood paperweight that said "Please turn me over," and when you turn it onto the other side, "Ahhh that feels so good." I laughed when I read that. Gloria must have been a woman after my own heart. Boots Carey, a giggler, operated the Kutz & Kurlz beauty salon in Wiley and made quilts in her spare time. Newcomer Peggy Massey called herself a "liberated woman" and said the world was changing. My cousin Vivian had been the Wiley High School football queen and valedictorian, a "high achiever, but never conceited," said my uncle Frank. My cousin Joan had been known in high school for "having strong opinions" and leading adventures like exploring abandoned farmhouses, driving jalopies through cow pastures, and shooting off bottle rockets on country roads.

There was more, but you get the idea.

As I read, in my mind I heard the voices of the people on the radio. It was as if they and the women were interchangeable, differing only in details.

In the end, I wondered, what did anyone's life matter, or the casseroles or quilts or jokes they made, or any of it? What difference did it make when you only ended up dead? For no reason?

Chapter 13
Scapegoat

The following Monday I dragged myself to work at 7:48, the usual time. I liked Mondays as a rule, because I didn't work on Saturdays, so first thing Monday I would have the Saturday business to process. I liked to have work ready to do. I would sip coffee while I looked over everything and then dive in. Time at work always went faster when there was a lot to do.

I felt wrung out, but pretty soon I got back into the routine, and the morning went fast. About 11:45, a shadow cast itself over my paperwork. I looked up.

"Hey, Billie." It was Alvin, one of the guys who worked in the yard. "There's somebody in a blue half-ton 3100 out there. Asked after you." He turned to go.

"A blue what?"

"Pickup truck?" he said, laughing.

The dumber I was, the more the men acted as if they enjoyed being around me. At long last, I was beginning to get it. And really, what did it hurt?

I wrestled the desk drawer open and pulled out my purse. "Going to lunch," I said to the boss's open door as I walked by.

When I climbed into the pickup, I noticed Clayton's forehead bandage was gone, leaving a crescent-shaped red mark. I guessed it would leave a little scar. I also saw that he had cleaned up most of the trash in the cab.

He was in Hutch to get a water pump, he told me, and would I let him buy me lunch.

"How did you find me?"

He smiled. "There's only two scrap iron shops on South Main, and I got lucky the first time."

"Oh, yeah," I said, embarrassed to remember my true confessions at the marker the day of the funeral. How bored he'd been. I cringed.

"Where's good?" he said.

"How about the R & B drive-in? It's close, C and Poplar."

The weather had cooled to a more seasonable mideighties, and it was one of those early summer days in Hutch when the humidity was negligible and there was a sweet breeze, the kind of rare day when being outdoors felt wonderful instead of itchy and buggy.

When we got to the drive-in, he switched off the pickup; it coughed a few times before it died. He shook his head. "Gotta set the timing one of these days."

Under the canopy, we ate our lunch of pork tenderloin sandwiches, fries, and Cokes. I felt young.

Clayton asked about Hutch, so I told him about the fifth-grade field trip we'd taken to the Carey salt mine. I remembered taking an elevator 350 feet underground into a cool, cavelike hole lined with rock salt crystals in many shades of gray; from there we rode in a cart into utter darkness. You could smell the salt and hear something trickling on the cave walls—

water, I guess. And we each got a souvenir piece of rock salt. It had an earthy taste.

"And I got a badge or certificate or something. 'Official Junior Salt Miner,' something like that."

He grinned. "You still have it?"

I lit a cigarette. "No, Mother never saved anything like that."

"Yeah. I don't have that stuff either."

I was embarrassed. I had forgotten about his absent father, his dead mother, his childhood of being moved from family to family. He had used the word "give"—"They give me to my uncle."

There was a silence. I mentioned the state fair, the new Cosmosphere, the national junior college men's basketball tournament. I mentioned Carey Park, only a few blocks south of where we were. The park had a swimming pool, picnic tables, a golf course. They were talking about putting in a zoo.

He nodded. After a silence, he said, "Didn't you tell me you're moving to Colorado?"

I took in a breath. "Maybe someday. You know, in the future." I tried to sound vague.

He took a giant bite of his sandwich and looked at me curiously.

"So anyway." It was a speech habit, one of those things you say when you can't think of what to say next.

He finished his sandwich and wiped his hands.

Just when I could no longer stand the silence, he put one hand on my arm. "Look, Billie. I come to . . ." His voice cracked, and he narrowed his eyes. "There's something I . . . Shit."

"It's okay," I said.

He turned to face me, and then he dropped his eyes and looked at his hands. "Well, see, I was in the wreck." His voice rose. "That's what I come to tell you." He let out his breath.

"What?"

He pulled back his hand, turned away from me, and scrunched

down in his seat. "I never told nobody." He punched his knee. "I need a beer." But he made no move to get one.

"What?" I said again.

"Fuck." Now he pounded on the steering wheel. I glanced around and saw people looking at us from their cars.

I felt myself rock a little, and my mouth watered. In a low voice I said, "You were in the wreck?"

"You guys done?" came the voice of the girl outside the window. No sooner had she lifted the food tray than Clayton started the truck, ground it into reverse, and backed out. He took a breath and more gently put it in first gear and left the drive-in. To my relief, he turned south on Main, but he drove past my work and into Carey Park. He found a spot under a tree and pulled up to it.

By that time, my hands were shaking. I didn't see anyone around, but I figured from here I could run someplace and flag down somebody if I had to.

"I'm sorry," he said, his upper body rocking forward and back. "I'm sorry, I'm sorry." He stopped rocking and reached behind the seat, retrieving a bottle of beer.

"I'm not sure that's a good idea." I used my mollifying voice, and it almost came out a question.

He opened the bottle and guzzled several swallows.

"Here's the thing." He was panting, and he took a minute to catch his breath. "What happened—everybody . . ." His face was red. His mouth worked.

"Everybody . . . ?"

He sighed, and then in a rush, "Everybody wants to know how come they was back there, on our road. Those ladies."

"Yes." My voice rose an octave.

"Well, fuck. It was my doing."

I stared at him.

He glanced away. "I feel like—I don't know."

For a moment I thought he wasn't going to finish. "It's all

right," I said, swallowing. "It'll be all right." Now he seemed—it felt as if he was on some edge. I was right there with him.

Abruptly he turned in the seat and lifted his right leg onto the seat between us. He leaned back. "The day before—Friday—I was working on this '62 Firebird, and then me and some of the guys went to this guy I know's house and had a few beers. Sitting around on the back porch, you know? Shootin' the shit."

I nodded. It was hard to breathe.

"Then pretty soon he brings out a bottle of Old Crow. Next thing I know, it's sunup. I'm sick as a dog. I take a piss in the backyard, upchuck. See, if my uncle found out I was out all night, let alone drinking like that . . ." He shuddered, raised the bottle, and drank. "I go to the truck, turns out it has a flat, and the spare's flat, too. I can't think. I'm sick, I want to crawl off someplace and die. I still can't think. I walk over to the house, peek into the back windows. Suddenly I see something move inside, and I about lose it. I go back of the garage, run the hose over my head, and set out for home on foot." He looked at his foot, and I remembered what he had said about having polio as a child.

"First three miles, I'm coasting on fumes—limp a while, walk a while, barf. And then, about two miles from the turnoff, I give out. I'm standing there, trying to think up some story to tell my uncle." He muttered *fuck* and swung his other leg up on the seat, bending his knees.

I watched him, trying not to think. I felt waves of heat, like razor blades, roll over my skin. Charlotte, making her presence known. She hadn't forgotten me.

"Well, then, here comes the Cadillac." His voice went high, and he cleared his throat. "She pulls up alongside me and waves me over. 'You need a ride, cutie?' I feel the AC through the window."

"Oh, my God." It was as if I were watching a movie. I saw it so clearly—Clayton, limping; the giant white car.

He moved one shoulder and then the other as if trying to scratch his back. His face was screwed into a frown. "'Nah, it's just a little ways,' I say. She says, 'Won't take long then, will it?'"

I tucked my hands under my thighs and remained still, afraid that if I moved at all, said anything, he would startle like a fawn.

But he didn't seem to notice me. "She starts up screaming/laughing. And then the rest of them. I look in there and see all them ladies, and I say, 'You don't have room,' and she says—she had this blond hair, almost white, this beehive—she says, 'Just climb on the bumper and grab ahold.' Screaming/laughing, pointing back with her head, you know, and I figure, *shit, take me an hour to walk it, stove up like I am, maybe this way I can get home before my uncle wakes up,* so I—So I—" He drank from the bottle.

"So you . . ." I willed myself to relax my throat, tamp down a wail, and listen. Just listen.

"Bumper on that Caddy's two foot long, must be, and it's got these little baby fins in back, you know? I tell her, take the next right and then hang a left at the half mile. Dirt road." He leaned his forehead on his knees. His next words, though spoken with a little buzz against his jeans, seemed to fill the cab. "She about threw me off when she turned off the highway, but I seen she was watching me in the rearview and she slowed down."

"God."

He looked up and seemed surprised to see me there. He blinked several times. "I never thought about—she didn't know our road. I never thought."

I cleared my throat. "So she drove, um, north on your road?"

He nodded. "She had her arm out the window, hanging down, waggling her fingers on the door, you know, like you do." He flattened one hand and drummed on the side of his thigh.

I saw myself in the car. I pictured their faces around me, their dresses, their shoes and purses, their glasses with the glittery plastic frames. I pictured Joan among them, laughing, rolling her eyes, swearing, smoking.

I made myself not say any of that. This vision, I knew, was courtesy of Charlotte. Comedy/tragedy, both or either, take your choice, it all hurts.

"So we're going along, and suddenly I think, *wait, where's she gonna drop me, what if my uncle hears the car, I shoulda told her to drop me on this side of the dike,* and then she sticks her head out the window and hollers something, I don't know what, and seems like she just floored it." His right foot pivoted forward from his heel, although he didn't seem to realize it.

He sucked in spit, swallowed, and now spoke rapidly. "We fishtailed for a second, but she come out of it. I heard them screaming. I couldn't tell if they was screaming/laughing or screaming/screaming. She come out of the skid, though. She come out of it. And I—you know how, when you come out of a skid, you feel lucky? Like you just missed a smashup? Like you almost lost control but you didn't? I was shaking, I almost pissed myself, but I thought everything was gonna be fine."

A moan made my lips buzz like a cello.

Clayton wasn't paying attention to me. He didn't seem to be aware of anything. "We was about a quarter mile from the dike, and I, all the sudden—*the fucking dike, the tree*! Now it seemed like we was *flying*, it was coming up so fast. I hollered at her, I pounded on the trunk, but all the sudden we was *there*, almost at the dike. And I jumped off. I just jumped off. And I—just out of habit, out of all them hours in the gym—I tumbled when I hit the ground. So I—so I spread out all that force over two or three, I don't know, three or four tumbles, five, like Coach taught me. And when I stopped I was laying in soft dirt at the edge of the field, in the volunteer wheat, all balled up. I thought I was dead, sure enough."

It felt as if I had sand in my mouth, digging its way into my gums, up under my lips.

"I swear to God, I actually thought I was dead." Clayton was cringing now, his arms folded across his chest, his eyes closed against the memory. "Couldn't get my breath, you know? Thought I was dead. I—maybe I passed out for a while, I don't know. I never heard nothing."

"Okay." The whole world was silent. Not a lick of wind, not an insect, nothing.

"Anyhow, inside I felt like I been kicked by a mule, but all I had was these scrapes and this cut on my head, bruises on my midsection." His fingers touched the scab. "I don't know how, but I snuck over the dike and down to where . . . the tree . . ." He closed his eyes. "I seen them." He moaned in the front of his mouth. To me it seemed like a young man's way to try to keep from sobbing. I stared at his lips, waiting for them to buckle.

But he was looking down, silent. To fill the empty time, the empty space, I reached into my purse and pulled out a cigarette. I held it toward him. He took it, and I lit it, along with one for myself. He sucked in the smoke and coughed.

I inhaled three, four, five times as hard as I could, in the seemingly desperate way I had seen Mother suck in smoke many times. I felt my mouth pucker, the smoke flow out of my nose. I felt everything above my neck turn red.

When Clayton spoke again, his voice was lower. "I walked up to the house, and, God damn, my uncle was still in bed." He shook his head. "I started doing chores. And when I heard the sheriff's car, I went back down in the slough and watched him. Pretty soon I walked over there. I made up a story about slipping and falling in the slough. Felt like I'd been kicked by a mule." He stubbed the cigarette on the sole of his boot and threw it out the truck window. Then he put the beer bottle to his lips, but it was empty.

He turned then and got out of the truck, tossing the bottle into the bed. I heard it hit the metal with a dull clunk, roll for a moment, and come to rest in grit.

I stubbed out my cigarette, pushed open my door, and when I was outside I leaned against the open window, looking at him across the cab.

He mirrored me. "So now you know how come them ladies was on our road," he said, his eyes cast down. "No good reason. Just a favor for a good-for-nothing hungover stupid son of a bitch. I'm the one should be dead, not them."

I lit another smoke with my hands shaking and watched the ragged gray edge where it was burning; a flake of tobacco stuck out the end and then was gone. A breeze cooled me. "Let me get this straight."

"What?"

I realized I had my head down. I looked up at him. All the air had gone out of me. I understood with a sickening jolt that I'd been hoping, just like everybody else—against all logic—that there would come a villain, or at least a scapegoat, or at least a *reason*, and we would all be satisfied. That there would be a goddamn moral to the story, that their deaths would have some goddamn meaning. Something to sand down the raw bleeding edge of randomness that mocked our pain and loss. "They gave you a ride, you jumped at the last minute, they crashed into the tree. Is that it?"

He nodded.

To me the question was self-evident. "How come you feel like it's your fault?"

Clayton obliged me as if reading my thoughts. "If I hadna gotten drunk and passed out in town, they wouldna been on that road," he said. "They woulda went straight to Wichita like they planned. They woulda did that singing deal. None of this shit woulda happened. All them kids would still have their mothers, like they ought to."

Well, yes, it had to be somebody's fault. It had to be. Or what was it all for?

I felt pain then, and for one little moment I let myself feel it instead of pushing it away. It crushed my ribcage. It took my breath.

Now I shook my head, swallowing. "You don't know that. Nobody knows that."

He leaned forward and bent at the waist, his head between his arms. His shoulders shook as if he were crying. "I don't know what to do."

I inhaled sharply. This was, of course, a different question. I blinked. "I don't see that there's anything *to* do."

He stood up straight and raised his head. "I read the papers, I see the TV. People want to know how come they was on our road."

I shook my head. "It doesn't make any difference how they got there. They're gone, and that's all that matters. It wasn't your fault. You— "

"I'm a fuckup. Always been a fuckup. Always— "

"It wasn't your fault, Clayton. You can't— "

"Don't tell my uncle, okay?"

I turned away from him and leaned against the truck. *Shit shit shit.* The implications of what he had told me began to creep into my consciousness. I knew something now, whether I wanted to or not. To me, his story was a simple thing, easy to imagine. I was Kansas born and bred; here, there was no such thing as walking for your health; if you were walking along a road, it meant you needed help; it never failed that every driver that passed would offer you a ride. I mean, it *never* failed. It was an everyday thing, something of no more importance than a thousand other things that happened that most people never thought twice about. No mystery, no villainy, no ill intent, no *meaning*. But I was by no means certain that the families would see it that way. Shit.

Like Clayton, I didn't know what to do. I now knew the very thing everyone was dying, apparently, to know: the big mystery of why the Cadillac was on Clayton's road. It was true what he had said—if he hadn't gotten drunk the night before, if he hadn't been limping along, trying to get home before his uncle woke up . . . if he this, if he that. If ifs and buts were candy and nuts . . . A thin thread for the meaning of seven lives—or seven deaths—to hang on.

But still, it was what everyone wanted—someone to blame, and a story. The accident wasn't random, not exactly; in the right light, you could see it as a story: the women were doing a good deed for a hardworking young kid, an orphan yet. A goddamn parable.

Clayton's shadow materialized in my peripheral vision, and I jumped. He was standing next to me now, and he placed his hand on my arm, just so. "Don't tell my uncle, okay?" he said again.

"How come you told me this? I don't want to *know* this."

He just looked at me. I swear he looked ten years old.

He swallowed. "I'll take you back to work."

He opened the door and took my elbow and helped me climb into the truck.

Back at the shop, I made myself a cup of coffee, got out the spiral notebook, and crossed out five-and-a-half feet's worth of inch-and-a-half by inch-and-a-half angle iron. Soon a truckload of mixed metal came in, and I weighed it full and empty and calculated the payout. A couple of crusty car batteries. An ordinary afternoon.

But every once in a while my heart burbled, and I remembered the accident, and I remembered I had the secret. Worse, I kept picturing it, frame by frame—the car, the boy, the leap, the dike, the tree, the bodies. I performed my work tasks, I made my cross-outs, I calculated my calculations, and underneath it all, just below my consciousness, ran a cold river of truth, indifferent and everlasting.

I left work an hour early, saying I had a headache. Which was true. But instead of going home, I went to the R & B and got a limeade and then drove to the park. I sat there in the Plymouth under the same tree, smoking and drinking the bittersweet soda, and when it was gone I ate the ice.

Now a handful of prepubescent kids streamed by, racing each other to the playground equipment, screeching and hollering. I lifted my paper cup and tapped the bottom, but it was empty.

My thoughts returned to Clayton. I pictured his face, hours ago, as he confessed to his part in the accident. I asked myself what I was going to do, what was the right thing to do, was I going to tell anyone. Around and around.

I tried to imagine what it would be like, for once, to be in everyone's good graces, to be the one who did right by the family and the town, to be seen as normal. To belong. But as I thought it through, I doubted that Clayton had any idea what he was in for if word got out. Not tell his uncle—how naïve could he get? Everybody and their uncle would know, and some of them would call for Clayton's head. He wasn't old enough to drink beer, let alone Old Crow, and he had in effect lied to the sheriff about what he knew about the accident. And wasn't hitchhiking itself illegal, notwithstanding everyone did it? It seemed to me that once they had their bad guy, they would have all kinds of things to charge him with. His uncle, a man who baked cakes and bought horses to please his sister's (probably illegitimate) child, would be the least of Clayton's worries.

To top it off, Clayton had let things go on too long, and now people had made up their own stories, maybe sexier than the truth. And if I was the one who told, wouldn't his silence reflect badly on Clayton? My instincts told me it would. But I doubted I could talk him in to telling. Why had he even told me? And so I was back where I started, talking to myself in circles.

I closed my eyes and pictured myself at the end of the dock at the lake in Colorado. Farther out, a breeze skimmed across the surface, rippling the water, creating a tessellated image—a thousand thousand triangles, in the sunlight and shadow of the current, constantly appearing, disappearing, reappearing. Nothing but texture: brightening/darkening triangles. There and not there, without ceasing, a pattern ancient as the mountains, seen for centuries only by birds and, possibly, angels. I felt a longing to be on the water, floating, rising, falling, my ears, at the last, full of nothing, Charlotte finally put to rest.

That night I dreamed I was back at the lake, and Joan rose from the waves, cold water streaming down her hair, her face, her neck. She looked toward me (I wasn't on the dock; I was floating in air), her eyes brilliant with revulsion, her mouth a single line curved downward. In the way of dreams, I could tell that she despised me.

I didn't have to ask myself how I was supposed to feel. I knew.

Oh, I knew.

Chapter 14

The Stranger in My House

After my lake dream, I slept a few hours. When I got up to use the bathroom at dawn, Mother was sitting in her green chair. Her eyes were open, but she didn't react when I took steps toward her. The cigarette between her fingers wasn't lit. There were six—no, seven—empties on the coffee table.

"Mother?" Still no reaction. I put my hand on her shoulder, and the feeling that passed between our two bodies made me shudder. It was a feeling of what, I didn't know. A feeling of vacancy.

"Mother?" Now I put my hand on her shoulder and shook her.

She blinked several times, and her head swiveled slightly. She took a breath and frowned. "What?"

"Are you all right?"

Her hand trembled as she lifted the cigarette to her mouth. "Of course I am. Why wouldn't I be?" She tried to take a drag, frowned, and reached for her matches.

"You don't look right."

She gave a hollow laugh, lit the cigarette, inhaled, and began coughing, bending double with the effort.

I thumped her on the back, but she waved me away with her free hand. "Get me a water," she croaked.

I hurried to the sink and back, and she took the glass. A few drops spilled out. She grasped the glass with the thumb and ring finger of her other hand, the burning cigarette still between her index and middle fingers, and she managed to control the glass enough with both hands to take a sip and then another. She cleared her throat. After another minute of struggling, she handed me the glass and lay back in the chair, swallowing air in gulps. I caught the long ash in one cupped hand and took the cigarette from her. I stubbed it out.

The skin on her face was gray, and her lips were pale purple.

"Don't you think you might be—might need to see a doctor?" I said.

She shook her head. "Don't be ridiculous."

"Just to get checked out."

"Absolutely not." Almost a screech. "I'm just tired. Go back to bed."

I knelt by the chair and placed my hand on hers. "I'll call them. I'm sure they can work you in."

She yanked her hand away. "You will do no such thing."

I rose, backed up, and sat on the couch. How many times had the two of us sat just this way, on this furniture, in this room, in this tableau? I watched as Mother fished another cigarette out of the pack and lit it. She didn't inhale, only quickly blew a little smoke back out.

Now I lit one for myself.

The two of us sat without speaking for about seven minutes, the length of time it took to finish one smoke. The room began to lighten.

"Go back to bed," she said again.

I stood up and yawned. "I can't sleep. I'm going to make

coffee." I filled the teakettle. While it heated, I smoked another cigarette. The first one hadn't quieted the heebie-jeebies. These days it took two for the relief to get all the way through to the inside of my skin.

When I had poured the steaming water into the coffeepot, I again heard Mother's ragged breathing, which had been muffled by the coffeemaking noises. I glanced across the room. She was shaking the empties one by one, apparently looking for a few last drops.

By the time I brought the two mugs over, she seemed to be breathing better. "Help me clear off these things, will you?" But when she tried to get up from the chair, her knees wobbled and she fell back down.

"I'll get it, just drink your coffee." Somehow I managed to gather the cans in my arms and lift the giant ashtray with my hands. On the way back from the trash can I grabbed a dishrag to wipe down the table. The cloth smelled sour as I dampened it in the sink.

Mother lifted the mug to her lips and drank a large swallow, wincing. She had done that for as long as I could remember. No one could drink coffee as hot as she did.

As I stood at the sink, I remembered what Clayton had told me. I was trying to work up the courage to tell someone, or commit not to. Or maybe I could dip a toe in—to try it out, detail by detail, to gauge the reaction or just to hear myself talk. I felt wrung out.

I pulled up a dinette chair to sit close to Mother. I began by reminding her of the people who had called in to the radio show. "Listening to the radio the other night, I—well, I thought about old times in Wiley. You know." Now I took a close look at her, and I was dismayed by how old she looked, how ill. When had her eyes become hooded like that? I had built such a wall around myself—my actual self, the self who was entwined with her with bands of steel—that I had scarcely looked at her since the night I rode home from the accident site and saw her sitting, ghostly, in the shadow of Frank and Wilma's porch.

"It shook me up, to tell you the truth," she said, her voice trembling. "It made me think of your dad. It happens so sudden, and then it's too late." She swept her arms in a broad gesture. "Everything. And anything. All of a sudden, it's too late."

I leaned in. She seemed to be thinking of something specific. "Like what? What do you mean?"

She dropped her arms. "You know. Things."

Her face closed, in the way it often did, as she dropped the thread between us that seemed to have been there a moment ago.

I swallowed and tried a different tack. "How come you didn't move there, close to everybody? After Daddy died." I took a sip of coffee. It tasted like dust.

She shrugged again. "This is what you want to talk about?" Her eyes were fixed on a spot just over my head.

"I've always wondered." Casually.

Her eyes went back and forth now. "They never liked me, his family."

"How come?" Now I had the same prickly feeling I'd had in Colorado, that night when she'd opened up about meeting Daddy and looking at the stars at the little airport near Wichita.

"That's a long story," she said.

"So tell me. I've got nothing better to do." *Don't wait until it's too late*, I said in my mind.

She looked at me for a minute as if reading my thought, and then she settled back and began. "Well, you have to understand. I was a change-of-life baby. You know, when you're older, and you think you can't get pregnant anymore. They were in their forties. He worked at the Wichita post office, and she kept house and had her friends. They had a happy life. And then, surprise!" She gulped the coffee, again wincing.

Her tone was matter-of-fact, as if she hadn't just dropped a truth that I had never known or imagined. I placed this piece into the mental puzzle I was building of her life, along with the few other pieces I had, all of them undifferentiated plain blue sky. If you know what I mean.

"They weren't exactly glad, I don't think," she went on. "They treated me like a pet, or like another adult. They always talked to me like an adult."

"Ah," I said. "I think I know what you mean."

She didn't take the bait; maybe she didn't get my meaning, or she chose to ignore it. "They took me wherever they went, not that they were gadabouts. Our house was a quiet one."

Now her eyes became unfocused, and she seemed lost in memory. "But they did play bridge with their friends, once a week I think, and they took me along sometimes. I'd bring a coloring book and color by myself in the kitchen while the grown-ups played cards." Her face relaxed, and she gave a little smile. "And then all the way home they'd replay the hands—'I had three to the jack-ten, and you thought I should raise to the two-level?' 'But how come you opened with a diamond?' 'No, four no-trump was Blackwood. Don't you remember Blackwood?' 'That's a drop-dead bid.' 'Since when?' 'What possessed you to ruff with the ace?' 'I was planning to cross-ruff, but you led trumps.'"

Bridge? They remembered the cards they'd held all evening, hand after hand? For the first time in memory, I was able to visualize my maternal grandparents. In their sepia wedding photograph, they wore the dour, frozen expressions I associated with the times they lived in. Now I pictured their faces, animated, in the car, and little Dixie in the backseat, sleepy but straining to hear, determined to remember everything. I pictured her father carrying her into the house when they got home, laying her gently on her bed, just as Daddy had done with me when I was little. I shivered. This was a closer look at Mother than I had experienced since Colorado, more than I had dreamed I would ever have.

"I myself never cared for cards," she said. "Hand me the afghan, will you?"

I walked to the couch and retrieved the afghan. Mother had knit it from a kit—three shades of blue in a chevron pattern. With all the nostalgia Web sites devoted to the sixties and seventies, you're bound to see a hundred of these exact afghans—three shades of blue, three shades of orange, three shades of brown—spread out on the backs of couches in the living room photos.

I tucked it around her lap and returned to the couch.

"My father's great passion was music, classical music, you know," she said, spreading the afghan over her legs. "We had a record player built in to a beautiful walnut cabinet. He must have had two hundred records—you know, the big ones. LPs."

"He did?" That walnut cabinet gleamed in my mind's eye.

She rolled her eyes. "You know that, I've told you a million times."

"No, you— "

"Anyway, he'd get home from work, hang up his hat, kiss Mother and me, and put on a record and light his pipe. Woe to you if you interrupted him while he was listening to his music." Now she was ignoring her coffee, and she seemed to have forgotten her pack of smokes. "Mother and I would go to the kitchen and talk while she made dinner. She had a portable radio in there, and she always turned it to a popular music station, but low, so it wouldn't bother him. Sometimes we danced in there, when I was little and she was still well." She swayed a little in her chair.

"Really?"

"They both died when I was a senior, but you know that. Mother first, cancer, and a month later he just turned his face to the wall and died, too, like a swan when the wife goes." She stared at the ceiling as if she saw swans there.

"I thought he had kidney disease." I remembered hearing that when I was a child.

She ignored me. "They'd made a plan for me to live with my best friend's family. You know her, Flossie Market. She was the one I was with at the café when I met Bill."

"They'd made a plan?" My antennae were up. It seemed there was something she wasn't telling me. It itched.

"What was the name of that place?" she said. "Some animal. Buffalo? Cow? Cow Café? No, that's not right."

"What?"

"Well, anyway, that's how I met your father. At that café where Flossie and I always went. The Rooster?" Now a genuine smile brightened her face. "Anyhow, Bill, he was like somebody threw a bucket of water in my face—too much, too loud, too strong, too everything. He was older than me, almost ten years. I hadn't ever known anyone like him. He made me feel so awake, so alive."

"You went to some airport that night, right?"

She nodded. "I fell hard for him." She sniffed the afghan and frowned. "He had a house, for one thing—you know, the little house on Halsey Drive. I don't know what he was doing in Wichita that day." For a moment her eyes glistened. Then she took a breath and looked at me directly. "Well, you know, I got pregnant."

"What?" My voice seemed to echo in the living room.

"You know. I told you that a long time ago."

"*Hell* no." She got pregnant? She was a senior in high school when she had me? Wait—

"You don't have to swear. You know I don't care for that kind of language." She put her mug to her lips and drank the rest of the coffee, frowning. I refilled the mug. "So anyway, that's why they hated me. The Enholms."

"You had me when you were a senior?" I could barely get the words out.

"We lost it," she said, as if she was talking about a piece of luggage.

"Oh." My arms twanged with some kind of cramp, seemingly of their own volition, as if they were separate from me.

"The baby made your grandparents furious, his mother especially. She never liked me. But me, I loved Bill to distraction."

"Grandma?" I tried to picture Grandma furious, but it wasn't possible.

"So much charm!" She threw back her head, her mouth opened wide, and for a moment she looked almost young again, almost beautiful. "Your dad could charm the spots off a leopard. Why he was interested in me, quiet like I was, I never understood. But he was. He was crazy about me. I never would have let him, otherwise. I never let anybody else."

Duly noted. As eager as I was for her to finally tell me these things, I began to feel apprehensive. What little remained of my moral sense, my sense of self really, seemed to be crumbling. And her insisting she had told me these things? I wondered if she had had long conversations in her mind and thought I was there. No wonder we were often talking in parallel. I lit a cigarette.

Now her face fell. "So after we lost it, I kept seeing him, and when your grandmother found out, she pitched a fit. So I told Bill, it was them or me." She looked at her hands. "I guess she screamed at him, called him every name in the book, and his dad stood by her. So he drove to Flossie's house, told me to pack a bag, and we drove to Hutchinson, and I moved in with him."

"And then you got married." There was no time to stop and picture a screaming match, to strain to imagine Grandma in such a scene, no time to make Mother think about what she was saying. For now, I had to keep knotting the thread before she broke it off in her teeth.

"Not at first," she said.

"Holy crap," I whispered.

She seemed unfazed. "He always had a reason he didn't want to get married. It wasn't me, it was . . ." She laughed through her nose. Some color had returned to her face. "He thought the state didn't have any right telling people what to do in their private life. It was none of their business. He hated the government, just hated it."

I blinked as my memories of him took on a new color.

"Anyway, he was selling his pans even then. He started out doing demonstrations at the local stores on Saturdays." Now she pulled out a cigarette and lit it. "He was a salesman, all right. Wasn't long before he was on the road most of the time. There was talk about him having a woman in every town, but I knew better. That was lies."

Surely she was sober, I told myself, after some sleep and half a pot of coffee. Or sober enough to know what was real and what wasn't. "He supposedly had girlfriends?" I said.

She coughed for a while and stubbed out her cigarette. "They thought so—the family. They always blamed me."

"I can't believe this," I said, half to myself. "It feels like everything I thought I—"

"His folks pretty much disowned me," she said. "They sent *him* birthday cards, they called once in a while, but if I answered they hung up."

I struggled to reconcile the Grandma I knew with the one Mother was talking about. Something didn't square.

"So that went on for a while," she said. "And then I came up pregnant again, with you. I told him this time he had to marry me or I was going to leave him."

I blinked. "Would you have? Where would you have gone?" Would she have found a back alley somewhere?

"He thought about it for a couple of weeks, and then one day—"

"He *thought* about it?"

"—here he came with flowers and a ring, and we drove to city hall and got married. I called his mother, and she said—I'll never forget this—'It's about time. You pregnant again?' And here pretty soon came packages in the mail, wedding presents and baby things. Like nothing happened!"

"Holy shit." Thing after thing after thing.

Now Mother's face looked peaceful. "That summer. It was the happiest time of my life. I kept getting bigger and bigger, and I was so happy to be expecting. I didn't care, boy or girl, as long as it was normal. Bill was home almost every Tuesday to Thursday, between fairs, and he took up taking care of me and the house. He set up milk and egg delivery—we already had the ice man twice a week—and even groceries. It was a happy time. A blissful time. He bought me that table fan!" She pointed. "It saved my life those last few weeks."

I got goose bumps. I had never heard any of this.

"And then you were born, and you were the prettiest baby I ever saw in my life. You were an angel—all that hair, and those eyes. They started out blue, they only turned hazel later on. Everybody said how beautiful you were. And so good! You never squalled, you just whimpered a little bit when you were hungry, and Bill would carry you over to me to nurse. You got the hang of it right away. You were an easy baby, in other words. Bill loved to cuddle you, change you, bathe you. He was like a kid with a new toy. I would lay there with tears in my eyes, watching the two of you."

This was the daddy I remembered. I allowed myself to relax, although my throat felt hollow with dread. There was no telling what might come next. For now, though, I was drinking it in, chugging it. It was like overhearing Mother talk to her friends, the woman who did her hair, the women from work. I wondered what was causing her to open up like this. I thought again about the voices on the radio. Maybe the accident had opened a crack in everybody's lives, exposing old mistakes, lies, truths, losses, sorrows, regrets. Maybe people were taking stock. Maybe, as Mother had said, it had brought home to us, in the most brutal way possible, that you never knew when it would be too late.

Maybe that was it, The Meaning everybody was looking for: you never know when it will be too late. What a cliché. What a tragedy.

"He got a girl to come in to help me—Polish or something, she could hardly speak English—and then he was gone. On the road, sometimes two weeks in a row." Now her face crumpled. "I felt like I'd woken up from a dream, you know? I couldn't sleep, and everything smelled bad—I don't know why. I was tired all the time. I didn't want to do anything but sleep. I was miserable all that fall. Everything smelled bad. I let the girl go."

Now her face brightened. "Then two days before Christmas he drove up with the car full of presents, a tree, lights, the whole shebang. He pulled me off the couch and danced me around, and we Christmas'ed it up like crazy—until the big day itself. Bill was on the rug rolling you around, and I was sitting there watching you, and I just busted into tears. Bam, bawling like a, I don't know what. He squinted at me and came over there and asked me what the matter was, and I said I didn't know, which was the truth, and he blew his stack. My God, hadn't he given me the best Christmas ever, the house looked like Santa's workshop, he'd spent a goddamn fortune. And I just sat there and bawled. He yelled, I bawled, you started bawling, and I got the first sick headache of my life. Lord Jesus, it was godawful. It was like I got shot in my right temple. I threw up, my right nostril started running, my right eye started tearing. I couldn't lay down, I couldn't sit up, all I could do was walk around, pace, and I walked into the bedroom and started banging my head against the wall."

"You what?"

She looked unseeing in my direction. "Bill came in and yelled at me for a while, and then he turned on the light and looked at my face. I asked him to call the doctor, the one who delivered you, and he said it was Christmas night, had I lost my mind, and then he grabbed you and pushed me into the car and drove us to the hospital."

I cringed. I tried to catch my breath. I saw snowflakes swirling in the pale yellow beams of the old Nash's headlights.

"Well, they said I was run-down and underweight and dehydrated. They hooked me up to a bottle of sugar water and gave me a shot of vitamins and then a shot to help me relax, and, thank God, it knocked me out and I slept until the next afternoon. By that time his mother was there. She was still mad because we hadn't come to Wiley for Christmas and brought the baby."

She was talking about me. I was the baby. She was giving me the babyhood I had lost long ago. It was a melodrama (to hear her tell it), but at least it was a story. The beginning of a story.

"They made me drink a strawberry milkshake. I threw it up, and I kept heaving, heaving, heaving, until they gave me another shot. Which is why I don't drink them to this day."

This was true. Even the smell of strawberries made her sick.

"So the doctor said I had pneumonia and hysteria, and he wouldn't let me go home until I could keep down solid food and gain five pounds. Bill's mother said she was taking you home to Wiley with her until I got out, and Bill said he was going back on the road as long as I was in the hospital. I was so weak, I just laid there. I had no idea. Everybody left, and I was in this strange world. I felt like I was in outer space. I couldn't sleep—they stood there *talking* right outside my room all night. How was I supposed to sleep? It made me tense, and the next evening I came down with another sick headache. The doctor wouldn't give me a shot this time, so I pulled the needle out of my arm and started banging my head against the wall. They hooked me up again and gave me the shot."

I felt drool on my chin and wiped it off. Evidently I had lost muscle control of my jaw. Charlotte, who had been banging all this time to be let in, stuck her foot in the door to my brain.

"The next morning they brought breakfast, and when I smelled the eggs, I threw up all over the tray. The doctor examined me for pregnancy, but that wasn't it. He thought it was just nerves." She lifted the afghan and wrapped it around her shoulders. "Long story short, it took me three weeks to gain the five pounds. I didn't have another sick headache in the hospital, thank God. I don't know what might have happened. In those days they would put you in the looney bin for 'hysteria,' they really would." She looked at me. "But you've heard all this before."

"Mother, I have not. I had no idea of any of this." I slurped saliva and focused on keeping my mouth closed.

She frowned. "I could have sworn we had this very same conversation before. The very same. I remember it. What do you call it? Daya view? Is there any more coffee?"

"So they released you? I was still with Grandma?" I retrieved the empty coffeepot and returned to the sink. It felt good to have a solid oak floor under my feet.

"Bill came and took me home. It was morning, I remember, and I was *so* tired. I rested a while, we had lunch, and he left the house. I sat at the kitchen table with my face in my hands and felt the bile rise in my throat, and I had the awfullest feeling. My *mouth* watered, and this *pain* started in my eye. It felt like ripping my eye open. I went into the bathroom and took four aspirin. I started pacing in the hallway. Then I walked back to the kitchen, and I opened the icebox. I thought a cold compress might help. And there was Bill's beer. I never had liked it. Now I thought, why not? I'm dying anyway. So I drank three bottles, one after the other, and it was like a miracle—the pain turned dull. Not gone, but not as terrible. I didn't feel drunk—I didn't know how 'drunk' felt, actually. I just felt—normal. No boiling stomach, just this dull pain in my eye, no runny nose, no tears, no need to pound my head against the wall. Just normal, more or less. A little bit euphoric, maybe, since I felt like I had beaten back the headache without a shot."

I returned with the coffee. "My God, Mother." I could only marvel. Whoever this woman was, she was—I didn't know what. I was meeting her for the first time.

She warmed her hands on the mug. "I laid down on the couch and fell asleep. When Bill got back toward evening, I felt shaky, real shaky, but all right. We ate some supper and went to bed. An hour later I felt bad, so I got up and drank two beers and felt normal again. I stayed up until four or five in the morning and fell asleep on the couch." She took a sip of her coffee. "That house on Halsey. I loved it so much. It was so pretty. It broke my heart when I had to sell it. I can still see every inch of that house. The curtains in every room—I made them all, you know. And the slipcovers, and—"

"I know. You—"

"There's no regret in life like wishing you were back in a house you had to sell." She glanced sorrowfully around the apartment. "Anyhow, that's how it started. When Bill was gone I ordered extra beer, and when the boy came with the box, I hid the bottles around the house. When he was home and I couldn't get my three beers after lunch, I had this constant hum in my head, this feeling of the dentist's drill against my teeth, this sense that my eye was drying out, scraping against my eyelid, you know? You can't imagine. I would send him out for something and drink a beer as fast as I could, and then I'd chew a cinnamon stick to mask the smell and lay down in bed facing the wall. When he came to bed later, I would wait until he was asleep and then sneak into the kitchen or even in the backyard and drink until the noises and drills in my head went away." She swallowed three mouthfuls of coffee.

"So you—"

"Then about a month after I came home from the hospital, I asked Bill when he was going to go pick up the baby. I wanted you back, of course. I knew—"

"You did?"

"—you were growing, and I didn't want to miss anything. I knew you were the only one we were going to have."

Bang.

"God, it's hot in here." She eased the afghan off her shoulders. "Don't tell me I'm going through the change of life already." She pretended to laugh. "*Anyhow*, he asked me if I really felt up to it. 'Of course, I'm well now.' But he just went back to reading his paper, and I had a feeling I'd better not push it. I waited a few days and asked again. Well, this went on for a while. I called his mother, and she put me off, too. And meanwhile I was fighting off these headaches."

I groaned.

"To tell the truth, I was afraid to push it. I was afraid . . . I would get hysterical, and they'd—I'd lose you for good. I think your dad went to see you in Wiley a few times behind my back, I really do. He was crazy about you, like I said."

"I do remember that," I said, meaning I remembered how he had enjoyed me. But then I pondered her words—"crazy about you." Not love, but madness. What was it about the word "love" that she was—they all were—so afraid of? Then words appeared before my eyes: *They think it's fire, but it's water.* Charlotte's words. The real Charlotte, the woman at the Garden of Eden, not the one who lived in my body. Now I thought I glimpsed her meaning: They think love is going to burn them up, but actually it's going to bathe them, cleanse them, comfort them, slake their awful thirst. Is that what she meant? I felt I was teetering on the verge of understanding.

Mother rolled her eyes. "Oh, please. You can't remember that. You were just a baby."

"No, I mean I remember he—"

"So one day when he was on the road, I took a cab to the bank and took out some money and walked to the bus station and rode to Wiley and walked into the house. I acted kind of, you know, breezy—'Didn't I tell you, I thought I told you, I'm here to get Billie.' I had a little bag with toys in it." She tossed her head and waved her arms, not a gesture she would usually make. "But you weren't there, which scared the hell out of me. His mother had gotten tired of chasing after you—you were crawling by then. Wilma had you. So I went over there. I grabbed you up, and you started bawling like I was some stranger, and I almost did get hysterical, but I swallowed it back."

Of course she did.

"I got such a headache on the bus on the way home, I thought I was going to die," Dixie said. "It was snowing and dark when we got into town that night, and there wasn't a cab, so I walked all the way home carrying you." Now she pantomimed cradling a baby against her shoulder, shivering, blinking. "It was—I almost thought we wouldn't make it. It was so dark. I've never been so cold." Her arms shifted as if folding a blanket around the baby. I couldn't tell whether she was caught up in the memory or just trying to make me see it more clearly. I saw it all right. I saw the gray/blue snow whitening under the streetlights, graying/bluing again as we pressed on; I saw her leaning into the icy wind; I felt the cold. It was like a Russian folktale.

"When we got home I laid with you on my belly for a while to warm you up. Then I scrambled you an egg and put you to bed and drank several beers and banged my head against the wall." She acted out laying the baby on her belly, scrambling an egg, drinking, and banging her head. "And somehow I made it to the morning. I drank some more, and after while it went away." She looked at me, beaming. "You were the best thing. So good. You just played by yourself while I laid on the couch. I slept for most of the next two days."

I felt a chill in the hot room.

"Bill was awfully surprised when he got home and you were there, but he was glad to see you, I could tell. I felt like it was all over, like I wouldn't lose you again, you know? I had to stay away from doctors and hospitals, for sure. I found out if I drank my beers it could quiet the buzzing in my head, send it into my neck and then down into my spine. *That* I could deal with. I started having one with dinner, then another one in the evening, maybe one more before bed. Bill never said anything. Nobody did."

She stared at her coffee mug as if seeing it for the first time. "Of course I don't drink like that now," she said breezily. "Haven't for years."

"Mother." *The hell? What was that armful of empties I just carried to the trash?*

"I started smoking, too, which I liked from the first time I tried it." She winked at me, leaned over as if sharing a secret. "It was easy to just take your dad's Luckies. I started ordering two cartons a week. They only cost a dollar or two in those days. Your dad always had cash for beer and cigarettes. He played cards on the road, and sometimes he brought home hundreds of dollars."

I sat there with my mouth open.

In this moment it felt as if she were like a porcelain teacup. If you set her down too hard, she might crack, even shatter. I spoke softly, off-handedly. "Mother, have you ever seen a doctor about your headaches? And losing your balance, like you do sometimes?" I knew the answer, but I had to ask.

"Huh! Doctors! I swore off doctors—didn't you hear what I said? They nearly *killed* me. Doctors!"

"That was twenty years ago. Maybe—"

"And then one day I got a phone call that he'd keeled over dead with a heart attack in Goodland. You probably remember that."

"I was eight, Mother. Of course I remember." *Probably?* What was wrong with her? Had she noticed me so seldom as all that? Or was I more like a neighbor child she fed out of Christian duty, a shadow in her peripheral vision, as her beery, lackadaisical attitude so often made it seem?

I tried to keep my tone conversational and not scolding or, worse, self-pitying. I didn't want to break whatever spell was keeping her talking, opening my own life to me.

She went on as if I hadn't spoken. "Wouldn't you know it, I only had about twenty dollars in cash, and sixty-some in the bank, when he died. I wrote it all down. I figured I could make one more house payment and pay the electric and gas and phone, but I didn't know where I was going to get money for food for the two of us. *Food,* Billie. I was never so afraid in my life. That's when the real war with the family started."

I was listening hard. Not a word about grief, loss, sorrow. Only money. Brass tacks. Food. Jesus. I shuddered.

"First thing, I called Slim Hightower. Hightower Funeral? Bill played cards with him for years. Years. My God, you wouldn't believe it. Three hundred dollars to bring his body to town, fourteen hundred for the cheapest casket—my God. You wouldn't believe it. Embalming, suit, visitation room, chapel, casket spray, memory cards, cemetery plot, digging the grave, some concrete thing for inside the grave, hearse to the cemetery, filling *in* the grave—I don't know what-all. I said no thank you, and I went to Goodland myself so I could have him cremated without all the folderol. I called Wilma—her, I got along with all right, not great, but all right. His mother called me back. They wanted me to have him brought to Wiley and have a second helping of everything *there*. Bury him in the family plot. Thousands of dollars. I started laughing. Might as well have been Monopoly money. I told her I'd already taken care of things, and I'd send her some of the ashes. She screamed at me. Of course they would've 'helped' with the money. They would've *helped*. I knew what 'help' was. They would've *helped*."

Now, to my surprise, she began crying. I jumped up, hurried into the bathroom, and returned with a length of toilet paper.

She waved it off. "I'm not exaggerating. I didn't know how you and I were going to *eat* after that handful of cash was gone." She gulped several times. "You can't imagine not knowing how you're going to eat."

"But weren't you working? I thought—"

She nodded and wiped her nose on her sleeve. "Part-time, while you were at school, three or four hours a day. And it only paid a dollar and a quarter. I needed to make at least two-fifty, full-time. I had no idea how to get a job like that, how long it would take. But Floy gave me more hours and a dime raise, God bless him."

There was a silence.

"I remember riding the bus to Goodland," I said. "I had that bad sunburn from the Garden of Eden, and I was peeling."

"Clear the hell and gone—Goodland," she said, nodding. "All these *people* to talk to. I drug you with me. I had to let them see the *situation*. I had a *child*." She shook her head. "Anyhow, it cost two hundred dollars, I think—or three hundred, something like that, I don't remember exactly—to get him cremated, so that's what I did. I made payments."

I swallowed. "How come you didn't let them help?"

"No. They just—they would have *owned* me for the rest of my life. Our life. No-siree-bob."

"Oh." I thought about the Enholms taking me as a baby and not wanting to give me back.

"Well anyway, Frank gave me some money later on, bless his heart. Told me not to tell the rest of them."

In the silence that followed, I heard my own breath. "I feel old."

Mother laughed through her nose. "Wait'll you're forty."

I closed my eyes and laid my head back. My stomach growled, and I felt light-headed. I was close to tears. "You hungry?" I said. "I could fry some eggs." That was Grandma speaking; food wouldn't fix everything, but it was worth trying. Couldn't hurt.

"He helped me sell the car, and the house, too," Mother said. "So we could eat until I got a paycheck and a cheap place to live. Frank."

"We're out of bread, looks like."

"I'm not hungry, but you go ahead. I'll keep you company." She lit a cigarette.

"Mother?"

"What?"

I turned to her. "I'm sorry for what I said to you after Daddy died. I had no idea of any of this."

She blew out a lungful of smoke. It curled lazily upward, like ghostly ribbon candy, and dissipated across the ceiling. "But I've told you all this before."

"No, you haven't." I reached into the drawer underneath the stove and pulled out the frying pan. "Maybe you've thought it all through, as if I was there. But you never told me any of this."

"Well anyway, I don't know what you're talking about—what you said after Bill died. It's all a blur to me now."

I stared at the shiny bottom of the steel pan and the script lettering "WonderWare Waterless" in the center.

What I said was, I wished it was you that died and not Daddy. The words were sharp in my memory, unsaid now, but hanging in the room between us. Maybe she hadn't heard me that day after all. Maybe she wanted it—all of it—to be a blur. Who could blame her really? I felt a pang, the first time I had felt something for Mother, other than exasperation, for a long time.

With three eggs frying, I had to raise my voice to reach her across the room. "When Daddy asked you what you wanted out of life? On your first date at—"

She blinked. "What I wanted?"

"You told him, a husband and kids and a house."

"I did?" She cleared her throat. "Well, I got what I wanted then, didn't I?"

"You ever think about anything else?"

"No, why would I?" She sounded defensive. "I tried to give you a happy life, you know. Remember that trip to Colorado?"

"Yeah, that's when you told me about the airport."

"I did?"

"Yeah, when what's-his-name was golfing." I frowned and stuck out my tongue.

"He wasn't so bad."

"Whatever happened to him?" She hadn't mentioned him, or seen him, after the trip. As far as I knew.

"He left the company." She dropped her eyes.

And then, at that instant, for the first time, it occurred to me that she had put up with him, even slept with him, to give me the trip to Colorado I had always wanted. How else could we have gone? Dear Lord. I felt my skin crawl, I felt ashamed, and, at the same time, I was overcome with wonder. What else did I owe her? How could I not have noticed things happening in front of my eyes? Guilt began eating away at the edges of my wonder.

I said nothing. What could I say?

After a while, she spoke again. "Why are you like this? So *sour* all the time? Don't you want to be happy?"

"Me? I'm happy."

"Are you? Seems like you hate everything and everybody. Hate this town, hate your job— "

"No, I don't. I never said that."

"You complain all the time."

I do no such thing. I shoved the pancake turner under the eggs, breaking all three. I began stirring them furiously. "Maybe I don't *drink* enough. To take the edge off."

"What did you say?"

"Oh, please." I lifted the heavy pan and then looked around. I hadn't gotten out any plates.

Mother spoke softly, so quiet I had to strain to hear. "You don't have to stay here, you know. You could find a place of your own. Move to Colorado like you've always talked about."

"Right." Holding the pan in one shaking hand, I opened the cupboard and pulled down two plates. "And who would take care of you, clean up after you, keep you from burning the house down?" I realized I hadn't quite formed these thoughts before, and now that they were in the world, I felt shame for how self-pitying they were. I felt as if I weighed three hundred pounds and had the face of a monster. I loathed myself.

I slammed the plates on the table, but when I went to pour the eggs—half runny, half scrambled—I lost control of the pan and it flipped, scattering the greasy fragments on the table, the chairs, the floor.

Fuck you, I said under my breath.

Mother said nothing, and when I looked up, she was on the floor. I set the pan on the stove and ran over to her.

She tried to stand but fell back down. "Give me a minute, you're hurting my arm. Just a *minute*." Her chest was heaving. She pushed me away, and when I gripped her harder, she hit me in my shoulder, my arm, my face. Carelessly and hard. "Let me get my breath—breathe me, breathe me. Give me a minute! Oh, my hip. Bring me a stamp, a stamp of water, honey?"

CHAPTER 15
YOU AND ME BOTH

The waiting room at St. Elizabeth's was pink and turquoise—pink in the sheer curtains hanging at the windows, pink in the robe worn by the giant Jesus in the mural on the opposite wall, pale pink in the lamb He held in His arms and those at His feet. Turquoise in the trim above the bank of windows, and in the boomerang-shaped Space Age soffit on the ceiling. The gleaming floor was laid with beige-speckled linoleum tiles.

Each chair was flanked by a standing ashtray, the type that looked like an urn on legs.

I settled into the beige chair, lit a cigarette, and dropped the match into the receptacle. When I pressed the button, the metal halves parted and the match fell through. I released it, and the halves clanged back together.

I sat for some minutes smoking, until my head snapped back and I awakened. The cigarette, gone cold, was burned down to the filter, and a foul smell hung in the air. I discarded the butt and tucked my purse on the arm of the chair to serve as a pillow.

I was awakened again when a young woman wearing a nurse's uniform stepped out of the hallway into the room. Her eyes strayed from her clipboard, and she looked over her glasses at me. "Mrs. Enholm? Are you with Mrs. Enholm?"

"Yes," I said, wiping my eyes and scrambling to my feet. "My daughter. I mean, my mother."

She nodded.

"What is it? Is her hip broken?"

"We'll know more after the workup. We've given her something to help her relax."

"What do I do?"

"Well, you can see her if you'd like," she said doubtfully. "She's been asking for you."

Mother lay in the narrow bed, her eyes closed. Her breathing was noisy, a wet growl deep in her chest followed by a kind of bumble against her lips.

I stood over her for a minute, not wanting to wake her. Then I took the seat in the corner. I lowered myself carefully, but the orange plastic crackled. Still, she didn't move.

The nurse—her tag said Leota—leaned over the bed. "You have company."

Mother startled, blinking, and fixed her gaze on the nurse.

"Your *daughter*."

Mother opened her mouth but said nothing. When I rose and walked toward the bed, her eyes darted around the room, landing at last on me. She stared at me. "I *told* you."

I laid my hand on her forearm. I felt the two bones under the skin. "How—"

"I told you! No doctors!"

"I thought your hip—"

"Out of here. Out." She flung her arms wide.

I looked at the nurse, who had stationed herself on the other side of the bed.

"She's been complaining she wants to go home." She leaned

down. "You can't go home right now. We have to. Do. More. Tests."

I glared at her. "Will you excuse us?"

"I have to take her vitals."

"Not right now. I need to talk to my mother. Privately."

The nurse sniffed and left the room, swinging the door hard so that I felt the air brush against my neck.

"They took my *clothes.*" Mother strained to rise but fell back against the bed. She began struggling with the blanket, which was tucked tightly around her.

"Here." I pulled on the blanket.

"*Stop,*" she said. "It hurts, it *hurts.*" She moaned.

"All right, okay, hold on." Working more gently, taking smaller handfuls, I finally freed her and spread the bedding out flat. Both of us were breathing hard.

I blinked. When had she gotten so tiny?

"I'm not broken," she said.

"You aren't?"

"They put this thing in me." She raised her arm with the IV. "It makes me feel like a horse."

"What?"

"A cereal bowl then."

"You're not making sense."

Her chest rose and fell, rose and fell. "I think me—they're . . ."

"You need to sleep," I said. "You've been awake all night."

"I have to feed the galoshes."

"No, it's okay. I'll do it. Go back to sleep, okay? Close your eyes."

"Don't think you're fooling me. You're not." But she closed her eyes, and I watched as her face relaxed.

"It's only the drugs, I'm sure," I said to no one. I didn't know whom I was trying to convince—Mother or myself.

"Well, Dr. Gable thinks it's lupus, but my money's on MS," the doctor said. "Stands for multiple sclerosis, s-c-l-e-r-o-s-i-s."

"I've heard of that." I felt my heart move in my chest, a kind of shudder as if a finger had been run over its slick, raw surface.

"I just *fell*, for crying out loud." Mother banged her palm against the overbed table.

"What did the tests show?" I said to the doctor.

"Well, with this kind of thing, it's more a matter of ruling out other things." He dipped his head left and right until there was an audible crack. "And her history is classic."

"I'm *fine*."

"What history?" I said.

His eyebrows went up. "Well, she's been sick for quite a while now." He rubbed the back of his neck with one hand. "Headaches, weakness and numbness in legs, balance issues, falling, depression, blurred vision. Classic."

I swallowed.

"The headaches . . ." He waggled his hand. "But—no skin involvement, no fevers, no hair loss. So, like I said, MS. Or it could be just nerves. But my money's on MS."

"I'm *fine*. I just *fell*." She frowned. "He's just trying to put his kids through college on my nickel."

"We could take spinal fluid to be sure, but Mrs. Disagreeable here says no."

I couldn't imagine what she might have told him. "Mother—"

"Don't use that tone with me." She shook her head, oddly smiling. "I'm fine."

I looked at the doctor. "What if you don't do the spinal thing?"

Again he shrugged. "Well, we don't have to, if she doesn't want it. I've got a steak dinner riding on it, is all." He grinned.

"Steak dinner! Hear that?" Mother said. "And *he's* telling *me* I'm the one that has to quit smoking. And drinking." She laughed.

"She can have a beer with dinner if she insists, but that's all she drinks anyway, she tells me." He looked over his glasses at me.

I pressed my lips together and said nothing.

"I'm afraid we don't have a lot to offer, as far as treatment," he went on. "The prescription should help manage her pain, but if she's having bothersome symptoms after you get home, give us a call." He paused. "We've given her something to stabilize her mood."

He glanced at his watch. "Well, I have a patient. See you in six months, Dixie." He tipped an invisible hat and smiled.

"Mrs. Enholm to you," she said. "Like fun you will."

He laughed and glided out the door.

"I like him," she said. "He has a sense of humor."

Leota entered the room and reached for the blood pressure cuff attached to the wall.

"She's being released," I said. "Where are her clothes?"

Leota pulled down the apparatus. "He's keeping her another day, for observation."

"But he just now said—"

"I *have* her chart," she said. "Why don't you go home, take a bath, get some sleep." Almost without my awareness she was ushering me to the door. "Your mom will be fine."

"I'll be fine, I'll be fine," Mother crowed.

As I left the room I heard her begin to cough, and in a moment she was gagging and choking. I turned, but then I thought better of it and began walking briskly down the hall. I was desperate for a cigarette, but I felt it was better to wait until I reached the waiting room, or even the car.

After a bath, as hot as I could stand it even in the hot apartment, I fell into bed with the fan on.

In my dream, Joan sits on a blue couch between me and Charlotte, who has on her Supersweet Feeds cap. Joan is wearing a wedding dress. "Ever see a body moldering?" she says.

Charlotte spits on the ground, which is covered in pale blue carpet, and says, "They'll skin you alive."

"No, they won't." I repeat *won't* five or six times. I feel myself about to cry.

"Daddy used to do tricks with me," I say. "I mean, he still does. No, wait, he's dead now. No, he isn't, that's a lie."

"I don't lie," Charlotte says. "Did you feed the cat?"

A telephone rings.

Joan laughs. "I lie all the time, you stupid idiot. I'm lying now."

"They think it's fire, but it's water," Charlotte says.

"Fair enough," I say.

Joan says, "Don't listen to your mother."

"He is *not* dead," I shout. Joan's hair is in flames. A telephone rings.

Charlotte extends a cottonwood twig toward me, but when I reach for it, it turns into a snake. A telephone rings.

The telephone had been ringing over and over. I fought my way out of bed and staggered to the phone, which hung on the wall next to the stove in the kitchenette.

"It's you," said the voice. "I've been calling and calling."

I cleared my throat. "Clayton. Hi."

"What's wrong?"

I cleared my throat again. "Nothing. Well, my mother's in the hospital."

"Fuck," he said. "What happened?"

"She, uh—we thought her hip was broken, but evidently it's not."

"Oh."

"What time is it? Can I call you back?" The wall clock read twenty-something after three. The windows were dark.

"Um, this'll just take a minute."

I stretched out the curly cord seven feet to reach my purse on the couch. I pulled out a cigarette and lit it. That first drag after sleep is so sweet.

"Billie?"

"Yeah, okay." Now I remembered what the doctor said.

"Listen, I'm worried."

"What about?" I coughed. *My money's on MS.*

"Well, you know."

I rubbed my eyes. "Yeah." The secret. I walked to the sink and ran a glass of water. The moment it touched my lips I realized how deeply thirsty I was. "Listen, is it actually three-something in the morning?" I thought about Mrs. McKutcheon and her children downstairs.

He cleared his throat. "Sorry."

I coughed and drank and refilled the glass.

"Listen, I've been thinking," he said. "I could maybe get in serious trouble."

I drank and drank. "Yeah," I said at last. "Maybe. I don't know."

There was a silence. I heard myself swallowing, and on the phone line I heard ghost voices, clicks, sonorous tones.

"I need, I need to know what you, um, are planning to do," Clayton said finally.

"That's a good question." I surprised myself by saying this. The casual cruelty of it took my breath away. "No, I mean—"

"Jesus, Billie."

"I mean—I have a lot of stuff going on. The wreck, your thing, my mother, stuff I just found out. I don't know what I'm going to do about any of it."

He sighed. "I'm sorry I ever told you."

"You and me both." It sounded harsh, harsher than I intended. "Look, maybe the thing is, you ought to come forward yourself."

"You don't know what you're asking."

"Your dad—I mean, your uncle—he might be mad for a while, but he's crazy about you, right? He'll stand by you."

"You mean mad at me for staying out all night drunk, or the other thing?"

"Well, both. But he would walk through fire for you, wouldn't he? Isn't that why you were trying to spare him in the first place?"

There was a long silence. "Yeah, I guess so," he said quietly. "But me, I've been in trouble before, you know? What if . . ."

I closed my eyes and leaned my forehead against the cupboard. "Maybe he would—you know—just let it go? Keep it just between the two of you. For your mom's sake."

"I don't know. I've thought about it. But it seems like a chickenshit thing to do. He's a straight shooter, you know? It would be like I was putting it on him."

"Yeah, I know. You put it on me."

"Yeah." The phone line clicked quietly for what seemed like a long time. "Listen, Billie. What if we went to Colorado, you and me?"

"What?"

"To get away. Wait, I don't mean that like it sounds. To go someplace where you'd be happy, like you said at the marker. You know."

All I could say was, "That's nuts." I put out my cigarette and coughed.

"Hear me out, though. I been asking around. I know a guy—well, my boss at the car repair, he knows a guy—who'll give me a job. In Limon, Colorado."

"Really." Even as I said it, though, my brain shifted to calculate mode. With two of us working, we might be able to make it. Rent a little place—

"Shit." I heard him swallow, a beer no doubt.

"What?" I said.

"Do you ever mean anything you say? Or are you just a bullshitter like everybody else?"

There was a silence. Me, who'd hated bullshitters for as long as I could remember.

Could it happen, though? For a minute my lungs cleared of

cigarette smoke, and I smelled pure cold blue air. I felt icy water drops on my arm; out of the corner of my eye I caught the flash of a silver trout belly.

"I'm sorry," I said. "It's the middle of the night. I don't think well in the middle of the night." It took an effort to form the words, and I spoke slowly. I wanted to make time slow down.

"Do you want to go to Colorado, or not?"

"That—that's not the question."

"What is, then?"

I lit another smoke and coughed for a while. The question was, of course, did I want to take off with some guy I hardly knew, and who scared me a little, to some blank, unknown future. The other question was, could I leave my sick mother to fend for herself. "Look, we can talk later. Call me back in the morning."

"I'll *be* there in the morning. I'm leaving, gonna get gas. I have some money."

"No!" It echoed in the room. "Mother gets out of the hospital tomorrow. I have to—"

"Pack your stuff." He hung up before I could say anything more.

I held the receiver away from my face and stared at the earpiece as if I could make something come out of it that made sense. "What the hell, Clayton," I said. Then I hung up and ran to the bathroom and peed like I would never stop.

I lay on the couch and tried to go back to sleep, but my brain was clicking and churning, burning, and that old sensation of insects crawling under my skin returned. Charlotte, angry. My face went red, my scalp burned.

I got up and paced, smoking, thinking. I did some dishes and ran the dust mop. I got dressed. I half expected that Clayton wouldn't show up.

But too soon, I heard the clanking muffler and the engine run-on. Then ticking.

Something I remembered from an old movie told me not to let him trap me in the apartment—it felt like I was operating on pure instinct—so I ran out the door. From the landing I saw him at the bottom of the steps. The sun was just rising, and he looked so young in the half-light. My teeth began chattering. I hugged myself.

He looked up at me and didn't say a word. As I stood there, he climbed the steps halfway up. I skipped down to meet him—I didn't want anyone to hear raised voices—and he stood with his left foot on one step and his right foot on the step below.

"You look beautiful," he said.

I sputtered; it was all I could do not to burst out laughing. If I had a hundred guesses, I couldn't have imagined him saying that. One, because it wasn't true, and two, because it sounded so corny.

He reached out to take my hand, and I pulled back and frowned at him. "I am *not*."

He grinned. I guess he thought I was flirting with him in a spunky-girl-movie kind of way.

Now my rational/suspicious/paranoid brain spit out an obvious question: did he want to get me out of Kansas so I couldn't tell people his secret connection to the accident? My arms broke out in goose bumps. Visions of murdered twenty-year-old women behind gas stations covered with tarps. I recalled his pleasure in that boy's broken hand, his efforts to smash beer bottles and rocks against the trees. *They give me to my uncle.*

He turned sideways and climbed past me, heading up the stairs, but I reached out and stopped him. "What are you doing?"

"Getting your stuff, what else?"

"No."

He looked down at my hand on his arm, and then he looked

me in the eye. "What do you mean, no? We're going." His face turned dark, and his tone was angry, and for a split second I thought he might throw me off the steps. I dropped my arm. My whole body wobbled.

Now he stepped down to just above me. "Don't you still feel like you did—like you need to get away from these, these small-town people?" He seemed to have memorized his pitch. "Don't you remember how great Colorado was, the snow and mountains and rocks and everything? Like you said?"

I opened my mouth, but no words came.

He drew a deep breath and let it out. "Don't you remember being a kid?" he said. "How bad it hurt—how bad it hurt to know you didn't belong where you was at?" His voice broke. His eyes glistened as he leaned toward me.

I shrank back. "Fuck. You don't know the half . . ." I saw myself standing with him in a mountain meadow. It was snowing, utterly silent, as the flakes swirled. Crisp, no wind. The nearby trees sighed.

A wisp of wood smoke stung my eyes. Broke my heart.

"I want to," I said, almost wailing. "I want to."

He brightened like daybreak. "Then let's go, Billie. We'll—"

I gripped the handrail. "Not *now*," I said, my voice—my self—both wavering and mollifying. "Not today. I can't."

His face crumpled, and he flopped down on the step.

Now my head was higher than his. I swallowed. "My mother has MS. Multiple—"

"I know what that means." He didn't sound surprised. At that moment I remembered he had told me his mother died young of breast cancer. We were both half-orphans.

"Well then, you know why I can't go. Not now."

"You don't want to go with *me*." The words seemed to savage his face.

"No, no, that's not it."

He dropped his eyes and stared at his hands. There was a silence.

"She'll get worse." I felt the breath leave my lungs. "She won't be able to *do* for herself."

He frowned, still looking down. "That's awful." He flicked something off one shoe. "But are you sure . . . you want to piddle your life away taking . . . ?"

I sucked air in. I shook my head. I told myself I didn't need to justify myself to him, I'd never promised him anything. But his words had sent me someplace I hadn't really been before. I remembered how Mother was behaving—was it only yesterday?—when I called the ambulance: unable to stand up, incoherent, angry, hitting me. She would get worse. I pictured her with a cane, then crutches, then a walker, then a wheelchair. I imagined her calling my name in the night. I imagined her incontinent, ashamed, raging. I didn't know if that was how it would be, but it seemed likely. It could be that way; it could be worse. And meanwhile, day by day, I would be turning more sour, bitter, dry. In a way, staying in Hutch with her was riskier than this wild idea of Clayton's.

I walked to the bottom of the stairs, and he followed me.

Not now, I had told him, trying to placate him; but it was clear as clear to me that it was now or never. If I didn't go now, I never would.

I looked around at our block, and I listened for a moment to the early birds chirping, and I knew it had to be never. It had to be. I didn't know why, I scarcely understood it myself, but I knew it had to be.

"You're not going," he said.

I shook my head and dropped my eyes. "I can't."

"You can, and you know it."

I couldn't look him in the eye, and so it was a surprise when he took my chin in his hands and kissed me. His mouth was surprisingly soft and sweet, and the kiss felt both tender and insistent. In a flash I saw the two of us, with a baby, just like Mother and Daddy, and I wondered, Could I? I thought of the things Mother had told me, the secrets, her suffering, her fears, and no. Just no. Not me. In my next life, maybe.

I needed something, desperately needed it—to quiet Charlotte, to find a way to gain the acceptance I craved. But this wasn't it.

Tears came. Clayton dropped his arms, turned away, and trudged to the pickup.

Even as he slammed the door and started it up and ground it into reverse, I longed to be sitting on that crackly, worn seat, bouncing out of town, setting out west in the early morning light. With a flower in my hair.

And then words came to me, absent thought: *I love her.*

What? my brain said.

I love her.

I thought, *Who am I even talking about?* But the feeling, the wonder of it, overcame everything. *I love her.*

This is what it feels like.

It hit me: it wasn't about being loved; it was about loving. The luckiest ones are the ones who find someone to love with their whole heart, or most of it. It was good to be loved, but it was necessary to love.

I don't know why it struck me like that. All I know is that something in me—some blood cell, some string of cilium, some crevice of bone marrow, some molecule of brain protein—zigged when it usually zagged, and I felt something, and I didn't suppress the feeling, and things changed.

Chapter 16

Not Long Wet, Not Long Dry

"My mom's having a baby." The piping voice came from a little girl who suddenly was standing knee-to-knee with me. I was sitting in the same waiting room and the same chair as yesterday. I had been up, fretting, half the night, and now Clayton was gone. I was nodding off, exhausted to the point of collapse.

The child was wearing dirty white tights and a faded Flintstones T-shirt two sizes too small. I saw her belly button through the cloth. She looked about four. "We don't know if it's a boy or a girl," she said. "Mom doesn't care, as long as it's normal."

"Oh."

"I want a girl." She eyed the afghan in my lap.

I hesitated. Children this age tended to be talkative. Well, it would help pass the time while they did the paperwork to release Mother. "Either way, you'll be their big sister."

"How do you know?"

"That's how it works." I wondered how Mother was doing. Were they dressing her yet? She hadn't wanted me in there while they were attending to her.

"You don't *know* me, though." The girl leaned her arm on the arm of my chair, her face close to mine. I glared at her arm.

She pulled back and looked around the room. I could see her thinking. "Gran wants a boy."

I lit a cigarette.

"Do you know my dad?" the girl said.

"No." I flicked my ash into the ashtray that stood next to my chair.

"We live at Gran's house now."

The child was becoming a nuisance. "You know, you shouldn't be talking to me. I'm a stranger. Didn't your mother— "

"My dad smokes," the girl said. "My mom and Gran don't. They think it's *filthy*."

"Did you hear what I said?"

"We have a cat. Gran says a cat will steal a baby's breath."

"I don't think so." What if Mother had trouble getting dressed? What if she didn't like the outfit I brought? I cringed as I pictured her arguing with the nurse.

"It's gray all over except for one foot is white." The girl did a clumsy pirouette. "Do you have a sister?"

"No."

"A brother?"

"No. Neither one." I glanced around for a magazine.

"My mom has a sister. She's my aunt."

"And your aunt's kids are your cousins."

The girl's eyes got big. "How do you *know* that?" She stared up and down my face, forehead to chin. Then she turned abruptly and began flipping the closures on the ashtrays, watching as the contents fell into—for all she knew—the bottom of the world. *Clang, clang, clang.* Then she backed up, feeling her way, and opened and closed the now-empty containers. *Clang, clang, clang.*

I watched her. The child was at the age before memory began. She had no patina, no "manners," no filter. She was like a talking animal. From some deep brain crease came an old memory. When I was four or five, I'd stolen a pipe-cleaner giraffe at a house belonging to friends of my parents, a couple who had a girl my same age. I felt terrible about taking it, and as soon as we got home I had wrapped it in newspaper and stuffed it in the bottom of the trash can in the kitchen. Now I envisioned this ashtray-clanging child as a toy giraffe, with a tuft of red hair on her forehead. I wondered, will I ever get over thinking up shit like this? Would Charlotte ever stop haunting me?

I blinked, and I jumped a bit when I realized the child was leaning in close again, her face inches from mine. "Are you dreaming?" she said.

"Would you mind?" I gestured, and she pulled back a little.

"Do people sleep with their eyes open?" she said.

"What?" I lit a cigarette and took a deep drag.

"Do you have any gum?" she said. "I didn't have time to brush my teeth."

"No. Sorry."

She leaned toward me again. "How do you keep from catching your face on fire?"

"One time I caught my sweater on fire."

"You did?"

"Actually it was my mother's sweater." It could be just nerves, but his money was on MS.

"You have a mother?"

"Yes."

"Where's she at?"

"She, um, she'll be here soon."

The girl sat back down. "Is she having a baby?"

"What? No." I got out a tissue and wiped my nose.

"Do you know my dad?"

"No, I don't. I told you."

The girl looked at me doubtfully. "He broke his shoulder. At work."

"Oh. Sorry."

"He had it in a—a—a thing. I forget." The girl sighed and leaned back in the chair.

A few minutes passed in silence, and then the girl slipped off her chair and walked slowly around the perimeter of the room. Then she extended her arms and pretended to fly like an airplane, her arms outstretched. After a moment she sped up, and she ran in circles on the floor, faster and faster. Her face turned red, and she smiled broadly. Such a simple game, one I had seen a hundred times. Kids did that. I myself had probably done it as a child. But the word that came to mind wasn't *simple*. It was *pure*. Pure flight, pure existence, pure feeling. Life wasn't complicated when you were four. When tears came, I surrendered to them. After all, I had only just realized that I loved my mother. Now I knew how it felt, but I was still contemplating what love was, what it required, what it demanded, what it promised, what it meant.

The girl widened the circles, and, when she approached me, she inadvertently kicked the ashtray. It tipped over and banged on the floor, and it opened and disgorged detritus and ash, but I saw only the child, whose airplaning changed abruptly to helicoptering. I leapt from my chair and grabbed the girl by the waist, and our momentum carried the two of us in a half circle until we stopped, and the child, breathless, let out a whoop too loud for the room, and we collapsed on the floor, laughing and snorting and hysterical.

My eyes full, I watched as the laughing girl turned into a giraffe, and I did not resist the hallucination. I just felt it. No thought, not really. I *felt* felt it. I was breathing hard, and inside

I was laughing/crying. I was hugging a giraffe, without a care in the world. Without a thought, an analysis, a comparison/contrast, a structure, a prediction, a prophecy, a thought experiment, nothing. Nothing. Nothing.

Now a nurse, a new one, middle-aged, materialized above us.

The girl stood up and brushed off the seat of her pants. She leaned forward, her eyes big. "Is it a boy or a girl?"

"What?"

Just then an older woman, wearing a pair of fluffy slippers and a trench coat over pajamas, emerged from the hallway. Her face was flushed. "Heidi," she said. "There you are. I been—"

"Gran!" the girl shrieked. She turned and ran to her, throwing her arms around the older woman's waist.

"We got us a wienie," the woman said, beaming.

"We did? The baby?"

Their excited voices trailed off as they walked away down the hall. The girl didn't look back.

The nurse addressed me, still on the floor. "Enholm?"

I nodded. I moved my arms as if to make a floor angel, but then I thought better of it. I crawled over and stood up the ashtray and then climbed into my chair.

"I need you to sign some papers," she said.

"You bet." I took the clipboard, and time stopped. Of course I kept moving, signing where I was told, chatting with the nurse—hadn't it been nice lately? Not as hot as before—but my mind was in another place. A place where time—the past, the future—was space, and so I had wandered, lost, I always had, and I had kept gathering and regathering my past and future pain all unawares, carrying it like the bee carries pollen. Present pain, which was always—is always—outside of time, was the worst of all, and that's why I had tried so hard to push it into the past or the future. I had been so afraid of the pain, and all my feelings felt like pain. And so I had always been afraid. The logic was inescapable.

They think it's fire, but it's water, Charlotte reminded me. I felt her words cascading over me, cool, pure, calming. Sweet.

Now I looked up, and there was Mother in a wheelchair being pushed by an orderly, a good-looking guy, young, wearing thick black glasses. Mother's hair was clean and brushed, and she looked rested, even radiant. She was laughing and flirting with the orderly, and he was smiling in a kindly way. I smiled, too, grateful almost to tears that he wasn't being condescending to her.

"There she is!" Mother said. "That's my daughter. I didn't know if she'd be here or not."

I let it pass. "You ready?" I stood up, extending the afghan. It stank of cigarette smoke.

"What's that?" she said. "Why'd you bring that ugly thing? What do I look like, some old lady?" She turned her face upward, murmuring something to the orderly, but I couldn't make out what she was saying.

I bent my knees and squatted in front of her, gripping the arms of the chair. I was trembling, and my voice was breathy. It was so, so hard. "Mother, listen to me."

She lowered her head.

"I love you," I said.

She frowned. "Of course I do. Don't be ridiculous."

I laughed a little and cried a little. Of course. It was not going to be easy.

"She has to stay in the chair until she's at the car," the orderly said. He pushed up his glasses.

I stood up and nodded. The nurse held the doors open as we emerged into the sparkling sunshine.

Far overhead, clouds shaped like fish-on-fish-scales extended across the sky. I hadn't seen clouds like that before. They were odd, white on blue on white, an aperiodic tessellation if I wasn't mistaken.

"Nice day," Mother said.

"Isn't it, though?" I said. "Look at those clouds."

She looked up, squinting. "'Mackerel sky, mackerel sky, not long wet, not long dry.'"

"Where'd you hear that?" I said.

She shook her head. "Long story."

"What does it mean?"

"Mean? Just what it says." She looked at me and frowned, and then she shrugged. "Whatever something is, don't get to liking it. It's bound to change."

I laughed. There was so much to learn.

Chapter 17
The Past

MS is a progressive disease. Within a year we had to move, because Mother couldn't make it up the steps anymore. We rented half of an old house on Avenue A that had been split vertically into a duplex; she slept downstairs in the living room, and I slept upstairs in the bedroom, except nights when she couldn't sleep. Then I sat with her, massaging her aching feet, her spasming thighs. I quit smoking early on, but I held the cigarette for her when she wanted it. For a long time I worked at the office in the mornings and brought the books home to work on in the afternoons, and when we were out of money I called Uncle Frank, bless his heart, who always sent a check. This went on for fifteen years, until Mother died in 1982 at age fifty-five. Frank paid for her cremation, and I took her and Daddy's ashes and scattered them under the stars at the crop duster airport out by Wichita. By some miracle it was still there. Lots of things like that, signifiers of some other life, are gone now.

Not gonna lie, taking care of her was hard. I had to learn how to laugh at things that used to make me angry, how to humble myself to learn things I didn't know (or want to), how to embrace imperfection and lack of control, how to let things slide off my back. Obviously this went against all my instincts. I had to accept, without understanding, that you could love someone and still be mad as hell at them, bored as hell by them, and disgusted by their body, their fluids, their words, and their actions. Toward the end Mother slid into dementia. She remembered things and then forgot them, told me things and then denied them, asked for things and then rejected them. But then she would get better, and she might be up and around for days—good days—and then not be lucid again for weeks. She might fly into a rage for no reason. And she grew more physically disabled day by day. I had never felt so tied to anyone—or so alone.

As her health worsened I was increasingly conscious that she was my last remaining immediate family member on earth. For the first few years I often thought about the baby she lost, whose existence I only learned about after the Bison Creek accident, and I wondered what it would have been like to have had a sibling. Would we have given each other what we didn't get from our parents? Would said sibling have been an oddwad like me? Would we have shared the burden of caring for Mother, or would he/she have reneged? Or would I have been the one to flake out? I had learned long ago that I could stand anything for a minute or an hour. But could I stand this existence for an indeterminate time? Pointless, of course, but there you go. Ruminating pointlessly has been one of my longtime hobbies.

What I needed in those years, among other things, was therapy. It seems obvious now, but for a long time I was repelled by the very idea. You have to understand that every person in the family, including Mother, thought the practice of psychiatry was, at best, quackery, and, at worst, *the work of the devil*—the scariest thing you could to say about something. They believed that people having mental health issues were faking; it was an excuse for not doing something you didn't want to do, or for doing something you wanted to do that you shouldn't. *Take what you can get and be satisfied.* And in my reading, psychology as a practice seemed to have a tenuous connection to the world as I knew it. So I had come by this revulsion honestly.

Thus, the first person I had to convince was myself. Change was in the air. Enlightenment—mass media be praised—was available. Oprah and Ann Landers—two actual, seemingly ordinary women who had made themselves rich and famous, who were on TV and in the paper every day—blasted the message on repeat: get help get help get help. Ann Landers even told you how: look up "mental health" in the phone book. It crept into my consciousness. I thought about it off and on. What if Charlotte, and all that flowed from her, was a brain thing and not a character flaw? Would she be amenable to strategic negotiation? If I went there, could I come back as myself? I wondered. But nope.

Then one day at work, when Mother was still alive, I started crying for no reason. I ducked into the bathroom and sat there sobbing quietly for an hour, the whole time asking myself what the hell was the matter with me, nothing had happened that morning to bring this on, stop this stupid *boo-hoo why am I crying* nonsense—really, if anything, it was *funny*—until my boss tapped on the door and asked if I was all right. I pretended I was sick and left for home, and I started crying again the moment I got into the car. In the driveway I sat in the car and smoked and cried and told myself, well, if you're batshit crazy, how are you going to take care of Mother?

I heard Charlotte cackling in the big elm tree out front. You can say a lot of things about Charlotte, but she was no quitter.

The pay phone at Dillons still had a phone book hanging by a coiled metal cord, and "mental health" took me to the number of the county mental health clinic. The woman who answered the phone asked me what was going on. "I started crying at work and couldn't stop." She put me on hold and then told me she could get me in tomorrow at ten-thirty. Easy peasy. At that first appointment I learned it would cost sixty-five dollars a session, and that day I applied for welfare, food stamps, disability (for Mother), the whole ball of wax.

God did not strike me dead.

Then every Tuesday at two o'clock I told Mother I was seeing the dentist, or meeting a friend for coffee, or picking up cigarettes, and I went to the therapist and slit my torso from clavicle to pubic bone and examined my innards. That was nothing new for me, of course, but now I had a trained professional to point out where to look. It made all the difference.

She asked me early on, "How did you feel when your father died? You were only eight."

Well, I could hardly get my breath. All I could think was, *my father died when I was only eight. My God.*

I burst into tears and cried for maybe twenty minutes, crying/laughing at myself all the while because I was being a big bawlbaby, and then crying some more. Okay, maybe longer than twenty minutes. She gave me tissues and sat calmly, and when I finally quieted, she said, almost drily, that evidently I had been holding that in for a while, and I laughed so hard I snorted spit and snot all over myself. "Our first goal might be for you to learn how to sit with your feelings," she said. I know you've probably heard that kind of thing all your life, and to you it may sound like psychobabble, but maybe you didn't have as ruthless a Charlotte as I had. To me it was a revelation. That you would be in pain and just let yourself feel it instead of ignoring it or suppressing it or denying you were feeling it or converting it into racking physical pain and naming it after a person you met once and could never forget.

My therapist kept telling me, week after week, that my feelings were real, they were true, they mattered, and I needed to respect them. Accepting that was hard for me, awfully hard. It seemed self-centered, conceited, stuck-up—all the things I had learned not to be, at home, at school, everywhere I had been. I struggled with it for a long time. I'm still not all the way there, and maybe I never will be. I have to sit with that.

I told her about the intense physical and emotional moods I sometimes got into, but I didn't describe them in detail or explain about the caterpillar on my brain synapses, and I certainly didn't tell her about naming the thing Charlotte, nor about that time on the roof with Joan. For the two years I saw her, I told her enough to get what help I thought she could give me. I feel sorry for therapists. It must be like trying to open a coconut with a toothpick.

But she did mention one day that it was common for MS patients to self-medicate with alcohol. It was known to relieve some patients' symptoms for a while.

Oh.

Mother's death coincided with the emergence of the home computer. I bought a Ferguson Big Board kit, which included a circuit board and an assortment of transistors and capacitors, and built one for myself, learning electronics along the way, and in the late nineties I was the one at work who installed and configured the PCs and software, and later Wi-Fi and whatnot, and eventually I got a job with a big software company you may have heard of, working remotely.

But there I go, getting ahead of myself again.

It took a while for us to find out what PCs were good for, which we figured out when the Internet came along. The net was just made for people like me, and naturally I was all over it (still am), slurping up information by the bucketful; and when I read people's stories or watch their videos about being on the northwest quadrant of the spectrum, I think I recognize myself. I don't know whether I am or not. I don't think anybody knew about it when I was in therapy, and certainly not when I was a kid sitting alone in the hallway puzzling over analogies and narrating my life in my head.

Believe me, it was a trip coming home from therapy and walking into the house and stubbing out the two or three cigarettes Mother had left burning in the big frilly ashtray on the coffee table. Two different worlds.

The other thing I got out of therapy was the need for everybody to find the people in the world who understand them. After much talking, I realized Daddy was one of those people for me, and Harriet from first grade was an honorary member; Grandma was a part-timer, although I've never solved the mystery of her and Mother's mutual dislike. Joan, I don't know about—if she had lived, maybe, eventually, we would have been close if we could have found a way to tell each other the truth about ourselves. I can't picture how that would have happened—God knows she had built a considerable shell around herself—but if it would have, our bond would have been spectacular. It's not wishful thinking to think that. I know enough now to know it's true, if unlikely.

Mother, sadly, wasn't one of those people for me. You get what you get.

About six months before Mother died, on impulse I bought her a parakeet, and she got so attached to that little guy—she named him Buddy—that I was flabbergasted. She talked to him endlessly in her gravelly voice. He picked up a few phrases. Pretty boy. Billy boy. Mommy boy. Buddy-buddy-buddy. She loved to free him from his cage and let him fly around the apartment and perch on the curtain rods or the TV or a windowsill and then take off and land on her finger while she made kissy sounds. She taught him to say "Buddy wanna beer," and she would stick her finger into the can and let him catch a drop just before it let go.

Mother slept in a rented hospital bed under the living room window, and every morning she insisted on getting up, getting dressed, and reclining on the couch to watch TV. She loved *The Price Is Right*.

One day while I was ironing in the living room and she was lying on the couch watching TV, she asked me to let Buddy out. He made his usual rounds and then perched on the back of the couch. He jabbered for a while and then slipped down onto her shoulder, and I looked up just in time to see him open and close his beak while he gently nibbled her cheek. Mother sighed and put down her cigarette, and she closed her eyes and smiled, and a tear gathered in the corner of one eye and found its way down her face. Then a remarkable thing happened. She seemed to lose the ability she'd always had to arrange her posture, her hands, and her expression to present as the ideal, stoic midwestern homemaker, and you could see her emotion on her face as clear as clear. Pure naked bliss—of all the feelings, probably the last thing she would want to reveal.

I set down the iron and stared. Buddy didn't seem to notice the tear, clinging now to her chin. He kept caressing her cheek, emitting a series of soft sounds somewhere between a purr and a chuckle.

It was as if a doll's face had cracked open to unmask a living human face.

My thoughts came fast: If Mother could have been my deliverer, she would have been. I got what I got, but so did she. Orphaned as a teen, pregnant out of wedlock, shunned by the only family she had, widowed young, sick for who knows how many years, struggling to make rent on a woman's pay—was it any wonder she was exhausted, inattentive, noncommittal? In a flash I understood that, in almost every way, I myself had fallen far short of the ideal daughter she had longed for. I saw how much I had in common with her—how much an outsider she, too, must have felt—and it took my breath away.

Almost the last thing she said to me—in the hospital, months later—was, "You'll never know how much I love you." For a split second I shrank back. Why now? Why not years ago? And why that half-assed "you'll never know," dooming me to writhe in that flattened, arid landscape, perishing of thirst?

But only for a split second. Then I was glad she had said it, finally, no matter how awkwardly, instead of waiting until it was too late. I extended my hand and touched her face lightly with the back of my index finger, caressing her cheek with my nail.

"I love you, too, Mother," I said to her, and the ends of her lips curled upward.

"Can you get me a cigarette?" she whispered.

"How about if I fix your lipstick first?" I said, knowing it wouldn't be long now.

One summer day about two years after Mother died, I was sitting in my car in Carey Park eating lunch when I saw a man drop off three kids, all boys, at the swimming pool. They jumped out of the SUV almost before he got it stopped. He leaned out the window and shouted, "Don't get wet, you guys!" and they rolled their eyes as they ran, their swim trunks flopping around their knees. Halfway to the pool the oldest one shouted, "Love you, Dad!" and the other two echoed him. "Love you more!" he yelled back.

It was as if they were enacting a scene from a TV sitcom. How extravagant. No real kids—no real fathers—said that kind of thing. As I may have mentioned, I had never heard anyone actually say "I love you" or even "love you" in the normal course of a normal day.

But now I had been to therapy, and so I asked myself, what if it wasn't a TV show? What if it was—what if it could be—actually real? Against all logic, I felt my hand pressing the car door handle, and I had to trot the last few steps to reach him as he was backing out.

"Wait," I said.

He startled, of course, but he stopped the truck and put it in park, his big hairy right arm draped over the wheel. A marine emblem tattoo peeked out of the sleeve of his T-shirt. He wiped his mouth on his shirt and smiled.

I could hardly breathe. I didn't know what to say. It felt like I was on fire. I almost said, "I think you may be one of my people, there aren't that many of us," but instead I said, "Hi."

"Do I know you?" he said in a friendly way. He had long Jesus hair, wavy, and red with one or two white glints. A full beard.

I shook my head. Honest to God, I stood there without moving. I was about to spontaneously combust, and I wanted to run away, but I couldn't move.

"You look like you're wound a little tight," he said, not in a judgy way but more to start a conversation.

"I do? I am?"

He reached down and shut off the SUV and got out. "Let's walk," he said.

I told him my name, and he told me his (Tom Lambert), and we talked about our families, school, weird dreams, work, revealed truth, the Garden of Eden in Lucas, giant dictionaries, food, Colorado, sports, animals—all the usual things. He was divorced, he told me, and he wasn't in any hurry to get married again, although he and his ex got along for the sake of the boys.

We walked along in the dry crackling grass, in and out of the sunshine, in and out of the shade of the big cottonwoods.

I asked him if he knew that some cottonwood twigs have a star inside if you cut them open on a growth line. He didn't. Lived in Kansas all his life and never had heard that. Wonders never cease, he said.

He looked at me. "What me and the boys like to do is, we go fishing on Cow Creek. I know a guy out at the Bible Camp. We load up our sleeping bags and Coleman stove, and we fish for bullheads with stink-bait. We gut 'em and roast 'em whole."

My gorge rose. "Don't they taste like mud?"

He smiled. "Don't overthink it, Billie. We hardly ever catch anything anyway."

I bent over laughing/crying.

He pulled out a hanky. "Want to have supper with us?"

I wiped my face. "I don't know. What are you having?"

He shrugged. "Probably frozen burritos. Wait, maybe there's some leftover KFC."

We got married three weeks later, no lie. When you look for something for thirty-eight years, you know it when you see it, speaking for myself.

We didn't move to Colorado—he has family we take care of nearby—but every summer we go for two weeks and have the best damn time. Sometimes with the boys and their wives and kids, sometimes by ourselves.

What surprised me the most was how hard I fell for the boys. I never would have predicted that. Let me put it this way. If you know what you don't know—in my case, how to (step)mother three rambunctious boys in a family where people express their feelings—there's no sense in acting as if you do know. You get glimmers now and then, and you hop from glimmer to glimmer and hope (believe) that your partner will snatch you back up when you fall through. Mine did. Does.

The boys were skittish around me at first, but they started to thaw when I showed them a few tricks I knew on the computer. Everything was text in those days—no mouse, no windows, no graphics, nothing very much fun for kids—but I showed them how to add a RAM card to the PC and make it run faster, and I taught them how to program an adventure game in Turbo Pascal. That got their attention. The youngest one, Eric, turned out to love card games, and he and I played slapjack and macaroni poker and canasta like Daddy taught me, and Eric taught me Poop on Your Neighbor, and sometimes the five of us played that one until all hours on a Saturday night. We all got yo-yos from Tom one Christmas, but even though I remembered the names of some of Daddy's tricks (like Walk the Dog, Around the World, Rock the Baby), I was too clumsy to do them, so the yo-yos were pretty much a bust. But the boys' first love was the computer and then of course video games, and they eagerly brought their hacking questions to me. All I can say is, don't believe everything you read about stepmothers.

One day the boys and I sat cross-legged in a circle on the floor—I was explaining some bit of esoteric computer lore (DOS versus CP/M; the difference between routers and switches, that kind of thing)—when I realized with a start that I must take after Grandma, who showed me how to roll piecrusts and do patchwork and embroider and defeat the Evil Eye and give your troubles to a worry doll. And she must have passed down her drive to know arcane things and make uncommon things to Daddy, who taught me how to play airplane and jacks and tetherball. The fact that I was too klutzy and impatient to quilt or skip rope wasn't the point, although I always thought it was. The point was in the doing and, especially in my case, the belonging. It had been right there in front of me for years, but I didn't see where I fit in—until I did.

And if Daddy had lived, I thought, I was sure he would have taught me how to do the trick, which he claimed made him plenty of walking-around money, where you bet the guy next to you in a tavern that you can cut this here ordinary cellophane cigarette wrapper with an ordinary single-edge razor blade (kept in your wallet for just such an occasion, the blade side covered in waxed canvas) such that you can pull the wrapper over your head.

And eventually, he would have showed me how to feel your feelings, the hardest trick of them all. Losing him, in the condition I was in, had cost me dearly.

Another thing Grandma said was, we are too soon old and too late smart. It was too late for Daddy, but thankfully not too late for the family I had chosen and that had chosen me.

I often think about the women who died in the Bison Creek accident, all seven of them, and all eighteen children they left behind, and how all that death jolted my mother out of her lifelong slumber and she opened up to me and little by little I found out what love felt like.

Somewhere in this house I have the special edition newspaper where they printed the profiles. I almost have them memorized. It's good to have that kind of record, but, in a way, those articles are pitiful. Quilting, chicken casseroles, school honors, all that stuff—that was only what they did, and not who they were. Who they were couldn't be expressed in any other way than in the living flesh and in the present moment, and that was the true measure of our loss. They themselves were the meaning, and their loss was the meaning, all by itself. You didn't need to decorate your pain with anger at some boogeyman so you didn't feel the pain so much. I'd mourned all my childhood because I didn't feel kinship with the community in which I was born, but, like everyone else, I too had suppressed my grief because I couldn't, or wouldn't, bear the pain. I know better now. Pain is the way you heal, to the point you can.

As for the role God played in the accident—a point of contention in Wiley for a long time—that's still a mystery to me. Like a lot of people, I have a lot of questions for God when the time comes. In the meantime, as I read the New Testament, Jesus was Zen as hell, answering questions with questions and speaking in riddles. I don't think we're meant to understand, only to let it wash over us. For me, and maybe for you, too, that's hard.

For years, Wiley had an annual pancake and sausage supper in the park to raise money for the children of those women.

After the youngest one graduated from high school, they stopped. They put up a granite monument with the women's names, and they named the park Wiley Memorial Park. A whole generation has passed since it happened. I've lived long enough to see it begin to fade into history. I'm awed by the privilege of that.

As for my cousin Don, his parents are gone now, along with two of his siblings. Facebook tells me he's divorced and lives in Idaho. He and I have differing political views. Did you know there's an option on Facebook where you're still friends but don't see their posts anymore?

I never heard from Clayton after that morning at the foot of the stairs to our old apartment off Main Street. I wrestled for years with whether to tell the family what I knew about the accident, but in the end I thought it was better not to. I still have mixed feelings about that. Wilma and Frank went to their graves not knowing. They all did. I don't know where they put their terrible grief. That's on me, and there's no resolving it, and I have to sit with that, too.

After things settled down that summer of 1967, I did write a letter to Ruth Adams, the Bison Creek neighbor who had called the police, and she said she'd be happy to cut my hair. I hired a neighbor girl to stay with Mother and drove two hours each way every six weeks to Ruth's place, and it was glorious. She told me all about what it was like marrying a white man in the 1940s. Offhand she mentioned it was legal then in Chicago, but not in a lot of places, and even though I had heard that before, I about swallowed my tongue. It's one thing to know something intellectually, but it's something else to see it and feel it in the living flesh. Illegal to marry somebody? Really? She told me about posting notecards in Bison Creek advertising her hair services and later finding them with slurs scrawled on them. But plenty of white ladies had her do their hair, she said, smiling at me in the mirror hanging there in the kitchen, and most all of the Black ladies. She was good at it, she loved the creativity of it, and she loved having the company. She told me about her children, grown now and grandparents themselves, and how they had hated being stuck out in the boonies on the farm when her husband was still alive, and how she had to go back to Chicago with them until they got over themselves, and how she wasn't with him when he died, and how that hurt. She had tried to sell the place afterwards, but she didn't get any offers, and so she moved back into the trailer; and it turned out that she herself was just as glad to live there, her and her brother Russell. She had a straight chair that she kept out in front of the trailer, and she always had her coffee setting there of a morning. Nothing so pretty as the song of a meadowlark, in her opinion, although she couldn't say as she liked the screeching cicadas like I did. I asked her, speaking of birds, did she know that Medora, Kansas, was the crow capital of the world? And that seeing two crows is good luck? She couldn't say as she did. Being with Ruth was the closest I ever got to being with Grandma again, and I didn't care how weird that was. Ruth died in 1975, and two of her children came to bury her, and I went to the funeral, my first one. At the time I didn't feel I had the right to cry, and so I held it back, thinking it the polite thing to do, but now I wish I had cried my heart out.

Sometimes I wonder what my obituary will say. Probably not much different from the seven women who died in the Bison Creek wreck. But the difference is, they were cheated out of their lives, and especially out of their grandchildren. When I think about that, my sorrow for them slices deep. Grandchildren make time stop in the most wonderful way. They can take all the love you have to give them. They don't think it's fire. In the wisdom they have not yet forgotten, they know it's water.

At the other end of life, where I am now, the beautiful thing about being "an old" (as the kids say) is that, for one thing, you're invisible, and, for another thing, you can commune with

Charlotte anytime you want to, and a lot of people just think you're eccentric. I've made friends with her, more or less. She's a part of me just like my stringy hair, the zigzag skin cancer scar on my chin, and my love of midcentury modern ashtrays. I've gotten pretty good at ignoring Charlotte when I'm around certain people, and I'm glad to have that option. No use borrowing trouble.

But with Tom there's no need to pretend. You can imagine that in the beginning, contemplating intimacy of the physical kind was, for me, complicated. But in the actual world it wasn't like that. It was funny and playful and, really, revelatory. Just lying there afterwards, gasping, I felt empty—empty of everything ugly and painful that I imagined or remembered. To be empty in that beautiful way—where you (as the song says) could have died then and there—was for me a new feeling, and I have often rejoiced in it. In the course of time Tom and I have had our good days and bad, but we deal with things in the knowledge of who we actually are, and that makes all the difference. I told him about Charlotte and everything, and he told me about the war and everything, and we sat with that. To be known for your true unvarnished self and be accepted, that's love.

Another thing I know is, one of the greatest days of your life is the day you forgive your parents for their shortcomings. It frees you to forgive your own.

As Tom says, don't overthink it. We hardly ever catch anything anyway.

A READING GROUP GUIDE

ABOUT THIS GUIDE

The suggested questions are included to enhance your group's reading of Elizabeth Hardinger's *Won't Be Long Now.*

1. Beyond what Billie says, why do you think she feels she doesn't belong in the same world as her parents?

2. What do you understand Billie to mean when she says that people's words sometimes "echo" in her mind? Have you (or someone you know) ever had an experience like this?

3. Billie often mentions the polka dot agate rock given to her by her friend Harriet. What do you think it means to Billie?

4. Why does Billie say that her grandmother is "natural"? What does she mean by that?

5. Billie tests at the level of genius and reads a thick dictionary for pleasure, and yet she is naïve about some things—for example, she thinks that the Garden of Eden tourist venue is the actual location where Adam and Eve once walked. How do you reconcile these two?

6. What role do you think the woman Billie meets at the Garden of Eden plays in the story? As off-putting as she is, why do you think Billie is drawn to her?

7. How do you think Billie's life would have turned out if her father had lived?

8. How do Billie's feelings about her mother change over the course of the novel? Does Dixie go through a similar change?

9. How would you describe Billie's feelings for Clayton? How does he feel about her?

10. Beyond abject grief, what do you think of the reaction of the Enholm family and the Wiley community to the ac-

cident that claims the lives of their loved ones? Did anything about it surprise you?

11. Billie's feelings about Joan are complicated. What aspects of Billie's life play into that relationship?

12. Do you think Billie made the right decision to stay in Hutch and take care of her mother?

13. Do you think Billie is, as she implies, autistic? How does that affect your view of her and her story?